The Outcasts

NANCY MANKINS HAMM

*To Jone —
God Bless!
Nancy Mankins Hamm
Isa 41:10*

Copyright © 2009 by Nancy Mankins Hamm

The Outcasts
by Nancy Mankins Hamm

Printed in the United States of America

ISBN 978-1-60791-899-8

All rights reserved solely by the author. The author guarantees all contents are original and do not infringe upon the legal rights of any other person or work. No part of this book may be reproduced in any form without the permission of the author. The views expressed in this book are not necessarily those of the publisher.

Scripture taken from the HOLY BIBLE, NEW INTERNATIONAL VERSION. Copyright © 1973, 1978, 1984 International Bible Society. Used by permission of Zondervan Bible Publishers.

Cover Photo
Copyright © istockphoto.com
Photographer Juan Estey
All rights reserved.

www.xulonpress.com

To courage—

I thank God who gives me courage through His Word. And I thank my husband, Gary; my friend and editor, Nancy Everson; my son Chad, for his expertise and help with the final proofread; and my family and friends, who encouraged me to write this book, and who stood by me every step of the way.

This book is dedicated to people who, like the characters in this book, have the courage to seek the truth and to take a stand against evil—no matter what the cost.

"Have I not commanded you? Be strong and courageous. Do not be terrified; do not be discouraged, for the Lord your God will be with you wherever you go." (Joshua 1:9)

Nancy Mankins Hamm served for twenty-three years as a missionary with NTM. She lived in Panama, reaching remote people with the gospel—until her late husband, Dave, and two colleagues were kidnapped from their isolated village and held hostage by Colombian terrorists. For eight-and-a-half years the three wives worked to obtain release for the men. Through this time, the ladies gained audiences with presidents, senators, congressmen, ambassadors, a queen, former hostages, and hostage experts—only to learn, after all their searching and waiting, that their husbands had been martyred by their captors.

Nancy has been interviewed on *Larry King Live*, *The Today Show*, *Focus on the Family Radio*, *Moody Radio*, and a host of local radio and television shows around the country. Nancy has shared her story of God's sustaining grace with audiences around the globe.

During that time of waiting by faith, Nancy wrote the book *Hostage: The Incredible True Story of the Kidnapping of Three American Missionaries*.

The Outcasts is Nancy's first work of fiction. No stranger to persevering through trials, Nancy shares this message through her books: God is able; He hears our cries; and He provides a way.

Currently, Nancy and her husband, Gary, live in Florida. Together, they have four married children, and are the proud grandparents of eight wonderful grandchildren—one of whom is in heaven.

Autographed copies of *The Outcasts* and *Hostage* can be purchased at nancymankinshamm.com

A note about this novel:

All persons, places, and events portrayed in this book are fictitious. The customs, beliefs, rituals, and traditions reflect various cultures around the world.

Chapter 1

Maamo rocked slowly back and forth in her roughly woven hammock, which had long since lost its vibrant colors. Her once-shiny black hair had faded to dark gray and now fell limply down her back. Deep lines in her weathered face accentuated her age, and her thin, four-foot-seven-inch frame was no stranger to hardship and hunger. However, a spark remained in Maamo's dark brown eyes—a spark that smoldered and refused to go out.

At age fifty-seven Maamo was the oldest woman in Ulgana. For generations the isolated village in the dense tropical rain forests of Central America had remained virtually untouched by the outside world—as though suspended in time...suspended, that is, until men from Ulgana had ventured farther upriver and discovered a small outpost town. The Nala people had believed that Ulgana and its sister villages were the total of humanity. It was a fearful thing to learn that *other* people existed—people who looked different and spoke an unintelligible language.

The Outcasts

Maamo remembered clearly the stories that had been told at night around her fire. Little by little, village men had begun to trade crops of plantain and avocado for items from the outside. Families now had plates, spoons, and large cast iron pots for cooking food over their fires. They valued their salt and matches, and the lucky ones even brought back cooking oil. The men now possessed machetes, files, and fishhooks. A few even had shotguns. So, as they ventured outside of their realm, life had begun to change. But they still had no idea at all about the vast world beyond the outpost town.

Maamo continued to sway in her hammock. She had never traveled even to the closest Nala village—except in her mind, that is. Often she tried to imagine her way along the dirt-packed trail that she envisioned from the stories she'd heard. In her mind's eye she tried hard to picture the steep, rugged path...snaking through the dense, green jungle, at times skirting the swiftly flowing river toward the village where her three sons and their families had lived for well over fifteen years. She certainly wasn't the only one of her people who had never visited even the nearest of the sister villages. *Most* of the residents of Ulgana had never ventured to make the grueling trek. The other two Nala communities, however, were so far away that she knew she couldn't begin to imagine them, so she didn't even try.

Maamo shivered. She pulled the musty, threadbare cover tighter around her. Years ago, her youngest son, Diego, had brought the blanket to her on one of his rare trips back to Ulgana.

She glared at the cold fire pit. *I'm out of wood, again. Why...why has my life turned out this way?* She closed her eyes and allowed her mind to take her back nearly forty-three years...

The feeble cry of a newborn pierced the semidarkness of the small hut.

"A girl!" Maamo's mother exulted. She laid the infant on a banana leaf to await the delivery of the afterbirth.

Maamo's joy was short-lived, however. More contractions wracked her body. "What's happening?" she cried out, as a second daughter made her way into the world.

"Twins!" her mother choked out.

"A curse!" rasped the grandfather, who had been standing outside the hut with Maamo's husband.

The room grew deathly quiet, except for the faint cries of two tiny infants.

"Nooo!" Maamo's scream pierced the night.

Quickly Maamo's mother wrapped each baby in banana leaves. Tears streamed down her face as she ran to the doorway and handed the tiny bundles to the men. Maamo's babies were whisked away into the dark night to appease the spirits.

"Nooo! Please don't take my babies!" sobbed the fourteen-year-old mother. Desperately she fought to break free from her own mother's arms to rescue her infants, but she could not.

"Hush. Here, take this," her mother said, quickly forcing her daughter to gag down a foul-tasting black liquid. Immediately it dulled her senses and gradually lulled her into a deep sleep....

How I wish I could have rescued them! Could I somehow have rescued them? Had my daughters been allowed to live, my life would have been so different.

One year later Maamo had given birth to a healthy baby boy. Her empty arms were filled, yet her questions and heartache remained. Two years passed and a second baby boy arrived, followed by a third boy two years after that. With each birth Maamo secretly mourned her baby girls all over again.

Then, an illness struck the village. Everyone knew the spirits had caused it. Over a third of the people died. Maamo's husband, both of her parents, and her only sister were among the casualties, leaving Maamo and her babies destitute. She had no family members left to haul large fire logs for her to cook on. With her babies in tow, she gathered sticks and twigs. With no one to watch her small children while she was gone, she struggled to maintain a meager garden and haul plantains and bananas. She had no relatives to gather building materials or to participate in the village projects, so her house was never on the list to be repaired. She could not replace the thatched roof or the bamboo walls when the harsh rains and hot winds took their toll year after year.

Eventually, at ages ten, eight, and six, her children were all able to help her plant and harvest food, haul fire logs, split wood, and repair the hut. But all too soon, it seemed, each son found a bride.

Why did all three boys have to find wives in Luwana? Maamo questioned, even these fifteen years later.

I begged Diego not to go! I pleaded with him to find a way to bring his bride here to Ulgana to live with me. She could still see the shocked expression on Diego's face, as if she'd lost her mind. His look unmistakably told her he would not defy the custom of living with the wife's family. He stared incredulously at her—everybody knew that the blood lines ran through the mother! As custom dictated, his new wife's family would gain a son-in-law to help provide for them. It wasn't his fault that his mother didn't have daughters who would marry and bring sons-in-law and grandchildren into her home. Maamo's fate had been sealed.

The spirits are never satisfied, Maamo thought bitterly. *They took my baby girls, my husband, and my family. Why should I obey them? Isn't there any other path to follow? Please, I want more for my grandchildren! There has to be a different way!*

Maamo had no way of knowing that in the farthest sister village to the west, another Nala woman's life was about to change forever.

⁂

The village of Namuro buzzed with activity. Dark gray clouds moved quickly overhead, masking the sunset. Outside of their huts, children frantically scooped partially dried rice into large homemade baskets before the huge, ominous clouds began to release their fury of rain. Clucking noisily, chickens vied for the kernels that fell to the ground in the children's haste. A loud clash of thunder sent toddlers rushing into their huts for shelter and comfort.

Inside Rosa's hut however, several women huddled silently. In the center of the circle, Rosa's sick daughter lay in her hammock and thrashed in pain, moaning incoherently. She no longer pleaded frantically for help, nor was she drawing up her knees and holding her lower right side.

"Poor thing," one of the women said.

"Poor thing, poor thing," echoed murmurs from the other sympathizers.

Rosa pursed her lips. "I placed the white medicine rock under her hammock yesterday. Why isn't it working? When will the chief arrive to chant over her again? I don't know what else to do. Poor little Paco…"

The Outcasts

Rosa broke off her sentence in the nick of time. She had nearly tempted fate, mentioning death out loud. The spirits would have been angered for sure. But she couldn't stop the thought that had entered her mind. *What will my grandson do if his mother dies? The spirits took his father, and now his mother, too, is close to death. Poor Paco.*

As the first drops of water dampened the hot, dry soil, an almost suffocating, earthy smell rose from the steaming ground outside. The muffled sound of rain landing on the thatched roof overhead accelerated into a dull roar as Rosa's sister, Ana, broke away from the group. Peering out between the split bamboo siding of the hut, she looked toward her own house to see whether her children had safely retrieved all of the rice. Satisfied, she returned to the group that was still hovering over her sick niece. She wouldn't think of leaving—none of them would. Their families would drink a banana drink which every family kept in large cooking pots on their fires. It served as a kind of staple meal—something to fill empty stomachs between intermittent hunting trips. They were fortunate to get meat once or twice a month, but plantains and bananas grew in abundance year-round. Grandmothers and older children would care for the younger ones. They would know that Rosa and her daughter could not be left all alone during their time of need.

The form in the hammock became very still. She let out a great sigh and then appeared to go to sleep.

"Is she well?" Rosa asked, looking around the group for encouragement.

"I don't know," one of the comforters stated uncertainly. "Perhaps we should get the chief."

"It's pouring down rain," another from the group interjected, wondering why she should even have to state the obvious.

Rosa poked her daughter's swollen abdomen and then laid her calloused hand on the young woman's skin. "She's hot. The heat is throughout her whole body."

"Ahhh, ahhh," responded the comforters, affirming the new dilemma.

In the already dim hut, light was fading quickly. At the other side of the primitive dwelling, the ends of three logs smoldered under a huge pot of banana drink. Rosa added dry sticks to rekindle the flame. Sparks crackled as the fire began to reheat the drink, as well as add some light to the room.

Minutes later Rosa used a hollowed-out gourd to ladle some of the hot, sweet liquid from the pot into a smaller gourd. She handed the drink to Blanca, the oldest woman in the group. Blanca quickly drank down the contents, wiped her mouth with the back of her hand, and held the gourd out for her hostess to retrieve. Another very large gourd filled with river water sat unsteadily on the earthen floor. Rosa used this to rinse the handmade cup. She then repeated the process for the next person.

The rainstorm brought a chill to the evening air. The ladies moved small stools into a semicircle, so they could sit with their backs near the warm fire and still face the sick woman in her hammock. Their small, carved wooden seats were barely eight inches tall, twelve inches wide, and eight inches deep. Rosa, however, swayed in her hammock next to her daughter and stared up at the smoke-stained thatched roof.

The group kept their silent vigil into the night. The chief didn't come because the rains didn't let up.

The first pink rays of dawn filtered into the twenty small huts of the village. A rooster crowed. One by one, families emerged from their homes, headed for the river, and began their morning routine. A trail led to each family's private bathing area. Older girls carried water back from the river. Some families used empty yellow five-gallon cooking oil containers for hauling water.

Rosa had shared her hammock with one of the women. Groggily, she got up and stood next to her daughter. Two other ladies stirred in the hammock they had shared. Soon they all were gathered again around the sick woman. Her beautiful brown skin glowed reddish and shiny with fever. Through the long night, she hadn't stirred—she still lay motionless in her hammock.

"I'm here. How did you greet the dawn?" The chief's loud voice boomed outside the door.

"No different," Rosa said. "And you?"

"The same, also," the chief replied.

"My daughter isn't thrashing in pain anymore. She is very hot though—the heat is throughout her whole body. Come, look."

Rico entered the hut and strode toward the hammock. With a flourish of authority he thrust his walking stick toward Rosa's sick daughter and then turned toward the nearest hammock and cast himself in it. From his throat resonated a special chant, a chant that was devised to chase away the evil spirits and heal the young woman.

For nearly an hour the ominous mantra echoed throughout their small village. A cloud of concern settled on the inhabitants of Namuro. They buried their doubts deep within their hearts, underneath their fear of contradicting the spirits. Their only hope lay in the chants, the medicine rocks, and the traditions handed down through generations. They tried to believe that surely she would be healed.

But the unthinkable happened.

In the midst of the resonating refrain, Rosa witnessed her daughter's last shuddering breath.

"No! No!" screamed Rosa. "Don't 'be no more'! Don't leave us! Don't leave Paco. No!"

The incantation ceased. Rosa's screams melted into the mournful wailing of hopelessness. Then the other women joined her. Finally, the chief's voice blended into the wailing. Like a wave sweeping through the village, the death wail crested higher as each villager joined in the lament.

Death, with its hopelessness and defeat, had again struck the lives and hearts of the Nala people.

The Outcasts

The mourners spoke in whispers. "Rosa...what will she do now? Poor thing...she has no husband, no daughters—only one son, and now a grandson to feed. Poor thing, poor thing."

Rosa stroked her long, stringy, black hair as she gazed at her daughter's lifeless form in the hammock. She wondered how she could provide the last meal for the whole village—the last meal to say goodbye to her precious girl. A taboo forbade anyone from ever again referring to her daughter by name.

Rosa's mournful weeping and haunting moans commenced once more as she expressed her grief the traditional Nala way. Then she collapsed into the arms of her friends.

With a cloud of dust, little Paco ran through the open doorway straight to his mother's hammock. "Mama, Mama!" he cried desperately.

Red-rimmed eyes looked on as he frantically tried to climb into the hammock with his mother. Nobody moved to stop him. Rosa, responding to her grandson's cries, opened her eyes, squared her shoulders, and moved away from the women who were consoling her. She had a job to do. Paco needed her; she would be strong for him.

"Paco," she said, "come here to Grandma, come."

"No!" shouted the confused little boy. Like many other toddlers in the village, he was naked and dirty. His little body was covered with numerous sores and bug bites. Paco darted away from his grandmother and ran back outside.

The Outcasts

Rosa walked to the opening and watched the little one disappear into his cousins' house.

"Fidel! Fidel!" she called out. She needed her son's help.

Fidel has always seemed just a touch slow, but he's a good boy. He has a gentle and quiet way about him. If only his father had lived long enough to teach him how to hunt and fish, she thought, *long enough to teach him how to be a man.*

Fidel is eighteen years old; he's ready to look for a wife. Soon he'll go live with his bride in her mother's home. They'll gain a son—another worker—hunter, wood gatherer, and basket weaver. I'll never have a son-in-law. But I can't think about that now.

Fidel ambled out of the hut next door. His gaze was vacant and sad.

"I'm here," he said quietly as he stepped inside the hut. He couldn't bring himself to look toward the hammock where he knew his dead sister lay.

"Fidel," his mother spoke urgently, "go and ask your uncle Esteban to take you hunting. I know he'll help us. We must have meat to prepare a last meal for…for your sister."

"Okay, Mother." Fidel's dark eyes involuntarily landed on his sister's form, then grew large with the realization that he would never ever see her alive again. He turned toward the door. He wanted to run, to cry, yet he moved away from the house with the same slow gait with which he'd arrived. He needed to obey his mother's wishes, to find his uncle, even though Fidel hated to hunt. He wasn't any good at it, not any good at all.

The Outcasts

Esteban was one of the few men in Namuro who owned a shotgun. Because of the circumstances, he agreed to take Fidel hunting, but Esteban knew it would be much easier if he went alone. It was already late in the day to start a hunt, but Fidel, machete in hand, followed his uncle up the path that led out of the village toward Kala.

In single file they hiked up and down small hills on the winding, uneven trail. Fidel, deep in his own thoughts, nearly missed seeing his uncle veer off the main trail to take an almost invisible footpath. Quickly, Fidel picked up his pace. Realizing that he easily could get lost, he forced himself to pay attention.

Carefully they trod across a mossy bridge made from a fallen tree, ten feet above an old, dried-up creek bed. Fidel shuddered at the thought of the snake dens that surely lurked below in the jumble of twigs and undergrowth.

Esteban halted on the other side. He listened and looked around for signs of game. At this time of day his only hope for a large animal was to come across a herd of wild pigs. As he trekked on, the footpath became more overgrown with each step. Fidel followed closely and as quietly as he could. Soon the sound of rushing water reached their ears and the trail ended at the river. Huge white rocks, almost as tall as the men, sat at the water's edge. Other rocks produced rapids toward the middle of the fast-running tributary.

As Esteban scouted the riverbank for tracks, Fidel watched and then followed him into the thick foliage where there wasn't even a footpath. Snap! Fidel stepped on a dry twig and got a sharp look from his uncle. Esteban crept further into the undergrowth of the forest and Fidel followed quietly. Suddenly, Esteban spotted a herd of wild pigs that had burrowed into the muddy underbrush. He pointed his chin toward them, alerting Fidel to their presence.

Esteban spotted the tusks of a boar. Slowly, he positioned his gun, aimed, and squeezed the trigger. The shot deafened Fidel and sent the herd running in all directions...except for the boar that lay dead—shot through the head so that no meat would be wasted.

Esteban nodded at Fidel and they each grabbed two legs and carried the heavy animal back to the open riverbank with the white rocks. To drain the pig's blood, Esteban used a strong vine to string the animal upside down in a nearby tree. Then he slit its belly with Fidel's machete and removed the entrails. They carried the carcass to the river and washed it out.

Fidel and Esteban took turns hauling the pig on their backs. They were sweaty and blood-stained when they arrived, but the hunt had been successful.

For three long and exhausting days the village mourned the loss of Rosa's daughter. Her body, still in her hammock, had been carried to the meetinghouse. Throughout the three days people came and went. They ate the final meal—the one provided by Rosa. They filed past the body or sat around on benches. The wailing continued. Some went home and slept while others stayed, but nobody went hunting or to his garden. Normal daily activities ceased.

The Outcasts

On the third day, the stench of the body was overwhelming. Everybody knew the dreaded time had come to bury the young mother. Fidel and Esteban each took one end of her hammock and carried her corpse to the edge of the river. Rosa walked behind them with Paco clutching her skirt. The crescendo of wailing reached its peak.

The forlorn group crossed the shallow river and climbed the steep bank on the other side. A freshly cut trail led them to the graveyard. Earlier the men had dug the shallow grave, which lay open, ready to swallow up Rosa's precious daughter. Gingerly they laid her body in the hole. Her handmade hammock had been fashioned for her shortly after she was born and had touched every day of her life; now it enshrouded her even in death.

As the first scoop of dirt fell onto her daughter, Rosa witnessed no more.... She never knew who carried her home and laid her into her own hammock—the hammock that she, too, would someday be buried in.

Chapter 2

Village life returned to normal.
Rosa stood and peered through the siding as her sister Ana and her five daughters filed by. *I wonder if they're going to harvest the rest of their rice*, Rosa thought enviously. *Esteban must have left earlier with his son-in-law. Luisa looks as though her baby will be born any day now—soon Ana will be a grandmother. She'll be caring for the baby and watching her daughters troop off to do the garden work. Why, only Nelsi has a smaller basket now. Maria has graduated to a full-sized basket along with the rest of the older girls. Ana has trained them well. Five daughters—and now I don't have even one.*

Ana and her daughters hiked barefoot in single file on the mile-long, earth-packed trail to their family garden. Without a word they joined Esteban and Timoteo who were already hard at work. An hour passed as they sweated in the heat and humidity, breaking off the stalks of rice and stacking them into piles on the ground. Wordlessly, Esteban began to bundle up the piles and neatly place them into the baskets. Using a bark band as a strap, the men helped each girl fasten the heavy baskets on their backs, anchoring the band around the lip of the basket and then around their foreheads. With her load on her back, Nelsi leaned forward into the strap and followed her mother and sisters. Even though their baskets were larger and heavier, they somehow made it look easy. In single file they followed Esteban and Timoteo, who each carried only his machete, as they briskly led the way back to the village.

Rosa stood at the siding once more and watched her sister's family returning home with their baskets brimming with rice. Paco napped in the hammock, and Fidel sat on a bench doing nothing at all.

As she entered her own hut, Nelsi was the last to disappear from Rosa's view. Luisa lifted the heavy basket off of her little sister's back. Nelsi was the first to grab a gourd, fill it with banana drink, and down it hungrily.

"Are we going to give some of our rice to Aunt Rosa?" Luisa ventured.

"They should have planted a crop," Esteban stated. "Fidel is lazy."

"Even if they had, as it turns out, they couldn't have harvested it. Now that Rosa is alone, she doesn't have any daughters to help her, and she has Paco to care for." Ana came to her sister's defense.

"We would have helped them harvest. Anyway, they could have helped us plant and harvest," Esteban said with a certain finality to his voice.

Luisa glanced sadly at her mother.

Esteban and Timoteo tied vines around each bundle of rice and hung them upside down in the rafters so they wouldn't mold or rot. When time and weather permitted, bundles would be cut down, and the kernels separated from the stalks and laid out in the sun to dry. When the kernels were dry, the girls would begin the arduous task of pounding the rice to remove the husks. Everyone anticipated the yearly crop of rice. It would be well worth all of this hard work.

The silence that had permeated Rosa's hut was finally broken. "Fidel," Rosa said, "we need meat. You must go hunting. Perhaps we can trade some meat for rice. I'm sure hungry for rice, and we didn't plant any this year."

Fidel sat silently staring at the fire for several long seconds before acknowledging his mother.

"I'm going to Luwana, leaving tomorrow," he said matter-of-factly.

"What?" Rosa spun around toward him. "What do you mean you're going to Luwana? We need you here. We need meat and firewood, and you promised to make me a basket. My old one is useless. What are you thinking?"

"Several guys are going to visit relatives. I'm going to find a wife. I promise you that I'll get permission to bring her back here." Fidel unfolded his plan calmly.

"Bah!" Rosa spat. "A girl never leaves her mother to live with her mother-in-law. Who would ever give you permission for that? It just isn't done that way."

"I'll get permission," Fidel said with a finality that was uncharacteristic for him.

Rosa lowered herself down onto a bench near the fire and stared into the flames. A small measure of hope began to flicker in her heart. *Who would have thought that Fidel—quiet, slow Fidel—would come up with such a plan. Perhaps I've misjudged him.* She stole a sideways glance at her son. *Maybe he moves like a slow, shallow creek, but it seems his mind runs deep—like dammed-up river water before the swift, dangerous rapids.* "Mmmm," she voiced aloud, with an ominous shiver that ran up her spine.

"When will you return?" Rosa ventured.

"In two weeks' time," Fidel replied.

Rosa wanted to ask whether he had a girl in mind, but she held her tongue. Fidel so seldom voiced any ideas, she was skeptical, to say the least. But she didn't want to discourage him if he actually had a girl in mind for this crazy scheme of his. Rosa wasn't accustomed to holding her tongue, but she could—if she put her mind to it.

The Outcasts

Roosters crowed as the first rays of the sun drifted through scattered clouds in the sky. The thud of an axe hitting its mark could be heard as someone splintered wood for kindling. The smell of wood smoke filtered through the village, and people began their morning treks to the river.

Rosa handed Fidel a gourd filled with warm banana drink. He downed the liquid and handed the gourd back to her.

Finally Rosa unstrung her son's hammock, laid his change of clothes in the center, and rolled it up. She sighed. *I wish I had some food for him to eat along the trail.*

"I'm gone," he said as he walked toward the door.

"Be careful." Worry tinged her voice.

Silently, Fidel exited the tiny hut and lumbered toward the group of young men who had already gathered at the edge of the village. Their wide grins mirrored their excitement as they anticipated the big trip to Luwana—two villages away! Fidel, however, displayed no emotion as he joined them.

Rosa watched her barefoot son in his worn-out trousers and dingy shirt. His unruly black hair stuck out at his crown. Slinging his hammock over his shoulder, Fidel followed his friends up the trail that led them into the jungle and out of his mother's sight.

Could he really bring back a wife? That's just not our way of doing things. Who would let her daughter leave her home to follow her husband to a distant village? How can I allow myself to think a plan like that might work? Whatever could Fidel be thinking? I fear that the dam is about to break loose, and my boy is on the verge of a ride down the rapids!

Hope faded and the reality of her desperate state once again set in.

Engulfed in his own thoughts, Fidel didn't realize that he'd slowed his pace and was lagging behind the group. The lush green jungle grew increasingly dense. The trail had narrowed to a mere footpath. He didn't even notice the beautiful orchids that grew here and there in the clefts of the tall trees. As usual, he wasn't watching for that fallen log that might be suitable to make into a canoe—a tree that had fallen long enough ago to be dry, but not so long ago that it was rotten—just the right fallen tree that was near enough to the riverbank so that it could be pushed into the river when the canoe was finished. His eyes weren't peeled for game that could provide a nice meal for his hosts when he reached the first village. Fidel didn't even realize that his friends *were* watching for or thinking and talking about such important things.

A whistle pierced the air, bringing him out of his reverie. Picking up his pace he caught up to the group and found them standing around together eating the food they'd each brought with them.

The Outcasts

Fidel sat on a fallen log and picked a thorn out of his calloused foot. He ambled to the river, knelt down, and scooped water into his cupped hands and took a drink. Somewhat refreshed, he rejoined the group.

"Let's go," sounded the self-appointed leader.

The young men pushed themselves, walking swiftly for the second half of their journey.

Proudly they crossed the river into Kala, their sister village, before the sun was halfway to the western horizon. They would spend the night here and finish their trip to Luwana the following day.

Children ran ahead of the visitors, proclaiming their arrival. The travelers split up, each looking for his relatives, who would offer him a meal and a place to hang his hammock for the night.

Fidel stood and surveyed the smaller village that he had seen only once before. A dozen well-maintained huts lined the bank where the river had created a horseshoe-shaped peninsula. The entire semicircle had been cleared and swept clean. Palm trees surrounded and separated the homes and more towered majestically around the meetinghouse that stood in the middle of the large clearing.

Fidel spotted his father's sister near her hut, and called out, "Aunt Dominga."

"Fidel," Dominga replied, "how did you greet the dawn?"

"Good," he said, "and you?"

"Good, too," she replied.

The Outcasts

"Mother sends her greetings," Fidel was obliged to say.

"How is your mother? We had word of your sister," Dominga stated sadly. "Alejo came back from Namuro the day after her burial. Poor Rosa—we heard how she fainted and all."

"We're okay," Fidel stated vacantly.

"Go inside and string up your hammock," Dominga offered. "Tell me about your trip."

Even though Fidel was thankful for a place to stay and hopeful for a good meal, he dreaded having to talk for the next few hours.

Entering the hut, the enticing aroma of soup simmering in a huge pot over the fire caused Fidel's mouth to water in anticipation. He hung his hammock and sat down in it.

Fidel wasn't disappointed—the stew was delicious! He savored the combination of venison, boiled yucca, and plantain. After he ate, Fidel went to the river for a long bath and some solitude.

When he returned, Fidel sat in his hammock answering more of the family's many questions. Finally the sun went down, and before the rest of the household had settled into their hammocks he fell fast asleep.

As the moon lit up the night sky above the twelve thatched-roofed huts, village noises diminished and jungle sounds prevailed. Bats swooshed through the open-ended peaks of the roofs while insects, frogs, and monkeys competed for the lead in their nightly chorus.

The Outcasts

Fidel stretched in his hammock as another day dawned. Although he would never admit it, he felt slightly sore from the previous day's hike.

Last night's soup simmered over the fire. *Another good meal before I go,* Fidel thought happily as he savored the aroma.

The sun was well past noon when the trail ended at the river crossing. The men waded through waist-deep water. Thirty huts peppered the perimeter of this peninsula, with one large communal hut in the center. Like the other Nala villages, the people of Luwana kept the ground free of weeds and swept clean, because they knew that this helped prevent snakes, rats, and other undesirable critters from invading their community. The pests that did show up would be more visible and easier to kill.

But unlike their arrival at Kala, no one was there to greet the weary travelers. Instead, raucous laughter emitted from the thatched-roofed meetinghouse. So the group walked silently to the gathering place.

Diego, the village chief, staggered out of the building and nearly plowed into them. In his drunken state he laughed boisterously and invited them to join in the festivities. One of the village girls had reached puberty. The customary drunken ritual for her was underway.

"We're glad you're here to join us," Diego slurred. "It just began last night—there's plenty to drink and we have two more days to celebrate."

As they entered the meetinghouse their eyes adjusted slowly to the darkened room. The acrid smell of fermented corn drink assailed their nostrils. Over a hundred people teetered and laughed and hung on one another.

In the far left-hand corner of the building Fidel spotted the small, temporary hut which he knew housed the girl who had just become a woman. She would remain in the hut for five to seven days. Her head, no doubt, had been shaved, and she would wear a head covering until her hair grew back. Then she would be available for marriage.

Fidel sought a log bench away from the crowd. He sat down and observed the people. For the ritual to be a success, however, everyone would have to get drunk.

And then he saw her—the chief's daughter. She was beautiful. Her long, thick black hair cascaded below her shoulders—even though it, too, had been shaved several years ago. She had a beautiful smile and a dimple in her right cheek—such an unusual marking, but somehow it made his heart leap.

He sighed. *She must be fourteen or nearly fifteen, perhaps. Victoria is even more beautiful than I was told,* Fidel thought. Suddenly his heart took over. He felt her beauty and sensed the connection between them that he hoped soon would become a reality.

He watched. Victoria was smiling across the room at a young man. The young man was smiling back. She giggled.

The Outcasts

Diego staggered toward Fidel. "Have you gotten a drink yet? Come, you must drink," he said in a loud and irritating manner.

"Okay," Fidel replied, standing up from the bench. He followed the chief to the huge cauldron in the center of the building.

Accepting the gourd, Fidel downed the foul liquid with a shudder. He despised these drunken festivals, even though he knew the necessity of the ritual. *I need to mill around, stay in a group, and not be noticed. Then I won't be forced to drink as much. It doesn't take a lot for me to become drunk.* Already he felt a bit unsteady—it was a powerful brew they'd made.

He moved toward Victoria but she didn't notice him. Her eyes were still glancing flirtatiously at the young man in the red shirt.

Fidel directed his attention to a conversation between two women who stood nearby.

"When will Victoria be getting married?" asked one woman.

"Raul has been sitting around our fire regularly," the chief's wife said in a proud, conspiratorial whisper.

"So, any day now he could slip into her hammock?" the woman countered as they both erupted into peals of drunken laughter.

One evening soon, Raul's friends would carry him into the hut and drop him into Victoria's hammock with her. She would, no doubt, scream and run outside. Everyone would laugh and the process would be repeated two more nights in a row. By the third night she would have to decide. If she stayed in the hammock she would be accepting Raul's proposal for marriage. The ceremonial process would begin.

The Outcasts

I don't have much time, Fidel thought. And then the plan solidified in his mind. For once, he realized he had to move quickly.

Fidel went straight to the chief and joined the conversation and laughter.

The party continued throughout the night and into the next day.

Meanwhile, younger children were not allowed in the meetinghouse. They were all fending for themselves in their huts. Hungry babies cried. Older children, accustomed to the routine, foraged for whatever leftovers they could find—cold banana drink, bananas, or avocados. They fed the little ones, and then themselves, as best they could. It would be over soon, they all hoped. But their nerves were on edge. They didn't like the noises and laughter, and they were afraid of the men who staggered around. Instinctively the children stayed in their own huts and remained as quiet as possible during the three-day drunken ceremony. Secretly, the older girls dreaded *their* turn in the little hut—but they knew it would come, all too soon.

Chapter 3

Fidel squinted tentatively through the slits in his puffy eyelids. Licking his lips, his tongue felt dry and too big for his mouth. He was queasy and his head throbbed. His mouth tasted terrible. Several seconds passed before he got his bearings.

He raised himself up off the dirt floor of the meetinghouse. Though most of the people had already disappeared into their homes, several men and women still lay passed out on the floor.

Fidel rose painfully, exited the building, and headed for the river, hoping that a bath and a change of clothes would make him feel better. Remembering the clothes that were rolled in his hammock, he turned around and entered the meetinghouse again. His roll was on the dirt floor near the bench he'd first sat on two days ago. *Two days ago*, he thought. *I can't remember anything after the first night. I've got to remember. Maybe a good bath in the river will help clear my head.* He picked up his belongings and stumbled again toward the door.

The cool river water felt wonderful. Fidel dunked his head and swished water in his mouth, trying to get rid of the acrid

The Outcasts

taste. The fogginess began to dissipate and he felt more normal and in control. As he sat on the shallow river bottom, letting the cool, refreshing current rush past his body, he willed his mind to remember his conversation with Diego. *Am I dreaming, or did Diego really agree to give Victoria to me for my wife?* He was afraid to believe it was true. *What if Diego doesn't remember? I'll have to be confident enough to insist. Did he give his permission for her to go with me and live away from her family and village? Am I dreaming this, or did he really consent?*

Fidel never moved very quickly, and he spoke as seldom as possible. Nobody realized that underneath, his mind was really very sharp. Fidel had a habit of listening to conversations and gleaning important facts about people—facts that he never forgot. Several years ago, Fidel had traveled to Kala for the first time. Diego, the chief of Luwana, was visiting during that same week and was therefore the subject of discussion around the fires each night.

Fidel learned that when Diego was very young, his father had died. In fact, a horrible epidemic had wiped out a third of Ulgana, the village where he was born. His mother had been left behind with three small boys to raise. When the time came for Diego, the youngest, to follow his new bride to Luwana, her village, his mother was left to live out her days alone. People felt sorry for his mother, Maamo—that life had dealt her such a hard blow. But, Diego had risen to become chief of Luwana, and he was respected in all the villages. He had overcome a very meager upbringing.

However, late one afternoon during Fidel's stay in Kala, he had gone for a walk on a little-used trail near the village hoping for some solitude—time without having to dialogue with his relatives. But along the way he'd overheard a ruckus in a nearby garden and had hidden among the thick underbrush. It had become all too clear that he had stumbled upon a clandestine encounter between a man and a woman. He'd waited. Finally a young teenage girl had rushed down the trail past his hiding spot, and a few minutes later a man had walked by. It was Diego! Fidel had hardly been able to believe his eyes. He hadn't been able to decide whether or not to expose the chief for who he really was. But Fidel, a young teenage boy—and a visitor at that—had been afraid that nobody would believe him. So he'd held his peace.

Even though drunk, Diego had remembered all too clearly the rendezvous in Kala...a severe lapse in judgment several years ago. Fidel's plan had been much easier to execute than he'd dared to hope. Diego was terrified to learn that Fidel had witnessed his indiscretion!

Yes, Fidel thought, *it is true. Diego gave me his word. Victoria is mine! She will be free to leave the village and begin her life as my wife. He told me the wedding ceremonies would begin in three days.*

Does that mean tomorrow?

Elated, Fidel rose quickly from the water with a rare smile fixed on his face. But his throbbing head soon removed the grin, and he crept slowly toward the shore and his clean clothes.

Except for the occasional squalls of babies who still hadn't been fed, the village was deathly quiet. Fidel wondered where he should go. He opted for the meetinghouse. Entering the building he strung his hammock between two posts, eased himself in, and closed his eyes. One foot remained on the floor, rocking the hammock back and forth in slow deliberate motions. He would enjoy this time alone to think and dream of his future with Victoria.

Fidel succumbed to a sound sleep. Many hours passed before Fidel awoke to the sound of people splitting kindling for fires that would soon be lit against the approaching dusk. Women were preparing meals for their hungry families. Dogs barked and children laughed as they ran past the open door of the meetinghouse. The villagers were awakening from the clutches of an evil ritual that held them captive.

Carefully, Fidel got up and stretched. He ambled outside and headed toward the chief's hut. His stomach ached with hunger and apprehension but he forced himself to remain calm, hoping that he appeared much more confident than he felt.

Nearing Diego's hut, Fidel called out a greeting to let him know he had company. Diego's wife appeared at the door with a disgusted look on her face and then disappeared quickly. Ominous mumblings emanated from inside.

"Come in," Diego rasped.

Fear assaulted Fidel as he stepped through the doorway.

The Outcasts

"Sit," Diego ordered, pointing to the hammock across from his.

Fidel sat down and faced the chief, wondering how he ever could have gotten himself into this mess. He willed himself not to show his anxiety.

"How did you greet the dawn?" Fidel asked.

"Okay," the chief said flatly, "and you?"

"Okay, too," Fidel returned.

"Good. It was a successful ceremony. The drink was potent and everyone got drunk. It was successful," the chief asserted.

"Yes, that's good," Fidel agreed. He glanced around the room hoping to see Victoria, but she wasn't there.

"Diego, do you remember our conversation?" Fidel began, wanting to get this torture over with as soon as possible.

"Um, yes." The chief cleared his throat and glanced toward his wife, who shot him a look that would have withered a lesser man.

"Victoria wants to marry another man," the chief's wife screeched. "You can't take her away from me to live in your village!"

Fidel paled. His own mother was known for speaking her mind, but under it all she had compassion and love. He wasn't used to this anger and open hostility. *But Victoria would be worth her mother's wrath*, he reassured himself.

"Be quiet!" the chief yelled back at his wife. "I gave him my word! I will not go back on my word. Just be quiet." The torment he felt inside didn't show in his stern eyes. Although he was enduring his wife's anger because of this decision, Diego knew it was nothing compared to what he'd face if she found out about the girl in Kala. That, plus his standing in the eyes of the whole village—his fate as their chief—all rested in buying this man's silence. Diego reasoned that he had no choice; he had been forced to betray his treasured daughter.

At that instant she entered the back door. Victoria had tied her wraparound skirt above her breasts like a dress—she'd been to the river and was dripping wet. With a five-gallon container of water balanced on her head she moved toward her mother, who lowered it to the ground.

"How did you greet the dawn?" Victoria greeted Fidel politely.

"Good, and you?" Fidel nearly stammered.

"I'm good, too," she said, looking toward her hammock and her clothes. Retrieving another skirt and blouse, she decided to go back to the river to get properly dressed and then go find her friend Elena.

"I'll be back later," she called out cheerily as she headed for the back door.

"You come right back here after you've dressed," her father commanded.

Victoria stopped in her tracks.

She tilted her head and looked at her father, wondering about his gruff command. It seemed unusual that he would want her to be around when he had a visitor from another village. Uneasiness filled her heart for a moment but she dismissed it lightly. *What a foolish thought—surely this man could have nothing to do with me. My parents know that I am going to marry Raul.* The mere thought of Raul brought a peaceful feeling to her heart and a slight smile to her lips.

"Okay," she agreed, floating toward the door lost in her own romantic thoughts.

Minutes later Victoria returned. When she entered she could sense that something was very, very wrong. Her mother sat stiffly on a stool, her eyes red-rimmed and angry-looking. The young man, whose name she couldn't remember, still sat across from her father.

"Victoria," her father began unceremoniously, "You will marry Fidel and go with him to live in his village. Fidel's mother is widowed, his sister is gone, and her son is orphaned. There aren't any other daughters, so you will be a daughter to her."

"*No!*" Victoria screamed, before she could think of the consequences.

Diego jumped out of his hammock and grabbed his daughter by her arms.

"You *will* marry him." His menacing tone was all too loud and clear. "Yesterday I gave him my word."

Fidel hadn't counted on a scene such as this. He couldn't move. Holding his breath he waited for Victoria's reply.

Victoria's head whirled as her mind fought frantically for a solution. She could not agree to marry this man whom she didn't even know. She loved Raul, she wanted him! But contradicting her father was forbidden. She had no choice. Her father would never go back on his word, not only as a man, but as a chief. How had this happened? Her life was ruined!

Victoria focused her eyes on Fidel with a hardness that turned him cold—a look which clearly flashed her thought, *I hate you for this. I hate you!* In that moment she built a wall around her heart.

Her long black hair flew over her shoulder as she jerked her head back toward her father. His hands were hurting her arms as he continued to grasp her tightly. The muscles tightened in her jaw. Her once-beautiful, soft brown eyes were wild with fear and hate. With all of her heart she wanted to die rather than succumb to his demand. But she had no choice—no choice at all!

She nodded ever so slightly. Her father loosened his grip.

Victoria's eyes filled with unshed tears. She clenched her jaw tighter and hardened her heart further, refusing to cry. As a child she'd learned her lessons well. Don't cry. Strong people survive. If you can intimidate others you will come out on top. *Except for* this, she thought bitterly. *Why can't I demand my right to marry Raul? Why can't I say no? What would happen to me if I crossed my father, the chief? Would I be driven away from my people? I could never survive as an outcast. But why, why is this the way?*

Gone was her innocence. Gone was her youth.

Unspoken anger filled the deathly quiet room. Diego returned to his hammock. Moments passed, but Victoria didn't trust herself to move or talk. Her heart still pounded out of control. She was afraid that if she moved at all she would bolt from the house. She only wanted to wake up from this horrible dream—if only it *were* a dream.

Diego looked at his wife as though it were now her responsibility to do something. She rose from her bench and announced that she and Victoria would be back shortly. Woodenly, Victoria followed her mother out the door and toward the river.

Near the bank they dropped down on a log. Neither spoke right away—each was deep in her own thoughts. Victoria wanted to plead with her mother to intervene but knew the request would be futile.

"Victoria..." her mother began, haltingly. Even though she too was angry and didn't understand this turn of events, she was wise enough to know that one can't cross certain lines. "I had never even seen your father before the day we began our marriage ceremonies. I too was promised to him by my father. That was the way things were done back then. You will grow to accept this. You will have a home, children, and he will provide you with food and clothes. This is life."

"What about love, Mother?"

"Love?" her mother questioned. "Life isn't about love—it's about survival. Besides, what you now call love is just an awakening to becoming a woman, a wife, and a mother. You will have that with Fidel. You will be content, even happy, if you let yourself."

"How can you let him take me away from here—away from you?" Victoria pleaded. "I've never even been outside our village. When will I ever see you again? You won't be with me during childbirth. I could even *die* and you wouldn't know."

"Victoria!" her mother reprimanded sharply, glancing fearfully around. "The spirits can hear you! Don't *ever* talk about *that*. You know better. You could put a curse on all of us! You have to stop this foolish talk and obey your father. He knows what is best for you, for us, and for the whole village."

The conversation had ended. Her mother rose and stalked back to their home. Blankly, Victoria stared at the dark, murky water running swiftly along its banks. *I wonder where this river would take me. What would happen if I...*but her thoughts were interrupted.

"Victoria," Elena whispered breathlessly.

Victoria looked up to see her best friend.

Elena sat down next to her.

"Victoria, the whole village is talking. Did your father give you to Fidel?"

"Yes," Victoria whispered numbly.

"Fidel is a distant cousin of mine," Elena replied. "He's from Namuro. Is it true that you'll go live there with him? Are you leaving us? Tell me it isn't true!"

"It's true, unless you can help me find a way out," Victoria said as she peered sideways at her friend.

Elena visibly recoiled from Victoria. She glanced around before answering.

"Victoria, don't, please don't ask me that. You have always had too many dreams, too many thoughts that contradict our ways. It's always scared me. Even this could be the spirits punishing you. You'd better stop before something worse happens to you, or us!" her friend whispered fearfully.

"Worse?" Victoria demanded, raising her voice. "Worse than not marrying Raul? Worse than being torn away from you and my family, to be married to a man I don't even know? Haven't you ever wondered whether we should have more choices in life—whether there's another way of doing things out there...somewhere?"

"Stop! Victoria, you're my best friend and I'll always love you, but I can't listen to this. I must go." Elena rose swiftly and ran silently up the path to the village.

Victoria sat, helpless, hopeless, and all alone—alone with her broken heart. No one would help her. She knew of no one who *could* help her. *Please!* Her heart screamed. *Isn't there anybody who can rescue me?*

Darkness would soon enshroud her, so she rose. Her head was bowed and her shoulders slumped in defeat as she haltingly made her way back up the path, dreading to go home. But even that dread did not match her fear of the spirits in the dead of night.

She entered the hut and looked around. Her mother was stirring the pot of banana drink. Her father and "the man" were gone. Relief surged through her weary body. At least she wouldn't have to look at him again tonight.

"Here," Victoria's mother said gently, handing her a gourd filled with the banana drink.

Numbly, Victoria accepted the cup, drank the hot lumpy liquid, and handed the empty container back to her mother.

Her sisters and brothers clamored noisily around the fire, eager for something to fill their stomachs which ached from the past three days of foraging for themselves. It was good to have their mother back at the fire to serve them, even if it was only banana drink.

Victoria ignored the hubbub and sought the solace of her hammock. She only wanted to sleep, to dream her dreams of the life she had anticipated.

Mercilessly, another day dawned. And with it came the realization that Victoria's dreams would never come true. Fidel had pushed for a quick wedding ceremony so that he and his bride could return to Namuro with the group. They would leave within the week.

Like a bad dream, the day passed by slowly. Victoria and her mother grabbed their baskets and hiked to their banana trees. A dozen or so "hands" or bunches of bananas sprouted from each large "head" or stalk. With fierceness she didn't know that she possessed, Victoria swung the machete and with one blow chopped off a large head of fruit. She continued to land her machete with equal force, severing each bunch of fruit from the main stalk. They divided the load and trudged home with their burdens. Victoria chose three huge hands of plantains, the type of banana used to make their drink, and took them down to the river to peel. When she returned, she cut up the plantains and dropped the pieces into a giant pot of water. She stoked the fire underneath the cauldron.

"We'll just have our household at the ceremony," her mother stated.

But tonight could have been the night, Victoria thought, picturing the grin that would be on Raul's face as his friends threw him into her hammock. Her dreams crumbled. It no longer mattered that she'd always imagined a houseful of guests listening to her father's words of advice and wisdom... The sidelong glances at Elena, trying not to giggle with delight... Wishing that the marriage could be consummated that evening instead of waiting the traditional week for her husband to prove himself to her family by hunting, fishing, and gathering wood....

"Okay," Victoria answered flatly.

Why? Her heart and mind cried out defiantly. *Why is Father doing this to me? He is my own father. Why is his drunken word more important than my happiness—my whole future? Is this all there is to life, as Mother says—just surviving? Nothing makes sense to me anymore, but I guess it never has.*

Victoria could not still the thoughts raging in her heart. She had never been able to stop her mind from questioning inconsistencies and wondering about forbidden issues.

Perhaps this is *my punishment*, she conceded to herself.

Chapter 4

One week later, Victoria stood outside of her childhood home. Her husband said, "Let's go," and headed down the trail after his buddies. It was well past dawn, an unusually late start for a trip. He hadn't seen the tears in his young bride's eyes. He didn't notice the chief turning away—retreating into the trees behind his hut.

Silently, Victoria turned from her sad mother and siblings and followed her husband down the path—toward an unknown destiny. She purposely lagged behind Fidel as they hiked away from the only life she'd ever known.

The basket on her back contained all of her earthly possessions: the beautiful hammock that her mother had woven for her when she was born, two wraparound skirts, two blouses that she had sewn by hand, and her one extra pair of underwear. She had her needle and various spools of thread that she had collected over the years. She also carried Fidel's hammock and his extra set of clothing, plus the food she had packed for them to eat today. On top of the load huddled her two chickens, their wings bound with cord made out of vine.

After the wedding ceremony her husband had left their house. Normally he would have been required to spend a week hunting, fishing, and gathering firewood. At the end of the week if he had proven himself worthy, he would have been accepted by the family and allowed to move in and share his wife's hammock. But even though Fidel hadn't been required to demonstrate his skills, tradition hadn't been totally ignored—he still had not been allowed to move in and share Victoria's hammock.

But that week of grace was past. She now belonged to him and would soon live in his home and in his village where everything would be foreign to her. She had no choice—she was a married woman now, and that vow could never be broken. *But I won't think about that now*, Victoria determined as she willed her feet to move.

The trees grew taller and the forest grew denser with every bend in the trail. Yesterday's rain had muddied the rugged path, yet she trudged on without complaint, mile after lonely mile.

When the sun was high overhead the group stopped near the river's edge. Fidel lifted the basket off of his wife's back and carefully set it down on the ground, propping it up against a tree. Victoria avoided eye contact with him and therefore she missed the loving expression in his gentle brown eyes.

He sat down on a log to rest while Victoria rifled through the basket in search of their meal. She handed Fidel his food and found a different log where she could sit alone. The rice and venison were wrapped tightly in banana leaves and tied with vine. Even though no longer hot, the meal tasted delicious, especially after the rigorous trek.

Fidel enjoyed his food immensely. *Having a wife is wonderful,* he thought. But it never occurred to him to voice his appreciation to his young bride.

The group was ready to move out again. Silently Fidel retrieved the basket and lifted it up onto Victoria's back. He placed the bark band around her forehead.

As the afternoon sun waned in the sky, they reached the village where they would spend the night. Victoria had heard many stories about Kala from her father and others who had traveled back and forth. She had secretly longed to experience visiting another village firsthand, and normally she would have been filled with curiosity and excitement reaching this faraway destination. But now she only wondered whose hut they would spend the night in. And at that thought her body trembled, fearing that tonight could be *the night.*

Word traveled quickly that Fidel had returned—with a wife! Victoria didn't like the smiles and stares that greeted them, and for the first time in her life she felt shy and awkward.

"Fidel," a woman's voice called out.

"Aunt Dominga," Fidel answered, picking up his pace toward the hut nearest them.

Victoria followed.

"How was your trip, Fidel?" the woman asked with a twinkle in her eyes.

"Good," Fidel answered. "This is my wife, Victoria. She's Diego's daughter."

"Hello, Victoria," Dominga said. "I am Fidel's aunt—his father was my brother. Come in, put your basket down. Sit and rest. You must be very tired from your journey."

"Okay," Victoria said quietly, as Fidel moved quickly to her side and lifted the basket from her back once again. It was the first time that she'd spoken since leaving her home.

They each strung their hammocks in the tiny hut. More than ready for a rest, they lounged back in their own hammocks and rocked slowly back and forth.

Their respite was short-lived, however, as Aunt Dominga began to interrogate them. "I'm surprised to see you so soon after your wedding."

Victoria remained silent, forcing Fidel to answer. "We're going back to Namuro to live."

"To live there, you say?" she repeated expectantly. She could hardly wait to tell the women she would visit tomorrow. After several frustratingly silent moments, she continued. "Fidel, I can hardly believe that Diego would give his blessing for his daughter to move to another village to live. Surely he wants her in her mother's home. It just isn't done any other way."

"Diego gave his permission," Fidel answered flatly.

Victoria turned, silently facing the far wall, and curled up in her hammock.

Dominga complained silently to herself. *I shouldn't have to ask at all. This information, and much more, should be freely given. Fidel at least could have found a talkative wife. Between the two of them I still can't get a halfway decent answer, let alone a conversation.* But on the other hand, she almost chuckled out loud, *my sister-in-law will make up for the both of them once they're home! Home—Diego let his daughter move away? There has to be something very wrong here. It can't stay a secret forever. I just wish I could be the one to know the truth first. I wonder what the others are learning from the visitors around their fires right now.* The older woman fumed silently the rest of the evening and into the night.

The next morning, after another uneventful night Victoria found herself trudging along the trail, a repeat of the day before. Along the way she discovered the largest and most beautiful orchids that she'd ever seen.

I wish Fidel's aunt would have had some food to send with us. Victoria's stomach growled, emphasizing her thoughts. *That break we took hadn't been nearly long enough, but surely it must have been the halfway point. If so, it can't be much farther,* Victoria told herself wearily. *It would help to know how close we are,* she thought but stubbornly refused to ask.

Finally, the trail ended at the bank of a swiftly flowing river which spilled into the branch they'd been following. Victoria could see that they would need to cross and pick up the trail again on the other side.

"We're nearly there," Fidel offered. "This spot in the river is deep. You'll need to carry the basket on top of your head."

Victoria stood still as he lifted the basket off her back and placed it on her head for her. She walked into the swift current in front of him. The river was deep and cold, but she walked across without incident. As she climbed the bank on the other side she could feel her husband's eyes on her and it made her angry. *How could he force me to marry him and bring me to this distant place? I hate him*, she thought. *I hate him.* After he had repositioned the basket, she waited until Fidel walked out in front of her once more.

Fifteen minutes later, on the opposite shore of the winding river that they had been following she saw the thatched roof of a hut. Dogs barked, signaling their approach. Victoria's stomach tightened into a knot, but she sullenly continued on behind her husband.

Minutes later they walked into the village. Fidel headed straight for the first hut, and Victoria sighed with relief that at least she wouldn't have to walk the length of this village amidst the stares of its inhabitants.

She followed Fidel into the tiny dwelling and waited for him to relieve her of her burden. Nobody was home.

Lifting the chickens out of the basket, Fidel cut the vines that had held their wings together for the past two days. They squawked noisily, and violently flapped their wings before fleeing outside.

Victoria was shocked at the disrepair of the house she would now call home. The roof was old and the bamboo poles that were tied together to make the walls were rotting—nearly falling down. An old and useless basket sat in the corner. Yet the floors were swept clean and what few possessions she saw were orderly and neat.

In bustled Rosa. She walked directly to Victoria and placed her hands on the young woman's cheeks.

Looking up at Fidel, Rosa said, "Is this your wife? Did you truly bring home a wife?"

"Yes, mother, this is Victoria. She is Diego's daughter," Fidel informed her with pride in his voice.

"Victoria," Rosa voiced almost reverently, as she gazed into her liquid brown eyes. "Good, it is *good* that you've come here. I'm happy that you're here."

After only a moment's hesitation Rosa blurted out, "But isn't Diego the chief? How on earth did you talk him into allowing his daughter to leave the village and come here to live with us?"

Victoria's shoulders sagged once more and she turned her back on the woman. Tears threatened to spill out of the pools that had formed in her eyes.

"How old is she?" Rosa continued. "Poor thing must be scared to death coming all this way, leaving her father and mother, not knowing when she'll ever see them again."

Victoria had nowhere to run, nowhere to be alone, so she built the wall around her heart a little bit higher, a little bit thicker. She didn't like this woman any more than she liked Fidel.

At that instant a dirty little boy who appeared to be about two years old ran noisily into the house. He ran straight into Rosa, nearly knocking her off her feet.

"Paco!" she yelled. "Be careful. What are you doing? Do you need something?"

Her grandson stood with his face buried in his grandmother's skirt, refusing to answer.

"Paco, your uncle has brought home a wife. You have an aunt. Her name is Victoria."

From the folds of cloth, Paco peeked out at his new aunt and quickly hid his face again.

Neither of them appeared to be impressed with the other and neither said a word.

"Well," Rosa said glancing back at Victoria, "you must be hungry. I've run out of food, though, Fidel, while you were gone. We need to go get some plantains. Never mind, I'll go borrow some food and tomorrow we can bring back what we need from the garden. Victoria, light the fire while I'm gone."

Rosa bustled out the door as quickly as she'd come in, with Paco close on her heels.

The Outcasts

At the front end of the hut, Fidel began to string up their hammocks—side by side, which didn't go unnoticed by Victoria. She spotted Rosa and Paco's hammocks at the other end, nearer the fire. She began searching the crooked shelf above the makeshift table for some matches—not that matches would do her any good without kindling. *I'm sure they must keep up with things better when Fidel is home*, Victoria tried to reassure herself.

Nightfall descended swiftly upon the tiny village. The inhabitants of Namuro had retreated into their huts. Muffled voices next door and a crying baby in the distance were the only people-sounds that Victoria could hear. Her trip to the river had been somewhat refreshing, yet she felt very exhausted...and weary—a feeling that she wasn't sure would ever go away.

She lay quiet and still in her hammock. Fidel was very close by in his. *Too close*, she thought.

Worried about approaching Victoria, Fidel was lost in deliberation. He couldn't quite get that look out of his mind—the look that had seized Victoria's face when her father told her she was to marry him. *Her eyes had looked like those of a wild animal backed into a corner by hunters with their dogs.* Fidel fought the image. *A trapped animal can be very unpredictable. It will be very humiliating if she rejects me—even worse if she causes a ruckus that the neighbors hear.*

I am married now, Victoria confirmed to herself, deep in thoughts of her own. *I have a duty. It would shame my family if I resist him and cause a commotion. I do not have a choice about this marriage, with all that it brings, so I will give myself to him—everything except my heart. Nobody can make me give him my heart,* she determined with a set to her delicate jaw.

She could scarcely breathe as Fidel got out of his hammock and came to her.

Morning dawned with the promise of another bright, clear day—in stark contrast to Victoria's gloominess. She took longer than usual at the river, thankful that nobody could witness the tears which finally coursed unchecked down her cheeks from her swollen eyes. She couldn't help reliving that dreaded event. She had steeled her heart and had endured the awkward advances of the stranger who was her husband. She had done her duty, but she felt violated—used!

The current, swift as it was, couldn't wash away the memory of an act which should have been special between two married people. Victoria once more contemplated floating down the river, allowing it to take her away...or to swallow her up. That thought alone seemed a relief to her tormented mind. *Perhaps somehow there might be an escape for me,* Victoria thought. A small glimmer of hope flickered from within, enough hope for her to continue on. She would allow herself to plan and scheme. She would question her life and her options.

Finally, she returned from the river. She looked around the tiny hut with dismay. At that instant she determined in her heart that in the meantime, changes would be made in this house. She also found her tongue.

"Fidel," she stated boldly. Three heads jerked toward her. "We need firewood, logs, and plantains—today!"

At least she isn't mute, Rosa thought to herself. *I was beginning to wonder whether the chief was relieved to get rid of her. She may even be a little spunky,* she smiled to herself.

Amazingly, in the three months that followed, Fidel and the village men had replaced the walls of the little hut, making the structure larger and much sturdier. They had thatched the roof with better and longer-lasting leaves. In the village meeting the other men had been amazed when Fidel spoke up, requesting that his house be next on the list of projects. Fidel never spoke up in the meetings—of course that was why his house was in such disrepair. They were doubly astounded when Fidel insisted on the best banana leaves for the thatch. Those leaves took much more time for everyone to gather. But they had agreed.

Fidel had even woven the two new baskets that sat in the corner near the fire, baskets that Victoria and Rosa used regularly to haul bananas, avocados, and the kindling that Fidel split for them. But, try as she might, Victoria could seldom get her

The Outcasts

husband to go hunting, and even when he did, he usually returned empty-handed.

At those times, with fishhook and line in hand Victoria would stalk up the trail alone and disappear from sight. She would return only after she had caught enough fish for the day's meal.

One day, fishing from the bank of the river Victoria began to long for venison stew. She sulked unhappily as her thoughts turned to home. *Raul would never have let me go hungry.* But her mind quickly turned from Raul to the real burden on her heart. *I haven't been feeling well for many weeks. I must be expecting a baby. I need to talk to my mother. If I am pregnant I can't eat venison anyway. I certainly don't want to tempt the spirits by eating meat from large animals while I'm pregnant. The spirits could claim the baby...it could be born with a deformity.* Victoria shuddered. *Fidel hasn't provided any large game since I've been here anyway,* her mind continued on, miserably. *I wish I could escape from here. I certainly can't leave now, though, not with a baby on the way. Besides, there's nowhere to run to. I would be an outcast in my own village or among any of my own people. I know there are other villages—towns where foreigners speak in a tongue I can't understand. But, if my family and my own people would reject and despise me, what would happen to me there? Why do I feel so lifeless and void? Why do I even exist?* The thought of another poor soul coming into this sad world didn't please her at all. She hoped that at least her baby wouldn't be a girl.

The Outcasts

The village of Namuro was different from the place where she had spent all of her life up until now. In Namuro, many people owned radios and listened to news from the outside world. Some men sold avocados, plantains, and rice downriver at a Latin town—a place that she tried hard to imagine.

As Victoria watched, Esteban and Timoteo floated out of sight in their canoe, which was filled with plantains. Secretly she yearned to jump in—to go along and witness firsthand the exciting and fearful place where people spoke Spanish instead of her native tongue.

She'd heard men talking to her husband around their fire, telling stories about the small stores that sold onions, garlic, oil, and delicious bread—something made out of a grain called wheat. One time Luisa had even given her a piece from a small loaf that had been brought back from that place. Victoria's stomach growled and her mouth watered as she remembered the delicious taste. It was hard to get used to the new sensations and cravings she felt.

The canoe floated around the bend and out of sight, so she turned from the river and walked back to her hut. She silently crept into her hammock to rest for a while.

Hours later, Victoria was jolted awake by Rosa's intense voice. "Victoria, some men are coming up the river. Their canoe is making a terrible, loud noise. The men are pale—they have no color at all! Hurry, we're taking the trail deep into the jungle. Our men will stay here in the village. Listen, can you hear the noise?"

Victoria froze. Yes, she could hear it! And then a warning call resonated throughout Namuro, setting off a frenzy of activity. Her face paled momentarily and then she took action.

"Rosa, where's Paco?" she yelled, grabbing her basket, some fruit, and two old blankets which had been thrown over the pole rafters. But Rosa was already out the door searching for the little boy who never seemed to stay put. Victoria followed quickly and caught up with Rosa and Paco as they, along with fifty other women and well over a hundred children, swiftly disappeared into the thick jungle that surrounded Namuro.

The terrified group, silent by instinct, fled rapidly toward one of the most distant gardens. There they huddled tightly in fearful silence, waiting for a signal that they could return.

Mother, Victoria thought, *I told you I could die and you'd never know!* She shuddered. *I'm the one who tempted the spirits. It's my fault. I brought a curse with me to this place. We are all going to die because of me. I'm sorry, I'm so sorry. Isn't there a spirit that can help us? If you're there, please, please help us!*

Chapter 5

The sun sat directly overhead as the frightened group remained huddled in the garden. Small children squirmed and whined because their bellies were empty.

Victoria peeled a banana for Paco and handed another piece of fruit to Rosa. Other women and children grew even more restless. Victoria was the only one who'd had the presence of mind to bring food.

Eva, the chief's wife, took charge—they were, after all, in a garden. She ordered three young teenage girls to go and find some ripe bananas. Several other women held up machetes which the trembling girls grabbed. Before disappearing into the jungle they glanced back furtively.

Soon the trio returned. Fortunately each of the girls had worn their work dresses under their wraparound skirts that day. Desperate not to have to make two trips, the girls had fashioned their skirts into makeshift baskets so they could carry the huge bundles of bananas on their backs.

The Outcasts

When the girls approached, children's eyes brightened. Bananas were divvied out quickly and devoured hungrily. All too rapidly, the food and the diversion were gone.

As the sun crept toward the western horizon fear stole through the group, fear of spending the night there—a dark night without shelter or protection. *The men, what was happening to the men?* As the ladies sat in tense silence, their faces reflected their tormented thoughts. The waiting seemed endless—yet far too quickly the sun continued its descent.

Suddenly, a low whistle sounded somewhere in the distance. Ears perked. The group stirred.

"Sshh!" an older woman hushed the others. She whistled. In return, another whistle pierced the air. Relieved, she stood in anticipation of the arrival of her husband.

She wasn't disappointed. He, followed by two other village men, entered the clearing and approached the group.

"The white men have no weapons. They speak Spanish, but we couldn't understand some of what they told us. They speak another language too, which makes them sound as strange as they look. They call themselves '*misioneros*,' and they brought us gifts of oil and matches. The chief held a meeting so we could decide what to do with them for the night. It's too late to send them away. We are allowing them to sleep in the meetinghouse. But our men will take turns standing guard tonight, just to make sure."

"How many are there?" his wife asked.

"Three. Come back to the village, but stay in your huts as much as possible. Stay away from the meetinghouse and go to the river only in groups. You children!" he said with brusque authority, "stay indoors with your families until these outsiders leave!"

The weary group rose stiffly from the hard, uneven ground of their hiding place and followed the men.

With fear and trepidation the exhausted assembly entered the village. Quickly the families dispersed into their own huts. They barely beat the darkness, and not one would venture to the river for her evening bath.

Relief surged through Rosa as she entered the hut and saw Fidel. She sat down on a small bench. Victoria laid her sleeping nephew in his hammock, stretched her aching arms, and joined Rosa and Fidel near the fire.

"Tell us about the men," Rosa whispered, as though the foreigners could hear and understand her.

"There are three men," Fidel began. Several infuriating moments lapsed before he continued. "They're ugly. Their skin has no color. The tall man's head doesn't have any hair on it at all, and his nose tilts up on the end like a pig's snout. One man's hair is the color of rice and his eyes are blue like a parrot's feathers. He doesn't appear to be blind, though. The third man has dark hair and normal eyes, but his skin, too, has hardly any color, and he's very tall. They call themselves misioneros.

"The men who've been making trips to the Latin town could understand some of what they said—something about wanting our permission to give our village a message that they have for us. But the White Ones didn't tell us what the message is. It doesn't make any sense.

"They gave the village two five-gallon containers of cooking oil and six boxes of matches. I can't figure it out."

Rosa and Victoria looked at each other. They were amazed at the story—even more amazed that Fidel had told this much without being coaxed.

"Are they dangerous?" Rosa ventured.

"No, I don't think so," Fidel answered.

"Why don't you think so?" Rosa plied.

"They have gentle eyes," Fidel responded. "Even the blue eyes have peacefulness about them."

Both Rosa and Victoria exhaled deeply, releasing some of their pent-up tension. Worn-out as they were, however, neither wanted to snuff out the fire and retreat to her hammock for the night. Each sat lost in her own thoughts until neither one could stay awake any longer.

※

In the morning, women and children moved toward their bathing areas in larger groups than usual. Their lives revolved around the river: it was their bathtub, their laundry, their water supply, and their toilet. Eyes darted to and fro for any sign of the outsiders. Each villager wanted to hurry back before the White Ones were escorted to their canoe to leave.

Like the rest, Victoria, Rosa, and Paco bathed quickly. Victoria filled a large gourd with water, balanced it on her head, and started up the trail with Paco and Rosa close on her heels. They entered the clearing just as the three misioneros, along with several village men, strode past. The blue-eyed man hesitated and smiled at Victoria. Paco screamed and ran away as fast as his little legs could carry him.

Victoria, both stunned and curious, felt her fear melting away and she returned the man's gentle smile. Sternly, Rosa grabbed Victoria's arm and propelled her away.

Even though her feet moved quickly, Victoria's wistful thoughts continued. *There is something about this outsider. He seems different. I would really like to get to know this blue-eyed man and his friends...I want to find out more about them.*

Three months passed. Victoria's middle had grown thicker. She lay in her hammock, aware of the baby moving inside her belly. *I wonder if Fidel has any idea that in four months he will be a father. Raul would have known. He would have been happy—we both would have been so happy.*

I just wish I could go home and talk to Mother, tell her I'm expecting a baby—tell her that she'll be a grandmother. I'm afraid—so many things could happen. Victoria's gloominess fed on itself.

Now that I'm pregnant, I don't want to risk making the spirits angry by eating meat from any large animals. I don't want anything to be wrong with my baby. Oh well, at least now it doesn't matter that Fidel hardly ever goes hunting.

Little one, Victoria's thoughts continued as she patted her belly, *I'll be there for you. No matter what, I'll protect you.*

Shouting interrupted Victoria's reverie.

"The white men have returned!" echoed from hut to hut.

Small children ran frantically toward the safety of their homes. Men headed toward the meetinghouse. Women stood in clusters, discussing the arrival. However, this time no one would flee. For three months the White Ones had been the topic of discussion around the fires at night. The inhabitants of Namuro were wary but they no longer felt threatened.

Victoria's heart leapt in anticipation. *They're back! Maybe they'll give us the message this time. I wonder how long they'll stay.* Bravely she straightened her skirt and headed for the riverbank.

Coming around the bend a canoe floated into view. Three men sat in the craft. *Blue Eyes, Tall One, and Smooth Head have returned,* Victoria noticed, certain they were the same three men she had seen before. *Is that a woman in the center of the canoe—a woman with a baby on her lap?* Astounded, Victoria shaded her eyes and strained for a better look.

The Outcasts

Village men appeared in a group upriver from Victoria, but the canoe carrying the misioneros pulled into shore at her feet. The young woman stood up in the center of the canoe. Her soft blue eyes gently engaged Victoria's. As Victoria watched, the woman nearly lost her balance as she tried to get out. Instinctively, Victoria waded into the water, reached for the baby and for the woman's hand—and both were given freely.

White skin is so soft and smooth, Victoria thought as she helped her from the boat. *What pretty sparkling earrings the baby has in her ears! Her clothes are so soft and clean. She must be about six months old. Her eyes are as blue as her mother's eyes, though, poor thing. She's chubby and soft and her skin doesn't have any sores on it. Her hair is the color of a baby chick. I wonder if she's sick. Mmmm,* Victoria thought, *is her father the one whose hair is the color of rice?* She scrutinized the woman next to her. *Her hair is like that of the cocoa bean. She's tall for a woman, but her muscles look soft and weak.*

"Hola," the baby's mother said in Spanish as she smiled cheerily at Victoria.

Victoria couldn't help but smile back.

Several village men appeared, greeted the white men, and guided them up the path toward the meetinghouse. Victoria followed, carrying the baby and leading the white woman.

She certainly is clumsy, Victoria thought to herself, as the young lady slipped around in her wet sandals. Laughing merrily, the woman finally flipped her sandals off her feet, picked up the offending shoes, and trod barefoot alongside her new friend.

"Linda," the woman said, pointing to her own chest.

Victoria stared at her. *Oh, maybe her baby needs to nurse.* She tried to hand the baby to her mother.

"No, no," the woman giggled delightedly. She stopped and patted herself again and said, "Linda." Next she patted the baby and said, "Kimberly." Then she patted Victoria, tilted her head, and didn't say anything.

Oh, could she mean names? "Victoria, my name is Victoria," she guessed tentatively as she thumped her own chest.

"Linda, my name is Linda," her friend mimicked Victoria's phrase with a strange sort of accent.

She sounded so funny! But she spoke our language—she tried! Victoria led the way toward the meetinghouse.

At the clearing, a crowd of women descended on them. Blanca grabbed the baby out of Victoria's arms. "A baby, a white baby!" she exclaimed, examining the infant's chubby arms and legs.

Kimberly wailed loudly.

"Give her back!" Victoria commanded. "You're making the poor thing cry."

Blanca wasn't accustomed to being talked to in such a manner, especially by a younger woman! She glared at Victoria, who stood her ground firmly as the baby continued to scream. Blanca handed her back.

Victoria immediately placed the baby in her own mother's arms and led her new friend straight through the crowd to the meetinghouse.

Hesitantly, Linda stood in the doorway and searched the crowd of men, trying to find her husband. Right away, the blue-eyed man caught her eye and advanced to her side. Even though Bob had described the village to her, Linda was overwhelmed. It felt surreal that in 1972, she was witnessing firsthand the primitive living conditions of these Nala people.

Intrigued, Victoria watched the couple, confirming in her mind that the man with blue eyes and hair the color of rice was indeed the woman's husband. *Why is he putting his arm around her shoulder and squeezing her? His eyes look so intensely into hers—almost as if he can read her thoughts. He's paying attention to her and not to the men! How odd.*

She turned to leave but was interrupted by Linda's sing-song voice. "Victoria."

She turned in response.

Linda, standing next to Bob, smiled and patted her husband's chest. "Roberto," she said.

"Roberto," Victoria repeated, looking straight into his smiling face.

Victoria left the meetinghouse and marched straight to her hut. Lounging in her hammock, she contemplated Roberto, Linda, and the baby. *I wonder how old Linda and Roberto are. They seem old to have only one baby. Maybe they have other children who stayed with their grandmother. I wonder how long they'll stay this time. I wonder how far away their village is. I've never heard about a village of white people before.*

Oooo... The low, resonant hum from the conch shell reached Victoria's ears. *The chief is assembling all of us at the meetinghouse!* Quickly she rose and straightened her skirt. Making her way back to the building, she pushed through the crowd that had arrived ahead of her and found a vacant seat on the women's side of the huge room.

"The White Ones have returned," the chief stated the obvious. The meeting was now in order. "The blue-eyed man wants permission for him, his wife, and baby to live here in our village."

"Here?"

"They want to live in our village?"

"Why?"

"What do they want?"

The murmur of voices cascaded throughout the crowd at this new information and then hushed in anticipation of the chief's next words.

"They want to learn our language..."

"Our language?"

"They want to learn our language?"

"Can other people learn to speak like we do?"

"How can they learn our language?"

The hum of voices was so loud that the chief had to shout to finish his sentence, "...because they have a message for us. They want to give us this message in our own language. It comes from a good spirit, they say, in a book."

Victoria's heart skipped a beat. *A good spirit!*

Time seemed to stand still for her. Her mind raced. *I want to know about a good spirit.* She struggled to concentrate on the chief's words, hoping she hadn't missed anything important.

"If we allow them to stay, they'll need a house."

"Where would they build a house?"

"Who would give them land? They don't have family here to build next to!"

The chief raised his voice again. "We don't know what will happen. Perhaps these foreigners could help us..."

"Or they could make the spirits angry with us!"

The chief's voice droned on for two hours, frequently punctuated by animated discussions.

Finally he announced, "We'll meet again tomorrow morning to decide together whether they can move here and live among us." The meeting was over.

Deep in lively discussions, men and women exited the structure. But Victoria remained seated. *I wonder where the White Ones will eat their evening meal. The chief said they'll hang their hammocks in here for the night. Linda looks exhausted*, she thought, as she watched the mother prop her baby up onto her slight shoulder.

Suddenly Victoria realized that she sat alone. She sped home to talk to Rosa and Fidel. When she entered the hut they were sitting by a newly-stoked fire.

"Fidel," she began, "where will the White Ones eat? Do they have food? Where can they build a fire to cook?"

Fidel searched her face, trying to understand. Answering just one question was a trial for Fidel, much less the two or three she had a habit of peppering at him all at once.

"We should prepare enough food for them, too," Victoria stated. "They looked very hungry and tired. I traded fish for rice the other day, and we can roast plantains and yucca over the fire. I have six eggs that I've been saving, too. It will be enough."

Rosa looked up. *Has that girl lost her mind?* "How are you going to talk to them? How do you plan to make them understand that they are to come here to eat?"

"I'll tell them," Victoria said, shutting out further discussion as she flung her beautiful hair over her shoulder and marched out the door.

Bravely she approached the meetinghouse. But when she stepped through the door her courage vanished. There in one corner of the large building stood the small group of White Ones—their heads were bowed.

What are they mumbling? she wondered, and turned around quickly to leave.

But Linda raised her head and called out, "Victoria!"

The Outcasts

Hesitantly, Victoria advanced toward the White Ones. *Why did I come here? How can I communicate with them? Maybe Rosa was right.* But with that thought she raised her chin. Summoning her courage she motioned to her stomach and then her mouth and pretended to eat.

Linda's sparkling blue eyes shone and her head shook vigorously in the affirmative. "Thank you, Lord," she whispered as she looked up toward heaven, "Thank you for this wonderful friend — the friend I've been praying for!"

Victoria peered skeptically up at the rafters then back at the strange woman. But it was too late to change her mind. Victoria watched incredulously as one of the men grabbed some shiny hard objects and a small, funny-looking shiny contraption. They all turned toward her. Not knowing what else to do, she exited the building and led the misioneros to her home.

"Sit down," said Victoria, pointing to the benches and hammocks. Rosa pursed her lips as she sat and stirred the large pot of rice that was beginning to boil. Their guests seated themselves and stole glances around the tiny hut. Tired as they were, they couldn't help but notice the details in this hut — the first Nala home they had entered. Meanwhile, from the baskets in the corner Victoria gathered yucca and plantains to take to the river to peel.

Rosa grabbed the large gourd from Victoria's hands and said, "I'll go to the river and peel these. *You* can *talk* to these people." With that, she grabbed the machete and stalked from her house.

The Outcasts

Victoria hesitated awkwardly, but after a moment she raised her chin and took a deep breath. Smiling at the baby, she attempted to say her name—*"Gim, Gim, Gimmer,"* and she laughed at herself. The White Ones joined in her laughter, but with no hint of scorn.

Linda rescued her, saying, "Kimmi."

"Gimmi," Victoria repeated, noting the approval on their faces. *I must have said it correctly,* she smiled to herself.

Bob took a small notebook and pencil out of his pocket and wrote something in it.

What's he doing now? Victoria questioned silently.

The baby fussed and Bob reached for her. She cuddled on his chest as her father leaned back in the hammock and rocked her to sleep.

How interesting—the way this white man treats his child, Victoria mused.

From his seat by the fire, Fidel quietly took it all in.

Pointing to Paul, the bald man, Linda said, "Pablo." She pointed to Joe, the tall man, and said, "José."

As though on cue, Joe remembered the cans of tuna he'd brought to offer their hosts. Sheepishly, he raised them in the air. Victoria stared blankly at the smooth shiny objects, unsure of what to do.

Linda retrieved the tuna and the opener, strode to the lopsided wooden table, and opened the can. Victoria sidled up to the table and watched, amazed. Linda waved the open can enticingly under her new friend's nose. Victoria's eyes lit up with delight when she breathed in the wonderful aroma of fish. Two more cans passed from hand to hand until they reached Linda, who opened them.

Suddenly Victoria had an idea. *Maybe, just maybe, I can convince Fidel and Rosa to let the misioneros live next to us!*

Chapter 6

After the meal, the weary group of missionaries thanked their hosts and made their way back to the meetinghouse to hang their hammocks. None of them doubted that they would sleep well after this long yet rewarding day.

Glaring at Victoria, Rosa threw the dirty dishes into a large gourd, to be washed at the river in the morning.

"That fish tasted good all mixed in with the rice," Victoria ventured.

"Humph," Rosa snorted.

"It would be nice to have neighbors who would share fish and other things with us. Linda could be another daughter to you, Rosa."

"Another daughter?" Rosa spat, incredulously. "This girl has lost her mind, Fidel. Talk some sense into her."

Victoria stomped over to her hammock. She loosened her skirt a little, peeled off her blouse, and crawled into her hammock. Covering herself with a blanket, she lay still and stared at the rafters as the rest of the household prepared for bed.

Fidel slipped into his hammock last. Soon he heard his mother's even breathing, so he looked toward Victoria in the dark.

"Victoria?" he whispered.

"What?" she replied, with an edge to her voice.

"We don't know anything about the misioneros. They could anger the spirits. I'm afraid for you—and for our baby." *There, I've said it.* Fidel exhaled deeply.

So he knows, Victoria thought. *It's no longer my secret.* "Fidel, haven't you ever wondered whether there is a good spirit?"

Silence.

"Yes, I've wondered," he said begrudgingly.

"This is an opportunity to find out. What if we never get another chance?" she beseeched.

Silence.

"Exactly what are you suggesting?" *I can't believe I asked that question,* Fidel thought. *It's hard telling what she'll come up with.*

Victoria leaned on her side, facing her husband in the darkness. "Let's offer to let them build a house next to us. They can be our family. We need more food and they can help us. We can teach them our language, and they will tell us about a good spirit."

Fidel shivered. *Nothing like this has ever been done before.* His heart skipped a beat realizing the last time he'd thought those words. He had taken a risk and asked Diego for Victoria. *That worked out okay.* "Mmmm," he said, trying to digest the possibility and formulate his own thoughts on the matter.

"The baby will be fine. Gimmi, the white baby, is fine. If the spirits haven't bothered her, isn't that a sign that it will be okay?" Victoria lay back again in her hammock. Her mind raced ahead, thinking about what it would be like when the misioneros came to live next door.

"Mmmm," Fidel said, ending the conversation. He was struggling to make sense about the white family merging with theirs—building next door. He hadn't actually heard much after that. A long sigh escaped his lungs as he closed his eyes and began to sort it all out in his mind.

☙

Voices exploded throughout the crammed meetinghouse.

"There isn't even a question here! Why should we allow outsiders to move into our village?"

"We can't risk making the spirits angry! No. Just tell them *no!*"

Victoria's heart raced. *Dare I speak up*? She looked across the room to the men's side and saw Fidel sitting silently. *Please say something*, she thought. *Or at least back me up if I do.*

Victoria stood up. Her knees shook but she squared her shoulders and said, "I think we should allow them to move in!"

An awkward hush settled over the crowd as they stared at her in disbelief.

"They can build next to our house," Victoria offered, not daring to look at Fidel or Rosa.

"Fidel!" a voice yelled out, "you and your mother agree with this?"

Victoria's heart beat wildly. *Don't faint, don't faint, stand firm,* she coaxed herself.

Fidel stood and looked his wife in the eye. *What am I going to do with her?*

They stared at one another.

What will Mother do to me?

An expectant silence permeated the room as every eye looked from Fidel to Victoria and back again.

Fidel turned from Victoria's gaze to the chief and said, "They can build next to us."

I can't believe my ears! Victoria exulted.

"What about Rosa?" blurted an angry man.

"I can't believe Rosa would agree," cried out another.

All eyes searched the large gathering for Rosa.

She stood up and glared at her daughter-in-law. Then Rosa shifted her gaze to Fidel. Something in his eyes told her she'd better not cross him on this one.

This was one of those rare times when Rosa thought before she spoke. *Whose house is it anyway?* she questioned gloomily. *My life has been turned upside down since Fidel brought Victoria home! But, if he'd gone to Luwana to live, where would I be? I am in debt to them. I owe them.*

She cleared her throat. "They can build on my property. We'll take them into our family."

"Did you hear that?"

"What are they thinking?"

"Okay, then!" boomed the chief, quieting everyone.

"Rosa, Fidel, and Victoria have offered land to build a house for the misioneros. Now we vote.

"Everyone who agrees to allow the White Ones to come live among us, stand."

Rosa, Victoria, and Fidel rose to their feet once more.

Luisa, with her new infant daughter in her arms, stood up next to Victoria.

Ana pulled on her daughter's skirt and whispered urgently, "What are you doing? Sit down! Sit!" But Luisa staunchly remained at Victoria's side.

"Now," the chief declared, "everyone who doesn't want them to move in, stand up."

The remaining assembly jumped noisily to their feet, talking angrily to one another about Victoria, Fidel, Rosa, *and* Luisa.

I can't believe it! Victoria thought. *I was positive that the misioneros would be allowed to come! All they needed was a family to take them in—and we agreed. This is unfair!*

Victoria fled to the sanctuary of her own home.

Rosa couldn't decide who to direct her anger to—she had been caught in the middle and was mad at everyone! She stomped from the meetinghouse in disgust.

Fidel stood his ground alone—enduring the scornful looks and disdainful comments.

※

Fidel ached for Victoria. *It's been months since the misioneros were sent away. At least most of the villagers are talking to us again. But Victoria still looks so forlorn. I just want her to be happy.*

"I'm here," Luisa called out at the door.

"Come in," Victoria said from her hammock.

Luisa entered and sat in Fidel's hammock across from her friend. As Luisa rocked gently back and forth, she nursed her baby. "Victoria, how are you feeling?"

"I'm fine," she answered sullenly.

"Good. I brought you some rice." Luisa pulled a small gourd filled with rice out from under an extra skirt that she was carrying. She handed the gift to Victoria.

"You're such a good friend." Victoria smiled. "I still can't believe you stood up with us!" she chuckled.

"I know. Mother didn't speak to me for a week. She was so mad!" The girls laughed.

It feels good to laugh. But at the same time I feel like crying, Victoria mused.

"Do you want to go fishing with me?" Victoria asked, impulsively.

"Yes, I'm sure Mother will watch Maria for me. I know Mother is hungry for fish, too. I'll take the baby home and change clothes. Just call out when you're ready to go." Luisa left quickly.

Feeling huge and heavy, Victoria eased out of her hammock, changed into an older skirt, and walked to the shelf to retrieve her fishhooks and line. "I'm going fishing with Luisa," she informed Fidel, who couldn't have missed the conversation.

As the girls headed upriver by trail, Victoria said, "It feels good to be outside and to walk."

"Your baby should be coming soon," Luisa said. "Are you scared? I was terribly afraid before Maria came."

"I wish my mother could be here," Victoria stated wistfully.

"You live with the midwife. Rosa will be right there no matter what time you need her."

"I know, but you still had your own mother with you, too, didn't you?"

"Yes. My mother hasn't had any more babies since Nelsi, and she's already ten years old. So it was safe for her to help. I don't know what I would have done without her!" Luisa declared.

"Then you should understand how much I want *my* mother!" Victoria said defensively.

"I do know, I was just trying to make you feel better." They both laughed.

"How will I know when it's time?" Victoria asked.

"You'll know!" They laughed again, nervously this time.

Fifteen minutes later Victoria led the way toward the river on a small footpath that had barely been visible from the main trail. Huge white boulders jutted out of the water. At the river's edge the girls turned over a large rock and captured small crayfish to use as bait. They climbed gingerly over the boulders and sat down on the largest one near the center of the river. Silently they baited their hooks and threw in their lines.

"Wow, caught one already!" Victoria said, as she pulled in a five-inch fish. Grabbing the vine she'd brought, she laced one end through the fish's gill. She poked a long stick between rocks and plunged it into the soft river bottom. Then she tied both ends of the vine securely to it, allowing the tethered fish to fall back into the cool, swift current.

"Have you thought about names for the baby?" Luisa asked. "Every time Timoteo returns from Cerro Alto he tells me new names that he's heard. Maybe I can help you."

Actually, Luisa was talking about nicknames, because Nala names were kept secret, and only nicknames were used. In the past, the Nala nickname described the person in some way. One woman in the village was called Red Girl because when she was born her skin was very reddish. Another man was named White because his skin color was so pale. However, when the Nala began venturing outside of their villages, they liked the idea of taking Spanish names for themselves and their babies at birth. They retained their custom of giving secret Nala names which were never spoken and would be known only by the immediate family throughout their lives and would be taken to the grave.

Victoria thought for a few moments and then commented, "I have some ideas, but I'd love to hear more names."

"Timoteo heard a woman call her little girl Susana. And the man who makes bread called out the name Melisa to one of his daughters."

"I like those, but what about boys' names?" Victoria desperately hoped for a boy.

"Franklin and Marvin are two names he told me about. Also, he heard one little boy called Yuri," Luisa shared.

Yuri," Victoria said. "That is different. I like that name."

Both women were lost in thought for a while.

"Luisa, do you ever wish you could go with your husband downriver to the Latin town?"

"I like hearing the stories when he comes back. Sometimes I lie awake and try to imagine the village there. But I never thought about actually going."

"I want to go someday. If Fidel ever makes a trip, I will ask him to take me, too," Victoria exclaimed.

"You're different. You aren't afraid to speak out. Are all of the girls in Luwana like you?" Luisa inquired.

Victoria laughed. "No. I am different, and I don't know why. I've always wondered about so many things. I feel a need to know why we do things the way we do, or whether there are other ways, other paths. Why can't we eat meat from large animals when we're pregnant? Would something bad really happen if we did? Why do the medicine rocks work sometimes, and other times they don't? Don't you ever have questions?"

"Yes. When Fidel's sister...didn't get well, I had many questions. She was my cousin—and closest friend. She was kind, she did things the right way—why would the spirits be mad at her? Why didn't the medicine rock heal her, or the chief's... Oh, I'm so sorry. I should never be talking this way!" Luisa cried out.

"That's okay, I feel the same as you. It helps to know I'm not the only one." But both girls looked around furtively, desperately hoping they hadn't offended any spirits.

Deep in their own thoughts and comfortable with each other's presence, they fished silently.

"We have fifteen fish," Luisa stated as she threaded her last catch onto the vine.

"I know, but I just want to sit here a while longer. I don't want to go back."

"I don't either, but I think Maria needs me."

"Okay. I'm very hungry, too," Victoria admitted.

From the footpath, the girls worked their way to the main trail and hiked back to the village.

"I'll clean the fish and bring some to you," Victoria offered.

"No, let Sebastiana and Teresa clean them. They've been sitting around all day. They'll bring some to you when they're done. You need to rest."

"Okay, thank you," Victoria agreed, feeling very weary all of a sudden.

Entering her hut, she found Rosa sitting by the fire.

"I'm boiling plantains and yucca for soup. All it needs is the fish," Rosa said. "You always manage to bring back fish."

"Sebastiana and Teresa are going to clean them. Soup sounds really good," Victoria said, plopping herself heavily into her hammock.

Pain woke Victoria from a sound sleep, taking her breath away. Her swollen abdomen slowly relaxed and she breathed deeply, willing herself to remain calm.

In the distance insects buzzed and monkeys howled. The cadence of even breathing filled the small hut as she stared into the darkness.

It's nothing. I'm going back to sleep, Victoria told herself, closing her eyes.

She was nearly asleep when another contraction assaulted her, and her eyes popped open in alarm. *Should I wake up Fidel and Rosa? Should I wait? My mother would know what to do. She should be here. I could call out to her and she would know whether it's time to run for the midwife. But Rosa is right here. I can wait because Rosa is the midwife and she's right here.*

Here comes another one. Victoria held her breath against the pain.

She thought the night would never end. Finally, roosters began to crow with the first rays of dawn.

Rosa rose from her hammock and made her way to the fire pit. She relit the fire, dressed, and headed for the door.

"Rosa," Victoria gasped hoarsely.

Rosa rushed to her daughter-in-law's hammock. "Is it time? How long have you been having the pains?" she questioned in alarm.

Victoria moaned.

"Fidel! Get up!" Rosa ordered.

Fidel roused. "What?"

"The baby is coming. Get some large banana leaves. Take Paco over to Ana's. Hurry!"

Fidel jumped out of his hammock, dressed quickly, and stole a fearful glance at his beautiful wife. Lines of worry etched his face. Grabbing Paco out of his hammock, Fidel disappeared from Victoria's sight.

"Why didn't you wake me up?" Rosa scolded.

Victoria moaned again as her abdomen tightened with an alarming force. Sweat broke out on her face. She looked pleadingly into Rosa's eyes.

"It's okay," Rosa's softened voice murmured. "It will all be over soon. You'll be okay." In her mind, however, she couldn't prevent the visions of other first-time mothers who had labored for days only to die before the baby could make its way into the world. Across her mind flitted the indelible image of the young mother who, after the birth of her second child, had bled to death before Rosa's eyes. She shook her head. Then there was the poor mother whose infant tried to arrive arm first. She shivered. *I can't think of these things, I must stop. Everything will be okay...Victoria and her baby will be fine—just fine.*

Fidel rushed back in with four very large banana leaves. He stood motionless in the center of the room, waiting for orders.

"Stand them up in the corner," Rosa snapped. "Help me string these blankets up to make a small room here around your hammocks.

"Good. Now bring the small stool and the leaves.

"Help me get her out of her hammock. Stand up, Victoria," Rosa urged gently, yet with an authority Victoria could not refuse.

"Throw her hammock up over the beam and lay out the banana leaves on the floor there. Never mind. Hold on to her, I'll do it myself," she said, grabbing the leaves from her son's hands.

Victoria leaned heavily on her husband as the pain shot through her. The contractions were relentless—she could no longer catch her breath in between.

This cannot be normal, Fidel thought, beside himself with fear.

The Outcasts

"Kneel on the leaves, Victoria," Rosa commanded. "Help her down! She can lean on the stool. Hurry up. Now get out of here, Fidel. Go!"

I can't do this. It hurts. I can't bear this any longer. Help me! Victoria's tortured mind screamed silently.

"Rosa, I'm here," called Ana from outside the makeshift room. "I've come to help."

"Come in," Rosa replied.

"Luisa sent me over—she wishes she could be here with you, Victoria. She thought I could fill in for your mother."

"Here, let me sit on the stool. Put your arms across my knees like Luisa did," she crooned.

Thank you, Victoria thought, as she leaned hard—pushing through another contraction. Her body demanded that she bear down. *It's almost over—I can sense it,* she thought.

Several pushes later, a lusty cry filled the air.

Ana wiped the sweat from Victoria's brow.

"A girl!" Rosa beamed. "You have a girl!"

Victoria endured several more light contractions which expelled the afterbirth. Finally she was helped into her own hammock. Her tiny daughter, swaddled in an old wraparound skirt, was laid gingerly in her waiting arms.

You are beautiful, little one, Victoria marveled. She stroked the baby's soft black hair and examined her tiny fingers and toes. "You're perfect, absolutely perfect," the new mother crooned to her infant as she snuggled the baby to her breast.

The Outcasts

Ana dug a hole in the corner and Rosa dumped the contents from the banana leaves into the hole and covered it with the dirt. The women pulled down the blankets and stood by Victoria's hammock to watch the new mother nurse her infant. Satisfied, Ana took her leave while Rosa started a pot of banana drink.

Fidel returned. He hesitated just inside the doorway and drank in the scene. Victoria was holding their baby girl. *She's beautiful—the softness in her eyes as she holds the baby—she's so beautiful!*

Victoria looked up from the infant. *He isn't even looking at the baby. Raul would have wanted to have a baby with me—he would have been happy.* Victoria forced herself to focus on the beautiful infant in her arms. Fidel moved haltingly toward his hammock and sat down slowly—almost reverently facing his wife and daughter.

"What name should we give her?" he asked. "She's so tiny." *I want to hold her,* he thought, as the picture of the misionero rocking his baby entered his mind.

Victoria laid the baby in her lap and said, "Up above my hammock wrapped in my skirt is a special blanket. Linda gave it to me before she left. It was *Gimmi's*. Will you get it for me?"

Fidel stood, reached up and brought down the skirt. He unfolded the cloth and produced the pink and blue baby blanket. It was soft and clean. He handed it to Victoria and watched as she tenderly wrapped the tiny infant—as though she'd been doing it for years. Without warning, Victoria handed the bundle to Fidel.

His eyes grew wide as he accepted his daughter. He felt awkward and foolish, but his heart melted as he gazed into the eyes of his firstborn. He relaxed as he leaned into his own hammock and snuggled her in the crook of his arm. He had never in all of his nineteen years felt this way before.

"What are we going to name her?" he repeated. Little did he know how long Victoria had agonized over a name for their baby. She had desperately hoped for a boy, but knew she must be prepared in case the baby was a girl. She thought about her mother and wished they could talk about a name, but her mother had not protected her when she needed her most.

"Rosalinda," Victoria declared.

A plate crashed to the table at the far end of the hut. Rosa retrieved it quickly and turned away so they couldn't see the tears that were pooling in her eyes. *Tears! What's the matter with me anyway? I've gone soft in my old age.*

Chapter 7

Rosalinda was one week old and visitors still arrived daily to see the newest inhabitant of Namuro.

"...heard you didn't make a sound," a toothless, gray-haired woman mumbled. She had entered the hut unannounced and plunked onto the nearest stool. "What'd ya name her—or is it a boy? No, it's a girl. They told me it's a girl and ya didn't yell out or make a sound. You've got spunk—'course everybody knows that, after the scene you caused over those White Ones. Had to laugh, I did. Myself, I like girls with spunk. When I was young, they used to beat it outta us. Well, gotta go. My fire's burn'n' and my husband'll be home soon. He better bring us some meat. I'll bring ya some meat if he had any luck. Ya gotta be hungry for meat..." the plump old lady continued her one-sided conversation as she hobbled out the door at the opposite end of the hut.

"Who was that?" Victoria asked.

"She lives in the farthest hut downriver. I've never taken you there. She's always been a bit strange," Rosa stated matter-of-factly.

"Why does she limp?" Victoria questioned.

"A snake bit her when she was a girl of maybe ten years old or so. She'd been out to the garden with her family and a snake struck her so fast no one saw it. Her father carried her home. Her leg swelled up twice its size and turned all black. The chanting lasted a week or more. She lived through it, but her bad leg never grew much after that.

"She's had nine sons and four daughters. They say she never made a sound either, not a sound—just like you."

Fidel entered the hut and deposited a freshly-butchered wild pig near the fire. It had been a successful hunting day for him.

"Wild pig!" Rosa exclaimed. "I'll start the fire."

"Thank you," Victoria said weakly from her hammock.

Fidel walked toward his wife. "How are you feeling? Does your head still ache?"

"I'm cold. Ana, Luisa, and Nelsi are sick," Victoria said through chattering teeth.

"Pedro and Ernesto's families are sick too," Rosa declared from her spot by the fire. "Plus, who knows how many others."

"I'm going back to the river to bathe," Fidel announced.

When he returned, he walked straight to the hammock and gingerly picked up Rosalinda. He held her in the crook of his arm as he rocked back and forth in his own hammock. Victoria closed her burning eyes. Shaking violently, she curled on her side, desperately hoping to fall asleep.

Fidel touched his daughter's skin and became alarmed. She too was burning with fever.

"Mother, what can we do? Rosalinda has a fever—she's sick, too!"

Feeling the baby's hot cheeks, Rosa shook her head in anguish. "Do you want me to go get the chief?"

"Yes," Fidel answered.

As she walked through the village, Rosa stopped outside each hut. At every house she learned that one or more family members had a headache, chills, or a fever. A cloud of fear hung ominously in the air.

"Rico!" Rosa called at the chief's hut.

"Come in," Eva summoned.

Rosa entered and without the usual small talk got right to the point. "Rosalinda is sick with the fever. Rico, will you come and chant?"

"Every home in the village is under attack. I've been waiting to assemble all of the men who are well enough to join me while I chant for the whole village," he declared. "I'll blow the conch shell soon. Several men were out hunting today but everyone should be back by now."

"Okay," Rosa said, leaving quickly. Fear crept into her heart. As she hurried home she tried to deny the ache she was feeling in her own head.

Victoria was not even aware of the delicious aroma of soup. Her small frame shook violently under her thin blanket.

Fidel held Rosalinda in his left arm while he ate his soup.

Rosa shook her head at the sight. *It doesn't seem natural for a man. But, I don't know...on the other hand, there's something about his love for that baby—and for Victoria. He would be devastated if anything happened to them. They have to get through this—they just have to!*

Rosa began to tremble. She was cold, yet her eyes burned. "Fidel," she croaked hoarsely.

He rushed to his mother's side and with his free hand helped her into her hammock. "Where's Paco?" *Sometimes I wonder if that boy even lives with us!*

Rosa didn't answer, so Fidel left the house to look for his nephew.

"Paco!" he called out.

"He's in here," Esteban hollered.

Fidel entered his uncle's hut and looked around at the hammocks filled with sick people. The mournful sound of the conch shell floated past their ears. "Are you going?" Fidel asked.

"Yes, Sebastiana can look after the rest of them. And you?"

"They're all sick, even Rosalinda," he said, looking down at the baby still cradled in the crook of his arm. "I have to stay with them. Paco, come on home—now!" The little boy followed obediently.

Chanting filled the night air. Rosalinda began to cry.

The Outcasts

"Victoria," Fidel whispered. "Can you nurse the baby? Rosalinda is hungry. Victoria?" Gently, he shook her arm, and could feel the heat through the blanket.

She moaned, shivered, and turned onto her back. As she uncovered herself to allow the baby to nurse she began to shake violently.

"Oh, Victoria," her husband moaned. *What can I do for her? How can I help her? If there is a good spirit, please, please help my family!*

Little did he know that the One True God—the God of all compassion—was listening to his cry, longing to save Victoria, little Rosalinda—and Fidel as well.

Throughout the night, Fidel rocked the baby. He checked on his mother and watched over his wife. Victoria's chills ended, but her fever soared. He pleaded with the spirit world to release his family. And he begged the unknown good spirit to help them.

Finally the blackness of night melted into the grayness of dawn. Exhausted, Fidel felt his wife's forehead. She was sweaty and no longer burned with fever! Next, he went to Rosa's hammock. She was very hot, but she was no longer shivering beneath her cover.

They seem a little better. "And you, little one," he said to the baby in his arms, "how are you?" But she was limp and unresponsive, the fever still ravaging her tiny body.

Worry lines traced Fidel's face as he paced the floor.

"Fidel," Victoria called out weakly. "Rosalinda needs to nurse."

"Here," he said, putting the baby into her arms.

"She's so hot! Wake up, little one," her mother coaxed gently, trying not to allow panic to seize her. She could barely hold her baby, she was so exhausted and weak. "Please wake up. Here," she said, urging the baby to nurse. But the infant lay still and limp in her arms. Victoria watched the baby's stomach rise and fall, reassuring herself that Rosalinda was still breathing. "What can we do? Please don't let anything happen to her," she begged her husband.

"I've heard some of the men talk when they come back from Cerro Alto. There is a 'sick house,' called a *clínica*, in that town, and a man who gives them medicine to make them well. We can take her there. It costs money, though, and we don't have any," Fidel informed her.

"You would do that? You would try the outsider's medicine?" Victoria asked, amazed.

"Yes, I will try anything for her, and for you. I'll go ask to use Esteban's canoe."

Fidel walked toward his uncle's house. Mid-stride, however, he stopped and listened. *A motor! It sounds like the misioneros' motor coming upriver.* He diverted toward the path to the river and trooped to the water's edge. He paced back and forth until the canoe finally rounded the corner and came into view.

Tall One, Smooth Head, Blue Eyes, and Linda smiled as the motor turned off and their canoe floated toward the bank.

"Can you help us? Hurry, our baby is sick," Fidel rattled off in Nala.

The Outcasts

The group looked from one to the other, desperately wishing that they could understand him, each sensing that something was terribly wrong. They disembarked and followed the trail to the village.

Victoria's eyes widened as Linda entered the hut. Tears stung Victoria's eyes, but she was too fatigued even to sit up.

Linda rushed to her side and saw the tiny, sick infant in her arms.

"Bob," she called urgently, "their baby is really sick. Come here. Hurry!"

Victoria couldn't understand a word and yet she felt such peace. *They'll help us—I know they'll help us somehow.*

"Paul," Bob said, "let's split up and go to the other huts and see if anyone else needs to go to the clinic in Cerro Alto. We have to get this baby to a doctor quickly. Her mother, too, I think. I wonder what they have."

"But my Spanish is so poor," Paul worried.

"It'll be hard for me to communicate with them, too." Bob tried to encourage his comrade. "They barely speak Spanish at all. Maybe the fewer words we use the better they'll understand anyway."

Paul prayed as he hurried to the nearest hut. *Father, please give me the words to say, and please somehow give these dear people understanding.* Hard stares and angry-sounding words drove him away from each Nala home.

Bob wasn't welcomed either. From each dwelling, he was turned away harshly.

With heavy hearts, both men returned to Fidel and Victoria's hut.

"I don't think they understood me. They all seemed so angry," Paul said.

"I got the same response," Bob replied. "Let's hope that Fidel will allow his wife and baby to go for help."

"We'll take you to Cerro Alto in our canoe," Bob said in Spanish, pointing toward the river. "There's a clínica and a doctor there."

Fidel looked at Victoria. He paused for a moment. "*Clínica...* Cerro Alto," he said.

"Yes," she smiled weakly. "Will Rosa come with us?"

"Mother," Fidel said, "come with us downriver to Cerro Alto. We're going to get help there for the baby and Victoria. We can get you help, too."

"No," Rosa said. "I'm getting better. My chills are gone. I'll stay here with Paco. You go if you think you should. We'll go to Ana's house. They'll take us in."

"Did Luisa get sick? Is Maria okay?" Victoria asked, fearful for her friend. "We need to ask before we leave."

"I think you'd better just go," Rosa stated flatly.

"I can't leave if Luisa needs help," Victoria cried.

"I'll go see," Fidel offered, walking out the door.

Moments later he returned saying, "Luisa is feeling better and Maria didn't get sick. Let's go."

Taking Kimberly from Linda's arms, Bob walked outside with Paul. Linda picked up tiny Rosalinda so Fidel could help Victoria get dressed. The process exhausted her. She couldn't get out of the hammock, so her husband lifted her in his arms and carried her to the canoe.

At least a dozen pairs of eyes peered through the cracks in their bamboo walls—nothing like *this* had ever happened before in Namuro.

Chapter 8

Linda placed two red vinyl cushions on the floor of the canoe and motioned for Fidel to set Victoria on them. Fidel sat down on the board behind his wife and she leaned against his legs, resting her head on his lap.

As the boat was guided toward the center of the Namuro River, Kimberly cried for her mother, so Linda handed baby Rosalinda to Fidel.

They floated downstream past the village bathing areas. The river deepened and the outboard motor roared to life, startling Victoria and Fidel. But their muscles relaxed as they remembered that this craft sped toward hope for their infant. Water lapped at the sides of the boat and the hot wind whipped at their hair and faces. Fidel felt exhilarated and somehow free as he moved away from the village toward the unknown.

Mile after mile the canoe dodged rocks and logs in the narrow tributary as Joe guided it through the deepest channels of the murky water.

The Outcasts

At last the Namuro River spilled out into the wide Grande River, and the boat sped on at an even faster rate. Fidel's heart seemed to race along with it as he thought about the outsiders and their village that he would soon experience first-hand. Looking up at the sun he realized that over three hours had passed.

How can I tell these misioneros that I don't have any money? he wondered. *This trip could be for nothing. People say that the outsiders demand money for everything.*

Soon houses came into Fidel's view. The sides of the buildings were made with flat wooden boards. Many had shiny roofs that looked like they were made from the same material as the cans of fish that the misioneros had shared with them. The canoe pulled up at a wooden dock, where hard, smooth, even steps led up to the town. Around his fire at night Fidel had been told that although the steps were smooth and uniform, they felt hard as rocks and didn't get muddy or slippery in the rain. Now the stories were becoming reality to Fidel, and he took it all in.

Linda stood on the dock and Fidel handed Rosalinda to her. He lifted Victoria in his arms and stepped out easily. As Fidel followed the misioneros to the clinic, he was painfully aware of the stares of the townspeople. Some of them had black skin and curly hair, and others had straight hair with skin color that was similar to the Nala. Although he had heard stories about these strangers, he was not prepared for the cold and hostile look in their eyes. Their gazes were not at all like the compassionate and peaceful look of the misioneros.

Bob took Rosalinda from his wife's outstretched arms and entered one of the wooden buildings with a shiny metal roof. Fidel followed. He was amazed that the floor was hard and shiny like the stairs. *This must be the clínica,* he surmised. Bob spoke Spanish to the woman inside. Fidel wasn't able to understand what followed.

As the nurse surveyed the Nala baby, and the Nala woman in Fidel's arms, she shook her head no. "We don't treat *them,*" she said disdainfully.

"They're sick. They could die! What do you mean you don't treat *them?*" Bob countered, attempting not to lose his temper.

"We don't have a lot of medicine and they never have money to pay. They wouldn't know how to take the medicine when they leave here, anyway. We don't treat *them.*" The nurse turned her back on the group.

"Wait a minute, hold on there," Bob said, drawing in a calming breath and praying for the right words. "We'll pay for the medications or treatments, and we'll make sure they're taken at the proper times. We need to know what's wrong with them. Many in their village have had high fevers and chills. The baby, too—she's very sick. We need to know what's wrong with them and what medicine they need. We'll take full responsibility. Please ask the doctor to look at them... Please."

The nurse raised her voice. "The doctor's not in. He won't be back until tomorrow sometime. But you have to leave this town before nightfall. They probably have malaria. We've been getting a lot of reports of malaria from the outlying area. We don't want it to spread here. You *have* to leave!"

Fidel watched the exchange between Bob and the woman. *Her words were as sharp as poisoned arrows!* Now he wished desperately that he could understand their conversation.

"Come on, let's go," Bob said, walking out the door toward Linda who was standing on the other side with Kimberly in her arms.

"Go where?" Linda reacted with sharpness in her voice.

"I don't know," Bob stated flatly, desperately trying to make sense of the predicament they were in.

"They won't allow us to stay here for the night?" Catching herself, Linda prayed. *Dear Lord, help me to remain calm. Fidel and Victoria can surely hear the tension in my voice and see it on my face. They have no idea what's happening and they're depending on us. I don't want to do anything to damage that developing trust. Please help us, Lord!*

Fidel set Victoria down on the grass and then sat down next to her. Bob handed Fidel his daughter.

"I'll stay here with them," Linda informed the group. "Why don't you guys go buy us some food and something to drink. I'm sure Victoria is getting very dehydrated. She slept most of the way here, so I didn't think to give her water."

"That's a good idea," Bob said, turning to Joe and Paul.

The Outcasts

Joe smiled and led the way toward the storefronts, anxious to check out more of this outpost community. Paul and Bob lagged behind their energetic companion, discussing the predicament.

Linda plopped down beside her friends. She looked at Fidel and Victoria sitting there in the grass with their sick child. Compassion wracked her heart and etched her face.

"They went to get us some food," she said in Spanish, making eating motions and pointing toward the men who were disappearing around the corner.

Victoria sat weakly and tried to nurse her unresponsive baby. Tears began to flow unchecked down her cheeks when Rosalinda remained lifeless in her arms. *Why isn't anyone helping us?* her heart cried out. *I thought this town had people who could help us! What are we going to do now? Rosalinda, hang on. I promised you that I would protect you—I promised! I have to do something for my baby!* Panic seized Victoria and her eyes flashed with determination and fear.

"Linda, do something!" she demanded in Nala.

Linda seemed to understand her plea and clearly saw her pain. *Oh, God, help me! What do you want me to do? Give me wisdom and help me to think this through.* Seconds later Linda remembered the liquid baby aspirin in the diaper bag. She also had a baby bottle with water in it. Opening the diaper bag, she located the aspirin and measured a quarter of a dropper.

"This is medicine," she said, wondering if they could understand her. She leaned toward Rosalinda.

Victoria hesitated, wondering about the strange red liquid she called medicine. *If she'd had it all along, why hadn't she given it to my baby sooner?* It was all very confusing, but Victoria was desperate for help, so she allowed Linda to put the dropper into Rosalinda's mouth. The baby stirred and gagged as the strange-tasting medicine was squirted in. She swallowed and then went back to sleep. Red liquid dribbled out of her mouth and Victoria wiped it away. Warily, she and Fidel watched their baby to see what would happen next.

Linda thought back to the first aid course she'd taken before coming to this country. *How much sugar and salt should I put in the bottle to counteract the baby's dehydration? We can buy sugar and salt at one of these stores. I'll wait until Bob gets back with the food. Maybe dehydration is her biggest problem. The aspirin should get her fever down. Perhaps that's why Victoria is so weak, too. In the canoe we have a cooler with water, and I have a glass jar. I'll put a little sugar and salt in that and give them both small amounts every fifteen minutes. I'll also give them as much plain water to drink as possible. We'll buy adult aspirin to take back to the village with us, and baby aspirin if the store here carries it. Even if we had any medication for malaria, I'm not sure if Victoria should take it while she's nursing, and the baby is surely too small for that medicine. If it is malaria, Victoria will probably have a relapse of the fever in a day or two. Perhaps treating them for dehydration and their fevers is the best that anyone can do. Now... can we make it back to Namuro before nightfall?*

Linda's thoughts were interrupted by her husband and two coworkers arriving with food and Cokes.

"Coca-Cola!" Linda smiled.

"Yeah, isn't that sad? Coke has reached these people before the gospel!" Joe interjected. "This seems like a town straight out of an old western movie. All we need are some horses tied up at hitching posts."

The other missionaries laughed, which only egged Joe on. "I expected saloon music from a player piano when I went into the store."

Fresh yeast rolls wrapped in brown paper were handed to Linda to be divvied out.

As the missionaries bowed their heads, Victoria and Fidel exchanged questioning glances. They listened as Paul spoke in what sounded to them like a low sing-song voice. The missionaries raised their heads and began to eat.

This is my first meal in days, Victoria realized as she savored the delicious flavor of the bread. *The wild pig! Fidel finally brought me home wild pig and I wasn't even able to eat any! At least Rosa and Paco have food while we're gone. This bread is delicious.*

Paul pried the caps off of two Cokes and handed them to Fidel and Victoria.

"I'm not sure what they'll think of that," he said. "I wish we could warn them."

Fidel watched the others drink from their bottles and turned his up to take a big swig. He grimaced and coughed.

Victoria looked at her own bottle cautiously. "What does it taste like?" she asked Fidel.

Fidel took another swig—only a sip this time. "I don't know," he informed her. "Try a *small* amount."

Victoria raised the bottle to her lips and sipped the dark liquid. When she chuckled at the bubbly drink, Fidel realized that it had been a very long time since he'd heard her laugh. His heart warmed and a loving smile lit up his own face.

Rosalinda stirred in Victoria's arms. She felt the baby's skin. "She isn't as hot!" Victoria exulted to her husband. She tried to nurse her baby, but the infant was still very weak and fell right back to sleep.

"Bob, I have a plan," Linda said to her husband. "If you can buy some sugar and salt, we can make a rehydration drink for the baby and Victoria. If I remember correctly, it is about 2 tablespoons of sugar and ½ teaspoon of salt per four cups of water."

"That's an excellent idea. I'll go back to the store while all of you get settled in the canoe for the trip back to Namuro," Bob said. "We talked about going on downriver and then to the city to a hospital, but we're worried about how they would be treated there, too—especially with the threat of malaria. I didn't realize how much the folks in this country discriminate against tribal people. It may be different in the city, but I don't know."

"I think you're right," Linda said sadly. "Oh, yes, and buy several bottles of adult aspirin, and if there is any liquid baby

The Outcasts

aspirin, buy that too. Perhaps the other villagers will still need help—and maybe even accept it—when we get back."

"Alright, I'll meet you at the canoe." Bob strode off again toward the store.

Linda, Joe, and Paul rose to their feet. Fidel picked up the baby and helped Victoria up.

"Are you strong enough to walk now?" Fidel asked.

"Yes, I feel better since I ate," Victoria said, as convincingly as possible.

She was relieved to reach the canoe and sit once again on the soft cushion. Her body and emotions were spent. *I can't wait to get home. I don't like this town and these people. They look at us as if they hate us—or like they might even harm us. I don't understand why they dislike us.* Suddenly another thought hit her like a thunderbolt. *Did I say "home"? Do I think of Namuro as my home now? But, I wish I could really go home. If anything happens to Rosalinda, my mother and father will never even get to meet her. How I wish I could really go home.*

Victoria's tumultuous thoughts ended in fitful sleep. She awoke off and on to the roar of the motor and the splash of water against the sides of the boat, only to drift off again into restless yet much-coveted sleep.

Victoria roused again as the canoe struggled up the swift current of the Namuro River. Since they first had passed this way it had flooded, making the rocks invisible under the swirling, dark brown surface. To complicate matters, darkness was descending rapidly. Silent tension filled the air.

"It's too dangerous—we can't go much farther," Paul called out from the front of the canoe. "At best we're going to ruin the propeller."

"Should we find a good spot and pull in?" Bob called to Joe, who was at the rear, running the motor.

"I guess we don't have any choice," Joe agreed.

"Pull in under those trees, behind that log," Paul called out to Joe, who guided the boat toward the undergrowth.

"No!" Fidel shouted. Joe reacted immediately, steering back toward the center of the river. Silently, Fidel pointed up at the tree branches which they'd been headed toward. All eyes followed.

Joe let out his breath, "Man, did you see that?"

"No," the others retorted. "What?"

"There's a huge snake up in that tree, right where we were going! It really blends in. I'm glad Fidel is paying attention." Joe grimaced and continued to shake his head.

Fidel calmly stood up and pointed, guiding them to continue upriver. The men took his lead. The boat struggled on for ten more minutes and finally Fidel motioned toward the left shore. Joe steered the canoe to the bank, and to their amazement, a thatched-roof hut appeared, thirty feet away.

"Aaa-ooo," Fidel called out.

"Aaa-ooo," echoed a reply.

The Outcasts

Fidel stepped out of the boat and walked toward the figure that had emerged from the hut. Few words were spoken between the two men, but it was understood that travelers could not continue on their journey after dark. The group would have a fire to sleep by...they would not be turned away.

The rest of the men disembarked and helped the women out of the canoe. They were astonished to find a rough-looking older man who spoke Spanish.

"Hola," the man greeted them.

"*Hola,*" returned Bob, in surprise. *He looks like a national. I wonder why he lives here.*

After exchanging names, the group hiked up the path toward a small hut.

Linda shuddered involuntarily as she followed the men inside. She was still thinking about the snake in the tree. However, when she entered the small, dark, one-room structure, new fears assailed her. She couldn't help but notice the cockroaches that roamed freely up and down the dilapidated bamboo walls. Chills ran up and down her spine.

Victoria collapsed into the nearest hammock and began to nurse her baby. *Rosalinda is so much better! She isn't limp anymore.* Victoria hadn't been aware of the spoonfuls of rehydration liquid that Linda had been feeding the infant every fifteen minutes for the last hour and a half. She barely recalled the sips of the liquid she herself had been given the few times she had awakened.

A rather plump Nala woman sat by the fire. She greeted Fidel and Victoria in their native tongue and stole uneasy glances at the White Ones. A small boy and a toddler huddled around her, obviously frightened by this invasion. At the far end of the room, a ten-year-old boy and his eight-year-old brother stared curiously at their visitors—rather excited that all of a sudden the evening promised to be quite interesting indeed.

So, Bob thought, *this Latin man married a Nala woman. I guess they aren't accepted anywhere, so they live out here on their own.*

Joe and Paul went back to the canoe to retrieve the rest of their gear, while Fidel silently hung hammocks.

Bob located the mosquito nets and tied them up around each hammock. He realized that they were all in danger of contracting malaria since it was now nightfall. He needed to get Linda and Kimberly under cover as quickly as possible, hoping it wouldn't be rude to their hosts. He also remembered that in their turmoil Fidel and Victoria hadn't brought their own hammocks.

"Alberto," Bob addressed the man of the house. "The women are very tired from the trip. They're going to rest in the hammocks. Thank you so very much for allowing us to stay here tonight."

"No problem," Alberto answered. He seemed to be a man of few words.

Bob directed his attention to Linda. "Come sit down in this hammock under the net with Kimberly."

The Outcasts

Chandi, the ten-year-old, leaned forward in his hammock. He listened in awe to the strange sounds of the white man. *Some of the sounds blend all together, but the rest glide around as though they can't find a place to land.* He listened for repeats of sounds and played them back in his mind. He was utterly fascinated.

Eight-year-old Antonio swung silently in the hammock next to his brother. His dark eyes didn't miss a move—they took in everything.

"Victoria," Bob said, this time in Spanish—pointing while he spoke. "You can have the hammock next to Linda." She stood up and hesitated. He walked to the hammock next to Linda's and held the netting up while he motioned to her. Victoria sat in the hammock with her baby still at her breast, wondering about all of the fabric around her. She was mystified, but figured that it must be alright since Linda's hammock looked the same. Victoria was just thankful to be sleeping in a hammock. *They have been so good to us.*

Paul retrieved two cans of tuna from a knapsack. "Do we have any bread left?" he asked.

"No, we ate it all," Linda said, her stomach beginning to growl at the thought of food.

"Alberto, we have this canned tuna to share with your family." Paul held out the cans toward his host.

Chandi held back a laugh. *He sounds like he's speaking his own language, only with Spanish words!*

Antonio studied the white woman. *I wonder why she's afraid. The muscles in her jaw are tight and her eyes flit around like she's about to run.*

Ignoring the cans, Alberto ordered harshly in Spanish, "Moya, food!" It didn't appear that the couple communicated in each other's language.

When they had come in, Moya had been roasting yucca over her fire for her family. But at her husband's command, she handed the plate of yucca with a large spoonful of coarse salt to Fidel. He rolled the yucca in the large granules and gave one to each of the misioneros. Linda broke hers in half and told her husband to give the other half to Victoria. To the hungry travelers, the smoke-flavored root vegetable tasted delicious.

From two large gourds in the corner Moya retrieved more yucca and some plantains and peeled them. She began roasting those over the fire. But the strange cans that the White Ones had set on the table she ignored.

After they had eaten, even though it was very early, everybody turned in for the night. Fidel slept in the hammock with Victoria and the baby. Alberto offered his youngest son's hammock to Bob, so Nelson doubled up with Antonio in his hammock.

Seemingly in vain, Linda tried to calm her heart and control her thoughts so she could sleep. *The mosquito net will keep the cockroaches, mosquitoes, and snakes away from us. Why am I so afraid? Lord, thank you for this house you've provided for us to stay in tonight. Thank you for the mosquito net. Thank you that*

The Outcasts

Victoria and Rosalinda are so much better. Fear isn't from you. Why am I so afraid?

Bats swooshed through the open ends of the hut. Wind rustled the leaves outside. In the distance, frogs croaked and monkeys howled. The rhythmic breathing of a dozen people joined the chorus. But Linda was unable to join them in their slumber.

What am I doing in this strange land of malaria, languages that I can't understand, and people who don't care whether others live or die? What about Kimberly? She could be the next one to get malaria. Could we get help for her if she needed it? Lord, are you sure you want us here?

Chapter 9

The canoe motor revved to life as the disheveled group began the last leg of the trip back to Namuro. They were anxious to arrive at their destination. They couldn't wait to get a bath and change their clothes.

Overnight the river had calmed, but it was still swollen and murky, obscuring rocks and debris—which would make the trip very slow-going.

Tired of being held, Kimberly fussed. She desperately wanted to try out her new walking skills. Bob retrieved her from Linda's arms and let her lean slightly over the side. The waves splashed at her chubby, outstretched hands and she squealed in delight at the much-needed diversion.

Victoria sat nursing Rosalinda, who had improved dramatically during the night. Fidel was relieved to be returning to the village with both his wife and his daughter doing so well. He would have enough to answer for as it was, and he dreaded the confrontation.

In the first laborious hour the canoe made very slow progress upstream. Over and over again, the propeller had to be raised out of the water to avoid the vestiges of rubble. The missionaries hadn't traveled this tributary under these conditions, and never with the extra weight of two more adults. The canoe lurched forward, floated backwards, and then lurched forward again. Fidel wished he had brought along some poles. The Nala don't have motors for their canoes, so they traverse the rivers using muscle power—lodging the poles against the rocks and forcing the canoe forward with their weight. He had been searching the shoreline for a specific group of trees, which finally came into his view—trees from which he might find the type of branch that he needed. He stood in the canoe and pointed toward the shore, motioning for Joe to pull over. At the bank he hopped out of the canoe. A few minutes later he returned with two eight-foot sticks. He handed one to Paul and then motioned for him to come from the front to the middle of the boat. Fidel then pushed off from the shore and jumped in and stood at the bow. He plunged his pole into the water and applied his weight, thrusting the boat toward the center of the stream. Joe lowered the propeller and started the motor. Fidel bounced his stick off of rocks, alerting Joe to their presence. When the propeller had to be raised again, Fidel inched the boat forward with his weight on the pole. Amazed, Paul gripped his pole tightly, stood up, and attempted to help. It looked easy enough, but his pole slipped off the rock. His arms flailed as he struggled to regain his balance and not soar into the water. His foot slipped and he yelped as his shin collided with wood. He was thankful to still be in the boat, even though blood trickled from his shin. Victoria couldn't help but laugh at this grown man who couldn't even pole a canoe. Nala children were fairly proficient by age six!

But Paul was not going to give up that easily. He stood again and thrust his pole into the water. When he felt it catch between two rocks, he cautiously began leaning on the pole. It was all he could do to hold his own, as Fidel's weight thrust the boat forward once more.

Bob and Paul passed the pole between them, attempting to help Fidel as best they could. Exhausted, they watched Fidel labor away, his sinewy muscles rippling as he relentlessly poled the canoe through the dangerous stream whenever it was too shallow for the motor.

Relief etched their faces as the first hut in Namuro came into view. Joe cut the motor for the last time. But as soon as the motor's roar ceased, the eerie sound of the death chant swept over them like a sudden chill. Dismay and apprehension shattered the short-lived relief of their safe arrival. Victoria paled. Fidel sought her eyes. *Who has died?* Each wondered in silent apprehension.

The Americans, too, felt the foreboding that wafted through the air in the ominous chant. Their muscles ached—muscles that were not accustomed to this form of travel. But their hearts ached even more with apprehension of the drama that was unfolding before their eyes.

Bob clapped Fidel on the shoulder and said, "*Amigo*, you're a good man."

Fidel smiled weakly and repeated, "*Amigo*." It was a word he knew. But the encouragement was short-lived. His muscles tensed as he turned away, hurrying ahead of the group to find out which of his relatives or friends had died. *Death. It could have been Rosalinda, or Victoria!* He shuddered.

He reached his hut and called out, "Mother? Where are you?"

Nobody was home, so he trotted toward the meetinghouse where the mourning was taking place. He entered and stood a few seconds, allowing his eyes to adjust to the darkness. Surrounding a hammock, which enfolded the lifeless form of an infant, were the members of the chief's family.

Rosa appeared at his side. "Their grandson. It happened at dawn. He was only two weeks old. His mother is at home—she's too sick to get out of her hammock." Rosa then looked around anxiously. Alarm tightened her voice. "Where are Victoria and the baby?" she asked anxiously.

"They're doing fine—they're here," Fidel reassured her.

Rosa let out a sigh of relief. For the first time since they'd left, Rosa's taut muscles relaxed.

The missionaries had hung their hammocks in the close quarters of Fidel's hut. They had been allowed to stay, so they solemnly witnessed the Nala rituals of death.

Linda collapsed into her hammock for the night. Exhaustion prevented her from even checking the mosquito netting. She just couldn't move a muscle, yet her mind wouldn't allow her the bliss of sleep. For three long days there had been no relief from the constant wailing. Like a throbbing headache, the mournful sound pulsed through her weary soul. It was the wailing of hopelessness. These people were lost, with no hope for an eternity with Christ. They lived in fear, a fear that Linda had never really known.

But nothing had prepared her for the silence that followed. The lack of wailing enshrouded her like a black veil—even though she'd felt she couldn't have stood another moment of listening to it. *Death...* she thought... *we Americans are so sheltered—even from the reality of death! Oh, Lord, I'll never forget that tiny, lifeless form being carried across the river and laid in that grave. Then, the dirt...!* She sobbed silently into the night.

Linda awoke to the sounds of village life. *The meeting!* she thought. *Lord, please let them vote for us to move here.* She couldn't help but hope that God would somehow use recent events to move the villagers' hearts. Perhaps the medical help and even the death of the baby would be enough to sway votes in their direction. *God, I know that You want these precious people to learn about You. I know that You want them to have the opportunity to hear Your*

Word in their own language. I know that You want to save each one! I pray, Lord, for Your perfect will to be done today.

Linda's prayer continued throughout the seemingly endless morning. Finally, low tones from the conch shell floated across the village, summoning the Nala to the special meeting.

Linda's stomach growled and sweat trickled down her aching back. She had been sitting on a hard, backless bench for over three hours. *I can't understand a word they're saying, but they all seem so angry. I don't understand—I thought they'd want us here.* Linda's mind wandered to the last few days and how grateful the people had been for the aspirin to relieve their fevers. *Now I can't tell who is for us and who is against us.* Her stomach complained again as she shifted her weight on the unforgiving wooden plank. *This is just miserable.*

Bob leaned toward her and whispered, "I've seen some of the women leave. Why don't you take Kimberly to Victoria's hut for a while? You must be exhausted."

"I'd love to, but I don't want to miss the vote," Linda whispered back.

With authority, the chief's voice rose above the others. The room grew silent.

About half of the villagers stood. Fidel, Victoria, and Rosa were among them.

The Outcasts

Bob and Linda exchanged meaningful glances.

One Nala man counted those who had risen. A word was given and the people sat down. More words were spoken by the chief and others stood up to be counted. Linda held her breath, wishing she had thought to count the first group. She found herself trying to count this one but then she lost track. As she braced herself for the verdict, time seemed to stand still. It was too close for comfort.

The chief stood and spoke in Nala and the room erupted in controversy. People rose to leave. Bob stood up and walked toward the chief.

"You can come," he stated flatly in Spanish. Without another word he turned and walked away.

Across the room Linda caught Victoria's sparkling eyes. They'd won!

Linda somehow realized though, that even though they'd won a battle, the war had just begun.

Chapter 10

Linda pushed open the heavy shutters and leaned on the rough-hewn board of her front-room window opening. She'd grown accustomed to her windows containing neither glass nor screen. Absentmindedly she gazed at the brown dirt around each brown hut and the thatched roofs that had long turned brown, too. It all fit her mood. The Nala village, where she had lived for three months, was now a familiar sight. Its houses, made from jungle materials, stood in three fairly organized rows. Today, however, she couldn't seem to focus on the pretty palm trees scattered around each hut. She didn't look up into the powder blue sky with the puffy white clouds. In fact, lately her ongoing dialogue with the Lord had digressed to complaining. Somehow she couldn't seem to help it.

Linda sighed wearily. *I'm so tired, Lord. I thought life would slow down after our house was built, but it hasn't. I'm tired of people being in my house all day long. I'm tired of hearing a language that I don't understand. Lord, I'm tired of being tired.*

Kimberly's sharp howl snapped Linda out of her silent prayer. She whirled around.

"Melita, what happened?" she asked the child in Nala. It was a phrase she'd learned early on. As she spoke, though, Linda winced at the sharpness in her own voice.

"I don't know," Melita replied. Guilt spread across her face as she hid Kimberly's favorite doll behind her back.

Several other children swarmed over Melita. An older girl grabbed the doll from her and victoriously held it out to Linda. The screen door slammed as Melita fled.

Linda slumped onto the wooden bench that served as their couch. *Why am I here, Lord? Sometimes I can't even love these dear lost children. I'm so sorry. Help me, God.*

"Linda!" Victoria's voice called out as she entered the house.

"How did you greet the dawn?" Linda said in customary Nala.

"Good, and you?" Victoria replied.

"Good, too," Linda said mechanically.

I wonder what's wrong with Linda today, Victoria thought. *She looks unhappy and tired.* "Linda, where is Roberto?" Victoria asked slowly, in simple Nala.

"In there," Linda replied, pointing toward an inner room. Since the house was finished, Bob had been studying the Nala language for eight hours every day.

"Ah," Victoria replied.

"Where is Fidel?" Linda asked, repeating the phrase in an effort to use as much of the language as she could. *I wish I could go back to the office and study alone for even two hours a day! But help me, Lord, to make use of the time that I have with people, too.*

"He went hunting with Esteban," Victoria said as clearly as possible.

"Ah," Linda replied with Nala inflection.

Little girls swayed in a hammock and squabbled over a book. When a page tore, a guilty silence fell. All eyes turned to Linda.

Linda got up and walked toward the hammock. She took the book from their hands and put it away. She then got some old magazines from a shelf and brought them out for the kids to look at. *I wish I had the words to ask them to be more careful, and to share with one another. Well, maybe by taking the book away, they'll at least understand that I'm not pleased about the page getting torn.*

As her mother walked by, Kimberly stood and held up her arms, wanting to be held. Linda realized that her daughter's naptime had arrived.

"Kimmi is tired," she said in faltering Nala.

Victoria, always quick to know what her friend wanted to say, said, "Gimmi is tired. I am taking Gimmi to her room."

"Kimmi is tired. I am taking Kimmi to her room," Linda repeated, walking toward her daughter's room, not sure exactly what the second sentence meant.

When she returned to the front room, all of the children had vanished. *I wonder what Victoria said to them? Lord, it's so frustrating not being able to really talk to Victoria. I want to truly get to know her and to understand how she thinks. I never dreamed how hard this would be.*

"Where is Rosa?" Linda asked, using the phrase again.

"At home," Victoria replied. "She is cooking soup."

"She is cooking soup," Linda repeated.

Victoria smiled. *I thought she would learn much quicker than this. Her ways are so different and I have so many questions. I wonder how long it will take before she can tell me the message they came to give us. But look how long it took for them to come back after they got permission to live here. It took them a long time to build this house and more time before they finally moved in! Rosalinda is a year old already!*

Both women sat and looked at each other, trying to think of something they could talk about. Victoria began looking at an old *National Geographic*.

"Panther," she said in Nala, pointing to the photograph of a panther.

"Panther," Linda repeated in faltering Nala, grabbing her notebook and pen from the counter. *I'm going to make the most of this time. I have to learn this language.* Linda sighed as she wrote down the word in Nala and in English. The small accomplishment did little to relieve her weariness.

"The panther is sitting," she said.

"The panther is on all fours," Victoria repeated, chuckling as she corrected her.

Linda's head began to throb as she wrote a question in her notebook. *This is just plain discouraging. Just when I think I understand some of the language I run into a brick wall. She didn't have to laugh.*

For the better part of Kimberly's nap, Linda and Victoria looked through magazines and Linda wrote down all of the new words that she'd gathered.

Finally Victoria said, "Do you have an onion?"

"Onion? Yes, I have an onion." She went to the pantry and took out one of her two remaining onions. She handed it to her friend, wishing she could be a more joyful giver.

"*Gracias*," Victoria said, using the Spanish word for thank you that she'd learned from Linda.

"*De nada*," Linda replied, politely. Then quickly she added in Nala, "How do you say '*gracias*' in Nala?"

Victoria thought. "Good," she said in Nala.

Good? They don't even have a word for thank you? I wonder whether they mean, good that you gave it to me, or it's good. Why do I feel so used, Lord? Why do they always want *something? We were having such a nice visit and then she had to ask me for something.* Linda thought of all the words she'd gathered. She couldn't help but roll her eyes as a small sigh escaped her. *I don't want to know about panthers and anteaters. I want to know how she feels and what she thinks.*

When will I ever get to that *point in this language?*

When Kimberly woke from her nap, Linda was busy cooking rice, setting the table, and frying wild pig meat.

Bob appeared from the office doorway with a smile on his face. "Something sure smells good."

"Thanks, but could you go get Kimberly while I finish this up?"

"Sure," he said, opening the door to his daughter's bedroom.

To the Nala, the house seemed extravagant. However, to Bob and Linda, it was very basic and plain. It had wood floors and inside walls, but no drop ceiling—open rafters held up the tin roof. The outside walls were made from split bamboo. Bob had built four shuttered windows in the front room, one in the kitchen, and one in each bedroom. The wooden shutters could be closed and latched at night, and when they left the village. But during the daytime they simply had to have light and air.

Next trip out to the city I'll buy some light-colored paint for the floor. Maybe that'll brighten it up a little bit in here, Bob told himself while he changed his daughter's diaper. *Maybe it'll lighten Linda's spirits, too. She seems unhappy lately. I guess there have been a lot of adjustments in the last three months. I'm sure she'll be fine. I'm so thankful that God brought us here! I'm thankful for this wonderful ministry among the Nala.*

As they prayed over their lunch, a scream pierced the air. Bob jumped up and ran toward the front door. Linda sat as if glued to her seat, dreading to find out who was hurt and how badly.

Timoteo carried Luisa inside and set her down on the hard bench. Fidel's cousin writhed in pain as she clutched her left hand and sobbed pitifully. The front room filled with concerned people.

"Let me see," Bob said in Nala. "Oh, boy," he exclaimed, reverting to English.

"What happened?" Linda asked Bob in English. "How bad is it?"

"Her index finger is crushed. It literally popped open. My guess is that she smashed it in the sugar cane press. I can't imagine how much pain she must be in. I don't think we can help her here."

Linda's stomach lurched as she plunked down onto a chair.

Bob looked at his wife's ashen face and asked, "Are you okay?"

"I think so," she replied faintly.

"She has to see a doctor. Do you think the clinic would treat her better than they treated Victoria and Rosalinda? This time it's an injury and not malaria—would that make a difference?" Bob asked his wife.

"I don't know. I would hope so, but I just don't know."

"Let's at least give her some aspirin for the pain, while we pray about what we should do." Bob looked toward his wife.

"I don't feel very well. It's in the pantry, honey. Would you get it?" Linda replied weakly.

While he retrieved the medicine and a glass of water for Luisa, Bob thought through the situation and prayed for guidance. He returned to Linda and said, "Sweetheart, how long would it take us to get ready to leave the village? I think we should take her out to the city, and I really think you could use a break too. I can't stand the thought of just sending them downriver—not knowing whether a doctor would even treat her."

In his heart he chafed at the thought of what a difference it would make to have two-way radios. *I wish we could at least contact the mission for advice.* Bob's thoughts drifted to a date sometime in the future when they would have not only a radio but an airstrip and a mission airplane as well. *Hey, I can dare to dream, can't I?*

At the thought of leaving for a break, Linda brightened up. She felt guilty as the first hint of a smile spread across her face. *Yes, I need a break.*

"I'll hurry. We can do it in an hour—maybe less. But can we get to Avanzada by dark? I hope the Smiths will be home so we can stay there. We told them not to expect us for another month." Linda felt a moment of thankfulness at what a blessing it was to have missionaries in Avanzada. "We'll have to catch the bus tomorrow morning. It leaves at six-thirty, doesn't it?"

"Yes, it leaves about then. I'm pretty sure the Smiths will be there, but if not, I believe they have a watchman who has a key to their house. It'll all work out. I'll tell Timoteo what we're doing. Hurry and get the food taken care of and pack what we need. I'll disconnect the propane and close the shutters."

The house emptied except for Luisa, who cried softly as she lay on the bench. The fog that had been hanging over Linda's mind for weeks cleared away. Moving swiftly and efficiently, she loaded the cooler with food and filled the thermos with water. She stacked some perishables on the counter to give away. Linda then packed Kimberly's clothes and a satchel for her and Bob as she mentally went over the long trip ahead. After a long canoe ride and a short night's sleep, they would need to catch the bus at six-thirty in the morning. Then they would be fortunate to make it out to the city by evening.

Again Linda had to fight for control of her stomach as she thought about how difficult this journey would be for Luisa. *Lord,* she prayed silently, *please provide Luisa with the help she needs. Please help her with the pain. Please Lord, I pray that she'll regain full use of that finger when it's healed. And thank You that I get to leave here for a while. Maybe I shouldn't feel this way...please forgive me...but, Lord, thank You for this break.*

Luisa's soft moans caught Linda's attention just as Bob entered the house. "We have to hurry if we hope to get there before dark. The chief gave Timoteo permission to go with his wife and of course, their baby."

"*Permission?*" Linda echoed with annoyance. "He had to get *permission* to take his wife out of the village for medical attention?"

"Yep, I guess there's an awful lot that we don't understand about this culture." Bob tried to sound lighthearted, but beneath the surface it scared him to death to think that he could have possibly put his own family in danger by not having a way to get them out for medical help if needed. He and Linda couldn't navigate the river alone, much less with Kimberly. He shook his head. *I'll have to meet with the field committee before returning. We really need partners. But could we get* permission *for another missionary family to come live in the village? Oh my, I think I'm the one who really needs the break!*

Chapter 11

Victoria sat near her fire, listening intently to visitors from Ulgana. This was a first...a first for the Nala from Ulgana to trek to this farthest village! And news from the place where her father was born! The last time she'd listened to stories by visitors from Ulgana, she'd been sitting around her mother's fire. Time almost stood still as her mind wrapped around all the news.

Victoria entered the conversation. "What about my father's mother?" She was careful not to mention her grandmother's name, in case she had died.

Silence ensued and Victoria braced herself for the worst.

"Oh...Maamo?" the young man asked. "She's still around, but I don't know why, or how. She doesn't have any real relatives left, but Julio still takes pity on her now and then. I don't think she'll last too much longer. Say, did we tell you that our chief's daughter is going to marry Raul, from Luwana?"

Victoria heard no more. Raul...was going to marry another chief's daughter. Raul...how long had it been since her heart fluttered at his name?

Days turned into weeks, but Victoria couldn't shake the solemn blues that weighed her down. First, Linda and Roberto had left. They said they would return, but it had been three weeks, and every day she listened for the motor but heard only silence. Then, she found out that her Raul was to marry another woman. *How could he? Why hadn't he saved her?* And then like a lightning bolt it occurred to her. *Why* didn't *he save me? What kind of man is he, anyway? Fidel went against the whole village for me, and for our baby. Fidel* would *have saved me…no matter what the cost! Do I love him? Do I really* love *Fidel?* A smile slowly worked into the corners of her mouth and the dimple in her cheek deepened. She blushed as she looked across the room at Fidel who was rocking Rosalinda to sleep in his hammock. *How could I not have seen this before? Raul would never rock a baby. Fidel is man enough to go against the stream. Fidel is my man and I love him!*

The look was not missed by Fidel. He sighed with relief that Victoria's mood had finally changed. He had been very worried about her lately. He even wondered whether they could be expecting another baby. Or was it the news of her grandmother in Ulgana? She hadn't mentioned it but he'd been thinking, and maybe now the time was right to talk to her.

"Victoria," Fidel ventured, "do you want to go fishing? We can leave Rosalinda with Mother."

Victoria tilted her head at her husband, who never ceased to amaze her. "Okay," she said, with another little blush.

Victoria caught her fourth fish while Fidel sat nearby, his mind clearly not on fishing. But Victoria didn't mind—she felt happy, and she hadn't been happy in a very long time.

"Victoria," Fidel began, "I've been thinking about your grandmother in Ulgana."

Victoria's head spun around to look at him, but she didn't say anything. She turned back toward the murky water and waited for him to go on.

"I've provided for my mother, yet your grandmother is suffering all alone. It isn't right that no one is caring for her in her old age. It isn't her fault that she didn't have any daughters."

Victoria could hardly believe her ears. She'd been so wrapped up in Raul that she'd barely thought of her own grandmother. She felt ashamed. She looked up at Fidel. "Grandmother did have a baby girl. I heard my father talking to my mother late at night. I think maybe my grandmother had…" Victoria glanced around furtively before whispering the dreaded words, "twin girls." She waited to see whether Fidel would rebuke her. When she glanced at her husband she could only see compassion in his large brown eyes. "But what can we do, Fidel?"

"Let's go to Luwana so you can see your parents again and introduce them to Rosalinda. She's getting old enough now—maybe you could even leave her there while we go on to Ulgana. We can get your grandmother and bring her back to live with us here."

Victoria was silent—she didn't know what to say, and she had to think about this. "But what if grandmother can't walk very far? Even the young men said it was a grueling trip!"

"We can take our time. We could even carry her back."

Victoria laughed at her husband...he had wild and crazy ideas, not unlike her own when she was younger. *Did that part of me die when I thought my world had been torn apart by marrying Fidel?* She mused. *Well, I did stand up for the misioneros!*

"We could carry her in her hammock on a long pole between us. Rosalinda could ride with her." Fidel laughed at the look on his wife's pretty face. "We can figure something out."

"When can we leave?" she asked, as another fish tugged on her line.

"I'll talk to the chief tomorrow. He wants to give a message to your father; I can offer to take that to him. We won't talk about bringing Maamo back. If we get fined we'll find a way to pay it, or we'll work it off."

They fell into a comfortable silence, each working out details of the conversation in their own minds. Victoria could barely contain the happiness and peace that she felt and the love that had grown so strong without her even realizing that she loved her husband at all. It was a mystery.

Three short days passed. Fidel and Victoria managed to sneak into the village of Luwana unnoticed, late in the afternoon. Victoria was about to call out at her parents' door when Rosalinda wailed! Victoria's mother looked out of the opening and ran to her daughter and granddaughter. The village came alive with the news. Rosalinda's aunts swept her up and passed her around to everyone. Finally she wailed again, desperately wanting to toddle around on her own two feet. Once free, she rewarded the group with a shy grin, which blossomed into a full four-toothed smile when everyone laughed at her.

Later, around the fire, Fidel announced that they would leave the very next day for Ulgana. Diego frowned at him, but before he could comment, Fidel somewhat redeemed himself by asking whether they would keep Rosalinda until he and Victoria returned. Diego remained silent, letting his wife accept for both of them.

Diego couldn't help but see his daughter's happiness, and relief flooded over him. He hadn't allowed himself to dwell on his daughter—it hurt him too much to remember the wounded look in her eyes when she'd left. Nor had he admitted to himself that it was his own fault, not Fidel's. And Fidel—he seemed different… but Diego was *not* ready to think about forgiving him.

The next morning at dawn, Victoria packed a light meal for them to take along on the trail. She hugged Rosalinda and wondered how she could leave her for two or three days. But she was glad that her mother could spend the extra time with her. She followed Fidel out the door and down the trail which would lead them to Ulgana.

The winding pathway snaked alongside the swiftly flowing river. As they walked, the hills became much steeper, and the farther they went, the denser the jungle became. At mid-morning they came to a break in the trail. It continued on the other side of the river. They pulled out their food and sat together on a log to eat. Victoria had left the large basket at her mother's, and they each carried only a hammock and one change of clothes. Even though they both missed Rosalinda, they realized that the trek was much less strenuous without her.

Silently, Victoria tried to imagine her grandmother. *I hope she's well. I hope her heart isn't broken from loneliness...or abandonment. I've heard that she was always strong-willed...*she nearly chuckled out loud. *I've never thought about it before, but maybe she's the one I take after. Perhaps it isn't just me.*

After quickly eating, they were both ready to wade into the water and cross over to the trail on the other side. From what they'd been told, it appeared that they were halfway to Ulgana. They should reach the village before noon if they kept up their pace.

Before the sun was overhead they heard a dog bark. They stopped and listened, and weren't disappointed, as the faraway hum of voices reached their ears. They walked around the next bend and saw the first thatched roof of Ulgana. Fidel whistled, signaling their approach. A flurry of activity ensued. Children ran to meet them on the trail and then dashed ahead of them, alerting the community that visitors from another village had arrived.

At the first hut, Fidel introduced himself and his wife and asked about Diego's mother and where her dwelling was. They were directed to the far end of the village, behind Julio's hut.

Walking through the shabby, broken-down village, Fidel and Victoria were stunned. They greeted each family and moved on swiftly. When they arrived at Julio's house, they were invited inside and directed to two small stools. Gladly, they sat and drank the warm banana drink offered to them by Julio's wife, Maria. Julio's first wife had died many years ago. She had been Maamo's sister.

"We came to visit my grandmother, Maamo," Victoria explained.

"Her place is out back," Julio said, pointing with his chin. "You're not going to want to spend the night there. I suppose you can hang your hammocks here for the night."

Victoria's anger flared within her but she kept her tongue in check. "We'll go visit her now."

The couple walked out and looked around for the hut behind the house but couldn't see one. They headed down the trail toward the river but no hut was in sight, so they came back again. Fidel called out to Julio, who came to the door. "*Where* is Maamo's hut?"

Julio ambled out the door and into the trees on a little-used, totally overgrown trail. A small lean-to appeared, one that looked more like a garden shack where people temporarily took shelter from the rains. "You have visitors," Julio called out tersely. He then turned and sauntered back the way he'd come.

Cautiously Victoria entered. "Grandmother, I'm Victoria, Diego's oldest daughter."

The frail form of a woman sat up unsteadily in her hammock. Slowly a smile crept across her face, interrupting the deep lines of her aged countenance. "Am I dreaming? Or, have I died?" She was almost startled to hear her own voice.

"Oh, Grandmother," Victoria wailed as she ran to her. "I'm so sorry that you haven't been taken care of properly. When was your last meal, Grandmother?"

The old woman chuckled softly, "I really am dreaming, and I don't ever want to wake up."

"No, we're real. This is Fidel, my husband. We came from Namuro to help you. We want to take you home with us." Victoria hadn't meant to overwhelm her grandmother within the first few seconds of their meeting, but her heart was broken at the conditions she was living in. She was furious with Julio and Maria—she was furious with her own father. How could they allow this?

Victoria marched out of the house and up to Julio's for a gourdful of banana drink. Maria handed over the drink, coldly looking into Victoria's angry eyes. As she stomped back to her

The Outcasts

grandmother's shack, Victoria chided herself that she'd eaten all of her own food that she'd packed for the trip.

Maamo devoured the warm liquid. Her eyes brightened a little and she sat up a bit straighter. Maamo surprised them by saying, "So, we're going to Namuro?" She looked at Fidel and then at Victoria's dumbfounded face. "You did say you were taking me back with you to Namuro, didn't you? Or am I really just dreaming all of this after all?"

Laughter rang through the small lean-to. Victoria saw first-hand that she and her grandmother had an awful lot in common. This frail little woman had spunk, and Victoria couldn't wait until she could get to know her better. It did Victoria's heart good to know that perhaps she was not, after all, a mere aberration.

"When *should* we go, Fidel?" Victoria asked with concern.

"I don't think a night here will help any of us," Fidel reasoned out loud. "But I'll have to get permission from the chief for you to move away, Grandmother."

"That shouldn't be a problem," the woman replied. "I'm just a liability and they'll be happy not to have me around anymore. My house fell down and the village never did put me on the list to build another one. I finally told Maria I was moving in with them if she didn't get her husband to put a roof over my head. So Julio built this for me. I've been worried about rainy season coming, though."

"I'll go talk to the chief. If we can get permission, let's head out now." Fidel hardly got the words out of his mouth before leaving the shack.

"Grandmother," Victoria said, "how well can you walk? You look very weak."

"I have a walking stick and I can still get to the river to bathe. But I haven't been anywhere else in a very long time."

"Okay, we'll find a way. What do you have to take with besides your hammock?" Victoria questioned as she looked around the pathetic lean-to. "Do you have a towel and other clothes, or a blanket?"

Maamo pointed to a small stash in the corner behind her hammock. Victoria retrieved the thin, worn-out blanket, tattered towel, and one stained and worn-out shift-type work dress—each had been washed, dried and neatly folded. Underneath the items sat a small bundle wrapped in vine. Victoria picked it up and looked questioningly at her grandmother. "My necklaces," she stated, and watched as Victoria carefully folded it inside the towel.

Fidel returned with a grim look on his face, but his words were, "Let's go."

"Do we have permission?" Victoria questioned, as she helped her grandmother out of the hammock.

"Yes," Fidel said, not wanting to elaborate that Maamo had been right. The chief had laughed at him and said the village would be better off without the worthless old woman. Fidel untied the hammock and retrieved Maamo's walking stick for her. He stopped mid-stride to admire the unusual cane.

"I carved it myself," Maamo proudly informed him.

"It's very unique, and elaborate...I really want to study it when we arrive at Luwana. So, women here in Ulgana carve?" Fidel laughed. *Life is going to get very interesting with Maamo around. Now I know where Victoria gets her spunk.*

Victoria rolled Maamo's meager possessions into the hammock, then added the roll to the one which was still on her back. Fidel carried his hammock on his own back—which didn't go unnoticed by Maamo. She reached for her walking stick and proudly followed Fidel out the door as Victoria took up the rear. They walked straight through the center of the village disregarding the curious stares of each and every inhabitant.

Once out of sight, Maamo's valiant attempt to hike all the way to Luwana began to fade. She tripped on a root and had to stop to catch her breath. Fidel directed her to a fallen log.

The old woman sat and looked sadly up at him and said, "This silly old woman isn't going to make it, but it sure was fun walking out of there as if I could."

"That's okay, I have an idea." Fidel strode into the thick tangle of jungle growth in pursuit of a long pole that would hold her weight. When he returned he took Maamo's hammock and tied each end around the branch. Victoria positioned one end on her shoulder and Fidel perched the other on his. Instructing Maamo to lie down in the hammock, they proceeded to hike for half an hour before stopping to rest. Before starting out again Fidel and Victoria each put a piece of clothing between their shoulders and the pole and continued on for another half hour. The trail was rough and the hills were steep. They were hungry and thirsty, yet they had never felt better about anything in their entire lives.

When the western sky cast pink and gray shadows above the treetops, Fidel and Victoria finally neared their destination, carrying their precious cargo. They helped Maamo out of the hammock. Fidel threw the branch into a vine-choked thicket, folded up the hammock and gave Maamo her walking stick. Proudly, the threesome entered Luwana, as Fidel called out to Diego that they'd returned.

Little Rosalinda toddled to her mother, but Diego stared incredulously at his. He was speechless and chagrined. *What on earth has Fidel done now?*

Maamo lifted her chin and walked toward her son with a greeting—as though she'd been expected to arrive from the house next door. Without further ceremony she entered the dwelling and eased herself into the first available hammock. The aroma of food overwhelmed her—real food. Maamo closed her eyes and for a moment wondered again whether this was all a dream...or had she really died. It seemed just too good to be true.

When Maamo opened her eyes again Victoria placed Rosalinda in the old woman's lap. "Grandma, this is your great-granddaughter, Rosalinda. Rosalinda, this is your very special great-grandmother." Dark eyes met and they sized each other up. Life was going to be very good indeed.

The three visitors slept especially well. At dawn they slowly awoke to the crow of a rooster, and the faraway thud of an axe splitting kindling. The aroma of wood smoke in their hut promised yet another meal, which put a large, nearly toothless smile on Maamo's face.

Outside, Victoria caught up with Fidel, who was heading for the river. "Did you tell Father the message from Rico?" she asked. When her husband ground to a halt, she nearly ran into him.

"Oh, the message…I forgot!" Fidel grimaced at his lapse. Diego wouldn't be happy with him for waiting the extra day. Being the voice between one chief and another was important business.

Once back from his morning bath, Fidel sought out Diego, who was lounging in his hammock. "Diego," he proceeded with a confident tone that he didn't feel, "Rico has a message for you."

Diego's brows rose, and just as quickly, a slight frown appeared on his stoic face. "Do we need privacy for this talk?" he asked.

"No, Rico is informing you that Namuro will be having a festival for César's second daughter, Blanca. It will have already begun, actually, uh today…but because César has relatives here in Luwana, the invitation has been extended to any who cares to join, if there is time…that is." Fidel's confidence lagged toward the end of the dissertation. He couldn't help but wonder what would have happened if they'd spent several days in Ulgana and he hadn't been able to present the message before the time of the festival had already passed. He swallowed hard.

"I'll inform the village this morning. Fidel..." Diego cleared his throat as he changed subjects. He chose his next words carefully. "What are your intentions bringing my mother here? This is not your responsibility to..."

"No," Fidel cut in, quite uncharacteristically, "I did not bring her here to live with you! I would never presume upon you in that way. We're taking Maamo home with us to Namuro, to live in our house."

Diego scowled and then he slowly countered, "I'm surprised that Rico sanctioned this." He scrutinized Fidel and observed him ever so slightly flinch. Just as he'd suspected, Fidel was acting on his own — without permission. An almost evil grin crept into the corners of the chief's mouth.

Chapter 12

Victoria sat by the smoky fire in her mother's hut, stirring a savory stew. This would be her last night before returning to Namuro. A deep sigh escaped her lips. *I'm going to miss Elena... yet I've changed so much. Elena can't envision Namuro...we've grown very far apart. I wish she'd at least consider coming to Namuro someday.*

Victoria had visited every household in her home village—including Raul's. She had discovered that, indeed, Raul was not the man she'd thought he was. Raul had decided not to marry Ramiro's daughter after all, because he didn't want to move to Ulgana. Raul, it seemed, was more interested in himself than anyone else, and Victoria was truly thankful that she hadn't married him. She'd been able to look Raul in the eye with no feelings at all for him.

A smile warmed Victoria's face. *I'm ready to go home. I sure hope that Linda and Roberto will be there when we get back. Yes, I'm looking forward to returning to Namuro with Fidel, Rosalinda, and Maamo*. Her thoughts then turned to her grandmother's village.

"Father," Victoria began, "why is Ulgana so run down?"

Diego had been sitting sullenly in his hammock. "I haven't been there for a long time."

"The houses are all in disrepair. It's sad." Victoria went on, even though her dad really hadn't answered her question.

"They've had a lot of sickness. Many people have died," the chief stated flatly.

"That is *not* the reason," his wife disputed sharply. "You know very well what happened in Ulgana. The chief fell into dishonor with that young woman from Kala! She had a baby; he looked just like Ramiro. It shamed him, and the whole village, too. Ulgana has never recovered. You can't have a weak leader — a chief who isn't respected. He should have turned the village over to another man."

Diego's jaw muscles tightened.

"Who is the woman? What happened to her and the baby?" Victoria's voice echoed her concern.

"They were forced to leave Kala and were sent to Ramiro in Ulgana," her mother alleged with a triumphant nod of her head.

Maamo grunted in contempt. "Ramiro didn't take care of them. He left that poor woman and her son destitute."

"What happened to them?" Victoria questioned anxiously.

"You saw my place — well, it looks pretty good compared to what they live in. She gets lots of 'visitors' at night, if you know what I mean. Her 'visitors' pay her with food. It isn't right, but I do feel sorry for the woman—she and her young one would've starved to death otherwise." Maamo shook her old head sadly. "If I'd had anything to share with them, I would have."

"That's terrible!" Victoria was outraged.

"I'll have no more of this talk in my house," Diego thundered. He rose from his hammock and stalked out the door. He hated the reminder of his own shame—and the fact that his rebel son-in-law held the upper hand with him. *I'm glad they're leaving tomorrow,* Diego fumed under his breath. *I can't stand having Fidel in my house. Everything was fine until that scoundrel came here—who does he think he is, anyway? What was I thinking? Why would anyone have believed him—I'm the chief!* Before Fidel showed up, not one time had Diego thought about the plight of the young woman whom he had violated. Not once had he wondered whether the baby might look more like him than Ramiro. But now, tiny beads of sweat stood on his forehead. *That boy must be four years old now...what if he* does *look like me?* He walked toward the river in hopes of washing away his new fears. He tried to reject the feelings of guilt and shame. *After all,* he reasoned, *it was a mistake—one stupid mistake.*

Diego was angry! He wasn't used to anyone having power over him. He determined to figure out a plan that would take Fidel down a notch or two. He'd have to be very careful so it didn't appear to come from him. It might take a long time, but somehow, someday, he wanted revenge.

Three days later, when they arrived at the outskirts of Namuro, Maamo was exhausted—as though she'd been the one hiking instead of lying helplessly in a hammock. Yet she eagerly grabbed her walking stick and stoically entered the village that she looked forward to making her home. She still felt as if she were dreaming. Never had she expected to actually travel to all of the Nala villages, yet here she was at the very edge of civilization—in her mind, the very end of the earth!

Fidel's mother sat at her fire, unaware of the changes that were about to take place in her life and home.

Rosa's excitement over Fidel's return was short-lived when an old woman followed him into their home. Rosa was so stunned that she actually fell silent as she was introduced to Victoria's grandmother, Maamo. Her toothless grin and genuine handshake did little to calm Rosa's racing heart.

Maamo spoke huskily through her emotions. "You have an extraordinary son. He rescued *you* from a life like *I've* been living since my last son left to marry. Now, he has rescued *me*, for whatever time I have left. It is good to have such a son. You, too, must be an extraordinary woman."

Rosa swallowed hard, while thoughts raced through her mind. *It's true, I was rescued—but along with that rescue apparently there's a price to pay. First, I've all but given up running my own household—though Victoria does manage things very well. And now, another woman is apparently joining our family—a woman older than me, and the matriarch from Victoria's lineage. How can the two of us co-exist? Things just aren't done this way! I will have words with Fidel—he could have at least warned me, given me some time to prepare for this.* Rosa stared at Maamo in utter disbelief.

Maamo continued the one-sided conversation with a chuckle. "I can see that Fidel must not have told you before he left that he was bringing me home with him. He's still extraordinary, but apparently he has a lot to learn. Does the chief know?"

Rosa found her voice. "If he didn't before, he has surely heard by now. First the misioneros, and now you..."

"Misioneros—what's that?"

"Ah, well, I guess they haven't filled you in on everything, either." Rosa relaxed, eager to give Maamo the whole story about *her* extraordinary granddaughter.

Wherever they went, Fidel and Victoria sensed the harsh stares of the chief and most of the villagers. A week had passed and tensions were running high. The misioneros still hadn't returned with Timoteo, Luisa, and Maria. Here they were replacing the roof on a second house since they'd been gone—Timoteo would face a steep fine as punishment for the work he'd missed while they'd been away. And besides, the majority wanted to know who the *misioneros* thought they were, anyway. Nala chiefs *were* medicine men, after all. And the subject of Maamo's appearance in the village—without permission—was still being discussed vehemently around various fires at night.

Perched on the top rafters of the chief's hut were eight older teenage boys. Young men filled the lower rafters, handing up the thatch and vines as well as making sure the knots were tied properly. Older men and younger boys scurried around below, taking the thatch out of the bundles that each household had gathered from the jungle, and cutting vines into proper lengths. They handed up the materials as well as gourds filled with water when needed. The roof was halfway finished when the sound of a motor stopped everyone in their tracks. They recognized the misioneros' motor and continued on with their project.

Victoria flew out of her house and down to the river, leaving Rosalinda screaming over her mother's quick departure. Rosa and Maamo exchanged quick glances and shook their heads as Rosa picked up the sobbing toddler and put her in the hammock with her great-grandmother. Realizing the banana drink was in danger of scorching over the hot fire, Rosa rescued the pot that Victoria had abandoned.

At the river, Victoria shielded her eyes from the sun and searched the brown tributary. She had heard the motor and knew they must be only minutes away. She wondered how Luisa's finger was, and couldn't wait to ask her all about the trip. Victoria had been very fearful that her good friend may have been treated poorly by the outsiders. And then dread assailed her, knowing how angry the whole village of Namuro was at all of them. She wished she could communicate better with Linda; there was a great deal that she and Roberto needed to know.

※

Victoria helped carry boxes to the misioneros' house and then visited for a while, but she couldn't wait to go to Luisa's. As soon as she felt she could leave politely, she trotted out of the house and straight for her friend's.

Amid the stares of the household, Luisa unwound the gauze, exposing the jagged, angry, red wounds on her swollen finger. She winced as she tried to move it and decided to bandage it up again.

The group sat spellbound as Luisa tried her best to describe the confusing world beyond their territory that none of them had ever witnessed before.

"We rode in a 'canoe' *outside* of the water! Twenty of us sat on soft benches totally inside the 'boat'—it had walls and a roof. The motor was loud, and 'chanting' blared in our ears."

"Who was chanting?" Ana questioned.

"I don't know. I couldn't tell where the sound came from. It was unlike anything I've ever heard. There were many strange sounds all combined. We were in that 'canoe' from dawn until noon. Everybody got out and ate a meal. We then got back into the craft. After that, the trail turned from small river rock to a hard surface, and after awhile *hundreds* of 'boats' moved around the trails at a horrific speed. Most were smaller and carried only a few people.

"There were houses made of the same hard stuff as the trails, and they were tall—some as tall as four of our huts stacked one on top of another!"

With huge eyes each member of the small assembly looked from Luisa to Timoteo for confirmation, wondering if Luisa had been given some strange medicine that had affected her mind. But Timoteo nodded his assent, and as one the group turned back toward Luisa and held their breath expectantly for her to continue.

Luisa did not disappoint them. "The 'boat' finally stopped and everyone got off. Then the misioneros and the three of us squeezed into a small 'canoe' that moved like a deer running though the forest on winding trails. It would stop quickly, then start with a jolt turning this way and that. There were many funny-looking houses with shiny roofs like the misioneros have. The 'boat' stopped at a house which was the color of a parrot's feathers, and we all got out and went inside."

Victoria lost track of time as her friend described lights that turned on and off magically and an indoor bathroom that literally took the water away like a waterfall! She was spellbound. It was too much information to take in all at once, yet Victoria found that she desperately wanted to be next to go to the "city" with Linda! Her reverie was interrupted by the cries of her own child and she flew to her feet and out the door. She was astonished that it was dark outside! She didn't want to miss the rest of the story, but then again she had a lot to tell everyone around their own fire. She knew that Luisa would recount her experiences many times, so she'd find out more tomorrow.

Bright and early the next morning, before the smell of wood smoke had even settled across the village, the conch shell blew.

"Rico certainly hasn't wasted any time calling a meeting," Fidel said as he and Victoria exchanged glances, dreading the looming confrontation.

Rosa's nerves were on edge, but Maamo seemed to enjoy the whole thing. "What can they do anyway?" the older woman stated with a chuckle. "It's a lot of bluff, it is. I've sat through more village meetings than you can imagine. Stand up to them with confidence. If you didn't have them worried they wouldn't be so upset. I wish I'd learned to stand up for myself years ago." Sadness crossed her features as she thought of her precious babies. In all these years they had never been far from her mind.

Rosa scowled at the woman she'd been warming up to. "That's all we need around here," she grumbled, "as if we aren't in enough trouble already. Don't encourage these two; they're out of control as it is!" With that, she grabbed her wraparound skirt and tied it over her housedress around her thick waist as she huffed out the door.

Fidel exited next and headed for the misioneros' house. After exchanging the customary greetings, he attempted to inform Bob of the village meeting and of their need to be there too. It was exhausting, but finally he felt he'd gotten through to the blue-eyed man. Fidel secretly wondered whether the man was slow in the head, whether he'd ever learn their language.

The conch shell blew again, so Fidel looked expectantly toward Bob, who sat smiling at him from his hammock. Fidel then stood up and moved toward an opened window. He pointed at the villagers who were flocking toward the large hut in the center of the village. Finally Bob understood. As he went for his notebook and pen, he explained to Linda where he was going, and then he followed Fidel out the door.

Four hours later Bob's stomach growled ferociously as he moved around uncomfortably on the hard bench. His mind had long ago given up trying to elicit new words, so the notebook sat idle in his lap. He wished he could leave, go home and do something productive. This was just a waste of time. First, they'd been out of the village for five weeks—and now, his first full day back, he couldn't even put in his eight hours of language study. He yawned and his stomach protested once more.

Voices became louder and it was obvious, even to Bob, that people were angry. Soon there was shouting from every side and Bob feared a riot would break out. He wondered what on earth had sparked the controversy. All eyes were on Fidel, Timoteo, and him—or at least the bench where they were sitting together. Then Timoteo rose and walked to the middle of the room and sat on a small stool. Angry voices seemed to berate him from all sides as he slumped in silence with downcast eyes. Bob's curiosity overflowed.

The chief's loud voice stilled the group, and he seemed to proclaim something.

Timoteo stood, nodded his assent, and returned to his seat.

Much to Bob's dismay, Fidel stood up next and walked to the small stool where he took his seat. Bob was transfixed and frustrated for the next half hour wondering why Fidel, too, was apparently being chastised.

Long past noon, the meeting finally ended. Bob stood up and stretched out his aching body. He looked anxiously at Fidel and then toward Timoteo, and wondered how he could learn this language any faster. He desperately wanted to know what had just transpired.

Two days later, Victoria sat in Linda's house. With machetes in hand, Fidel and Timoteo had left at dawn to begin working off their fines. They had been sentenced to clear weeds from the trail, halfway to Kala...the villagers usually cleaned it together several times a year. The project took all of the men and teenage boys over four hours to complete; it would take the two men nearly two weeks.

"Where is your husband?" Linda asked, with one of her Nala phrases.

"He's cutting the trail," Victoria answered.

"Ah," Linda countered.

"He went with Timoteo," Victoria informed her, rather sadly.

"Timoteo and Fidel went to cut the trail," Linda put the words together.

"Yes!" her friend was rather encouraged.

"Good," Linda said brightly.

Victoria slumped a little, and wondered whether this misionera understood or just mimicked like the parrots of the jungle. She decided to tell her friend, "You stayed away too long. Timoteo only had permission to be gone for two weeks."

Linda blinked helplessly. She retrieved her notebook and asked Victoria to repeat the words. She wrote strange marks on the paper, marks that her friend thought were foolishness—it certainly didn't seem to be serving any purpose that Victoria could see.

The two sat in silence for long moments, each lost in her own thoughts. Linda decided to pull out some magazines, and soon they were rifling through the pages of a new one that Linda had recently purchased.

Victoria stopped at one page and stared in disbelief. Linda giggled and said in Spanish, "They're twins." Victoria's startled expression made her wonder whether twins had ever been born in Namuro. She then remembered her photo album and the picture of her twin nephews, so she quickly retrieved the book from her bedroom and showed the snapshot to her friend.

"You keep them?" Victoria questioned.

Linda blinked. She wrote the phrase down and walked into her husband's tiny office. "Honey, what does this mean?"

"It means, do you keep them," he answered. "How was it used?"

"I showed her the photo of Tommy and Billy. We saw twins in the magazine and she seemed quite astonished." A shiver ran down her spine.

"Wow, I guess we'd better write this up in our culture notebook. I hope they don't...I hope they don't have a taboo about twins." Bob rubbed his forehead, wishing for the millionth time that he could learn this language faster.

Victoria wished desperately that she could tell Linda not to show the magazine or picture to anyone else. As it was, the chief was furious that Bob hadn't responded to any of the accusations about him. The village couldn't find a way to punish the misioneros, because they couldn't even understand they were in trouble! But Victoria was really afraid that if anyone saw those pictures, the misioneros would be kicked out of the village for sure. Just then Kimmi cried, so when Linda walked from the office to the bedroom, Victoria quietly tore the page out of the magazine and hid that as well as the snapshot inside her skirt. She fled outside hollering, "See you later!" as the door slammed behind her.

Chapter 13

The powerful smell of damp earth assaulted Maamo as she lounged in her hammock. It had been over a year since she had moved to Namuro. With each new storm, she still shivered at the thought of what life would have been like for her had she still been in Ulgana.

Gusts of rain hammered loudly on the misioneros' tin roof—twenty feet from her hammock. Through the cracks in the walls Maamo watched Victoria standing under the shiny eaves, catching fresh rainwater in the five-gallon container that sat on top of her head.

Paco and a half-dozen other children were bathing under the water that fell from the roof. Maamo assessed the white woman as she leaned out her window and handed a sliver of soap to the children. They giggled and smiled as they bathed in style—with soap, a luxury few households could afford. Each girl lathered her hair with it and smelled the wonderful white sliver before passing it on to the next child.

Linda stood at the window-opening of their front room, still amazed that kids would consider bath soap an amenity. Her mind recalled the privileged children in the U.S.A. who would scoff at the thought. Of course, how many ever would have wrapped a tin can in a rag and pretended to have a baby doll? Linda had witnessed firsthand many things that most Americans would never even hear about. People here appreciated the small things in life—the basics.

But this was not paradise. They lived in fear. They were oppressed by taboos and customs designed to appease spirits—they needed to know the one true God!

Bob and Linda had studied hard in the year and a half they'd been living in Namuro. They could communicate very well now and were gleaning many things about the culture in which they lived. Soon, they hoped, they would be ready to determine the alphabet for the unwritten Nala language. From there they would translate simple primers, and then, Lord willing, they would begin translating the Scriptures.

Linda felt such an urgency to tell her friends about God and His Son, Jesus Christ. But she also knew that this message needed to be shared with the proper words and to be backed by Scripture. Unless it was understood, it would be given in vain. Linda feared, however, that another death would occur before they were ready to share the gospel. That would break her heart, because they were so very close to delivering God's message to these dear people. She was filled with apprehension as she rubbed her swollen belly.

The Outcasts

In only two days they would be leaving the village to spend the remainder of her pregnancy in the city near her doctor and the hospital. Bob wasn't sure how soon they should return with the new baby, either. *We could be gone for five months!* Linda sighed. *Part of me is ready and very eager to leave, yet part of me never wants to go again. I feel as if I have a foot in both worlds.*

From Luisa's house came the vigorous cry of her baby. Mateo had come into the world three months ago, and he seemed to have been hungry ever since.

Linda turned away from the window as Victoria walked away to her own house with the full container of fresh rainwater on her head. Victoria entered her hut, and Rosa lifted the heavy container from her daughter-in-law's head and set it on the floor in the corner.

Victoria changed her wet clothing and then, hoping for a midday nap, she lowered her slight frame, which was now heavy with child, into her hammock. She hadn't recalled feeling so tired, or being so huge with Rosalinda. But her thoughts were lulled to sleep with the ceaseless thundering of the rain. Before she awoke, the dark and dreary afternoon had slipped into evening.

Bob sat in his office daydreaming. Rainy season would slow down the progress on the airstrip, and he was determined to get the mission plane flying in and out of Namuro before they returned with the new baby. They were fairly close to having all the trees felled, but he knew he'd be making several river trips alone back to the village to oversee the project while Linda and Kimmi stayed in the city. Next would come clearing any remaining stumps from the huge runway and then cutting down the weeds. Bob planned to bring a lawn mower in to keep the weeds and grass cut low and even.

It hadn't been easy to convince the people of Namuro that an airstrip would benefit everyone. He'd informed the people that some supplies for the village could be brought in, and he'd offered the chief a ride in the airplane, too. Fortunately, permission had already been granted and the airstrip was half-cleared when the mission plane flew over Namuro, giving the Nala their first glimpse of air travel. Bob chuckled. *I'm not sure that promising Rico a ride would have been a help where his vote was concerned! I saw his face pale when the Cessna buzzed the strip!*

At least it's progress, Bob thought, a little sadly. He hadn't been able to convince the village to allow another missionary couple to come and join them. He smiled, thinking, *I can't really blame them. We've certainly made our share of blunders!* He knew they'd been oblivious to the villagers' rules and expectations, yet he still had no idea how many times they would have driven the missionary family away from Namuro—had the Nala been able to communicate with them!

The next day, at the misionero's house, Victoria sat visiting her friend. "Is your baby coming any day now?" Linda asked.

Victoria wondered whether she'd heard her right. "No," she ventured, "not for another month. And yours?"

"Oh," Linda replied, trying not to show her surprise. "Mine is due in three months." Then, Linda remembered again about the photographs of the twins—the ones that had disappeared when Victoria fled from their house. All of a sudden she felt a little faint, and cold perspiration appeared on her upper lip. Her face paled as she realized that Victoria *could* be carrying twins! Linda's stomach lurched at the horrible thought that, possibly, these people kill their twins—and she wouldn't be in the village when Victoria delivered.

Victoria scrutinized her friend. "Are you feeling well?"

"I'm fine," Linda said, trying to recover from her gloomy thoughts.

"Linda," Victoria ventured slowly, "you came to tell us about a good spirit. You talk well now. Why haven't you given us the message?"

Linda hesitated, agonizing over what to do. *Their language doesn't have all of the words that I need to share the gospel.*

Victoria's disappointment showed clearly on her face. She remained silent.

The missionary's heart pounded as she prayed for wisdom from above. She *had* to tell her friend about Christ—she couldn't leave here, knowing she'd had this opportunity and hadn't at least tried to give the gospel to her friend.

So she began, "Victoria, we have learned that you believe in spirits. Is that true?"

"Yes, there are many spirits."

"Are you afraid of the spirits?"

Victoria shifted uncomfortably. "Yes, we are."

"There is one true 'Good Spirit' named *Dios*," Linda said, using the Spanish word for God, because there was no word for God in the Nala language. "Dios lives in a wonderful, perfect place up in the sky, and He wants all of us to go live with Him there when we die.

"We've learned that you believe in a place where you will go to after you die, right?"

"Yes, a good place. If we're good Nala, we will go to the good place," Victoria affirmed.

"Well, Dios says that none of us are good enough. We have all done bad things, every one of us. He calls these bad things 'sin.' Stealing, lying, and hating are just a few sins."

Victoria's crestfallen features showed Linda that she understood, so she went on. "For that reason, Dios sent his only Son, *Jesús*, to earth to die in our place. Jesús took our sins upon Himself and paid the price so we could go to the good place and live with Him forever."

"So the Good Spirit is a man-spirit?" Victoria asked.

"His Son came as a man." Linda tried to clarify.

But before Victoria could formulate even one of her many questions, a commotion broke out in the village. Dogs began to bark, people started yelling, and Victoria bolted out the door to find out what the problem was.

Linda began to weep. She knew that the enemy desperately wanted to protect his stronghold in Namuro and that the battle lines were drawn. They were so close to presenting the gospel—in fact, she just had! But Linda realized that it had been very superficial and had left many more questions than answers. She began to pray, *Lord, please give Victoria understanding from what I shared with her just now. We don't even have a word in their language for Your name! I did the best I could, Lord. Please, somehow, use what I said for Your glory. I pray, Lord, that the seeds that have been sown today will produce fruit in her life. I know that You love Victoria and want her to accept You as her Savior. I pray that soon she'll come to know You, Father God. And, Lord, please, if Victoria is carrying twins, please spare their lives!*

Two days later, Bob and Linda were packing their household possessions in fifty-five-gallon barrels for storage. During the months they would be gone from the village, they needed to protect their things from insects and the elements.

Kimmi colored in her coloring book, chatting happily in Nala with her little friends, who all vied for space so they could color with her. Kimmi tore out several pages and handed one to each of the girls. With crayons in hand they all giggled and slid to their tummies on the smooth hard floor.

Linda watched with a smile on her face. Kimmi would be fluent in English *and* Nala someday! She prayed that her daughter would grow to have a heart for missions. A twinge of pain reminded her that she was not looking forward to eight hours in the canoe tomorrow and then eight hours more the following day in a very loud, bumpy bus. *It is* indeed *time for us to leave here. I hope that when we return it will be in an airplane!*

Despondently, Victoria sat in her hammock, mulling over the conversation she'd had with Linda. *If the spirit Dios had a man-spirit Son named Jesús, Dios, too, must be a man-spirit. How could Dios or Jesús be good spirits if they're man-spirits? All spirits are feared,* Victoria thought, *but most can be appeased. The only spirits I've ever heard of that were in the form of men, though, were the dreaded spirits who had been so angry that they killed off nearly an entire Nala village hundreds of years ago. The man-spirits invaded the village and took all of the women's gold necklaces and gold earrings. The Nala rose up against them and fought to the death! Only two young girls escaped into the jungle and fled to Ulgana to describe the massacre. The man-spirits had men's faces and hands but their bones were on the outside of their bodies, like an armadillo's. And they had shone like the sun.* Victoria shuddered, but her mind continued with the account that had been passed on from generation to generation.

The chief of Ulgana had prepared for an attack, collecting all of the women's gold necklaces and earrings. He'd hoped to give the gold to the dreaded man-spirits and save the lives of the villagers. But the attack never came.

Gold jewelry is scarce now, Victoria thought. *The gold for our jewelry used to come from a secret spot in the river of the sister village—the one that had been destroyed. And nobody has ever dared to return. Our people still fear the man-spirits and wish to appease them however we can, if they ever return. We still look diligently for shiny rocks in the river, but very little is ever found.*

However, despite all that she had been told before, Victoria refused to be dismayed. *I'm sure that I just didn't understand Linda. After all,* she thought, *I've asked for help from the Good Spirit many times in the past. I've felt in my being that He exists— almost as though He somehow calls out to me. I want to know so much more! I want to learn more about Dios and Jesús, I believe they exist, and they must be good spirits. I have so many questions that I need to ask Linda.*

Victoria also wished she could tell Fidel, Maamo, and Rosa what she'd learned, but she still had far too many questions. Mainly she was afraid to tell them that the Good Spirit could be a man-spirit, so she kept it to herself. Victoria sighed deeply. *Linda leaves tomorrow. I'll have to wait until she returns to find out more.*

Fidel and Timoteo had permission to help the misioneros get as far as Avanzada, and then they would bring the canoe back up, the way that they had done many times in the past year and a half. It had become their job. The outboard motor was kept in a shack that Roberto had built on the other side of the river. Fidel hauled the heavy motor up and down the steep, slippery bank for Roberto. Fidel had also learned how to clean it and put in just the right amount of gasoline and oil for the trip. Even though the rest of the villagers were jealous that Fidel and Timoteo received goods for working for the misioneros, the two had been allowed to continue. After all, Roberto always brought back kerosene, oil, onions, and matches, which were shared with anyone who asked. So, the chief had reasoned, it was a fair trade.

Victoria gyrated out of the hammock with difficulty. Her stomach tightened in rebellion. She held her breath until the sensation eased. Next, the familiar kicks against her ribs nearly took her breath away. She would be glad when the time came to have this baby—she felt certain he must be a boy, a very big boy! Deep in her thoughts, wondering whether she should go to Linda's to ask her questions, she didn't hear Fidel enter the hut and lay the skinned rabbits down in the corner. But Rosalinda's cheery exclamation brought Victoria out of her reverie with a start. She was ecstatic at the sight of the good meat—small game that she could eat! Her eyes held the love and thankfulness that she felt toward her husband, and she flew into action, starting the fire in anticipation of rabbit stew! It was already nearing dusk—it would be a late meal.

Victoria ate the rabbit stew hungrily. She stacked all the dishes in a huge gourd on the floor to wash at the river in the morning.

She decided to go visit Linda and ask her questions, but when she peered out the cracks she saw the kerosene light at the misioneros' house flicker out. So she reconciled herself to a good night's sleep instead. She was apprehensive about Fidel leaving for two days. But, in exchange for his work Linda would buy things for them in the city. Even though Linda said that she wouldn't come back until after the baby was born, she said that Roberto would return without her. Victoria had asked Linda for cloth, fishhooks, panties for Rosalinda, and a new blanket that they desperately needed. She was very pleased that Fidel was able to work for those items. Victoria had also asked for two new wraparound skirts, which she would give to Maamo and Rosa as gifts. She wanted to ask for three, but Linda didn't seem to want to make her funny marks in her book even for the two. Perhaps another trip would earn a new skirt for Victoria herself. She enjoyed telling Linda all the things she'd like to have, and wanted to make sure it was a complete list, even if Linda only brought back half of the things she wanted. Victoria was never sure why sometimes she received more and other times fewer of the items. Fidel's list had included a new machete and file, plus shotgun shells that he could either trade with Esteban for meat, or use to hunt if Esteban allowed him to borrow the gun.

    The new day dawned with fog lying heavily over the village, which to the Nala signaled that a bright and sunny day would emerge. The smell of the misioneros' coffee wafted into the hut and Fidel's mouth watered. He'd learned to like coffee, so he headed next door for his daily cup.

Soon the misioneros' house was filled with Nala, each there to say goodbye and wish them well—though not in words, but each with his or her presence. The strange White Ones were tense and rather unfriendly, but they always seemed that way before a trip. It was very hard to understand them.

Actually, Linda was frustrated. She'd packed all their cups except the two they would take on the trip. There was barely enough coffee for the two of them and yet the house filled up with people expecting a morning cup of coffee. She felt as if she could never leave this village without feeling used by these people and glad to be on her way. Why couldn't she just have the last day to herself? It was hard to close up the house, it was difficult being out of food, and she was so tired...and not at all looking forward to the uncomfortable trip back to civilization.

Chapter 14

By dusk on the second day, Victoria wondered why Fidel and Timoteo had not arrived. She was worried, frustrated, and…in labor! She'd hidden the pains for many long hours, waiting for her husband. She wondered whether she could be mistaken about the months—the baby certainly seemed big enough! But, no, she knew that she had one more full moon to go. Nervously, she rocked back and forth with a scowl on her face. One strong painful contraction after another assaulted her. Victoria knew there wasn't much time left, yet she remained stubbornly silent.

Rosa stoked the fire—the air had cooled down and it smelled like rain could be in store for them shortly. Victoria's sullenness was getting on Rosa's nerves, even though she too was upset that the men weren't back. It was a fearful thing to be on the river past dark. Intermittent storms and flash floods could hit without warning. She decided to visit her sister's family for the evening, so she spoke to the room at large, "I'll see you later. I'm going to Ana's." Paco was, of course, nowhere to be seen, but Rosalinda followed her grandmother out the door. She loved going to her cousins' house.

Maamo studied Victoria. If, over the past few hours, she'd been reading the signs right, Victoria was about to have her baby. She'd wondered why the young woman was so secretive about it, but she'd held her peace. Maamo had helped deliver several babies—out of necessity—but she'd never been the official midwife in her village. She'd been watching Victoria closely over the past months, and she'd thought that her granddaughter was wrong about when this baby should arrive.

Lightning and thunder crashed close by, followed by torrential rain. Victoria could handle the pains no longer. She sought Maamo's eyes...pleading silently for understanding and help. When the strong contraction ended she whispered, "It's time."

Maamo's stiff legs sought the earthen floor and she fought for balance as she threw her hammock up over the rafter. "We don't have banana leaves, girl. You could have given us some time to prepare. Well, I can't blame it all on you—I've known for several hours and I sat there in silence too. The two of us, we're a lot alike, you know."

"I hoped Fidel would arrive." Victoria gritted her teeth, bracing for the next pain.

"I know dear, I know," Maamo crooned.

When she could talk again, Victoria directed Maamo to a cardboard box above her own hammock. Maamo took down the container and found a plastic tarp inside which Linda had given to

Victoria. She spread the sheet out on the floor and placed a stool in the middle. Victoria slid off her hammock and leaned heavily on the bench as she pushed the baby from her body.

As another crash of thunder erupted from the sky, the newborn cried weakly. A flash of light momentarily illuminated her tiny body. Victoria and Maamo exchanged wary glances at the small infant—they had both expected a large and robust boy.

Victoria labored on, trying to expel the afterbirth, but nearly ten minutes later a second baby girl was born. No cry was heard as she slid onto the plastic. Victoria panicked. "Help her, Grandmother, please help her!"

Picking up the slippery baby by her heels, Maamo patted the little one's back. She turned her over. Maamo slid her finger around inside the baby's mouth. Next she gently bent the baby's chest toward her tiny legs as if folding her in half. At last the baby cried...it sounded more like the whimper of a wounded animal, but she was breathing.

Finally, the afterbirth was delivered and then buried in a corner. Maamo and Victoria were petrified. They couldn't speak—or even look at one another—they both just knew that neither could harm those babies. But, what future would they have? What would the village do? What would Rosa say? And Fidel....

Maamo retrieved Rosalinda's old blanket plus a brand new one that Linda had left for Victoria, and they each wrapped one of the babies and snuggled them to their mother's breasts. Both tiny girls began to nurse.

Lightning and thunder crashed again and the rains continued for another hour. The babies slept peacefully. Finally Victoria said, "Grandmother, would you get the box down again? Inside there are pictures, pictures of twins. The White Ones don't kill their twins. Why should we?"

Maamo found the snapshot and the page from a magazine. She took them close to the fire so she could see. "It's good," she said. "I had twin girls before your father was born. Your great-grandfather and your grandfather buried them in the jungle, and they were never talked about again. But I've never forgotten them—and I've never forgiven myself. I will not allow it to happen again!"

"Grandmother, Linda told me about the Good Spirit named Dios. He must allow twins to live, but I don't know how to call out to Him."

They fell silent for a while. Victoria couldn't think. She was exhausted from the long day's silent labor as well as this new fear for her babies.

"We'll face it all head-on. Don't fear. You have a good husband who will stand with us." Maamo knew that they could be in for the fight of their lives…but fight they would.

With those words, even though distraught, Victoria was too exhausted to resist the sleep that claimed her.

Embers glowed and sputtered in the fire pit. The rain stopped and Rosa crept back into the quiet hut with Rosalinda asleep in her arms. Paco had been left in a hammock with two cousins. Rosa headed straight for her hammock and slept unsuspectingly with the toddler. After several hours, however, she awoke with a start to the cries of an infant. Rosa sat straight up in her hammock—"I hear a baby!" she exclaimed.

"Yes," Maamo interjected in the dark. "You missed the birth during the storm."

Again a baby cried and Rosa said, "Well, Victoria, aren't you going to feed the child?"

"Yes." Victoria struggled to get the second infant settled to nurse at her other breast.

"Is he a boy?" Rosa asked excitedly, contemplating getting up to see. But she didn't want to awaken Rosalinda—and it was very dark and cool. It would be of little use to get out of her warm hammock at this hour.

"No, girl..." Victoria choked away the plural on the end. *Do I tell her tonight? I feel so deceitful. I can't tell her tonight!*

"And Fidel missed it. He'll have a big surprise when he gets back tomorrow!" Rosa exclaimed.

Little did she know that *she, too,* would have a huge surprise when the sun rose over the unsuspecting village of Namuro.

The faint aroma of wood smoke drifted into their hut moments before daybreak. Foreboding seized Victoria's heart as she awoke to the plight of protecting her babies. She feared Rosa's response. Desperately she wished for Fidel to arrive quickly—surely he would defend her and their baby daughters! She wanted to run to the river with them in her arms and wait for her husband's return.

She was so weary, so hungry, and still so weak. She felt as if she could barely breathe from the terror of it all.

Rosalinda jumped out of her grandmother's hammock and trotted out the door, back to her cousins' house. Rosa stretched and yawned. "Oh, the baby! Was I dreaming, Victoria? Did you really have the baby last night while I was gone?" Almost like a young girl, she hopped out of her hammock and hurried over to her daughter-in-law.

Rosa nearly fainted at the sight before her eyes...not one, but two little bundles were snuggled, one on each side of Victoria. The woman reached out for a post, ready to collapse. Maamo pulled a stool over for her to sit on. Rosa's face grew pale and her hands trembled. She looked frantically from Victoria to Maamo and back again. She couldn't speak, she couldn't voice her anger or fear, or whatever it was she was feeling.

All that Victoria could think to do was hand one of the babies to her. When the infant gazed into her grandmother's eyes, it was enough. In defeat Rosa whispered desperately, "What are we going to do?"

Sleep had escaped Maamo throughout the long night. "I may have a plan," the matriarch offered. Two pairs of terrified eyes focused on her, so she continued. "Why not put up birthing curtains this morning. It will keep any visitors away. We'll just have to keep these babies from crying. Maybe we can stall long enough for Fidel to get back."

"It isn't a long-term solution, but it sounds like a good plan for now," Rosa declared. Color returned to her face as she stood, very happy to at least have something to do.

Chapter 15

Shortly after noon, the faint sound of a motor announced Fidel and Timoteo's return. The three women, still huddled in the small, curtained section of the house, looked into one another's eyes.

Fidel ran excitedly toward his hut, having learned that Victoria was about to give birth. Apprehension filled his heart, knowing her time wasn't for another month yet.

"I'm here!" he called out at the door.

"Come in," Rosa responded from the inner room.

Fidel walked in cautiously, making sure the blankets were hiding the event. To his surprise Rosa held open the covering and waved him inside. Confusion registered on his face, then his heart pounded in his chest with the thought that perhaps Victoria had…. had not lived through the ordeal. He hurried into the birthing room and willed his eyes to adjust quickly to the darkness. When they did, he saw his precious wife, safe and sound, with a baby in her arms. He reached joyously for the infant, but then something in Victoria's face stopped him in his tracks. Something *was wrong*.

Victoria's eyes shifted toward Maamo, averting Fidel's gaze in her direction. To his utter disbelief, a *second* baby was sleeping peacefully in her arms. Fidel couldn't move. He couldn't think straight. He couldn't quite shift from his initial fear to complete joy and then back to dread and fear once again. He sat heavily on a small bench. Victoria's eyes pooled with unshed tears...her inner being pleaded for her husband to be the hero she knew him to be. The thought of their babies being rejected was more than she could bear—and the seconds seemed to her an eternity.

Finally, Fidel collected his thoughts and was able to speak. "When were they born?"

"Last night," Victoria said.

"Nobody else knows..." Fidel stated rather than asked, trying hard to formulate their next move. "How did you manage to keep it a secret?" he asked, amazed. But before anyone could answer he continued. "Never mind, we'll have lots of time to talk. We have to decide what to do." Then he reached gingerly for the baby in Maamo's arms and Victoria's heart soared. Fidel had not let her down.

"I think we'd better gather our belongings and head for the river. When Luisa met us at the bank saying you were in labor, I left the canoe without putting the motor away. The best thing is to leave the village. Perhaps, when they're a little older, we can return. But we just can't take the risk now," Fidel informed the women calmly.

"But where will we go?" Victoria asked.

The Outcasts

Rosa began to protest, "I've never been outside of this village..." but she stopped short when she looked around at the family who had all become so dear to her. Besides, Maamo had survived huge changes. Rosa determined that she could do whatever she had to do to stick by this family. They would all need one another.

Fidel stood and handed the infant into Victoria's free arm as he looked at Rosa and Maamo. "You need to gather all of our things quickly. Where are Rosalinda and Paco?"

"They're at Ana's," Rosa explained as she retrieved her own stash of possessions.

Within minutes the family's worldly goods were packed into two cardboard boxes; three hefty baskets; a very large, sooty kettle which held various gourds as well as their few dishes, cups, and silverware; and finally, an empty five-gallon oil container.

Fidel returned with the children, well aware that at any minute visitors could arrive to see the new baby. He grabbed the heavy pot and the oil container and trotted out the back and down their river trail. He'd never been more thankful for the private and secluded path that couldn't be seen from other huts. When he returned, they all quietly fled behind him down the path. Even Maamo, with her walking stick in hand, was laden with a basket on her back.

Once at the river they packed the canoe, quickly settled in, and began to float downstream. They could barely breathe, and their hearts raced, knowing they'd pass every other family's bathing spot. They couldn't put the motor down until the river became deeper. Hopefully, the element of surprise would be enough to keep people from stopping them.

Around the first bend, children playing in the river stopped to stare as the canoe floated by. Two boys ran home with this mystifying news. Alerted, people sprinted toward the river, but when they arrived, they could only stare speechlessly as Fidel propelled his entire family out of sight beyond the last bend.

The conch shell blew and adults flocked into the meetinghouse to discuss the situation. Ana and Luisa were crushed. They couldn't imagine what had happened, yet all eyes were on *them*, searching for answers. Finally, the two boys who had first seen the boat were called into the meeting for questioning.

"What, exactly, did you see?" the chief asked gruffly.

"We saw the canoe with the misioneros' motor on back. There was Fidel, his mother, that old lady, and Victoria," the boy recounted slowly.

"Paco was with them," interjected the second boy, "and Rosalinda."

"Was Victoria holding a baby?" The chief wanted the valuable information.

"Oh, yes, I saw a baby wrapped in a blanket in her arms...and uh...another one in Rosa's," the boy recalled proudly.

"No!" the chief shouted. But his shout was lost, along with all control of the meeting.

The crowd settled down, however, when a teenage boy ran in. "I looked through their house and everything's gone—it's empty. Well, except for these. I found them lying inside on the floor."

The chief's face reddened as he focused on the page from a magazine and a photograph of...twins! "That's *it*—" he thundered, "those misioneros have caused this! Fidel and Victoria pushed to have them move here in the first place, and now the spirits are angry! How could Fidel allow those babies to live? We're in danger of the curse coming down on all of us!"

The meeting had cost them precious time. Fear of angry spirits kept the villagers from chasing the family. In desperation, hoping to appease the spirits' wrath, they decided to burn Fidel's house to the ground. They would deal with the misioneros' house later...perhaps they would burn that one, too. But one blaze would be dangerous enough, especially when daylight would soon be fading. They'd had a good rain the night before, so hopefully the sparks wouldn't ignite other roofs. But just in case, the villagers began a bucket brigade to soak the dwellings nearest Fidel's, and they would all keep a very close watch.

Eerily, angry faces watched as hungry flames consumed the walls. And then, like a torch, the thatch caught fire and flamed viciously in the darkening sky. Ana and Luisa wept for their loss. Secretly, Luisa wished she could have seen the babies...and said goodbye.

The Outcasts

The motor began to sputter and Fidel knew they were running out of gasoline. He hadn't had a chance to fill it up before fleeing the village, but he also knew that the misioneros kept a fifty-five-gallon drum of fuel, as well as motor oil, at Alberto's place. "We'll stop at Alberto and Moya's for the night," Fidel informed his family.

About fifteen minutes later, Fidel deftly poled the canoe into the nearly invisible landing and called out. "Aaa-ooo!"

However, nobody responded, so Fidel called out a second time while helping his family disembark.

The exhausted group walked the thirty yards toward the hut and called out at the door.

A boy holding a baby opened the door for them and they entered the dark dwelling. Moya was seated near the cold fire pit with two young children by her side.

"Where's Alberto?" Fidel asked.

"I don't know," Moya barely whispered.

"How long has he been away?" Victoria questioned her.

"Going on two weeks. He went to Cerro Alto to sell the last of our rice and avocados so he could buy supplies. We haven't seen him since, and I have no idea what to do. He always returns the same day...there's nowhere to stay in Cerro Alto." Moya was distraught.

Fidel said, "I'm going to get our hammocks."

"Okay," Moya said. "I don't have any food, though. We ran out days ago and I haven't gone back to the garden since." At the very mention of food the two scruffy children at Moya's side began to cry.

Paco and Rosalinda stared at the weeping children, who appeared to be near their ages. They longed to run and play after the long canoe ride, but instinctively they stood quietly by their grandmother's side. Rosalinda's shiny thick black hair hung to her petite shoulders. Her eyes sparkled and her cheeks held a healthy glow. Paco, although in desperate need of a bath, also had a head full of hair and a robust look. Moya's children, however, had sores covering their skinny bodies, and their unkempt hair had no shine at all.

Maamo lowered herself stiffly onto a bench. Rosa and Victoria were holding the babies, who both began to fuss. Victoria was anxious to have her hammock hung so she could sit comfortably and nurse her twins. She wondered why Fidel was taking such a long time. But finally he entered the door with one of the large baskets and a box. He set them down and left to retrieve another load, while Rosa hung the hammocks at the far end of the house.

Victoria lounged and nursed her babies. She asked Moya, "Are you out of firewood and kindling, too?"

"Yes. Alberto wouldn't just leave us like this. I have nowhere to go. What am I going to do?" she cried. She was so despondent that she hadn't even noticed the twins, or didn't care. Moya had barely averted her downcast eyes from the cold fire pit.

"We'll figure something out tomorrow," Victoria tried to reassure her.

Maamo looked at the motley crew and said, "Maybe we should start our own village for people who have nowhere else to go."

"That sounds good," Victoria said with a chuckle. "Of course, we don't have any money, and there won't be any way to support ourselves until we can plant and harvest food. No house to live in! But, still, it sounds good!"

Halfway through the conversation Fidel entered with the rest of their belongings and said, "What sounds good?"

"Grandmother says we should start our own village…a village full of outcasts!" Victoria nearly giggled. She was far too tired.

"I moved the canoe up the creek that winds around the back of the property. It'll be out of sight if anyone comes downriver tomorrow," Fidel informed the women.

Night had fallen and the hut was dark and cold, so everyone sought his hammock for the night.

Victoria's thoughts turned to the misioneros. *I wonder whether Roberto and Linda will be allowed to return to Namuro? But even if they do, how will we learn more about the Good Spirit? Could it be that the Good Spirit Dios is the one who helped us escape? Is He stronger than the bad spirits? He must be, here we are. My babies are still alive! Oh how I want to know more about Dios and His Son Jesús. Our lives have changed forever—there's no turning back. I don't know why, but I think I've changed, too.* Victoria felt hopeful. *Perhaps we* will *start our own village—a village for outcasts. And maybe, somehow, Linda and Roberto will be part of it, too.*

Peace filled her heart and mind, extinguishing the anguish and fear that had engulfed her. And Victoria slept.

Chapter 16

Finally, the long night gave way to a new dawn. Fidel had not slept much at all, and with good reason. He had not been able to bridle his thoughts about this household, which now consisted of three babies, four small children, two older women, his wife—who'd just given birth, two boys, who were about twelve and ten, plus Moya. Survival would mean hard work—hopefully the boys, Moya, and Rosa would be up to the tasks at hand.

Babies began to cry and the small children were whining for food when Fidel sought the haven of the outdoors. But Chandi, the oldest boy, had preceded him.

"How did you greet the dawn?" Fidel asked.

"Good, and you?" the boy countered.

"I'm good, too," Fidel stated.

"If I remember correctly," Fidel said, trying to size him up, "you're about twelve years old, right?"

"Yes, I'm twelve." Chandi said, standing a bit taller.

"You're a hard worker, too, aren't you?" questioned Fidel.

"I am. I work with my dad. Usually I go to Cerro Alto with him, too, but he made me stay home because of the baby and all," Chandi explained. "I wish I'd gone with him."

"Well, we can't do anything about that, but you sure can help your family now. Your dad would want that, you know." Fidel tried to bolster the lad.

"Okay, I'll help," Chandi determined.

Antonio walked outside and wordlessly joined them.

"Let's go get some wood and split some kindling. Lead the way." Fidel realized he would need, somehow, to encourage these youngsters as best he could. They headed toward a storage shack where machetes, an axe, and the drum of gasoline were kept.

Inside, Rosa took control. "Moya," she began, "your kids are hungry—we all need food. Leave the small ones here and take me to your garden. Grab your basket."

Woodenly, Moya obeyed, leading the older woman out the door and up the narrow trail that led past the shack and into the dense rain forest. Silently, they trekked along the damp, musty-smelling trail until they entered a rough plot. Typical of the jungle gardens, only natives would recognize the plants which produced their food. There were no neat rows; instead, yucca and other root vegetables were interspersed around and beneath banana and plantain trees.

The growing season was past, however, so Moya and Rosa began to forage for whatever precious food had been missed while

The Outcasts

harvesting the last of the crops. Fortunately, bananas and plantains produced year-round.

Soon, the pair trudged back to the house with their baskets laden with a variety of produce. When the women entered the hut and relieved each other of their loads, the children's eyes lit up at the bounty.

Rosa handed out bananas, which the children quickly devoured before she could even unload the two baskets. She sorted the vegetables and fruits and eyed the amounts—wondering how many days they could exist on this food. She was encouraged, though, because she'd seen more plantains that would soon be ripe. They could survive on banana drink if they had a good supply of firewood.

After cutting and splitting wood, Fidel, Chandi, and Antonio entered the house. Their stomachs were growling, so their eyes brightened at the pile of food in the corner, and they happily devoured the bananas that Rosa handed them.

"We have wood to be hauled," Fidel informed Moya. She nodded and went for her basket once more. Rosa wasn't far behind with hers. Out the door the five went, returning shortly with their burdens.

Around the fire that night Victoria reminded her husband that their baby girls needed names. Each with an infant on their lap, they studied their identical daughters. Silky black hair covered their heads and a miniscule dimple in the right cheek of each one made their parents smile. The girls were so tiny...but also perfect in every way.

"Do you like the name Isabel?" Fidel ventured.

Silently Victoria played the name through her mind. "Yes, I like that. I've been thinking about Susana or Melisa."

"Susana," Fidel repeated. "Susana and Isabel are very nice names."

"But," Victoria hesitated, "which one gets which name...and how will we tell them apart?"

The couple looked at each other and chuckled over the dilemma.

Surprisingly, it was Moya who spoke up next. "I have beads and string. We can make the girls each a different colored bracelet."

"That's a wonderful idea!" Victoria exulted.

"Do you remember which one was born first?" Fidel asked.

"She was," Victoria said, pointing to the infant in her husband's lap. "I kept the new blanket on her, and Rosalinda's baby blanket on the second-born."

"Then let's name the firstborn Isabel and the second Susana." Fidel gazed adoringly at his babies.

Victoria's face glowed with love and delight. She felt relieved that her babies had names. Somehow, it seemed like a protection. They had lived long enough to be named—surely no one would harm them now...would they?

After a long silence Fidel spoke once more. "I need to take the canoe to Avanzada and get a message to Roberto. I don't know how to talk to the other misioneros, though. I can't figure out what to do."

"Do they speak Spanish?" Chandi asked, almost shyly.

"Yes. But I don't," Fidel said, staring numbly at the fire.

"I speak Spanish with my dad, and Nala with my mom," Chandi informed him.

"You do? Now *that* is a help indeed!" Fidel's spirits soared as once-vague plans became clear in his mind. "Tomorrow you and I will go to Avanzada. We can bring back supplies from Cerro Alto. Chandi, do you know how to buy supplies?"

"Yes." The boy smiled proudly.

"Good. That's good." Once again Fidel was encouraged.

Victoria piped up then, "Fidel, we don't have any money. How can you *buy* anything?"

"Roberto gave me this when we left him in Avanzada," Fidel said, pulling some bills out of his pocket. He had no idea of their worth, however. "He told me to pick him up in one month, and take him back to Namuro so he could check on the airstrip. He left gasoline and oil, but he said I should take this in case the motor broke or we got stuck anywhere and needed food. I figure we're stuck. I'll let him know in the message we give to the other misioneros in Avanzada."

Victoria and the others felt reassured, and began to talk among themselves as they settled in the little ones for another night.

Fidel took that opportunity to go outside for a breath of fresh air underneath the starlit sky. Maamo followed him.

"I guess the time has come," she told her wonderful grandson-in-law.

"What?" Fidel queried uncertainly.

"I've had a secret," Maamo whispered conspiratorially.

Fidel led the older woman to a nearby stump and helped her ease herself down. His curiosity was piqued as he waited for her to go on.

To his surprise, she said, "This walking stick is very special."

Fidel had often admired the top of the staff, which had been carved into the shape of the head of a toucan. Its long beak formed the sturdy hand-piece. He had often wondered just how large or oddly-shaped the original piece of wood must have been. The head of the bird was unique, with two black eyes that protruded in a very distinctive way. The body of the bird gradually blended into the rest of the sturdy stick.

Fidel waited for her to continue.

"If you look closely at the eyes, you'll see it's a dowel that holds the small head on above the beak. It was all one piece until I carved a hollow spot down through the top of the head and a few inches into its body. Then I carved a new head and fitted it over the top of the old one and put the dowel through, to hold it in place. Inside, I've hidden some gold nuggets." She waited for a response, but when it didn't come she looked toward Fidel in the semidarkness.

Finally Fidel managed to say, "Gold? Where did you get gold?"

"You remember hearing about the 'lost village'?" she stated with a soft laugh. "I think I discovered it...long ago. I'd heard stories about it when I was a young girl. I determined to find where that village had been, and when other kids my age were playing in the river or out fishing, I scouted the area...farther and farther upriver, until one day I found gold nuggets glinting from the bank of the river. I returned often, and each time I scooped out more and more of the riverbank at that spot. One day, I found gold coins and more gold nuggets. I never told anyone. You can imagine the trouble I'd have caused. So, I just buried the gold in a special place. Years ago I carved this walking stick, and then one day I got the idea about making the secret compartment for the nuggets. Of course, the gold coins wouldn't fit, so I pierced holes into them and made two necklaces. They're inside with my belongings."

They fell silent.

Fidel continued the conversation quietly. "I know that gold is coveted, but I have no idea how its value compares to paper money. But Maamo, I do believe you've saved our lives."

"You saved *my* life," the older woman proclaimed fondly to Fidel. "I can never thank you enough. Maybe this gold can get us through until we can start a new village...to help others who have nowhere else to turn. I'd surely like that."

"It will be a big help!" Fidel said, as relief began to wash over his weary mind and body.

It would be Fidel's turn for a restful night's sleep.

Chapter 17

Rosa was the first one up the following morning, greeting the first rays of dawn. With only two remaining matches, she very carefully laid slivers of kindling in the center of the cold fire pit and surrounded those with slightly larger chips of wood. She struck one match and held it close until the flame crackled as it was fueled by the dry chips. Satisfied, she added a couple of larger pieces and then pushed the ends of the three large logs closer to the fire. Once the three ends began to burn she would place the cooking pot on them, to reheat the banana drink. *We only have one match left. We'd better keep the fire going until Fidel and Chandi return. But, these logs will be burnt out in two more days. I sure hope they can leave early and return yet tonight. What if the chief sends men to come after the babies and we're here alone? Maybe I can talk Fidel into not going. But...we only have one match left...* Rosa couldn't tame her thoughts and fears.

Babies cried, children stirred, and then suddenly the household bustled noisily as the day officially began. Fidel, Chandi, and Antonio headed for the shack to ready the boat and motor for the trip. Victoria and Moya nursed their babies, while the children gathered around the fire, anxious for food. With her walking stick in hand, Maamo worked her way toward the door.

Several minutes later, she reentered the house along with Fidel and the boys.

"What supplies do we need?" Fidel asked.

"Matches," Rosa stated. "There's only one left."

"We're out of kerosene, sugar, and coffee," Moya said. Seeing Fidel's eyebrows raise slightly, she quickly added, "But we can live without those."

For the first time, Fidel realized that life away from the village was indeed going to be different. Without sugar cane, and without a press to squeeze out its sugary liquid to sweeten the banana drink, they would in fact need to buy sugar. And, Alberto no doubt had been accustomed to drinking coffee and buying kerosene for a hand-made lamp. This household had been used to luxuries that, before the misioneros' arrival, the Nala had known nothing about.

Fidel looked at Chandi and asked, "Does your dad have any more .00 buck and birdshot shells?" He'd seen the shotgun in the corner.

But Antonio was the one to answer. "No, dad was bringing some back. We're all out. We also need fishhooks and fishing line."

"Do you have any salt?" Rosa asked Moya.

"No," Moya stated flatly. But she was puzzled. *The salt just seems to disappear at times, along with matches. I can't figure it out,* she thought.

Fidel waited a few seconds before asking, "Moya, do you have a shelter in your garden?"

Moya looked up in surprise. "Yes."

"Victoria, I want you and the children to go to the garden while we're gone. Mother, you, Paco, and Maamo need to stay there with them too.

"Antonio, will you take all of our hammocks to the shelter and string them up there for us? If anyone comes here while we're gone, I don't want them to know that our family has been here."

Antonio agreed with the nod of his head.

"Moya, the rest of you can remain here or go with them, but just don't tell anyone we've come here, okay?" Fidel warned.

"I won't," Moya assured him.

"Antonio, take care of things while we're gone."

Antonio nodded again and then answered, "I will."

Fidel was ready to leave, so he and Chandi quickly downed the lukewarm banana drink.

Victoria was grateful that they had a plan. *I can't wait to get outside. I didn't realize that I felt this way, but even though walking won't be pleasant, I really need some outside air.*

Fidel fingered the half-dozen gold nuggets in his pants pocket. Maamo had secreted them to him outside. He had no idea whether he'd need them for this trip, but it felt wonderful to know they were there. Lovingly, he looked at each of his daughters and then at his beautiful wife. "I'm gone," he said, and strode out the door.

Chandi followed him. "I'm gone."

The four women exchanged glances, trying to feel brave. They handed out banana drink to the children, as Antonio unstrung the hammocks.

"Are you staying here?" Rosa asked Moya hopefully.

"No, I'll go with you to the garden shelter," she decided.

Now, how am I supposed to keep this fire going? Rosa fumed silently. *She'll just have to trek back here and stoke it. This banana drink had better not scorch.* The heavy cauldron was too hot to move, so Rosa scraped some of the wood away from the center to slow down the fire, and hoped it would smolder until Moya could come back.

The simple shelter was nearly a mile away from the house. The structure, which was used only as a temporary refuge from rain, had posts and rafters with a new thatched roof. But like most garden shelters, it had no walls or furnishings of any kind. The group settled in for the long day, very thankful for their hammocks, which provided places to sit. But, never far from their minds was the impending night, which they all knew they could not spend in the garden without walls to protect them.

The Outcasts

Rosalinda and Gina played together a few feet from the shelter where the women lounged in hammocks. Gina, at three and a half, was almost a year older than Rosalinda. Nelson, it turned out, was five years old, a half year older than Paco, even though he looked much younger. The boys were roaming farther away; they had been drawn to the edge of the creek and were throwing pebbles into the water. Antonio had disappeared up the trail and deep into the jungle.

Victoria breathed in the fresh air as she rocked and nursed Susana. Maamo cradled Isabel as they swung slightly to and fro in her hammock. Moya sat on a small stool that she'd carried with her. She stared blankly into space. Rosa was tired of sitting, frustrated at having nothing to do. She wished she could go clean the house...in her estimation Moya was lazy.

And then, Rosa's keen eyes took in the surrounding garden and she zeroed in on several large bushes in the distance. She walked from the dwelling to inspect further and came back to the group very excited.

"Moya, I found your cotton bushes! The cotton is ready to pick. In fact, it's going to rot with any more rain. We need to bring it in today."

Maamo's ears perked up at the news. "I really like to spin cotton into yarn. Moya, you have a new hammock to make for the baby. What did you name her?"

"We named her Amalia," Moya said. "I planted cotton seeds when we first came here. I don't know why—I don't know how to spin cotton or weave hammocks. Alberto bought hammocks for each of the children in Cerro Alto. He was bringing one back for Amalia...."

Rosa and Maamo were surprised, but Rosa quickly found her voice. "Can we pick the cotton and use it to make a hammock for the twins?"

"Okay," Moya said.

Rosa grabbed her empty basket, but before she left she told Moya, "You need to go back to the house and check the fire. Bring back some banana drink for our midday meal."

Moya met the eyes of the older woman. "It's hard not knowing about Alberto. I can't stop wondering whether he's sick or hurt. I've felt isolated for years, but never hopelessly abandoned. We didn't have a canoe or any way to leave here to search for him or get help. I almost lost my will to go on. But, with all of you here, I'm trying to feel hopeful again—to get some energy back. I *am* trying."

Rosa felt pity for her. *Maybe Moya wasn't as lazy as it appeared. But her house was a mess and nearly falling down. Of course, this family was all alone with no village to help them build and repair.* Then Rosa shivered. *Perhaps we're all about to find out how hard that can be.*

The Outcasts

Fidel and Chandi had been traveling for nearly an hour and a half when Cerro Alto came into view. Fidel guided the canoe to the now-familiar wooden dock at the bottom of the concrete stairs. Chandi securely tied the front end of the canoe to a piling.

Fidel felt a bit nervous about buying supplies, but they'd already discussed what they needed and Chandi said he could handle the buying. Fidel pulled the wad of bills from his pocket and handed them to the boy. Chandi peeled each one back looking at the denominations and raised his right eyebrow.

"This is a lot of money. Keep these two bills in your pocket, and you'd better not show them to anyone," Chandi, who was wise beyond his years, cautioned. "This money will buy everything we need, plus some extra items, if you want."

Fidel put the two twenties back in his pocket. He patted the gold nuggets. *It doesn't seem like we'll need to use these*, he thought gratefully.

The two jaunted up the stairs and followed the cement sidewalk to the left. Six rough, weathered wooden structures with rusting tin roofs lined the walkway facing the river. Fidel followed Chandi into a *bodega*. At an uneven plank counter, the boy asked the clerk in Spanish for matches, salt, sugar, fishhooks, fishing line, and .00 buck and birdshot shells.

The middle-aged Latino man hesitated, looking harshly at Fidel, then back to Chandi. "Where's your dad, boy?"

Chandi answered politely, "We haven't seen him for two weeks, sir. Was he here?"

"Yes, yes he was, about two weeks ago. He purchased exactly what you've asked for, plus a hammock, I think. But, he never made it home, you say?" The clerk was curious.

"No. This man is a friend of ours and he's helping us until my dad comes back," Chandi explained.

The clerk glared one more time at Fidel. When he looked back at Chandi, the boy had two bills between the thumb and forefinger of his right hand, which he rested on the countertop. Begrudgingly, the cynical man turned to the untidy shelves behind the counter to retrieve the requested goods. He weighed the sugar and the salt on the white porcelain scale that hung down on chains from a rafter.

Chandi walked to the back of the store, pretending to look around at larger items that sat on dusty plank shelving. He was glad that Fidel had followed him—he didn't want to speak Nala in front of the store owner. When far enough away he whispered to Fidel, "Do you want kerosene, cooking oil, or anything else?"

Fidel was amazed that the two bills could buy all of these things. He'd spotted some hand soap so he told Chandi to buy the soap along with all of the other items he'd just mentioned; "...and coffee," he added impetuously.

Chandi walked back to the clerk. Fidel was amazed as the boy once again spoke the odd language so easily.

The clerk found an empty mason jar and filled it with vegetable oil. He then stuck a funnel into the slim neck of a dirty old bottle and poured kerosene into it. He pushed a cork into the top and then scribbled numbers onto a brown paper bag.

Chandi handed the owner the ten and five dollar bills and was given back three ones and two quarters. They gathered each small brown bag containing the salt, sugar, and coffee, as well as the brown paper bundle that contained the rest of the supplies, the mason jar, and the bottle of kerosene.

Outside, the aroma of freshly baked bread assailed them. Chandi looked at Fidel hopefully and Fidel nodded his head and followed his young comrade into another store. Fidel spied Coca-Cola and quietly told Chandi to buy two of those and as many of the yeast rolls as the rest of the money would buy.

Soon they were back in their canoe and speeding downriver toward Avanzada. They sipped their cola, and each ate two of the fresh hot buns. Chandi sat at the bow with the wind blowing his hair. He thought about his missing father. *He made it to Cerro Alto...but what happened on the way back home? I've been searching for any signs of our canoe. We have to find him! He has to be alive!*

The sun was directly overhead when, four hours later, they arrived in Avanzada. Fidel, familiar with the dock, guided the canoe to shore. Chandi tied up the boat and hopped out. He followed Fidel up the bank to the door of the building, taking in the neat-looking block house with the shiny tin roof. Fidel knocked on the smooth wooden door, feeling a bit foolish...but that was how the misioneros got the attention of the owners of the house.

The Outcasts

An American lady wearing a bright green dress opened the door. She smiled broadly as she greeted Fidel in Spanish. "Hola, Fidel!"

"Hola," Fidel repeated, nearly exhausting his repertoire of Spanish words.

"Hola," the woman smiled at Chandi, "my name is Paula. What's your name?"

"My name is Chandi," he informed her.

"Chandi—that's an unusual name. I've never heard it before," Paula said.

"Actually, my name is Santiago, but Santi for short. My mother is Nala, so she pronounces it Chandi, and that stuck," he said with a bright, good-natured smile.

"I like it. So, you speak Spanish. That's good. Come in, both of you, come in," Paula said, leading the way.

Chandi was amazed at the white walls. The cement floor was shiny and clean. Red and white checked fabric hung at the window openings. The benches looked soft with a shiny fabric covering them. In another room, Chandi could see a table with four wooden chairs. A curious-looking large, shiny, white box-type thing caught his eye.

Fidel started speaking to Paula in Nala, so Chandi quickly began interpreting for the woman. Soon she understood that Fidel needed to get a message to Bob and Linda, so she grabbed a notebook and paper and jotted things down as they spoke.

The Outcasts

"Let me repeat this to you to make sure I got it right," she said. "Victoria had twins, so the whole family had to leave Namuro for the babies' safety. Fidel's family is staying at Alberto and Moya's, but Alberto is missing. He didn't return from Cerro Alto, where he went two weeks ago. Fidel had to use some of the money Roberto left with him so they could buy supplies. Should Fidel still meet Roberto here in Avanzada in a month, as planned? Fidel isn't sure whether the village will allow Roberto and Linda to go back to Namuro, but Fidel knows that he and his family cannot return." Paula looked to the boy for affirmation that she had all the facts right. Chandi nodded.

"I'll get this message to them, but it won't be for another week," Paula informed them.

"How will we get a reply?" Chandi asked. "Should we come back in a month?"

Paula thought for a moment. "Do you have a radio?"

"No," Chandi stated simply, but he'd seen and heard one in Cerro Alto.

"I have an extra radio I can give you, and some batteries. Just a minute." Paula went into another room and came back with an aqua-colored plastic radio and eight batteries.

Chandi's eyes lit up with excitement.

"It's set for Radio Día. See right here, if this knob gets turned you have to turn it back to this, 910. The batteries go in this way." She pointed to the proper ends as she inserted four C batteries into the box. Chandi and Fidel followed her every move. Paula turned the radio on. It crackled slightly and then filled the air with a salsa tune.

"Every afternoon at 3:00 Radio Día reads messages to people. Roberto and Linda will send you a message over the radio. You'll have to listen every day from 3:00 until 3:30. Here are four extra batteries. When the radio stops working, put these new ones in."

Fidel watched Chandi, who had begun to look at his feet. Something seemed to have gone wrong. Paula noticed it, too.

"Oh," it finally dawned on her. "Do you have a watch?"

"No," Chandi said. "The store clerk has one, and my dad talked about buying one someday."

Once more, Paula was deep in thought. Finally, she left the room again, in search of the watch that her son had received as a Christmas present several years before. It was a Mickey Mouse watch, one he didn't use anymore. Before bringing it out, she set the proper time.

"Here, it has to be wound like this," she said. "Then you press it back in, like this."

There was a tension in the air. "You can have it," Paula said to Chandi.

The boy's eyes widened, and then he handed it over to Fidel. As a child, he could never presume to own a watch when Fidel and his father didn't even have one.

Paula tried hard not to smile as Fidel proudly fastened the bright-colored watch onto his wrist. She went to his side to show where the hands would be at 3:00, and then explained to Chandi that it would be 3:00 when it was still dark and they were sleeping and 3:00 again in the afternoon. At 3:00 in the afternoon they should listen to the radio program.

The three of them were worn out.

Paula excused herself and went to the kitchen for lemonade. Chandi watched as she opened the door of the big, shiny, white box. He couldn't see what she was doing, but she brought them glasses filled with the ice-cold beverage.

Fidel and Chandi hid their surprise as they tasted the liquid that gave them the chills, each wondering what the funny cubes were that felt so strange against their lips and tongues. It didn't take long, however, before they felt refreshed and knew they'd miss that special drink. The bottles of Coke had been cool to the touch, but this was cold!

Fidel signaled to Chandi that they had to leave.

"Gracias," Chandi said, "Thank you for everything. We have to go so we can make it home before dark."

"Should you spend the night here?" Paula offered.

Chandi interpreted for Fidel, even though sure what his answer would be. "No, we have to get back tonight."

"Do you have flashlights?" Paula asked with concern, "...so you can see if you don't make it back before dark."

"No, but we'll be okay." The boy was already embarrassed by the woman's generosity.

"I have two extra flashlights. Here, take them," she insisted. Even though Paula knew that too many possessions or too much money could upset the fragile economy of outlying villages, she felt compelled to help them. They had, after all, fled from their home and were fighting to survive. This circumstance was different.

Fidel and Chandi smiled and nodded. "Gracias," Chandi said, once more.

The two sprinted down the bank to the canoe, very concerned about making it back before nightfall. Fidel filled the gas tank from the red metal gas can that he'd brought along. The motor revved to life, and they headed upriver as fast as the outboard would take them.

They passed Cerro Alto without even slowing down. Going upriver had taken an extra hour. The sun was setting in the western sky before they arrived at the mouth of the Namuro River. It was a dangerous section of waterway where the Namuro gushed into the strong current of the Grande River.

Chandi was poised at the bow, long pole in hand, bracing himself as they were turbulently propelled across the currents. Fidel slowed the motor, then sped up at just the right moment so they could ford safely.

The river had demanded their full attention, so neither had noticed the faint glow and the sliver of smoke from a fire on the opposite shore of the Grande.

Chapter 18

The sun was setting quickly and the garden shelter was growing darker by the minute. Fidel had told them to stay there until he returned, but they simply couldn't spend the night in the open without any protection.

Just before dusk, Antonio returned, as mysteriously as he'd left. The children were cranky and hungry and beginning to sense the fear that was building up in the women. Finally, Rosa took charge.

"Let's get these hammocks down. We're walking back to the house while we can still see the trail," Rosa said with authority. She continued talking under her breath as the group moved quickly to gather their things. *Why'd we wait so long anyway? We all knew we couldn't stay here after dark. There are snakes, among other things. We'd better not see one along the trail. What was Fidel thinking, anyway, telling us to stay here no matter what?* "Is that it? Everybody ready? Hand me that baby, Victoria—you can't carry two."

The Outcasts

Rosalinda began to cry. "Come ride on my shoulder," Antonio offered, and knelt close to the ground in front of her. He lifted the child up on one shoulder and slung a hammock over the other. He then led the way down the footpath toward the house.

Maamo hobbled along the rough trail in the semidarkness with Victoria close by her side on the narrow pathway. They lagged behind the fast-moving group. When they were only halfway there, Antonio returned alone, machete in hand, to guide and protect them.

"You're a good boy," Maamo said. "Life's going to work out just fine for all of us—I can feel it in my bones."

Antonio didn't reply, but the compliment remained in his heart.

It was dark before they reached the hut. Inside, Rosa sat at the cold fire pit, struggling to rekindle the embers which had gone out despite Moya's efforts at noon. *I should have come back myself,* Rosa fumed. With children fussing and crying, Antonio started stringing up the hammocks.

Victoria laid the babies down as soon as she could, and began filling gourds of cold banana drink for the children. They drank hungrily and climbed into their swinging beds for the night. Victoria shivered at the thought of how many days it had been since she'd bathed her children in the river. If she couldn't keep them clean, they too would soon be covered with sores.

"Aaa-ooo." A signal sounded from the river.

It was Fidel! "Aaa-ooo!" Antonio called, as he hurried out the door to help them.

He could hear that they were poling the canoe up the creek to the shack, so he headed that way. Then he saw two lights shining from the canoe! Lights! He ran to meet them.

All smiles, Fidel and the boys entered the house with their parcels. They shined the beams of light from their flashlights around the room, to the delight of everyone inside.

Chandi searched the crooked shelf above the wobbly wooden table, looking for their handmade smudge lamp. It was a baking powder tin. They'd poked a hole into the lid and stuffed a wick through the hole. Chandi filled it with kerosene and dropped the wick into the liquid, pushing the lid down tight. He retrieved a match from the parcel and lit the tiny lamp. It provided a dim light in the very dark room.

Fidel reached into another paper bag and handed a fresh bread roll to each of the women and children. He and Chandi ate the remaining two—they were very hungry!

Victoria savored each bite—it was delicious.

Maamo had never tasted anything like it before, and her mind began working overtime, wondering how they could learn to make it themselves.

Antonio inspected a parcel and found the shells, fishhooks, and fishing line. He smiled.

The fire finally flamed to life and they settled in to listen to the account of the trip. At the end of the dissertation, when

Fidel recounted the strong current turning into the Namuro River, Antonio was the one who spoke.

"That's it! That's exactly what I've been thinking happened to Dad! The day before he went to Cerro Alto, the Namuro River flooded. I remember because he put off going for an extra day. Lots of logs and debris floated down and emptied into the Grande. The day he left, the river was no longer flooding, but the current was still very strong. Maybe he capsized...but he could have made it to shore. We have to go search for him tomorrow. We *have* to!" Antonio insisted.

Antonio and Chandi looked expectantly at Fidel, who said, "Of course we will."

Rosa said, "I'll go fishing tomorrow. Nelson and Paco can help me."

"Good," Fidel said. "We all need a good night's sleep, then."

Within minutes, each of the fourteen people in the tiny hut was fast asleep.

The next morning, Fidel again sat in the back of the canoe by the motor. Antonio, the lightest, was at the bow, and Chandi in the middle, each poling the canoe through the creek toward the Namuro River. They eased out into the current and floated to the mouth of the river. Before reaching it, however, they tried to pull to the side so they could look across the expanse of the Grande.

The Outcasts

The current was too strong—it sucked them viciously into the larger, deeper waterway. Chandi and Fidel fought to steady the canoe, but Antonio's eyes skimmed the currents and searched the farthest bank across the expanse. Their boat followed the current downstream toward Cerro Alto, and Fidel fired up the motor. Once the current settled down, he turned the boat around and headed back upstream along the right-hand shore. Alberto would have been poling a canoe along that bank, so they headed slowly upriver, surveying the marshy land and dense jungle for any signs of Alberto or the missing canoe.

A piece of land jutted out—an ideal place to catch debris. Fidel cut the motor, and then Chandi and Antonio stood and plunged their poles deep into the muddy river bottom to prevent the canoe from moving backwards downstream. They inched forward, searching and calling out. But there were no signs of the missing man.

Fidel fired up the motor once more and sped upstream past the mouth of the Namuro River. He quit the motor, and the boys plunged their poles into the river bottom. Fidel stood and put his weight to a pole on the opposite side, allowing the boys to push off and turn the canoe around. They used their poles, slowing the boat's progress while they looked at the shoreline from this direction. Again, they called out.

They heard a dog barking, but all too swiftly they rounded the bend past the Namuro River again. When it was safe, Fidel started the motor, turned the canoe around, and headed back upriver to the place where the land jutted out. He cut the motor and they poled up past the jut and then allowed the current to push the canoe into the bank. The land behind the boat rose above the marshes, so Antonio and Chandi got out to look around.

"I have to stay with the boat," Fidel said. "Be careful, and don't go very far. Here, take these machetes. There's bound to be a lot of snakes in there. Call out and listen, but don't go too far!"

The boys climbed the small rise. "Aaa-ooo," they called.

The barking continued, so they followed the sound into the thick trees. Antonio watched closely, so they could find their way back. He had natural tracking instincts and used them.

"Aaa-ooo," Chandi called out.

"Aaa-ooo," came a faint reply.

They forged their way through a maze of tree roots and underbrush. Mosquitoes covered their bare arms and faces, but they hurried on relentlessly. The barking became louder and guided them to a wooden shack in a small clearing. Inside on a crudely built bed lay their father. The boys were shocked at how thin he was.

"Papa! Papa!" they called as they ran to him.

Alberto didn't have much strength. "You found me," he whispered.

Chandi and Antonio jumped at the sound of another man's voice. "You boys his sons?"

A huge black man stood in the doorway. "My name's Andrés. *Rey* (King) here found your daddy pinned under his canoe," Andrés said, pointing at the dog. Your dad busted his leg good. He hasn't talked much, mostly slept since I tried to put it back into place. He did say, though, that he lives across the river, in that direction. I've seen the smoke from your place—he pointed it out one night."

Chandi spoke up. "Thank you for helping him."

"I've been patching up your dad's canoe, but the waters will have to get a lot higher before I can get it back into the river."

"Papa," Chandi roused his father again. "Fidel brought us over in his canoe. He's waiting for us. Can you make it to the river?"

Alberto attempted to sit up and the color drained out of his face.

"I splinted his leg, but he can't put any weight on it yet. I think I can carry him that far though," Andrés informed them.

As carefully as he could, the large, strong man lifted Alberto to his feet. The injured man groaned loudly and then passed out from the pain. Andrés hefted him over his broad, bare shoulder. Antonio led the way and Chandi followed, sadly watching his father's head bounce limply on Andrés' back. He wondered about Andrés' curious accent—he didn't sound like his father, or the people in Cerro Alto.

Fidel was very relieved when he heard people coming back. He was surprised when a large black man, carrying Alberto, followed Antonio from the thicket. Fidel nodded, wishing he could communicate with the man who'd obviously saved his friend's life.

Fidel stood deep in thought, unsure of how to help get Alberto into the canoe without further damaging his obviously injured leg. After a few seconds he told the boys to get into the craft and hold it steady. Fidel jumped up onto the bank and helped to ease

Alberto off of the giant man's shoulder. He cupped his arms under both of Alberto's legs while Andrés cradled his upper body. They stepped down into the canoe, lowering Alberto onto the bottom between the front and middle benches—but he was too long. Antonio grabbed his father's ankles as gingerly as he could and guided them underneath the middle bench seat.

Fidel spoke to Chandi. "Tell the man he's welcome at our house any time." Then he realized it wasn't really *his* house.

But Chandi relayed the message to Andrés, who nodded with a curious grin on his face. "I'm a loner, but thank you."

Fidel, Chandi, and Antonio leaned heavily into their poles, dislodging the canoe and poling into deeper water, where Fidel started the motor and headed toward the opposite shore and the Namuro River.

Chapter 19

Three exhausting weeks had passed—weeks of vigilance, as they hid from the villagers who were, no doubt, still hunting for the frightened family.

Victoria was bent over, sweeping her dirt floor with a handmade whisk broom. Billows of dust floated in the air. The secluded garden shelter now had split bamboo walls, and had become their new home.

Building the walls had been a tremendous amount of work for Fidel, Chandi, and Antonio. Fidel and Victoria had taken village life for granted and were finding out firsthand how helpful it had been for all of the men to gather materials and work together on each house. They now also understood why Alberto and Moya's house wasn't in better shape.

Alberto was thankful to be back in his own home. His misshapen right leg remained too painful and weak to walk on. He hobbled gingerly from his hammock toward the fire, using the crutches that Fidel had fashioned from two long, forked sticks. Moya watched him thoughtfully. He had changed. Even though she and her husband had never learned one another's language, Alberto had always conversed freely with the children. He'd even taught Chandi and Antonio from his old school books. Now her husband was silent and sullen, even with the boys. Moya wondered again about his past. Someday, she purposed, she'd ask her sons if they knew. For now, she was just glad to have him back. For her, his presence was enough.

Alberto was so grateful to Fidel and Victoria for taking care of his family when he couldn't, that he had gladly given Fidel's family the garden shack for their home.

Alberto recognized that it would be a long time before he could hunt, make repairs, or be of much help with anything—if ever again. Even his canoe was gone—he felt totally useless. He cringed at the thought of life without another family to share the workload with Chandi and Antonio.

Scrutinizing the rotting patches of the thatched roof, Alberto realized he should have replaced it long ago. He ran his hand across the rough and dilapidated bamboo siding and he wondered why he'd been so lazy. And now—now he couldn't do the things he'd only wanted to put off doing before. Alberto realized that the truth was that he'd never truly adjusted to this way of life. He'd been raised in a city, not the outback jungle. However, this life, he knew, could be far less cruel. So why hadn't he put himself wholly into it?

Chandi sat on a bench near the crackling radio. It was 3:00—the highlight of his day. Fidel had entrusted the wristwatch to him, because he had to monitor the radio at the proper time.

"Rodrigo Vasques sends this message to his wife, Anita. Meet the bus at 10:00 Saturday morning. I'm sending rice, and clothing for the children. I need plantains." The radio announcer read the note quickly and went on to the next.

"Mother is in the hospital. Come out to town as soon as you can...."

"We need plantains. I have one more week of work, then I'll return...."

And then, after all the weeks of listening, Chandi finally heard, "This message is for Fidel and Victoria from Roberto and Linda. Meet me in Avanzada one week from today. Pablo and José will be with me."

Chandi turned off the radio and hurried out the door. He ran up the path to tell Fidel.

"Good," Fidel said. "That's good! We need more supplies from Cerro Alto, but I didn't want to use Roberto's motor without his permission unless I had to. Ask your father if you can go with me." Fidel chuckled. "That is, if you want to go with me."

"Of course I do!" Chandi confirmed emphatically.

"That's good, because I need your help," Fidel stated genuinely.

The Outcasts

"Where's Antonio? I'd like to ask him if he'd stay here while we're gone. I haven't seen much of him lately. Is he off hunting again?" Fidel asked.

"He's been gone a lot. He's been acting pretty strange, too. I don't know what's going on with him," Chandi replied.

"I'll watch for him to come by here. Maybe I can talk to him," Fidel offered.

Rosalinda crawled into her daddy's hammock and sat on his lap while he rocked slowly back and forth.

"Victoria," Fidel said, "what supplies do we need from Cerro Alto?"

"We need matches, salt, and fishhooks. I'm also concerned about planting a garden and growing rice for next year. We need our own plantain and banana trees, too. I really miss our chickens and eggs. I'm so thankful for all of the meat that Antonio brings us—without that, we'd be very hungry," Victoria stated.

"You're right. I'll see what we can buy in Cerro Alto. It isn't going to be easy. We're starting with nothing. But, we do have a roof over our heads—and walls on our house!" Fidel teased his wife.

"And Isabel and Susana are safe and healthy." Victoria looked lovingly toward the twins, who were lying head to head in her hammock, fast asleep. It seemed hard to believe that they were almost a month old already.

Less than an hour later, Antonio ambled by the hut. That, alone, was unusual for him. Peering from the cracks in the split

The Outcasts

bamboo walls near his hammock, Fidel watched the boy. He stood up and exited his house.

Antonio looked up, with a troubled expression on his face.

"Antonio," Fidel began, "go with me to the shed, okay?"

Wordlessly, Antonio followed Fidel into the shack that smelled like a mixture of gasoline and oil.

"Next week I'm going to Avanzada to pick up the misioneros. I'd love to take you with me sometime, but you're such a big help here. Would you stay with Victoria and my family while I'm gone?" Fidel asked him.

"Okay," Antonio agreed.

"Antonio, is anything troubling you? You can talk to me," Fidel coaxed.

Antonio's expression was unsure...anxious. It was very unusual for the laid-back boy. While he waited, Fidel began wiping down the outboard with a rag. He'd already cleaned it after the last use, but he needed something to do while they talked.

Several moments later, Antonio began. "I have a secret that I'm afraid to tell. I said I wouldn't...so how can I go back on that?"

"Mmmm," Fidel said. "You have to be careful giving your word. But sometimes, as hard as it is, you have to do what's right."

"I've tried to convince her..." Antonio's eyes widened.

"Her?" Fidel asked in amazement. "You'd best tell me, son."

Antonio sat on a small wooden stool. Minutes passed by. Not for the first time, Fidel was amazed that the boy was only ten years old.

"There's a place I found, about a year ago. I go there whenever I can. It has old block buildings with concrete floors, like the town hall in Cerro Alto. But it's been deserted for a very long time. The block walls are sturdy, but some of the tin roofs have caved in. The ones that are left are brown and have holes in them. And, there's a huge, long concrete trail. It doesn't lead to anywhere! It's uneven and broken up in places. I can't figure it out.

"A couple of months ago, when I went to my place, I heard people talking. I hid in one of the buildings and waited. They were the voices of a woman and a boy speaking in Nala. The boy was telling his mother how hungry he was and she began to cry.

"I called out to them and they got real quiet. They hid. But I started talking, and I told them my name and age. The boy, Pepe, came out. He's five years old.

"Since then, I've been taking them meat when I hunt, and wood and matches so they can cook. I always take bananas, plantains, and sometimes salt. Dalia finally started to trust me, but she told me that I could never tell anyone that they were there.

"Today, though...she's giving birth. Pepe is scared—he said she's been like that since yesterday. He asked me to get help, but Dalia screamed at me that I'd promised not to tell anyone."

Fidel stared at Antonio. He was dumbfounded, speechless.

Antonio looked up into the older man's eyes, hoping for reassurance.

"You did the right thing telling me. I'll get my mother...she's delivered lots of babies...and you can take us there. We have a few

The Outcasts

extra matches and some food we can take along. I'll get the flashlights. Go tell your parents I need your help tonight so they won't worry about you. Let them know you'll be back in the morning."

Fidel hurried to his house to tell them about the woman who needed their help. Rosa, anxious to leave, gathered a few supplies. Antonio returned, and the three hiked as quickly as Rosa could manage, up the trail and into the thick green jungle. In the basket on her back, Rosa carried her hammock, the blankets, food, flashlights, and other items that would be needed. Fidel and Antonio carried their own hammocks and their machetes so her load wouldn't be too heavy.

It was cooler underneath the thick canopy of trees, and the pungent smell of damp earth filled each breath as Rosa trudged along between Antonio and Fidel. She refused to stop and rest, fearful of the young woman's plight.

Finally, Antonio stopped and turned around. "We're very close."

He stepped out of the dense jungle and led them into a clearing where the wide and very long concrete trail was. They walked to the center and stopped. They looked up and then down the trail. It truly led to nowhere—it simply ended. On the other side stood seven concrete block buildings.

Antonio called out, "Aaa-ooo!"

"Aaa-ooo!" came Pepe's reply.

Rosa stood and gaped. She tapped her bare foot on the cool hard surface. Rosa had never seen concrete before. Fidel urged his mother to continue on. When a woman's frantic scream pierced the air, Rosa flew into action. Pepe led them to one of the smaller block buildings, where his mother lay on the hard concrete floor, writhing in pain. Her haunted eyes became wild with fear.

"No, no, go away!" she cried, when she saw people outside the doorway.

Rosa took the basket off her back and walked into the dwelling. The men sought refuge in another block structure, busying themselves by hanging hammocks around beams that were still sturdy enough to hold weight. Fidel and Antonio gathered wood and built a fire on the concrete floor. They shared food with Pepe, careful to save some for Rosa and Dalia.

Rosa approached the woman, who appeared to be in her mid-twenties. "My name is Rosa. I've come to help you. What's your name?"

"Please go away!" she moaned.

"How long have you been in labor?" Rosa questioned her.

"Yesterday morning..." but Dalia couldn't go on. She screamed in agony.

Rosa called out for Fidel, who came running to the doorway. "I need water to wash my hands, and a flashlight."

Fidel returned with a flashlight and a large gourd full of river water that Pepe had filled earlier in the day.

Rosa could see that they were in trouble. The baby's bottom was preventing the delivery. As the contraction eased, Rosa pushed on the baby's buttocks, but before she could do any more, Dalia bore down with another pain.

"Don't push!" Rosa urged. "You have to wait and not push, just for two or three more pains."

Dalia's stomach relaxed once more and she took a deep breath. Rosa pushed the baby's buttocks again and sought a leg. She pushed up on the woman's abdomen with her free hand—as hard as she could. She pulled the leg down. Another contraction was starting and she gruffly ordered the mother, "Don't push! You'll lose this baby for sure if you push!"

Dalia forced herself to breathe, to relax, to breathe. She willed herself to be calm.

Rosa got her fingers around the other leg and slid her fingers to the ankle. Gently, she pulled the baby's other foot out of the womb.

"Okay, next pain you can push. Push with all your might."

Another scream broke through the air as the infant was expelled into the world. And then the hearty cry of the newborn. Much to Rosa's relief, the positioning of the baby had caused most of the trauma to the mother, and not to her child. She was a large baby and was very much alive.

Fidel walked toward the door opening and asked, "Is Dalia okay?"

"Dalia, so that's your name," Rosa crooned. And then she called out to her son, "I think so. This has been hard on her, but

I think she'll be okay. The baby is a girl and she seems to be healthy."

"Good," Fidel said, taking the news back to the waiting boys.

Soon Dalia was rocking luxuriously in the softly woven fabric of the hammock with her infant at her breast. Pepe brought her a piece of wild pig meat and a roasted plantain that he'd rolled in coarse salt. Tears flowed from Dalia's eyes. It had been far too long since she'd sat in a hammock, or had people take care of her. Except for Antonio…she looked at the boy from across the room and said, "You saved our lives, Antonio. You did good."

Antonio nodded, relieved to know that he hadn't failed his friends.

When Dalia woke up the next morning, Rosa told her that the men had gone home, but she would stay until Dalia could walk back with them.

"I'm not going with you," Dalia stated in alarm.

"Why not?" Rosa asked, indignantly.

Dalia was silent.

"You can't raise two children out here all alone in the wild. Our family will take you in." Rosa hoped to talk some sense into the woman.

"No," she stated with finality.

Rosa pondered the situation silently. This woman had obviously had a very hard life. She didn't trust anyone. Rosa decided to tell her their story.

The Outcasts

"Fidel and his wife just had *twins*." Rosa said in an ominous tone.

Dalia's eyes widened.

"We lived in Namuro, but fled so they wouldn't kill the babies."

Dalia drew her own infant a bit closer.

"Now we live next to Antonio's family. His mother is Nala, but she married his father, who's an outsider. The village ran them off. They can never return."

Dalia could relate to that and she waited for more information.

"We would love to have you join our village for outcasts!" Rosa exclaimed.

"I don't have anything. I don't have any way to pay for food. I…" But Dalia couldn't explain any more.

"Who's your mother?" Rosa questioned. But she was met with silence. "Which village did you live in?" More silence. "Dalia," Rosa said, slightly exasperated, "between all of us in our household we've been to every village. Your past will come out. It's best that you tell me now."

Dalia set her jaw defiantly. She deliberated in her mind. *I might as well tell her everything now. She'll probably leave us here, but better now than later. I'd rather face her with the truth than face the whole family.*

"Okay, I'll tell you. I'm Dalia, originally from Kala. When I was thirteen years old, very important visitors came to our village.

The Outcasts

It was so exciting to see those men, two of whom were chiefs, and listen to their stories around the fire. One of them paid attention to me and I felt so special! I went out to a jungle garden with him because he promised me a gift. I had no idea what would happen, and I couldn't stop him. He was strong, and I was afraid because he was so important. Afterward, he threw a necklace on the ground by me, and I cried as he strode away. Before I could bring myself to get up and go home, one of the other men found me, and he, too..." Dalia cried softly. She couldn't go on for several moments.

"I became pregnant and the village had a meeting. They sat me in the middle, humiliated and berated me. They demanded to know who the father of my baby was. The first man was Ramiro, the chief of Ulgana, so I named him. I could not admit that there had been another.

"The very next day, I was sent from the village. Two of our men took me to Luwana, and the following day three men from Luwana took me to Ulgana. By the time I arrived, I knew that life as I had known it was over. I thought it couldn't ever get any worse, but it did. Ramiro would have nothing to do with me. He called me a liar. They built me a small shelter on the outer edge of the village. I had no food, no garden, nothing to cook with. I only had my hammock and one change of clothing that I'd been allowed to bring with me.

"Men started visiting me at night. They brought food...for a price—a very high price.

"Pepe is five years old now. I couldn't stand the way I had to live in front of him. And, I was pregnant again. I decided that I would leave...even if it cost me my life. I couldn't go on.

"One day, a group of men was going to the outpost to sell their crop of avocados. I told Pepe to follow me to the river. We watched as their canoe floated downstream, and I realized that the river would take us away from there. I made up my mind that anything would be better than the way I had been living. It was no life at all.

"The following day, Pepe and I went down to the river early in the morning. I took my hammock, pretending I was going to wash it. But when we got there, I told Pepe to get into a small abandoned canoe. It was old and dilapidated, but we got in and I pushed off with a pole that I'd left nearby.

"We floated downstream slowly. Finally we reached the large river, but we were sucked into the swift current so quickly that we nearly capsized. I looked behind us and I could see the shiny roofs of the buildings that I'd heard about, where the Ulgana villagers go to trade. But it was too late to go there, the river was too deep and swift. All we could do was hang on. For hours we sped down the swift current, and then another river spilled into it. Our canoe capsized and we were slammed into the muddy bank. I hadn't let go of Pepe—somehow we had stayed together. Of course we lost the hammock, but we had survived. We crawled up the bank looking for drier ground. We walked deep into a stand of large trees and then came out into this strange clearing. Several days later, I feared that we would die here, but that's when Antonio found us. He saved our lives."

Rosa was very touched by the story. "We won't turn you away. I'm very sorry that you've been mistreated. This is your chance to start a new life."

"But I have nothing to offer. I would rather die than go back to that kind of life," Dalia said vehemently, afraid that any men in their group would abuse her.

"Can you sweep floors and wash clothes?" Rosa asked.

"Yes," Dalia said.

"Can you haul plantains and firewood?" Rosa asked again.

"Yes," Dalia affirmed.

"Then you'd be part of the village…and part of our family. We need another young woman. I'm getting too old for the hauling. Victoria's grandmother can't work anymore, but the two of us can watch the babies while you young women work. We need you as much as you need us," Rosa declared with finality.

Dalia was afraid that this was all too good to be true. "Are you sure?" she asked.

"I'm sure," Rosa declared.

The following morning, Antonio returned to guide Rosa, Dalia and her newborn infant, and Pepe home. The two families had discussed the newest outcasts who would join their "village." Nobody had questioned whether they should rescue them—none would have considered turning them away.

The Outcasts

Before noon, Antonio led Pepe and the two weary women into Fidel and Victoria's house. Victoria held out her arms for the new baby that would now be a part of their family. She greeted Dalia and smiled warmly at her.

Dalia sat in a hammock and began to relax a little. But, when Maamo entered the hut, the young woman drew in her breath sharply. The color drained from her face. Maamo, however, barely flinched. She'd been told that a woman named Dalia and her five-year-old son, Pepe, were outcasts in need of a home. She'd known right away who they were, but she'd held her tongue.

Maamo walked to the hammock. She leaned her cane against the wall and cradled Dalia's face in her hands as she said, "Another granddaughter!"

Dalia was horrified—she wanted to run. *Maamo is Diego's mother! Victoria is his daughter. I can't stay here.* The bitterness that had grown within her through the years surfaced with a vengeance. *I hate Diego as much as I hate Ramiro! I don't want to have anything to do with his family.* She sat dejectedly, trying to think of a way out. Though tormented, she realized that it had been a very long time since she'd sat comfortably around a fire—with happy family sounds, and the delicious aroma of food. She would bide her time.

Fidel swung in his own hammock, deep in turmoil. *Could Dalia be the girl who had been with Diego? Could Pepe be Victoria's half brother? Can I keep Victoria from finding out?*

Chapter 20

Bob, Paul, and Joe floated downriver in silence. After being picked up in Avanzada, they'd had a good night's sleep at Fidel's, and then had taken the canoe up to Namuro to check the progress of the airstrip. They had been praying that the uproar over the twins wouldn't affect Bob and Linda's ministry in the village.

At the riverbank, however, the chief and half a dozen angry men confronted the misioneros, and told them to leave Namuro and never come back. They informed them that Bob and Linda's house had been burned to the ground! When Bob asked whether he could look at the house—whether he could retrieve the barrels in hopes that some items may not have been destroyed—the Nala men had brandished their machetes at the three and told them to leave.

As the canoe made its way back to Alberto's landing, Bob prayed and sought God's will for his future ministry with the Nala people. He was very thankful that he'd taken most of his language and culture materials with him to study while he was in town—the thought that he could have lost a year and a half of work was almost more than he could bear. But, what if his ministry with the Nala was over? He had believed that God wanted him to reach the Nala with the gospel—had God changed His will? Was God closing the door, or was this from the enemy?

Little did Bob or the other two missionaries know, but the chief was calling a meeting to alert the inhabitants of Namuro that the boat and motor which Fidel and his family had escaped in were now back in the hands of the misioneros. Roberto must know where the twins are. Now the villagers would have to determine whether burning the houses had been enough.

An hour later, the missionaries guided the canoe toward the riverbank at Alberto's place and disembarked. The three weary men called out at the first hut to let Alberto and Moya know they were back. Then they walked up the trail to Fidel and Victoria's house.

Victoria sat by the smoky fire. *I wish we had some root vegetables to thicken this broth and make it more flavorful,* Victoria thought, as she stirred the venison soup. *But, how can I complain? Venison! It's wonderful to have this meat!*

Antonio, it turned out, was the best hunter of the group. The day before, Fidel had brought back buckshot, so Antonio had disappeared into the jungle with the shotgun. He'd returned with a small buck which he had butchered and skinned so he could carry it home. The meat had been divided between the two families.

The Outcasts

The missionaries had paid Fidel and Chandi for making the trip to Avanzada to pick them up. With his wages, Fidel had purchased supplies in Cerro Alto.

Chandi, too, had purchased necessities for his family. Much to the delight of Antonio, Chandi had also brought back a pair of men's rubber boots for his brother. Antonio had talked about Andrés' rubber boots nearly every day since seeing them. Chandi was glad to be the one who got to go on the trips to town, but he felt bad for Antonio that he couldn't. Even though he knew that Antonio preferred the jungle and hunting, he couldn't imagine being left behind. Also, Chandi was very thankful for all of the good meat that Antonio supplied. So the boots were a special gift to his brother. He was glad that Antonio would have some protection against snakes, scorpions, thorns and other hazards while he tromped around in the dense underbrush.

Dalia took gourds filled with soup to the three white men sitting in their hammocks. She handed them each a tablespoon which Fidel had purchased. Dalia averted her eyes from them and was thankful to go back to the hammock that she'd been using since she'd joined the household. As she sat and swung slowly, she thought, *I really don't feel threatened by the white men; they don't look at me* that way. *Fidel doesn't either.* But, Dalia was afraid to let her guard down too much. To her, men simply could not be trusted. Others had acted the same around their families... but when alone... *Don't trust any of them!* she warned herself.

When the men had finished eating, she hurried back to retrieve the dishes so she could wash them out and fill them again for Fidel, Maamo, and Rosa.

Once everyone had eaten the noonday meal, the adults lounged in their hammocks. Little Rosalinda, with her long black hair and beautiful large brown eyes, ran straight for Bob, who picked her up and swung her in his hammock. She was all smiles and won the heart of each of the missionary men. She wore a hand-me-down dress of Kimberly's, which made Bob miss his own little girl even more.

"Roberto," Fidel said, "can you and Linda come here to live? We want to hear about the Good Spirit. We've waited a long time and you speak very well now."

"I don't know. I'll have to talk to our leaders," Bob told him.

"Ahhh," Fidel said, understanding all about leaders and needing permission.

"Would Alberto allow us to build on his land?" Bob asked, wanting all the facts to take back to the mission.

"I have another location in mind," Fidel stated.

Interested, Bob sat up in the hammock. "Where?"

"Antonio discovered a place that has old abandoned buildings. We've been talking about starting our own village," Fidel laughed. "A village for outcasts."

Bob perked up. His curiosity was piqued. "How far away is it? I'd love to go there."

The Outcasts

"We could get there and back before dark," Fidel said. "If I can find Antonio—he needs to lead the way. He's the one who discovered it."

Fifteen minutes later, shotgun in hand, wearing his black rubber boots that went almost to his knees, Antonio led the way up the trail. The three missionaries followed in single file. Fidel, carrying his machete, was close behind them.

Soon it seemed as if the dense jungle had swallowed them. A thick canopy of broad leaves and gigantic trees hid the rays of the noonday sun. The underbrush never saw the light of day, retaining dampness with the musty odor of decaying foliage. No one could see a trail of any kind, and the men were amazed that Antonio could find his way.

Nearly an hour later, the group stepped out of the rain forest and seemingly into another world. The missionaries were flabbergasted. Bob didn't have the Nala words to relay to Fidel that the place looked like it might have been a World War II airfield—with a concrete runway! Bob was able to tell them that the concrete "trail" was an airstrip.

Paul, a history buff and a veteran, exclaimed in English to his comrades, "I can't believe this! Years ago I read about several old abandoned World War II camps in this country. The U.S. moved out several decades ago, and apparently the military here wants nothing to do with this area. They do have a small outpost at the border, but I've heard that the few troops who guard the border get sent there as punishment."

The five of them trekked in silence across the width of the airstrip, stopping in the middle to look up and down the length of it, which appeared to be around a half mile. They walked on to the seven block buildings, which differed in size and were in varying degrees of disrepair.

Paul led the way into the first building on the right, and said in English to his companions, "This looks like it was the two top-ranking officers' quarters. There are two individual rooms. The rafters are shot—the rusted tin is lying on top of ceiling beams. Wow, unbelievable." In each room there was a metal desk, chair, and a metal chest of drawers.

They walked into the next building. Paul spoke again. "My guess is that this was the officers' quarters." They counted six rooms; each still contained two bed frames with rusty springs, a metal desk, wooden chair, and two metal chests of drawers.

The third building proved to be the mess hall. It had a kitchen built in the back, complete with an old wood cookstove. Countertops and open shelves above them had been made from cinder blocks covered with cement. A very old refrigerator stood in the corner. The servicemen had left tin plates and tin cups, as well as silverware. Lower shelves housed cast-iron skillets and pots in various sizes. It looked as if some could be salvaged.

In the main part of this building were the remains of five tables and thirty-six chairs, made out of wood. There had to be enough parts left to make several good tables and chairs. An inside wall separated one third of the room, making an area which must have been for the officers.

The fourth building was the second-largest. Paul said, "This must have been the enlisted men's quarters." He tried to open the heavy wooden door, but something was in the way. Bob and Joe added their weight, and the door moved enough for them to peer inside. It was one large room, but the tin, rafters, and most of the beams had fallen and lay on top of dilapidated bunk beds and metal chests of drawers. It looked as if about two dozen men may have been housed there. Now it appeared to be more of a rusty haven for snakes or rats.

The five continued to scout around the property. One small building which sat behind the officers' quarters may have been the officers' club. It had a bar and shelves that still held some liquor bottles. There were several small tables and a dozen more chairs.

To the left of the enlisted men's quarters stood two more structures. One very small building could have been the radio command center, and the other had been the mechanics' shop. Bob whistled when he entered and saw two generators, some work benches, tools, and parts. He was sure that many useful things could be salvaged.

Paul said, "It's very overgrown, but somewhere around here they probably dug underground bunkers to store drums of aviation fuel and possibly ammunition. This is just amazing."

Bob spoke to Fidel in Nala: "You're thinking of moving here to start your village?"

"Victoria and I have discussed it, but we haven't talked to Alberto and Moya about it yet. We need to have a meeting. Victoria and I haven't planted our garden, but Alberto and Moya's is an hour from here. It would be a lot of work for them to start over, too. What do you think about this place?" Fidel was curious.

"It's amazing! It would take a lot of work, but this would be a wonderful start for a new village. You'll need tin, wood for rafters and beams, and new doors of some kind. But the block appears strong and the concrete floors are good. And the airstrip! We could fly in and out. This is great!"

Fidel was encouraged.

Then Bob frowned a bit. *It is fantastic, but they don't have any money. We can't afford to fly tin and wood in for seven buildings!* Then he said, "Fidel, it cost us a lot of money for the tin and wood to build our house in Namuro. It was expensive flying the materials to Avanzada, and then we had to pay for the gas to haul it upriver. Maybe there's a way for you to build rafters the way you do for your homes and then thatch the roofs."

Fidel nodded, but didn't answer. *Roberto doesn't understand that it would take many men to gather all the materials and thatch all those roofs. Should I show Roberto the gold nuggets? Can he find out what they're worth? I need to know how much the gold is worth.*

Fidel, Chandi, and Antonio walked behind the buildings, through a large stand of trees, and finally came out at the Grande River. When they looked back, the camp was hidden from view.

Fidel shook his head. *How many times have I gone by this very spot?* Among the trees, Fidel found a stream that flowed into the Grande. He studied the tributary's path and decided that it must run to the west of the camp and airstrip.

He looked at Chandi and Antonio and asked, "Would you two follow the creek in back of your house to see whether it runs into this one? Maybe we could get your dad here in a canoe."

At that possibility, the boys' eyes lit up, and they agreed to check it out the next day.

The three walked back toward the buildings where the misioneros were standing together talking. Fidel said, "We need to leave. We don't want to be on the trail after dark."

Bob interpreted for his buddies, and the group headed back across the airstrip. Before stepping into the jungle, though, the missionaries just had to turn around and look at the World War II camp one last time.

While Victoria was preparing food, Fidel sat in his hammock and explained in great detail about the camp that Antonio had found. Chandi and Antonio sat and listened, and then went to their own house to share the day's events with their family.

After a meager meal, Fidel spoke to Bob. "Roberto, I need to talk with you outside."

"Okay," Bob agreed, quite curious. Fidel had never asked to speak privately with him before.

They walked down the path to the shed. It was dark, but Bob had a flashlight. Inside the shed, they sat on small stools.

"Roberto, I need your help. Maamo gave me some gold nuggets that she found years ago. I don't have any idea what they're worth. I don't know whether I can just buy what I need with them or whether they have to be turned in for paper money," Fidel said.

"Gold?" Bob questioned. "Do you have them with you?"

"Yes." Fidel reached into his pocket. In his palm he held out the six gold nuggets.

Bob picked up one and studied it carefully. The piece was oddly shaped, smooth and shiny, yet it had some rugged corners and areas with small pockmarks. "It sure looks like gold to me! It could be an ounce. They measure gold in troy ounces." Bob had to use the English word for troy and the Spanish word for ounce. "A troy ounce could be worth about $250.00. I'll have to check. That's a lot of money, Fidel."

The men sat quietly for a few minutes, each deep in thought.

"It would be better for me to cash them in the city. I don't think it would be good to show gold to anyone in Avanzada. These six nuggets could be worth $1,500.00, maybe even more," Bob explained.

Fidel had no way to put that into perspective. He was encouraged, though, that it seemed to be a lot of money.

"What do you want to use the gold for?" Bob asked, not wanting to assume he would use it to fix up the camp.

"It's very hard to live outside of a village. Gathering poles and thatching is very hard work. It takes a lot of time. Chandi,

Antonio, and I are the only ones who can do that. We don't have a garden—no rice, no plantain or banana trees. I'd like to use this gold to put roofs on those buildings and to start a new village. Then we'd plant our garden near the camp," Fidel informed him.

"There could be some things that you can do for food until your garden and trees produce. You can buy large bags of rice, and we can teach you how to bake bread. In Avanzada you can purchase chickens so that you'll have eggs. You could buy dozens of baby chicks, too," Bob stated.

"Those are great ideas. Let's go back and you can tell us more about it. Victoria will want to hear." Fidel was encouraged. "But I need to know how much I can buy with $1,500.00."

"I'll make a list tonight. Prices haven't changed much since we built our house. We'll figure out how many roofs you can put up, plus the supplies you'll need, and the cost of flying those supplies in," Bob offered.

"Let's go, then," Fidel suggested.

The two men walked back to the hut, where everyone was lounging in hammocks.

Fidel started the discussion. "Roberto has some ideas for us."

"Fidel told me that food will be a problem for you until you can plant crops and grow banana trees. You can buy large sacks of rice and we can teach you how to make bread. You'll need to buy flour, yeast, sugar, salt, and oil. You can make an oven—a thing to bake bread in—out of a fifty-five-gallon drum." Bob laughed. "You may not need that. There's a stove at the camp. Instead of cooking food over your fire, you can cook on the stove, or bake inside the stove." His comment was met with blank stares, but he continued. "It's kind of like your fire pit—only different. I can show you. You could also buy some chickens in Avanzada, or dozens of baby chicks. Then you'd have a lot of eggs," Bob suggested.

Victoria's mind began to whirl. "Tomorrow I want to go see the place," she said with excitement in her voice.

"Tomorrow Chandi and Antonio are taking the canoe up the creek to see if it connects to a river branch that runs along the camp. If it does, we all can go. Alberto and Moya need to see it, too. Then all of us will be able to discuss the possibilities and make plans," Fidel told her.

"That would be wonderful, to have Moya *and* Alberto join us," Victoria remarked.

The next morning, Chandi and Antonio took off in the canoe. They poled the craft up the narrow, shallow stream. It was very slow going for the first half hour, and then they reached the river branch that flowed into the creek. At that spot, the tributary flowed downstream in two directions—their creek, and possibly the river branch that would take them to the camp. They pulled the canoe tight to the left around the bend and headed downstream. The water was a little deeper and swifter, so poling the canoe was much easier. Within another half hour they spotted the camp! Near the west end of the airstrip, they disembarked and pulled the canoe safely up onto land so it wouldn't float down into the

The Outcasts

Grande River. They couldn't resist another look at the camp. After a quick tour, they got back into the canoe and labored upstream. At the Y they pulled the canoe sharply to the right around the bend and then poled downstream to the shack. They arrived home before noon.

Fidel met them on the trail. "What did you find?" he asked.

"We *can* get to the tributary that runs past the camp. It's slow going. This creek is very shallow. If the canoe is too heavy, we'll never make it," Chandi said.

"Okay, are you up to making another trip tomorrow morning?" Fidel asked.

"Yes," both boys said in unison. "We'll let our dad know," Chandi told him.

"Okay—Maamo and your dad can go in the canoe; your mom and Victoria can walk. Antonio, will you lead them, and I'll go with Chandi?"

"Okay," Antonio readily agreed.

"Dalia and Rosa can stay here with the little children. And the misioneros can go by trail if they want to, or stay if they'd rather," Fidel stated.

The following evening, the two households gathered together at Fidel and Victoria's. The misioneros would leave in the morning, and Fidel wanted to have a meeting before they went. Antonio had shot a rabbit on the way home from the camp, and Moya had brought plantains and yucca, so Victoria sat at the fire stirring a large cauldron of rabbit stew. The aroma wafted through the hut, enticing everyone.

Fidel began the meeting. "We've all been to the camp. I'd like to know whether or not fixing it up and moving there would be beneficial for all of us. Chandi, would you tell your dad, Pablo, and José what I'm saying?"

"Okay," Chandi said, interpreting Fidel's words into Spanish.

Alberto continued to look at his feet. He said, "I don't feel like I have a say."

Chandi interpreted for the Nala speakers.

Surprise registered on Fidel's face. "Why? You have as much say as the rest of us—if not more."

Chandi interpreted. His father looked up.

Fidel went on. "This is your land—you took us in when we had nowhere else to go. You gave us this house, and you've been sharing your food with us. We've taken in Dalia, the baby, and Pepe. You're housing and feeding them, too. We're all in this together—we're starting our own village, unless you've changed your mind."

Chandi explained in Spanish once more.

"Yes, I want to be part of the village. But, all I have to offer is this land. If we move, I have nothing more to provide. I can't work anymore." Alberto looked back down at his feet.

Chandi spoke in Nala.

The Outcasts

After a few moments it was Victoria who spoke up. "I've been thinking. The misioneros said they will teach us how to make bread, like the rolls we buy in Cerro Alto. Alberto, do you want to bake bread for all of us?" She paused. "Besides," she continued with a twinkle in her eyes, "your son Antonio *is* the one who found the camp!"

Chandi interpreted for his dad.

Alberto thought about it, and then he looked up again with a bit of confidence that he hadn't felt or displayed since his injury. "Yes," he said. He was beginning to realize he had more stake in this than he'd thought. After a brief pause he added, "I watched a man in Cerro Alto take the buns out of an oven that was made from a fifty-five-gallon drum. It smelled wonderful. And he sold them for ten cents each. I'd like to learn to make bread."

Chandi explained in Nala, with a smile on his face.

Moya spoke next. "Those houses have hard floors. Some have separate areas that are all very small. We've always slept in one room and had a fire to keep us warm."

Chandi relayed his mother's concerns.

Fidel said, "We can build fireboxes, so that we can still have our fires. If you want to, your family can have the largest building without the separations in it. That one is in the worst shape, but we can clean it out and get a roof on it."

Chandi spoke for the Spanish speakers.

Moya nodded, somewhat satisfied, but still a little unsure of all the changes that would come.

Rosa spoke up next. "What about Moya's garden? It'll be very far away. And we don't have one yet. Food is already scarce, trying to share."

Chandi repeated in Spanish.

Fidel answered, "That has been one of my biggest concerns, but today we were able to travel by canoe from here to the camp, so we'll be able to haul produce in the canoe once a week until the new gardens are ready. We'll also buy rice, and chickens so we'll have eggs, plus the bread that Alberto will bake. We won't be depending solely on the garden any more."

Once Chandi had interpreted, everyone nodded. And then all eyes turned toward Fidel.

He said, "Okay, then, everyone in favor of moving to the camp, stand up."

Chandi repeated Fidel's words.

All of the adults, except for the three misioneros, who didn't have a vote, stood up. It had been decided.

Fidel spoke next. He told the group that he would find out how long it would take to get tin and wood to fix the houses, and that for now, they could clean out the debris and clear the area of weeds. He also suggested that they plant bamboo along the bank where they were currently landing their boats so that in the future, their homes would be totally hidden from view. He had asked Maamo ahead of time whether he could tell about the gold nuggets. She had agreed, so he explained how they were going to pay for the repairs. He told them that Roberto said that they should have enough money to repair two buildings, possibly three, if the beams were usable. And they would also have money for food until their new gardens began to produce.

Fidel then spoke about the misioneros. He explained that Roberto and Linda were interested in moving to the new village with them. The other two misioneros were helpers who would visit once in a while, but they lived in town and had families there. After his dissertation, which Chandi interpreted throughout, another vote was taken—whether Roberto and Linda could join their village. Again, all the adults stood up in agreement.

Bob spoke to the group, saying how much he and Linda wanted to come. He then explained that first his leaders would have to give their permission.

When Bob finished talking, Fidel ended the meeting.

Suddenly, the thought occurred to Fidel, *Am I the chief?*

Chapter 21

The Nala Nation was in an uproar.

In Ulgana, the villagers had discovered the disappearance of Dalia and Pepe, as well as the old abandoned canoe which had obviously been used as their means of escape. Ramiro had held a village meeting, but apparent apathy had prevented any action. The men were very sorry that Dalia was gone, but couldn't show it. The women were ecstatic to be rid of her, but didn't want their husbands to know that they knew the truth about them. So the village as a whole went on as if nothing had happened.

However, word of Dalia and Pepe's strange disappearance did eventually spread to Luwana. In fact, on that very same day, another visitor also arrived, but from Namuro, reporting to Diego that his daughter had borne *twins*—and had fled the village with them! Diego was furious! He had been elated that Dalia was finally out of his life; and then, only hours later, he was reeling from the news of his daughter and Fidel! Diego couldn't stop berating himself that he hadn't put an end to Fidel long ago. Diego's wife, on the other hand, was distraught that she had two grandchildren whom she would never see...she might never even know whether they were girls or boys—and in fact, those babies' lives must still be in imminent danger. Questions pounded in her aching head and she sought her hammock, hoping for relief.

Days later, in Kala, Dalia's mother was mourning her daughter and grandson's disappearance. Over the past five years, she'd tried desperately to put them out of her mind...Dalia had always seemed like such a sweet child. The mother had wondered many times where her daughter had gone wrong...but she kept her broken heart to herself. If her husband felt any pain, he didn't show it. Life would go on.

The village of Namuro was split as to how to deal with Fidel and Victoria's babies. Half of the village was prepared to hunt down the twins and kill them. Ana and Luisa rose up, however, and were joined by the rest of the people in Namuro. They contended that the little ones were a month old already—no doubt they already had names. This group refused to be a part of murdering the babies. They pled that the two houses had been burned, the offenders had fled, and that surely the spirits had already been appeased. After all, they surmised, nothing bad had happened—*so far, anyway.*

Chapter 22

Two weeks later, Fidel, Victoria, Dalia, Chandi, and Antonio returned from a long day of cleaning up the camp. Rosa had a full pot of hot banana drink waiting for them. Exhausted, they sat wearily in hammocks and drank their fill.

Ever since Fidel and Chandi had returned from taking the misioneros back to Avanzada, the worn-out group had been working hard at the camp. They had hoped to have the buildings roofed before the heavy rains arrived, but it appeared that time was about to run out. The mess hall and the officers' quarters had the best beams, even though the rafters were shot. They had salvaged the best of the tin and roofed those two buildings. All of the furniture that had any possibility of being used in the future they'd moved into those two structures. The group had laboriously cleaned out the enlisted men's quarters, preparing that dwelling for new beams, rafters, and tin. They'd made two huge piles of rubbish, one to be burned and the other to be buried. But, even after they moved, they didn't want a fire to alert others to the existence of the camp. The burn pile would have to wait.

"I'm here," Alberto's voice called out as he neared the hut.

"Come in," Fidel replied with a look of wonder on his face. Alberto rarely made the painful walk to their place.

Alberto entered and smiled broadly as he handed Fidel a plate piled high with freshly baked yeast buns. Somehow, Alberto had balanced the plate as he hobbled with a crutch under one arm.

As they gathered around him, the household was abuzz with delight and wonder. Alberto's first two attempts at bread making had failed miserably. He'd been sure that Chandi's verbal instructions from the misionera in Avanzada had been wrong. In fact, he'd had rather harsh words with his son after both attempts. If he'd been able to figure out another use for that huge bag of flour, he would have given up altogether. Now he was very glad that he'd given it one more try. As Fidel and his household savored Alberto's wares, the baker soaked in the compliments and didn't miss the pleasure reflected on each face. For the first time since the accident, he felt productive—like he might have something to offer after all. He would take his fifty-five-gallon barrel oven with him to the camp when they moved. Already, he'd made up his mind that he didn't want to learn to use the cookstove that was there. It had been hard enough to learn how much wood to keep in the barrel in order to bake the bread and yet not to burn it. He'd also learned that uniform size of the buns mattered, so he needed to work some more on that.

The Outcasts

Midmorning on the following day, the sound of a small plane flying low overhead sent all of Alberto's and Fidel's families running outside. They looked up into the sky and saw the misioneros' airplane circle around—returning to buzz their houses. Listening carefully, they realized it had headed toward the camp and it was landing there.

Upriver, in Namuro, the sound of the airplane did not go unnoticed either. Rico leaned forward in his hammock. As chief of Namuro, the previous day he had welcomed Diego, chief of Luwana, into his home—though he had arrived unexpectedly and unannounced. Rico sat back again and contemplated whether the misioneros' airplane could be nearby, and whether it could have anything to do with Fidel.

Meanwhile downriver, Fidel, Chandi, and Antonio grabbed the gun and machetes and rushed up the trail toward the camp, hoping to find the misioneros waiting for them.

When they arrived at the airstrip, the plane had been unloaded, and Bob and the pilot were touring the camp. Shiny new sheets of tin lay on the ground near the building that would be Alberto's family's house. Nearby sat a neatly stacked pile of two-by-fours, a keg of nails, a box of metal gusset plates, a roll of chicken wire, a roll of screen, and a fifty-five-gallon barrel.

Bob and Fidel smiled broadly at one another.

"My friend," Bob began as soon as Fidel was near, "your gold was worth $1,855.00! This tin and wood should repair the largest structure. You have more money, but the plane could only carry this load for today."

"Good. This is good," Fidel said, still smiling.

"I see you've been working hard," Bob went on. "Rainy season will be in full force soon. I know you want the roofs on two of these buildings as soon as possible." Bob pointed toward the mess hall. "So, is that the other structure that you want to fix?"

"Yes," Fidel affirmed. "Alberto's family will live in the larger one, and we'll take that one."

"I'll measure yours today, then, and bring in what you need in three days. Fidel, I have a group of men who'll come in and help you build. Three days from now, we can fly in the materials for your house, and then the next morning fly back with José, Pablo, and two more men, along with Juan the pilot, and me. We can spend two nights, so we'll have three days to work," Bob offered.

"Do I have enough money to do all of this?" Fidel questioned.

"Yes. Today's materials cost $246.50, and the flight is $162.50, so you've spent $409.00 so far. Your supplies and next flight should cost about the same, because we might as well fill it up with materials that you'll need, even if you'll use them on other buildings. We'll pay for our own flight in to help you build." Bob was excited about the project. "And," he said with another huge smile, "we have permission to move here and live in your village!"

Fidel smiled broadly. "Good. That's good!" He stared at the buildings—and then asked, "Which house do you want?"

The Outcasts

Bob turned toward the block structures. The largest building was the next-to-the-last house on the west side. If he remembered correctly, it had six small rooms. Bob knew the Nala didn't care for separate rooms, so he felt free to ask for that house, which would be best for his family. "Let's go look at that one," the missionary said, pointing with his chin in the direction of the building, as he'd learned from the Nala.

The two men entered the twenty-four by twenty-four-foot officers' quarters. Walking down the hallway, they looked into each ten-by-seven-foot room. Bob would have to play around with this floor plan and take out walls to make the space more usable. He thought about building a second floor for bedrooms and knew that would work.

"Can we have this one?" Bob asked as he looked at his friend.

"Yes," Fidel answered simply.

"The inside walls are wood, so we'll have to take some of those down. Now that I think about it, if you want this bigger building, we could take all the walls out for you," Bob offered.

"No, we'll take the other one," Fidel said.

"If you're sure, then we'd like this one." Bob paused for a moment and then continued. "Fidel, I brought some of your money with me in case you need it. The rest I have in a safe place for you. If you have a list of supplies that you want me to put on your next flight, I can do that."

Fidel made a mental list of their provisions. *We aren't really low on supplies yet...but...we have the money, and the plane can bring them in. That's a good idea,* he decided. "We want more flour, yeast, oil, and sugar for the bread that Alberto has been making...and rice, coffee, kerosene, matches, bath soap, fishhooks, batteries, .00 buck and birdshot, and several dozen baby chicks," Fidel rattled off.

"Uh, wait," Bob stammered. He grabbed a piece of paper and the stub of a pencil from his shirt pocket. "Could you repeat that?"

After Bob had written down those items, Fidel added a few more. "Four wraparound skirts. Also we need fabric, thread, and needles for the women to make blouses." Fidel's thoughts turned to his wonderful wife. *Victoria got wraparound skirts for Maamo and Rosa, even though her own skirts are worn and stained. She hasn't made a blouse since we've been married. In fact, all of the women's blouses are worn out, and I haven't seen any of them sewing. I'll give Victoria two skirts and one each for Moya and Dalia.*

Bob was out of his element. "So, uh, what colors, or how much? For Victoria and Rosa?" He wasn't at all sure about fabric, or skirts, for that matter.

"Linda will know what they'd like and how much to get. Victoria, Rosa, Maamo, Moya, and Dalia all need new blouses." Fidel felt good inside—it was wonderful to have the means to provide for his family and friends. "The children could all use underwear, too, but I don't know what sizes. If Linda knows, have her buy underwear, too." All of a sudden, Fidel realized the list could go on and on. They all needed underwear. They could use rubber boots, and the boys needed trousers and shirts as badly as he and Alberto did. He thought for several moments before he asked, "How much do clothes cost? Chandi and Antonio need trousers and shirts. Alberto and I do, too. But I don't know how much it costs. We need to fix the houses and eat—more than we need clothes."

They were interrupted when the pilot called to Bob in English. Bob and Fidel walked to him. Fidel watched while Bob explained that the pilot was siphoning extra gasoline into the drum. Bob would have a cache of fuel for his boat motor—and, if the pilot ever needed extra, he would have some here.

While Fidel watched the process, he had no idea that a canoe was rounding the last bend before Alberto's landing.

Chapter 23

Rico ordered the young men to pull in at the small, rundown landing where, on more than one occasion, his scouts had seen signs of Fidel. Diego and Rico stepped out of the canoe, followed by two more men. Two teenagers, long poles in hand, stayed in the boat waiting for a quick getaway.

The two chiefs led the charge as the men stormed into Alberto's hut. Moya's scream sent the household into chaos.

Alberto stood from his hammock and spoke as if to the intruders, knowing they wouldn't understand his cryptic Spanish. "Go alert the others to run."

Diego thundered in Nala, "Where's my daughter Victoria?"

Diego and Rico stepped farther inside the dark dwelling to look around. Nelson, who'd understood his father, darted out the door with Paco and Pepe at his heels, but the men outside grabbed two of the boys. Paco escaped their clutches and ran up the trail toward his house. The men watched him disappear on the path that led into the trees.

Paco ran into his house, startling the women with his gasping words. "Victoria...your father...is here."

Victoria paled. Rosa's eyes sought first the twins lying in a hammock, and then Victoria's terror-filled face. Maamo looked around the hut and realized they didn't even have a machete to defend themselves. Fire flamed in her eyes, and she took action through her words. "Paco, take Susana and run toward the camp. We'll find you when it's safe. Go!"

The scared little boy obeyed Maamo. Susana screamed as he grabbed her and rushed out the door.

"Victoria, take Isabel and run into the jungle in the opposite direction. They need both babies," the wise old woman ordered.

Victoria hesitated—she was paralyzed with fear and anger.

"Hurry!" Maamo demanded.

Victoria grabbed Isabel and ran. Men's voices and the thudding of running feet reached her ears as she put the baby to her breast to keep her quiet. Victoria stepped noiselessly into the thick green underbrush. Every muscle in her body tensed, ready for action. Her heart pounded wildly in her ears. She willed her mind to think clearly.

Diego stormed the house as Rico and two men stood guard at the entrance. "Where's Victoria?" he shouted.

"She isn't here!" Maamo spoke harshly to her son.

Dalia cowered in a dark corner, cradling her own baby in her arms. Diego reached for the girl, thinking she was Victoria. Dalia screamed and scratched his face viciously.

Diego recoiled in horror as he recognized Dalia—even though the years and her harsh existence had changed her tremendously since their last encounter.

"Give me the child!" he ordered.

"She's mine!" Dalia screamed.

"Where's the other one?" Diego demanded, as he snatched the baby from Dalia's arms.

"Noooo! She's mine, give her back to me. I hate you! You ruined my life once and you *will not* ruin it again!" Dalia screamed as she attacked Diego. "Ramiro raped me when I was thirteen years old—and then *you* raped me too! You ruined my life! I've been used by nearly every man I've known since then—until I came here. I hate you and I've tried to hate your mother and daughter because of you. But now I can see that they aren't like you. But you and Ramiro—I'll always hate you two. Someday I'll get even!"

Dalia lunged at Diego. But she was afraid of hurting the baby by pulling her from Diego's strong arms.

Maamo was astonished by Dalia's allegations. She handed her walking stick to Rosa, who struck Diego from behind. Dalia grabbed her baby and then held her ground in front of the chief, who had fallen to his knees from the unexpected blow.

Diego stood up, probing the back of his bleeding head with one hand and running the other along the deep scratches on his cheek. The hate in Dalia's eyes mirrored his own. She had exposed him! His secret was out, and there was no turning back.

The Outcasts

Dalia handed her screaming baby to Maamo and grabbed the walking stick from Rosa's hand.

With narrowing eyes, Dalia swung the walking stick at Diego, but he grabbed the end before it reached its mark. He shoved her out of the way, throwing the cane at her as she hit the ground. Diego didn't see his small granddaughter peeking out from behind Maamo's skirt with horror in her innocent brown eyes. Diego exited the dwelling.

Once outside, Rico and his followers stared at Diego in disgust. All respect for him was gone now that his dark secret had been revealed. Rico took over the lead. "We have to find those twins," he hissed. "I'll deal with you later, Diego!"

Thunder crashed loudly as a bolt of lightning struck a nearby tree. A huge branch fell and smoldered at their feet. At that same instant, dogs began to bark. The intruders turned to face a huge black man rushing toward them with two animals, ready to unleash their fury.

Wide-eyed, the now-fearful group rapidly retreated down the trail toward the waiting canoe.

Chapter 24

Andrés watched the retreating men for only a moment before rushing into the hut. He stood dumbfounded as Rosa helped Dalia from the floor to a hammock. He desperately wished that he could communicate with these women, as he tried to understand what had just happened.

Rosa asked Dalia, "Are you hurt?"

"I'm okay," Dalia said.

"You did good," Maamo praised from her hammock. She laid Dalia's baby next to her and helped little Rosalinda climb up into her lap. She held the trembling child close.

"I have to find Pepe!" Dalia cried out, realizing for the first time that her son could be in danger.

The room grew deathly still, however, as the women became aware of the huge man with dark skin who had entered so quietly.

"I'm Andrés," the man tried to explain. He knew that he'd scared them. "I want to help you." But they couldn't understand Spanish.

"Andrés," Rosa repeated. In her own language, to the others she said, "He must be the man who saved Alberto. Fidel told us about him. Dalia, leave the baby here with Maamo, and we'll go find Pepe. Then we have to find Paco and Victoria. Dalia, you have to name that child—we can't keep calling her 'the baby.'"

Andrés followed the women as they walked cautiously down the trail toward Alberto's house. When they arrived, they could see that the men and the canoe were gone.

"Alberto? Moya? Where are you?" Rosa called out.

"We're inside," Moya answered.

Entering the hut, Rosa and Dalia found Alberto and Moya with hands and feet bound with vine. Little Gina's wide eyes mirrored her terror as she sat close to her mother, with her baby sister on her lap. Pepe and Nelson were tied to posts.

Andrés took out his hunting knife and cut loose the little boy whom Dalia had run to. Tears streamed down Pepe's face as he hugged his mother. Next Andrés freed Nelson, Moya, and Alberto. When Andrés had first arrived and found the family tied, he'd wanted to free them, but Alberto had implored him to go and help Victoria and the babies first. Andrés couldn't imagine why those Nala men had terrorized these families. He was anxious to get back to his reclusive house and uncomplicated life.

The entire group returned to Fidel's house. Andrés listened as Alberto explained to him about the twins and the Nala's pursuit to kill them. He also told the man Dalia's story. Andrés' emotions

The Outcasts

battled within him. He didn't want to feel the pain that others were going through—he just wanted to go back home.

Rosa and Dalia called out to Victoria and Paco, letting them know that they could return. Victoria stepped into the clearing, but Paco could not be found.

Victoria looked up at the threatening sky. Not only was evening fast approaching, but storm clouds darkened the sky with each passing moment.

Fidel and the boys hiked swiftly from the camp, trying to beat the weather home. Halfway down the trail, Antonio stopped in his tracks.

"What is it?" Fidel asked.

The three fell silent.

Whatever sound Antonio thought he'd heard was no longer audible, so the three set out again. They moved a little more swiftly, not understanding the apprehension they each felt.

Ten minutes later, they stopped again. The faint sound of barking dogs reached their ears, so they picked up their pace. Soon, they met the dogs and Andrés on the trail. Andrés filled Chandi in, and he quickly translated for Fidel. They all began calling out to Paco, as they searched fervently for the young boy and Susana.

The dogs barked loudly and then bolted into the dense jungle. Antonio swiftly followed through the tangle of underbrush.

Howling, the dogs stood still before the small boy who was sitting on the ground with a sleeping baby in his lap.

Later that evening, both families and Andrés sat quietly processing the day's events that had been shared around Victoria's fire. They were all hungry, exhausted, and terrified of the future. Rain fell relentlessly, and thunder clapped loudly in the sky.

"I think we should move to the camp tomorrow," Fidel stated.

All eyes looked at their leader. They nodded, grateful that he had a plan.

Victoria's dark thoughts about her father were crushing her. But she was exhausted, and simply couldn't sort through everything.

Until they could take him back home in the canoe that he'd returned to them, Andrés was stranded with the group. Even though he was more than willing to help them move, Andrés was uneasy around all of these people.

Paco sat happily by the fire, petting Rey with one hand and Reina (Queen) with the other. The stray female dog had joined Andrés and Rey several weeks ago.

They'd brought the hammocks up from Alberto's. It was understood that his family wouldn't return to their house.

Tomorrow, the camp would become their home.

Chapter 25

The next day, using their father's canoe, Chandi and Antonio transported Alberto, his oven, bread-making supplies, and the heavy cooking pots, as well as plantains and bananas, to the camp. In the smaller vessel it was much easier to traverse the shallow creek.

They returned for Maamo, Rosa, the twins, Gina, and Rosalinda. Dishes, gourds, and other supplies were added to that canoe load. So Antonio could lead the others on foot, Fidel took the boy's place in the canoe with Chandi. The rest of their worldly possessions were carried in baskets on the women's backs.

On the second day, Chandi and Antonio returned by trail to retrieve the larger canoe, boat motor, gasoline, oil, and kerosene from the shed. At the last minute, the two resourceful boys thought about the cooking logs and kindling, which had been left in both of the houses. They hauled it all to the canoe and set out on the laborious trip in the heavily laden boat.

The following day, when the mission plane landed on the airstrip at the camp, John the pilot was surprised to see a very tall black man, Alberto's family, as well as Fidel's entire household. The pilot told Alberto that he would return the next day—weather permitting. Alberto already knew about the group of men who were going to come in with Bob to help them put roofs on two of the buildings.

As soon as the plane was unloaded, the pilot was ready to get back into the Cessna and take off for the second leg of his flight. But Fidel wanted to talk to him, so he asked Chandi to translate. The three stood near the plane as Chandi interpreted for the pilot: Fidel wanted Roberto to buy two shotguns to bring in the next day when they came. John's eyebrows rose slightly, but he assured Chandi that he would relay the message to Roberto.

Once in the sky, John radioed his wife with his takeoff information, and gave her the message about the shotguns so she could let Bob know. He wouldn't have much time to shop before tomorrow morning's flight. As busy as the man was getting the work crew together, John knew this message wouldn't be one that Bob would want to get. But there had been something in Fidel's demeanor that made John unable to ignore the seriousness of his request.

Fidel and the boys hauled the supplies into the kitchen portion of the mess hall, which ran the entire length of the back of the building. They set the boxes on the concrete counter which spanned the back wall of the room. Two deep sinks were plumbed into the center portion of the countertop, complete with a water pump handle which was bolted into the concrete. A wood cookstove sat against the wall to the right of the countertop. At the opposite end of the kitchen and next to the back door sat an old propane refrigerator. The inside wall was lined with wooden shelves, some of which still held canned goods, and a doorway which led into what used to be the dining hall.

This was the structure that was divided by a wooden wall which had separated the officers' and enlisted men's eating areas.

Fidel, Andrés, Chandi, and Antonio had moved most of the tables, benches, and chairs which had previously been stored there into another building so they could hang the hammocks in both sections.

Without the warmth of a fire and the glow from its flames, however, this strange block house felt cold and desolate.

Chapter 26

The mission plane landed early the following morning, before the storm clouds could roll in. Each missionary had been praying for good weather, and for each person involved in the work project.

Tools, jugs of water, and coolers filled with food were unloaded from the plane and into waiting hands. Fidel watched. Finally the shotguns came into view. Fidel relaxed for the first time in days, as Bob handed him the shotguns that would not only provide their camp with more food, but more importantly would protect his family. Fidel smiled and nodded as he stroked the shiny new wooden stocks of the single-shot weapons.

Without wasting any more time, Bob showed the crew the structure that they needed to work on, and the men efficiently began the building project. Four hours later, however, a torrential downpour sent them running for cover. Bob searched the coolers for the lunch that Linda had prepared for them. To each of the workers he handed out sandwiches which Linda had wrapped in waxed paper. He filled brightly-colored metal cups with ice water

The Outcasts

from the Igloo and handed one to each man. As they bowed their heads, Bob led them in prayer.

Nearby, Paco, Nelson, and Pepe sat on the floor watching the men. Soon Gina and Rosalinda shyly joined the group. The men felt uncomfortable, wondering whether the children were hungry, too.

Bob knew that Linda hadn't prepared enough food for over a dozen extra people, but when he looked around, he realized they didn't have any cooking fires yet. Tin lay above him, flat on the beams—there would be no way for the smoke to escape the building. He went back to the cooler for more sandwiches and handed a half to each child. He didn't know whether they would like Western food, but the ravenous kids relished the sandwiches. So Bob got them some more.

Well into the evening, rain thundered on the tin. Chandi and Antonio strung six more hammocks into the already crowded rooms. They lit some of the old kerosene lanterns that Dalia had cleaned, and placed them on tables. One group lounged around the warm glow in Alberto and Moya's half, while three of the missionary men talked in Spanish to Alberto and Andrés about God and the Bible. Chandi and Antonio listened intently, and periodically Chandi asked questions. Moya sat quietly, watching the beams of lantern light dance through the dusty air. She couldn't understand the discussion, but she was glad to hear her husband conversing. He'd been so quiet for such a long time.

"I was told that I had to obey all the commandments and rules," Alberto said, "but the people who pounded that into me didn't obey the Ten Commandments themselves. I'm better than they were, but I don't see how any person can be good all of the time."

Paul replied, "In His Book, Dios tells us that everyone is a sinner. And the law of Dios demands that we be perfect, all the time."

"Nobody's perfect!" Chandi protested.

"You're absolutely right. Yet people do all kinds of things to try to make themselves acceptable to Dios. A person might think they're good if they loan their canoe, or give money to a person who's in need, or if they don't drink liquor or smoke cigarettes—but, even though all of those things seem good, Dios says that all our attempts to pay for our sins are absolutely useless."

"Only Dios can make a way for us to be saved, and He has done that by sending His Son, Jesús," Joe said.

"Who is Jesús?" Chandi asked.

"Jesús is Dios. He's perfect, sinless in every way," Joe said.

"In His Word He tells us that He calmed storms just by speaking. He healed people and helped people, showing them that He is truly Dios Almighty," Paul added.

"That's amazing," Chandi said intently.

"*He* is amazing! Dios knew from the beginning of time that all people would sin and would need someone to save them from the penalty for their sins. That's why He let Jesús die on the cross," Paul said.

Paul looked at his listeners and realized that they were trying hard to process what he had said to them. He wanted to share

The Outcasts

so much more—but realized that this was a very good first step toward knowing the qualities and character of the One True God.

Joe spoke up. "In the Bible, Jesús tells us, 'For Dios so loved the world that He gave His one and only Son, that whoever believes in Him shall not perish but have eternal life.'

"Jesús died on the cross for our sins, He was buried, and He rose again, because death could not hold Him in the grave," Joe said.

"Dios accepted Jesús' death on the cross as payment for our sins. Nothing else will do—the only thing we can bring to Dios for our salvation is to admit we are sinners, and to put our faith in what Jesús did for us," Paul said, praying that his listeners had understood.

"I've known too many bad people who claim to be religious," Alberto stated.

"That's my point," Joe contended. "It takes more than religion. You need a personal relationship with Jesús."

"How can that happen?" Chandi piped up.

"The Bible says, 'Believe in the Lord Jesús, and you will be saved—you and your whole household.'" Joe quoted Scripture. "When you believe and accept Jesús as your Savior, His Spirit changes your heart and enters your life. You then have a personal relationship with Dios, not just head knowledge about religion."

Andrés listened to the men silently. *If Dios could have calmed the storm that took my wife and daughter from me, why didn't He?* the tormented man thought.

The Outcasts

Alberto spoke up once more. "I was raised in an orphanage. They claimed religion and forced us to pray daily and to ask forgiveness for our sins. But the things they did to us.... I swore I'd never have anything to do with religion again."

"Dios will deal with them someday. He'll deal with each one of us separately. You can't change them, but you shouldn't allow their sin to keep you from seeking Dios and spending eternity in heaven with Him. You alone have to make that decision," Joe said.

On the other side of the wall, Bob finished sharing the same concepts in the Nala language. He was thankful for the many hours he'd studied to prepare for translating the Scriptures into Nala. He taught them the new Nala terms for God.

"How many good spirits are there?" Fidel asked.

"There is one true 'Perfect One'. He is three persons in one—the 'Perfect Father', the 'Perfect Son', and the 'Perfect Spirit'. They are the Perfect One. He is totally different from the spirit world that you believe in. The only Good Spirit is the Perfect One of the Bible," Bob said to his listeners, using the new Nala words.

"Linda and I have been praying for all of you since before we left the village. Linda felt perhaps you would have twins, Victoria, and she feared for them. The Perfect One protected your babies from death. He loves every one of you and wants you to know Him personally—to believe that the Perfect Son died on a cross for your sins. Believe in Him and you will be saved—you'll become a child of the Perfect One," Bob pleaded.

"Will the Perfect One allow nothing bad ever to happen to me again if I believe in Him?" Dalia's barely audible voice asked from the hammock farthest away.

"I wish I could say that's true, but it isn't," Bob said with a sigh. "The Perfect One's Word tells us that in this life we'll have trouble, but that He will see us through with His power and strength. Even though we'll still go through problems, we'll have hope and peace that will make the problems much easier to bear."

They all fell silent. Bob tried to fully recall a favorite quote — something he'd heard once at a conference. After a few moments, he continued. "For people who haven't accepted the Perfect Son as their Savior, the things that happen in this life are the best they will ever know, with the worst yet to come — an eternity in hell. For those of us who are saved — those of us who've put our faith in the death, burial, and resurrection of the Perfect Son — whatever happens to us on this earth is the worst we'll ever experience, with the best yet to come — an eternity in heaven with the Perfect One!"

Dalia began to sob. "I want that. I want the Perfect Son."

Victoria said, "I've believed there was a Good Spirit since Linda talked to me, and I believe He's helped me, but I didn't understand as much as I do now. I want to know the Perfect One. I believe what you say is true."

Maamo said, "I've called out many times, asking if there was a Good Spirit. I've known that there had to be more to life. I've wanted more for my descendants. Now I know that the Perfect One has sent you to tell us about Him. I believe."

Bob was overwhelmed. He asked each woman again whether they understood that they were sinners, and that the Perfect Son paid the full price for their sin by dying on the cross. He stressed again that the Perfect Son not only died, but He rose from the dead, and that He lives in heaven with the Perfect Father. Tears streamed down his face as he led in prayer for each woman to confess her sin and accept the Perfect Son's death on the cross as payment for that sin—to accept the free gift of eternal life.

Fidel and Rosa remained silent. It wasn't that they didn't want to believe, but they had so many questions. Fidel was sad, though—he felt that he was being left behind when his wife prayed.

In his hammock, Bob swung slowly back and forth, deep in thought. *We know so little about how the Nala think. I know that we've only touched the surface of their view of the spirit world. A lot more teaching is needed for them to understand who You are, even though they now have some spiritual terms in their language, and Nala words for God, Jesus, Holy Spirit, and sin. I know that it's only a start, Lord, but please bless Maamo, Victoria, and Dalia—the first three Nala believers. Lord, help us to teach them clearly in their own language. I pray, Lord, that soon I'll be able to begin translating your Word into the Nala language. Thank You, Lord, thank You for these new believers.*

Each person fell asleep to the cadence of rain on the tin roof. Bob praised God for the three new believers, the first Nala to come to know Christ! He couldn't wait to tell Linda how God had answered their prayers.

Andrés was the last one to close his eyes and allow sleep to claim him. He played the conversation over in his mind many times. But, he reasoned, if Dios were good, how could He allow all the heartache and pain that was in this world? Andrés' mind went to his wife and daughter...to the last time he'd seen them, clinging for their lives to the broken-down raft. He couldn't get to them through the raging flood waters. He couldn't save them!

Andrés' body jerked and he awoke in a cold sweat. He was used to it; nearly every night for the past three years, he'd relived the horror of that day.

Chapter 27

The dreary morning turned into another rainy day. Not to be daunted, however, the work team made the best of their time. Two men explored the needs of the long-abandoned kitchen. They primed the old pump and, much to Victoria's amazement and delight, clear water eventually flowed freely into the kitchen sink.

Instead of building, the missionaries washed dishes and silverware, scoured pots and pans, and scrubbed and bleached the countertop. Their wives had gone the extra mile thinking of every useful supply to send with their husbands.

Andrés watched as José dismantled, cleaned, and reattached the stovepipe and built a fire in the wood-burning stove.

After washing his hands, José set out ingredients on the countertop. He worked efficiently as Victoria and Dalia watched his every move. They were mesmerized as he measured, poured, and stirred a strange-looking concoction. In amazement, they watched him pour the thick liquid into a skillet. And after it bubbled around the edges, they stared as he flipped the now-solid substance. They never tired of studying how each pancake was poured, turned over,

The Outcasts

and finally placed on a plate and slathered with butter. And then, to the delight of everybody's taste buds, a sweet liquid was drizzled over the top. For the first time in many days, everyone had a full stomach and felt satisfied. Dalia secretly hoped that someday she would have the opportunity to try to make that delicious food.

After lunch the rains let up, so the men went back to Alberto's house to work on the rafters. Fidel, Andrés, and Chandi worked with the men, learning how to use the necessary tools so they could build the next roof by themselves.

Antonio had been asked to go hunting. Even though he enjoyed the roofing project, he was thankful to be away from the crowd and back into the quiet jungle.

The crew worked until the last sliver of light faded in the western sky. Unless the weather looked bad, the pilot planned to leave the next morning at about ten-thirty. The missionaries desperately wanted to complete Alberto and Moya's house before they left.

The following morning, the weather held long enough for the men to nail the last piece of tin into place. Broad smiles and slaps on the back were thanks enough for the hard work.

Gathering their few belongings, the missionaries left the tools and even their extra work clothes for the men. Andrés could easily wear Joe's clothes. Other used clothing had been sent in for the boys and children, but Fidel hadn't opened the bags and boxes yet. Everyone waved at the Cessna as it roared down the runway and lifted into the darkening sky.

The Outcasts

Fidel, Andrés, and Chandi unstrung Alberto's family's hammocks and moved them to their new house. Dark storm clouds rolled in, threatening another downpour. With the previous storm, they'd been fortunate to have only a few leaks. But each of them knew that if the winds were too fierce, the old tin could blow off easily. So when Alberto offered for everyone to move to his secure house, Fidel agreed. Quickly, everyone carried their hammocks and meager possessions to the new location.

Andrés and Fidel placed fire logs in the center of the house, where the smoke would rise to the peak and escape through the open gables. For the first time since the move, Moya lit her fire and relaxed.

For the two large windows, the missionaries had fashioned shutters out of tin. To allow light and fresh air inside, sticks held the shutters out away from the house. As the rain began to pound on the tin roof, Chandi ran to each opening and lowered the tin, hooking the shutters into place with latches. Lightning flashed across the sky, and booming thunder echoed loudly. As torrents of rain pounded on the new structure, the winds kicked up and the air cooled down.

Victoria helped Moya put a large cauldron of leftover soup over the fire. The day before, Antonio had brought home a wild pig. They'd already cooked the stew on the cookstove, but their mouths watered as they thought about the smoky flavor that would be added by reheating it over the real fire pit.

The Outcasts

The deluge continued throughout the day and night and into the following day. By late afternoon, the rain let up enough for Andrés and Antonio, with the dogs at their heels, to walk to the Grande River for a look. The sight left them dumbfounded. They stared across the expanse toward the peninsula that Andrés called home. It was under water! Trees were visible, but muddy water ran swiftly over the land. Logs and debris rushed past the flooded banks. No one said a word as they stared at the brown torrent. Andrés felt a shiver run through his body as he remembered the flood that had taken his family. He turned from the scene and walked silently back to the house. He wondered again about Dios, who opened up the floodgates of heaven at will. Andrés had once again been spared, but why...why hadn't Dios protected his wife and little girl?

Another type of storm was brewing in Luwana.

Diego had left Namuro in disgrace. Rico had denounced him publicly for his impropriety with Dalia, and for hiding the truth all of these years.

When Diego arrived home, he'd had no choice but to call a meeting and confess his past. But nothing had prepared him for the consequences.

The people of Luwana voted in a new chief and banished Diego. He and his family were to be exiled to Ulgana.

The Outcasts

Diego's wife, Flora, would not speak to him. Despondently, she sat in her hammock deep in thought. *Adolfo is seventeen—old enough to go his own way. But...what way can he go now? He, too, has been banished—for his father's sins! And Lucinda—*a low moan escaped Flora's throat. *Lucinda had hoped that any day now her young man would be carried to her hammock. Just like my Victoria, Lucinda's heart will be broken, too. Diego! How could you do this to us?* She wasn't sure what she should do. Normally, Flora wouldn't have even considered another option—after all, no woman ever left her husband willingly. If she did, she would be on her own, and no man would ever marry her. *The younger ones I'm not as worried about, but I'm a woman—alone, I can't provide for them.* Yet Victoria kept coming to her mind. *Victoria—my Victoria saved her babies! My grandchildren! Are they girls or boys? She saved them, and now her family is in exile. But they are in exile for doing* good*—not* evil! *Diego has not followed the Nala way either! Oh, Victoria, I failed you, yet you've remained strong. I want to be strong, too. Could there be another way—could there be more than one path? But, how can I find Victoria? She's downriver from Namuro in a house near Alberto and Moya's...that's all I know. Could I ever find her? I've never been outside of Luwana...I have six children to feed and care for....* Victoria's mother withdrew further into her shell of silence. As they packed their belongings into the large baskets that Flora and her daughters would carry to Ulgana, Flora would not even look at her husband.

The Outcasts

Diego had no idea that his wife even had another option to consider. He only wanted to get away as quickly as he could—away from the humiliating stares of the people who had once respected him as their leader. Diego felt that he could deal with his wife's anger later.

Diego sat in his hammock. His mind went back to his childhood in Ulgana—memories that he'd tried hard to forget. From his earliest recollection, his family consisted of his mother, Maamo, and his two older brothers. His father, grandparents, and aunt had all died of a sickness that had ravaged their village and claimed many lives. He cringed at the thought of the gnawing hunger pangs that had kept him awake at night. Diego also remembered the hard work in the gardens—women's work! He had been so humiliated—trudging in from the gardens with his brothers and mother, carrying loads on his back like a girl. And now he was returning to that horrible village, returning in disgrace. He'd provided so well for his family. He'd worked so hard to become respected. And now—now he was going back to where he started.

Torrential rains exploded in the late afternoon skies. The trails would be muddy in the morning, making their journey even more miserable. Diego looked at his wife but quickly turned away. Flora's face was even darker and more ominous than the fierce storm outside.

The Outcasts

The last rays of light were quickly retreating in the western skies as Andrés sat despondently in a borrowed hammock. His heart thundered and his mind allowed him no rest. Finally, he exited the house and swiftly walked with his dogs toward the river once again. Rey and Reina charged ahead, barking loudly as they disappeared into the trees near the water's edge.

Hearing the dogs, Chandi and Antonio ran to meet Andrés. The river had overflowed its banks and flooded fifteen feet of tree-studded land. Still barking loudly, the animals stopped near a tree twenty feet away. The threesome turned to look.

An overturned canoe lay on top of an unconscious man. Andrés and the boys sprinted swiftly to the craft. Another hand became visible, sticking out from underneath the boat—possibly the hand of a woman. They felt beneath the canoe before tipping it away from the bodies. In the semidarkness, they couldn't fully make out the features of the Nala family—how many were there? Were they dead or alive?

Chandi whistled loudly—signaling the camp of a need. Flashlights in hand, Fidel, Victoria, and Dalia rushed from the house. Fidel whistled and Chandi signaled once more, indicating to them which direction to go.

Andrés hefted the unconscious man over his shoulder and carried him to Alberto's house. But when he returned for the woman the group was no longer standing over her. Andrés heard voices and saw lights about twenty feet away. He arrived to see them hovering over two tiny forms, whose faces were barely

The Outcasts

above the surface of the murky water. Victoria picked up one small child, and Dalia lifted the other from the mud that had cushioned their landing. The children's cries pierced the night air—whether from pain or fear, nobody knew. Andrés rushed back to the woman and carried her in his arms as he led Victoria and Dalia back to the house.

"Are there more children?" Chandi questioned.

"I don't know," Fidel stated flatly.

"The dogs will find them if there are," Antonio declared.

Rey and Reina sniffed around tangled heaps of logs and branches. They ran upriver and then circled back downriver. Cold chills ran up and down Fidel's spine. He shined his flashlight around the quagmire and waited for the dogs to return to their sides. *They're Nala,* Fidel thought, *but I don't recognize them. Now the location of our camp will no longer be a secret. Has trouble found us again?*

The dogs howled loudly, and the three followed the sound. The dim rays of their lights were insufficient to guide their way safely in the deepening water. The dogs appeared to be standing on a fallen tree.

"Antonio, I need your boots. You and Chandi look for a long branch to use to pull me back if the water becomes too deep and swift."

Wordlessly, the boys obeyed. When they came back with the pole, Fidel grabbed one end and waded farther into the current. Across the log lay the misshapen form of a young boy. Fidel's eyes filled with tears as he hoisted the child over his shoulder. Using the pole, Chandi and Antonio pulled them back to safety. The dogs followed—content, it seemed, to return to the house.

Inside Alberto's home, all of the camp's inhabitants watched over the Nala family. Each victim had been undressed, laid in a hammock, and tenderly covered with a warm blanket. Each one, that is, except the body of the boy whose lifeless form now lay in a hammock in Fidel's house.

Eerie shadows from the cook fire danced across the tin ceiling, adding to the haunted looks of the adults and the confused expressions of the children. The only sounds that pervaded the room were the soft crackles of the flames. Unanswered questions hung heavily in the air as the night watch began.

Chapter 28

Several hours later, all the children slept peacefully in hammocks. Victoria added wood to the fire.

In a barely audible voice Dalia said, "They're from Ulgana."

Ears perked up and all eyes looked toward the young woman who so seldom spoke. They waited quietly for her to go on.

"Carlos and Edilma are their names. The two little ones are Ana Maria and Alicia. I think they have two boys—there could be another older boy still out there..." Dalia's heart beat wildly, old feelings returned—feelings that she'd hoped were behind her forever. *When they wake up they'll recognize me. Our camp is no longer a secret...and the twins! What will happen to us now?*

Alberto groaned, remembering *his* ordeal. Unconsciously, he rubbed his leg. In the dark back corner of the room, Andrés lowered his head into his hands as he sat in a hammock. Fidel's heart sank, wondering whether he should have stayed outside hunting for other children. He looked at the dogs sleeping peacefully near the fire. *Surely the dogs wouldn't have stopped searching if the other boy had been close by. But…his mind nagged at him…but, what if they were my children?*

Wordlessly, Fidel rose from the hammock and walked to a table near the door where they kept supplies. He put the remaining fresh batteries into his flashlight. Andrés and the boys joined him and waited for their leader to speak.

"We have to go back out and look for the boy," he stated.

All three heads nodded in the affirmative.

"It's getting more dangerous out there in the dark, with snakes and debris. Andrés, you have boots. Antonio, if I can use yours, I think you and Chandi should stay here." He could see the disappointment in the boys' eyes, but they lowered their heads in compliance.

Fidel loaded the older shotgun and handed it, extra shells, and a flashlight to Andrés. Donning Antonio's boots, Fidel grabbed his own flashlight and a machete.

A low whistle from Andrés brought the two dogs to the men's sides, and together they exited the house into the darkness of the night.

Chandi leaned against the table and looked at his brother. "The older boy would have been in the front of the canoe." In silence, each boy tried to imagine the flood, river currents, and possible scenarios of the accident.

"He could have jumped out at the last minute and floated downstream until he could catch a branch and climb up into a tree," Antonio offered. "It wasn't totally dark when we found the canoe."

"Wouldn't he have called out for help?" Chandi asked.

"I don't know how far downriver he'd have gone before catching hold of something," Antonio said.

"Yes," Chandi affirmed. "He could've grabbed onto a log in the river and floated way downstream. He could still be floating...."

"Maybe tomorrow the river will be calm enough to take the boat and motor and look for him. I don't think the dogs would've come in if he'd been nearby," Antonio said hopefully. But they both knew that the flooded river would take days to recede.

A commotion caught their attention and they hurried back to the fire. Edilma was waking up. The fearful woman tried to sit up as she gestured wildly. She groaned, held her head, and lay back down with wide eyes staring at the blur of people surrounding her.

"Your canoe overturned, and we found you," Victoria said gently.

"Where are my children?" Edilma asked.

"The girls are over there..." Victoria pointed to a hammock close by.

"And the boys?" she asked. "My husband, where is Carlos?"

"Your husband is here. Please rest," Victoria tried to comfort the woman.

"But the boys...where are Rodrigo and Mateo?" she pleaded.

"They need for you to sleep now. We're going to take care of you. Please go to sleep," Victoria crooned softly as she gently rocked the woman's hammock to and fro.

Outside, rain began to fall once more. The dogs stayed near the men and didn't run ahead.

Fidel called out, "Aaa-ooo! Aaa-ooo!"

Only the sound of the unleashed fury of rushing floodwater resonated back from the ominous darkness.

The two men walked downriver, parallel to the flooded bank, until they reached the tributary that fed into the Grande from the west. They had no choice but to give up for the night and continue the next day at the crack of dawn.

Disheartened, they trudged back to the camp to wait out the darkness.

Chapter 29

At the first rays of the sunrise, Fidel, Andrés, Chandi, and Antonio walked toward the still-raging river. Logs and debris rushed along the murky torrent. The river was far from safe, but they didn't have time to wait.

"We should cross the river branch and follow by land along the Grande," Fidel said. "Antonio, have you ever been down there by land?"

"No," Antonio answered.

"I think that only two of us should go." Fidel was deep in thought while Chandi translated for Andrés. Then he continued, "Andrés, will you go with Chandi? Antonio and I should start building the roof on my house. With all the extra people, we need to have another house ready soon."

"Yes, Chandi and I will do our best to find the boy," the big man said, barely able to keep the emotion out of his voice.

Fidel handed Andrés the shotgun, extra shells, and one of the long, thick ropes that he'd found at the camp.

The Outcasts

With machete in hand, Chandi interpreted once again. He hoped that someday they would all be able to communicate in one another's language—not that he ever tired of translating. It appeared to him that Andrés was beginning to understand some Nala, but he never attempted to speak it. *Maybe,* he thought, *maybe I could teach them and not just translate.* Chandi's mind explored the possibility of teaching while he interpreted, perhaps in a way that nobody would realize what he was doing.

"Here," Antonio said, shoving his boots at his brother, who didn't appear to be paying attention to anything.

"Oh, good," Chandi said, realizing he needed to focus on the job ahead of him.

Although barely into the trees, Andrés and Chandi sloshed through ankle-deep water until they reached the stream to the west. The twosome, along with the dogs, traversed the swollen waterway. Once on the other side, they had to back farther away from the Grande, because the water was up to the top of their boots. It would be slow going—trying to stay close enough to the riverbank to be able to see or hear the missing boy. Rey and Reina ran ahead and sniffed at branches and logs which were out of the water. For nearly an hour they walked, diverting around flooded coves, climbing over downed trees, looking under mounds of debris. They whistled and hollered, hoping desperately for some response.

The Outcasts

Chandi climbed a tree and explored the surrounding area. "Andrés, if you float down the river on a log, would you stay on this side, or could you end up floating to the other side?"

"I don't know," Andrés responded flatly. "If he didn't hit his head and go under, he could still be hanging on. I hope he's hanging on!"

"Well, it seems to me if he floated downstream all night long he'd be in Avanzada by now, don't you think?" Chandi asked.

Andrés put his hand on his head, discouraged at that thought, discouraged at the thought of anything except a miracle. *A miracle...Dios, please lead us to that boy. I can't believe I'm asking You; I haven't talked to You since...since You let my family die. You let my wife and my daughter die!* Tears began to course down the giant man's face. For the first time, he allowed them to flow freely.

Unaware of Andrés' anguish, Chandi switched around in his perch up in the tree to view the embankment they had been walking along. He looked upstream, then downstream. The ridge became steep at the next switchback, and he could see a logjam in a cove which had probably been burrowed out by the flood. *This could be it!* Chandi thought as he descended.

"Andrés, there are some logs up ahead that are lodged in the bank. Let's go look." Chandi was oblivious to the fact that Andrés had to swipe the tears from his face before he could follow. Chandi spoke as he moved quickly toward the alcove; however, he could no longer see the spot from the ground.

The last twenty feet were treacherous. Andrés tied the rope to a tree and then around Chandi's waist. As Chandi edged through the mud toward the steep bank, Andrés held the slack in the rope. Chandi felt the earth give way beneath him, but there wasn't anything nearby to grab hold of.

Andrés felt the rope cutting into his palms, but he held firmly as he called out, "Chandi! Are you okay? Do you want me to pull you back up?"

"I'm fine," Chandi stated breathlessly as he dangled from the line. "Let me down, but slowly, so I can stand on a log—but don't let go. It doesn't look stable," Chandi informed his friend.

Andrés slowly lowered the boy until he felt the rope slacken. He braced himself in case Chandi needed to be held or pulled up quickly. Sweat beaded on his brow and an involuntary prayer poured from his heart. *Dios, please protect Chandi, and please help us to find the boy! Please, Dios!* It was a voluntary prayer that followed. *Please forgive me for my silence, for my anger. Dios, I believe in You, but I don't know enough about You. I want to really know You, Dios.*

Chandi's voice broke through Andrés' epiphany. "I see something! I have to get closer to the bank...oh..." Again, Andrés felt the boy's full weight on the rope, and he held tight.

"Thanks," came Chandi's voice. "These logs are slippery. I see someone in the debris—it's a tangle of branches that are closer to the bank. I have to walk back..."

Again the rope gouged into Andrés' hands, and he held on tightly until Chandi regained his footing and the tension was released. "You okay?" the man's voice bellowed above the roar of the river.

"Yes." Chandi sounded winded. "I need a little more slack, but I'm afraid these logs could give way before I reach him." Chandi grabbed a root growing out of the side of the bank. Gingerly, he traversed another log that rolled with every step he took. Andrés released more of the rope as Chandi moved along. He reached the tangled branches that had caught the boy's body. Chandi stepped tentatively onto the fallen tree where the unconscious—or dead—boy lay. It felt firm, so he sat down next to him and tugged on the rope for a little more slack. The boy appeared to be about eight years old. Chandi didn't know how he could get him up the bank.

"Andrés?" Chandi called.

"What's happening?" Andrés asked.

"I don't think I can get him through these branches and up the bank. This tree we're on feels secure, though. Can you go get help?" Chandi pleaded.

Andrés felt paralyzed with fear at the thought of leaving the boys. *The gun...I should shoot the gun, and Fidel will come,* Andrés thought. Then he said, "I'm letting go of the rope, Chandi. I'm going to fire the gun a couple of times to signal Fidel."

"That's a good idea," Chandi replied. He felt the release of the rope.

Seconds later, Chandi flinched at the boom of the shotgun blast. Moments passed, and then he heard the faraway sound of another shotgun report. Andrés fired once again and they both knew that help would soon be on the way. Andrés whistled for his dogs. They hadn't caught the scent of the boy, so they'd been off on their own. But both dogs soon returned to their master and began barking.

When Fidel and Antonio arrived, they found Andrés sitting on the ground, next to a large tree. The rope was tied around the tree, and Andrés held the line in his bleeding hands.

"What happened?" Fidel asked him.

Antonio stepped in quickly to interpret for the two men.

"Chandi found the boy, but they're down there, and Chandi can't get him up by himself."

"Chandi?" Fidel called down the bank. "Is he alive?"

"I don't know. I can't get close enough to his chest or face. I really need my machete. And I don't think I can hold his weight for both of us to be hauled up there."

Fidel was quiet for several minutes while his mind pondered the problem. Everyone waited patiently for the solution they were sure that their leader would come up with.

"Okay," Fidel said. "Antonio, you go back for a hammock and another rope."

"Okay," Antonio said as he sprinted away, wishing he had his boots.

Fidel climbed a tree that was ten feet away from the one that the rope was tied to. He climbed out onto a branch, hoping he could see where the boys were. The logjam had cut an alcove into the bank between the two trees. He scooted along the branch until he could see the boys in the quagmire below him.

He climbed down and went in search of a vine. When he returned, he secured Chandi's machete to the long vine. Fidel climbed the tree again and lowered the tool to Chandi.

Eagerly the boy untied the machete. He stood up and then slowly and cautiously cut away the branches that enshrouded the child.

When Antonio returned, Fidel threw one end of the second rope up over the tree branch. He tied the end of the rope to the hammock. Then he climbed back up and scooted out on the branch. He lowered the hammock down.

Carefully, Chandi worked the hammock under the boy's body. But unsure, he called out, "Would the branch and the rope hold both of us? I'm afraid he'll fall out if I'm not in the hammock with him."

"It should hold," Fidel shouted back.

Chandi worked the hammock back out from under the boy and secured the rope to the ends of the hammock. He sat in the middle and then scooted the boy in with him, leaning the child's torso up against his chest. Chandi wrapped his arms around the lad's waist, holding him securely.

"We're ready," Chandi yelled. "No, wait! I have to untie the first rope that I still have around my waist! Okay, I'm ready now."

Fidel climbed down the tree and told Antonio go up to watch the hammock's progress from the branch. Fidel wound the rope around another tree and grasped the end firmly with both hands. Andrés stood between the two trees and took hold of the line. First he drew up the slack in the rope. The hammock slowly encased the boys. Antonio signaled that they were ready. The giant of a man heaved with all of his bodyweight and strength. The hammock lifted the boys above the logjam. Fidel efficiently took up the slack in the rope and then held on firmly once again, using the tree as a stopgap for safety.

Andrés' muscles rippled and sweat poured down his back as he hauled the boys upward. Tensely, Antonio supervised from the tree. Fidel again took up the slack and secured the rope. Antonio signaled for more and Andrés heaved again. Finally, the hammock rose above the bank and Fidel tied off the rope. He drew up the first rope and tossed the end to Antonio. Fidel instructed Antonio to tie it loosely around the rope that the boys hung from. The knot slid down and Andrés grabbed that rope and pulled the hammock in over the safety of land. Fidel slackened his rope to lower the hammock to the ground.

Andrés leaned close to the pallid form in Chandi's arms and saw the shallow rise and fall of his chest. "He's alive!" the huge man exulted. Andrés picked up the boy to carry him home.

The Outcasts

The dogs barked and ran ahead while the others followed close behind.

Dios, I don't understand Your ways. I don't know why You save some and allow others to die. I do know that I need You and I want to know You—truly know You! Andrés didn't fully understand that he was about to travel another trail—as a son of the living God!

Chapter 30

Six weeks had passed. The new roof on Fidel's house was finished, and enough materials had been left over to re-roof the small two room building for Andrés. It had once been the top ranking officers' quarters. Andrés was a wonderful help to the group, but he stayed to himself unless he was assisting in some way. Using old tin, they'd patched up the six room officers' quarters that they'd been using for storage. They'd cleared out one of the rooms for Carlos and his family. They'd also loaned them three hammocks.

Out of necessity they cooked joint meals. Dalia, who had been enamored by the cookstove, proved to be a very creative and good cook. She learned to use the pots and skillets, and even recreated the pancakes that the misioneros had served them. Of course, they'd long since run out of butter and syrup. They also used their cooking fires for banana drink, and for soup—when they had meat.

Even though the Nala weren't accustomed to sitting down together for meals, the tables and benches served everyone well.

Alberto and the boys enjoyed it, and as time passed, the others began to appear to eat with the group instead of staggering in separately. Everyone except Carlos and his family, that is—they took food back to their own house and ate alone—much to Dalia's relief. Andrés was beginning to participate in mealtime discussions. After each meal, Victoria and Rosa washed and dried the dishes while Maamo took care of Susana and Isabel. The twins were five months old, and Maamo realized she wouldn't be able to contain them in her hammock much longer. Her heart overflowed at their bright smiles and loving cuddles. For the first time, she felt peace about her own twins as she lived vicariously through these two precious great-granddaughters. With the little dimples in their chubby cheeks, they looked like their mother. Their thick black hair already hung a couple of inches below the napes of their necks. They were secure and happy babies.

It was a bright, sunny morning and Fidel had gathered everyone together for a meeting. The men and children proudly wore the wonderful clothing that the misioneros had given them. Everyone except Carlos' family that is—they had refused to accept any gift from the others.

Carlos sat scowling at the group. Edilma sulked quietly on a bench behind the other women. Although their injuries had healed, their hearts had not.

"We want to go back to Ulgana," Carlos demanded as he stood before the meeting. "*We* are *good* Nala. We don't want any more of the spirits' curses to come on us because we're staying with you. Our canoe overturned at *your* camp! Our firstborn son 'is no more,' and look," he said, pointing at Rodrigo, "the spirits have cursed the boy! You aren't walking the Nala way—you kept those...*babies*! You joined with Moya, the outsider, and their mixed offspring. And all of you treat *Dalia* as if she is one of you—she was banned for..."

"That's enough!" Fidel shouted.

Eyes widened at their leader's uncharacteristic sharpness. The room was deadly silent as Fidel continued. "You are free to leave. We aren't holding you here. We were helping you in your time of need."

Fidel had hoped that Carlos and his family would fit in, but they'd been a constant aggravation to everyone. All except Rodrigo—wordlessly, the boy had bonded with his rescuers.

"We don't have a canoe. We're so far downriver that we couldn't pole back to Ulgana even if we had one," Carlos complained.

"We can take you up to a trail that leads to Namuro," Fidel suggested abruptly. However, as soon as he'd spoken, he realized he hadn't thought through the consequences. He was frustrated and eager to see Carlos and his family leave, but acting impetuously could put all of them in serious danger.

Carlos' eyes narrowed menacingly. "You have a motor for your canoe. We won't tell where you are if you take us back to Ulgana *by canoe*."

Carlos and Edilma expected a fight, or at least the normal heated discussions that that were customary events at village meetings. But the group sat deep in thought.

Fidel's features hardened with determination, but he spoke calmly. "We'll consider that, and we'll let you know soon. For today, we have other decisions to make."

Carlos stomped out of the house in disgust. Edilma gathered her daughters and followed him. But Rodrigo remained seated next to Chandi. He had slowly learned to walk again, but the boy never spoke. A dull and sad expression remained on his face as he hung his head low and kept his hands in the pockets of his threadbare pants. His mind fought hard to fully understand what his father had said. He already knew that his family no longer accepted him, and somehow he only felt contentment when he was near Chandi and the others in the camp who helped him and loved him. He could hear, he could feel, and sometimes old memories would flash momentarily into his mind. But his voice was locked inside his brain—he couldn't figure out how to put his thoughts into spoken words. Exhausted from the effort, Rodrigo's mind slipped gently into a quiet place. He sat idly and patted Reina, who lay at his feet.

The meeting continued somberly. Since the work group had left, the misioneros and their airplane had not been seen, and supplies were running very low. It was decided that Fidel, Chandi, and Antonio would use the motor to take the canoe to Cerro Alto the next day. Andrés, who had become the newest member of the village, would stay behind with Alberto. They had the shotguns, and the men were always on their guard. But with Carlos' open hostility, they felt even more vulnerable—from within their camp.

Early the next morning, Fidel and the boys readied the canoe and motor. They waved good-bye to the small group who'd gathered by the river.

When they neared Cerro Alto an hour-and-a-half later, they were overwhelmed by what they found. Fidel turned off the motor and stood up in the back of the canoe. "There's been a mudslide," he stated, in awe of the destruction. "That flood destroyed Cerro Alto!"

The tall, unstable riverbank had collapsed, wiping out all of the stores that had lined the ridge of ground above the Grande. The cement stairs and dock had vanished. From their view, no buildings—not one home—remained standing. The town appeared totally devastated and deserted.

Chandi and Antonio stared silently. Fidel wasn't sure what to do. To stop the craft from floating downriver, the boys leaned harder into their poles.

"It looks like we have to go on down to Avanzada," Fidel voiced.

The two nodded.

"I hate to worry everyone by being gone so long, but we won't make it down and back before sundown unless we continue on. Let's go," he said.

The boys guided the canoe toward the middle of the river and Fidel revved the motor to life once more. Involuntarily, all three looked back at the devastation they were speeding away from.

Fidel faced forward once again, deep in thought as he opened up the throttle. *Maybe some survived—maybe they took refuge downriver because their food and source of income are gone. Hopefully some were able to escape.*

As they turned the bend, Antonio glanced back once more. *Are those animals...or children?* he wondered, before trees obscured his view. *Surely small children haven't been left behind!* He thought for a few seconds before he spoke up.

"Fidel," he yelled back above the roar of the motor.

Fidel slowed down. "Yes?"

"I saw something in Cerro Alto as we rounded the bend. It may have been dogs, but...it may have been children." Antonio's voice was hesitant, yet urgent.

"Let's pull over to the bank and talk about this," Fidel said, uncertain whether he'd heard correctly.

To stop and hold the canoe at the bank, the boys once again leaned into the poles.

"What did you see?" Fidel asked the younger boy.

"We were pretty far away, but it could have been several children sitting near the bank watching us...it could have been a pack of dogs though," Antonio said.

"If they're dogs, they're probably hungry and dangerous. That flood was six weeks ago. Surely small children couldn't

The Outcasts

have survived alone. But we'd better go back and find out. We brought the gun and machetes. Watch for a place to tie up the canoe. I don't want you two going up there alone," Fidel said as he started the motor.

Minutes later, after tying the canoe to a tree, the threesome disembarked. Fidel took the lead as they climbed up the steep bank on the downriver side of the town. As they reached the top, they heard scurrying sounds.

"Anybody here?" Chandi called out in Spanish. "We're here to help you."

The three looked around. The mudslide had started with the collapse of the heavily wooded hill behind the town, and it had leveled everything in its path—all the way to the river. Not one structure remained standing. The stench of decomposition threatened to gag them. But they walked resolutely toward what had once been the center of the small town.

At the muffled cry of a baby, their ears perked.

"Who's here?" Chandi repeated. "We want to help you."

"We're over here," a small voice said, as a tiny girl peeked out from behind a pile of debris.

Chandi took the lead so he could talk to the child. He found five small children and an eight-month-old baby. They were filthy, and what clothes they had were ragged and torn. Their dark brown eyes blended into the dirt on their faces, and the mud in their curly black hair was caked and dried.

"What have you been eating?" Chandi asked.

"We used the cans of food that we found. We ate bananas, but the trees were destroyed and we can't find any more," the oldest child explained, and she began to cry.

"Are there any adults here?" Chandi asked.

"Everybody but us died," the little girl sobbed.

"Are these your sisters and brothers?" Chandi asked again.

"She's my sister," the little girl said, gesturing to the baby in her arms. "The rest aren't. We found each other after all the buildings collapsed. Other people have been here but we were afraid of them, so we hid. But the food has been gone for days and we're very hungry," she said.

Chandi looked at Fidel and relayed the story. Fidel said, "Tell her we'll take them home with us."

We really don't need six more mouths to feed. Fidel rubbed his head. *Should we take the kids back home and go down to Avanzada tomorrow, or should we go down with the kids and get supplies and come back?* Looking at each sad, exhausted child, he knew they should take them home.

Chapter 31

The women froze in stunned silence when Fidel and the boys led six filthy, sad-faced children into the house. Staring at the heartrending sight before them, Andrés and Alberto followed and sat down in hammocks.

Fidel and Chandi explained what had happened in Cerro Alto, as everyone gazed at the children who'd huddled together in the center of the room.

"They speak Spanish, so it seems like they should live with us," Chandi said.

Alberto looked angrily at his son. "This isn't your decision!"

Moya searched her son's face and he explained to her in Nala what he'd said.

"There are *six* of them!" she screeched, feeling no further explanation was needed.

Next, Dalia spoke up. "I'd like to take them, even though we're already a burden to all of you. They can learn Nala. I think we should all learn to speak each other's language anyway." Dalia blushed and lowered her eyes. She was unaccustomed to voicing her opinions—in fact, this was the first time she'd voiced her own views of anything since Carlos and his family had been at the camp.

Andrés stared at Dalia as Chandi once again interpreted. *That's what I thought she said.* His heart pounded with the desire to take in these dear children who looked so forlorn. *My daughter! She could have been orphaned and afraid—left alone after a flood tore apart the only world she'd ever known. I speak their language, but how can I take on six children? A woman would do a better job.* Andrés remained silent.

"We're all in this together," Fidel reminded the group. "Let's get these children some food while we figure out what will work best for everyone."

Dalia and Victoria headed for the kitchen.

Rosa went in search of extra clothing, towels, and soap. *These children are filthy. We're already sharing the few hammocks we have. Where on earth are we going to sleep six more children—six!*

Carlos stared out of the window in their house and relayed to his wife that six more outcasts had arrived at this cursed place. "We have to get out of here—soon!"

Dalia returned with avocado slices and bananas that would be quick nourishment for the children. She handed the plate of food to a child and then smiled at the oldest girl. Gingerly, Dalia took the baby from her arms. She sat on the closest bench and put the baby to her breast to nurse her.

The Outcasts

Dalia spoke to Chandi, who still hovered near the group. "Tell them there's more food, but they must eat only a little bit for now. After they bathe they can eat some more. Let them know that their stomachs will hurt if they eat too much food all at once."

Chandi complied.

Rosa arrived with soap, towels, and extra clothing. She shook her head slightly and ushered the five children toward their bathing spot. Dalia followed with the baby still in her arms. Whooping and laughing, the rest of the little ones rushed happily ahead. Chandi and Antonio followed behind, with Rodrigo close beside them. Maamo and Victoria stayed at the house with the four babies.

From their window opening, Carlos, Edilma, and their girls gawked at the procession.

Edilma was the first to speak. "Carlos, maybe we shouldn't have asked them to take us back in the canoe. We don't want the angry spirits to follow us home!"

"I have a plan," Carlos sneered. "We need to appease the spirits. Ramiro is a strong chief. Ramiro will know what to do with them." Carlos nearly growled, "Fidel is the leader here—without him and the two older boys, this group will die away along with the curse they've called down on themselves."

Chapter 32

That evening by lantern light, another meeting assembled in Fidel's house. Carlos and Edilma had not been asked to join them. The ten younger children and five babies had settled into hammocks and were blissfully allowing much-needed sleep to claim them.

Fidel cleared his throat. Chandi took the cue and assumed his role as interpreter for the group. The room quieted in anticipation as Fidel began. "One pressing issue is supplies. Tomorrow Chandi, Antonio, and I will go to Avanzada."

"I have enough flour for one batch of bread. I can make it tomorrow," Alberto offered from his seat at one of the tables.

"Good," Fidel said. "Bread will feed everyone until we return."

"How much money do you have?" Maamo asked from her hammock as she gently rocked the twins back and forth.

Fidel reached into his pocket. "Roberto is storing the rest for us, but he gave me this when he left."

He handed the bills to Chandi, who counted them out loud. "Twenty, forty, fifty, sixty, seventy, eighty, eighty-five, ninety, ninety-five, one hundred. There's a hundred dollars."

Fidel mentally approximated the amounts of money they'd spent before in Cerro Alto and Avanzada, and knew that a hundred dollars was a lot of money. "Good," he said, and then changed subjects. "I know that we need to decide whether to take Carlos and his family back to Ulgana or up to the trail that leads to Namuro. But for tonight the more important issue is the children and who they will stay with."

Dalia said, "I want the children."

"Your space is too small for all of them," Rosa piped up practically, in her usual brusque manner.

Dalia was very thankful for the portion of the house that had once been the officers' dining room. It was a private area for her family. But Rosa was right; there wouldn't be room for six more children. She lowered her head sadly.

"When Carlos leaves, we'll have an empty house," Andrés offered as a possible solution. Chandi translated, but it hadn't gone unnoticed that Andrés had understood the Nala and had answered in Spanish.

Victoria said, "She would be alone in a house with six small children and two babies! Dalia, would you feel safe at night?"

Dalia didn't know what to say—she desperately wanted to care for the children, but the thought of living in a separate house terrified her. "You're right, that wouldn't be good," she whispered.

The Outcasts

Chandi translated for the Spanish speakers. Everyone remained silent, deep in thought.

Maamo spoke next. "You have a good heart, Dalia. You're a good mother. But taking on six besides your two would be too much for anyone to handle alone. We *are all* in this together and we need each other. The baby and her sister Elisabet could stay with you. Little Angelina still needs to nurse, and you can nurse two babies. I think Rodrigo is going to need a home, too. He should stay with Alberto's family. He's so attached to Chandi and Antonio...he'll need them if his family deserts him—and I'm sure they will. That leaves four more." Maamo stopped, deep in thought while Chandi translated.

"I can take Nacio and Miguel," Andrés offered.

"We could take Alegría and Felicidad," Victoria proposed.

"Good," Fidel stated. "Does anyone object to this plan?"

Nobody disagreed, so Fidel closed the meeting by adding, "We have many more decisions to face soon. Without Cerro Alto, Namuro has nowhere to trade. Nobody there has a motor to get down to Avanzada and back. Carlos and Edilma can't be trusted to keep our camp a secret. We have to make big decisions. *But*," Fidel emphasized, "we will talk about this *after* Carlos and Edilma leave."

Everyone understood what Fidel meant, and the seriousness of the matter. They also understood that the meeting was officially finished.

The following evening, Fidel, Chandi, and Antonio returned from Avanzada, just before dusk turned into a moonless night. The motor had alerted the camp, so all able bodies met the canoe at the river branch and hauled the supplies to Fidel's kitchen. Carlos and Edilma peeked from their window, in awe of the boxes and bags of supplies. *Where did the money come from to buy all of that?* Carlos wondered.

Andrés hoisted the motor up onto his shoulder and carried it to the small building nearest the creek, where they kept it along with the drum of gasoline and several containers of kerosene. Fidel walked with him and showed him a padlock that he'd purchased to secure the structure. He gave Andrés one of the two small keys for safekeeping. Both men knew that hard times could bring out the worst in people, and thieves might soon be ravaging the area. Little did they know, however, that an hour before dawn, Carlos would attempt to enter the building, to steal the motor and then abscond with one of the canoes...but the lock would hold strong.

The next morning, Fidel called another meeting. Again he excluded Carlos' family.

Fidel opened the meeting by saying, "We have to decide where to take Carlos and Edilma."

Rosa spoke up next. "We need to get them out of here soon. They don't have a problem eating lots of food, and I just don't trust them."

"I think we should take them up to the trail and let them walk back. Why should we use the motor and the gasoline to take them by river?" said Alberto.

"Well," Fidel began, "I've been thinking about it, and the problem is that if they go to Namuro first, they'll tell them our location. But if we take them back to Ulgana, we'll have more time to decide what to do before word gets back to Namuro and everyone knows where we're at."

Murmurs of assent rose throughout the room. Nobody had thought about it that way.

"Will you take Chandi and Antonio with you?" Andrés asked.

"I think I'll take Chandi and leave Antonio here. You'll need meat. We'll have Carlos to help get us upriver, and coming back down will be easy. So, Chandi and I will be able to do it alone." Fidel had obviously been thinking it through.

"When will you leave?" Victoria asked, not anxious to have her husband gone again.

"Day after tomorrow, if the weather holds. I need a couple of days before going again," Fidel said.

"When will you tell Carlos?" Alberto asked.

"After the meeting I'll let him know," Fidel replied. "Now, let's talk about the supplies. I bought four more hammocks and blankets—enough for each household to take care of the extra kids. I bought a pair of boots for Chandi, and a pair for me, too. Now we won't have to borrow Antonio's.

"Rodrigo," Fidel said, looking at the boy who sat on the floor near Chandi's feet.

Rodrigo looked up at Fidel.

"I bought you some fishhooks and fishing line. We need a good fisherman to help supply us with food. I think you're just the one for that job." Fidel smiled at him with confidence.

A faint smile crossed the boy's lips as he lowered his head and mulled the words over in his mind.

"The rest of the supplies are the normal provisions. You know where we keep everything, and you can supply your own houses as you run out." Fidel stopped talking and looked around the room at each adult. "Do you have any suggestions or concerns?"

Dalia spoke up. "I'm worried about you going to Ulgana. Ramiro is evil. He's dangerous…" She couldn't go on.

"She's right," Maamo affirmed.

"We don't have a choice," Fidel said, ending the meeting.

Like a dam in the river of life, Nala tradition had held fast against change. But the floodgates had finally opened—and now the dam burst, accelerating change at an alarming speed. The unsuspecting group had no idea that yet another crisis threatened the Nala Nation.

But God knew—God knew, and He heard the cries of people who were lost in darkness.

Chapter 33

Two days later at dawn, Andrés hauled the motor to the canoe while Chandi siphoned gasoline from the fifty-five-gallon drum into the gas can.

Carlos, Edilma, and their two girls seated themselves in the center of the canoe. Rodrigo stood on the bank, but his parents turned their heads away from him.

Fidel arrived, having said good-bye to his wonderful girls and beautiful wife. He would miss them on this dreaded trip. Deep in thought, he almost missed Rodrigo's misery. In his heart, Fidel had known that Carlos would be a coward and not even try to explain to his boy why he was abandoning him.

Fidel knelt by Rodrigo. "I'm sorry, son. Your parents are going back to their village. They don't understand what they'll be missing by leaving you behind, but we love you and we're glad you'll be part of our family now."

Chandi set the gas can in the boat and then sized up the situation. He turned to Rodrigo and said, "I'll be back soon. After I get back, we'll go fishing together. Okay?"

The Outcasts

Rodrigo nodded, but he felt uneasy. His eyes darted from face to face, looking for Antonio. When the troubled lad saw that his friend wasn't getting into the canoe, he walked to Antonio's side. Unable to process the enormity of what was taking place, Rodrigo simply allowed his mind to shut down. He was not alone—he was with Antonio; that was enough.

Fidel sat down by the motor, and Chandi, pole in hand, walked to the front of the craft. He shoved off, sending them drifting toward the Grande River. Fidel directed Chandi to guide the canoe down the Grande instead of fighting the swift currents from the Namuro River which joined the Grande upstream from them. Fidel revved the motor to life, and when the river bend straightened out, he made a wide u-turn, beginning their journey up the large watercourse.

Fidel had no idea how long they would travel before the next river would appear—the river that would take them to Ulgana. He had never been up this far before.

Fidel studied the sky, which promised a clear day. He watched the banks for signs of animals or people. The trees grew taller and thicker the farther they traveled, but they passed no visible signs of trails or huts.

The motor droned on as the sun grew higher in the sky. Fidel noticed footpaths and thatched rooftops interspersed with trees, and he wondered who lived this far away from Cerro Alto.

More time went by, and Fidel grew anxious.

"Over there—on the left." Carlos pointed to the river ahead of them. "That will take us to Ulgana."

Fidel sized up the currents and safely navigated the turn. He was deep in thought as he looked up at the sun. *I wonder if we can get there and back down to the Grande before dark. I don't feel good about spending the night in Ulgana. I'd like to find a trail and let them out before we get to the village, but I don't know whether there are any. Why didn't I ask Dalia about that?*

The river grew shallow, so Fidel turned off the motor. He threw a pole to Carlos and grabbed another one. For the next two hours, the three leaned into their poles and laboriously moved the canoe up the river. Furtively, Fidel searched the shore for signs of gardens or trails, but none came into view.

Their poles began sinking into deeper water, but Fidel didn't turn the motor back on. He was in a quandary—he wanted to make better time, but he didn't want to alert the villagers to their arrival. Before long, the river got shallow again, so Fidel was glad that he hadn't used the motor. The sun was halfway to its western descent when a bathing area came into view.

"Pull it over," Fidel ordered.

"No, up farther!" Carlos exclaimed.

"Over!" Fidel commanded once more. Carlos sat down, and Chandi and Fidel poled the canoe to shore. A young woman and several children sat washing clothes. They turned to look at the approaching canoe.

The Outcasts

Carlos and Edilma stared at the group whom they'd never seen before in their village. Carlos was so shocked, he forgot his plan of whistling to alert the village of their arrival.

"Fidel?" the young woman questioned. "I'm Victoria's sister, Lucinda."

Fidel was surprised. "Are you visiting Ulgana? Or did you marry someone from here?"

Tears welled up into her pretty brown eyes. "Oh, Fidel..."

Carlos whistled a loud warning, and Fidel and Chandi knew they were in trouble. "We have to go!" Fidel shouted, as Carlos and his family bounded out of the canoe and sprinted toward the center of the village in search of reinforcements.

With his pole, Fidel held firm the back of the canoe, while Chandi pushed the front of the boat downstream.

"Wait! Take us with you! Let me get my mother," Lucinda cried. She ordered the three children who were with her to get into the canoe. As she turned to run to their nearby lean-to, Fidel noticed a huge black and blue mark across her cheek.

Adolfo and his brothers had just returned from gathering thatch for the house that the village was going to build them. The brothers had left very early in the morning and were the first to return. The rest of the men were still gone. Lucinda told Adolfo that Fidel was there with a canoe—and they had to hurry! Without questioning, Adolfo lifted his mother out of her hammock and carried her to the waiting craft. As soon as they were all in, Fidel and Chandi gave mighty shoves and propelled the boat downstream. Adolfo grabbed a pole and helped speed them away from the terrible place where they'd lived for the past six weeks.

Fidel wondered about Diego...he couldn't imagine what had happened, but he didn't like the bruises that he saw on Lucinda and her mother. There wasn't time for questions, so he continued to thrust the canoe swiftly on its way to the Grande, where he could use the motor and get them safely back to the camp.

They reached the mouth of the river at dusk and were able to maneuver into the Grande. Although it would be a moonlit night, Fidel knew it wouldn't be easy to navigate into their small tributary—even with a full moon in the sky.

When Fidel was convinced that they hadn't been followed and couldn't be overtaken, he shut down the motor and filled it with the reserve gasoline from the can. Then he revved it to life again, and they sped toward home.

Finally the Namuro River came into view. Moonbeams illuminated the way, and Fidel navigated safely through the current, around the bend, and into their river branch. The three poled up to the landing. Adolfo picked up his mother and the rest disembarked, following Chandi and Fidel to one of the strange-looking houses.

Victoria could not believe her eyes! "Mother! Lucinda? Oh... you're *here*? How can this be? But...but, what about father? Oh, no! You're hurt—you're bruised! What happened to you?"

Victoria's mother hadn't spoken a word since leaving Ulgana. Tears spilled down her cheeks. Adolfo set her in the nearest hammock and the complete story unfolded.

"Your father was banned from Luwana. We had to move to Ulgana because he and Ramiro violated that young girl—Dalia," Flora explained.

"Mother," Victoria interrupted. "Dalia is here with us."

Flora's eyes widened, and for a few moments she looked like an animal that wanted to run. An awkward silence enveloped the room as Flora's emotions battled within her. *How can this be? I'm tired of hurting...I don't want to be around that girl who's turned my life upside down!* Seconds slowly passed. *No...wait...she isn't to blame. Lucinda was going to be forced to marry Ramiro. He wanted my girl for a second wife—and it wouldn't be her fault. She would be forced, just like Dalia must have been forced.* And she felt sympathy for the girl. Her eyes softened and she looked around the room.

Head down, Dalia came forward and stood in front of Victoria's mother. Flora's hand reached for Dalia's chin and pulled it up so their eyes could meet. There were no words...but the understanding was clear. It was enough.

Flora continued her account, "We had to pack our belongings and leave Luwana. We were all exiled for your father's wickedness. Adolfo was going to marry Cecilia in Kala, and Lucinda wanted Mateo. It was like watching *your* agony all over again, Victoria! I should have helped you—I was wrong!"

Victoria stared at her brokenhearted mother. "It's okay, mother. I'm happy. I love Fidel. It all worked out for good."

Flora gathered her strength once more. "Lucinda was so angry that she told your father she would not go to Ulgana. He struck her across the face. I yelled at him and stood between them and he struck me too. We knew that we had no choice, so the next day we hiked through the mud to Ulgana. It's a terrible place. Ramiro is very evil and your father has become even more like him."

Victoria was horrified—she could barely take it all in.

Tears slid down Maamo's weathered face. She couldn't bear hearing that *her son* had become such a wicked man. She had no words to express her sorrow to Flora, so she remained silent.

"We've been living in a lean-to. Ramiro and your father decided to join forces as co-chiefs. Ulgana is very small and run-down. They decided they want more wives, and through that will build up the village," Flora said.

"More wives? What do you mean?" Victoria asked.

"Ramiro wants to marry Lucinda and have her for his second wife." Flora broke down into tears.

"No!" Victoria gasped.

"Lucinda told her father, 'Absolutely not,' and he struck her again. It sent her across the floor. So I intervened. As you can see, he gave me a very severe beating. I could not fight him." Flora sighed.

Lucinda broke into the conversation. "He was going to make me marry Ramiro next week! I was so afraid, because I had no way to escape. But Fidel came—just in time!"

Victoria spoke up angrily. "Why do they think they can break our Nala laws and have more than one wife, but we shouldn't break another of our customs in order to save our daughters' lives?"

"The babies! They're girls? I want to see my grandchildren!" Flora exclaimed.

Rosa retrieved Isabel from Maamo's hammock and handed the sleeping baby to her newly-arrived grandmother. Then she went back for Susana.

Reverently, Flora held the baby girls. She hugged and kissed them and allowed the tears to course down her face once more.

"Victoria, you did the right thing saving these babies! You are on a good trail—there must be more than one after all," Flora said as she gazed into the sleeping faces of two of her precious granddaughters.

Rosalinda wasn't about to be left out. Her black hair bobbed down her back as she pranced toward the hammock. With a huge smile and shining eyes, she said in little-girl talk, "Hi gramma... I'm Rosalinda...they're my sisters." The two-and-a-half-year-old couldn't remember meeting her grandmother before. And she wasn't disappointed; her grandmother laughed in delight at her adorable Rosalinda.

Fidel watched in silence, but fear for their future weighed heavily on his shoulders—it assaulted his very being.

Chapter 34

Dalia and Victoria brought food to the hungry travelers. Everyone in the camp had already joined the group, so as soon as Fidel finished eating, he began the meeting.

"We have to decide whether we should stay at this location," Fidel announced.

"Move?"

"Where would we go?"

"Start all over again?"

Fidel ran through the list of dangers. "Carlos knows exactly where we are. Diego will want his family back. Namuro could still be looking for Isabel and Susana."

"If we move, how will the misioneros find us?" Dalia lamented.

Andrés spoke next. "What would it take to start a trading post like Cerro Alto was? Namuro needs a place to buy and sell. If we could fill that need, maybe they would no longer be our enemies. Surely they would see that bad spirits have not hurt you for allowing your twins to live. On the contrary, don't we have

The Outcasts

much more than anyone in Namuro has? I'm not Nala, of course, but this is how I see it."

After Andrés' words were translated, Maamo cleared her throat, and the room quieted for the matriarch. "I think we need to stand our ground. What would it take to make this camp secure?"

Fidel thought for a while. "In Avanzada, many of the houses have fences around them—some even have walls. I don't know how much that would cost.

"I like the idea of trading and selling. It would help everyone. We have $1,000.00 left...but I don't know how much money it would take to start out—to buy enough goods."

Chandi spoke up next. "I can work on a plan for that. If we buy the crops from Namuro, we could sell them for more money in Avanzada, and we'd make a profit. We could also keep what we need and not have to spend as much time planting and harvesting our own food."

"The problem with that is that the motor belongs to the misioneros. I don't know how much a motor of our own would cost," Fidel explained.

"I wondered how you got that motor," Adolfo said, feeling at home already. "How much is $1,000.00? We get $50.00 when we sell a canoe load of plantains."

Chandi explained that twenty loads of plantains would be worth $1,000.00.

"Where did you get that much money?" Adolfo exclaimed.

Fidel looked at Maamo to see whether she wanted to tell where the money had come from.

Maamo laughed, and her toothless grin made everyone smile. "See my walking stick?" Maamo waved the cane up high for all to view. "I carved this myself, and I made a secret compartment in it. When I was a girl, I found the *lost village*."

Maamo paused to take in the wide eyes and rapt attention of her new audience.

"I used to go there alone. One day I found *gold* and I buried it in a special place. Several years ago, I carved that secret compartment in my walking stick and hid the gold nuggets in there. I gave Fidel six of the gold nuggets, and he's used the money to feed and clothe all of us and to fix up this camp. I wanted to start a village for people who had nowhere else to go, and that's exactly what this place has become. I still have a few more gold nuggets and the gold coin necklaces." Maamo's eyes sparkled. "Fidel, do you think that would be enough to build a fence, buy a motor, *and* start a store?"

Everyone laughed. The tension that had filled the room suddenly dissipated.

"Is everyone willing to stay here for a while longer? We can fortify the camp and find out whether Namuro wants to trade with us. There are still a lot of problems to face...but maybe moving again isn't the answer, at least for now." Fidel decided to take a vote. "Does anyone want to move now?"

Nobody stood up.

"So, does that mean we aren't moving?" Paco questioned, as his head darted from person to person in the room.

Everyone laughed again.

"No, we aren't moving. We can stay here," Rosa reassured her young grandson.

"Good!" echoed lots of little voices from around the room.

Andrés was next to address the crowd. As always, Chandi was interpreting for the group. "Until we get a fence or wall built, I think we need a plan in case anybody comes to cause a problem. The children can take turns being lookouts at the landing. The dogs can stay with them. We're going to have a litter of pups soon, so in time we'll have more dogs to guard us. We need a signal...and when that signal is heard, all of the women and children should head for one of the bunkers. We can clean it out and keep some food, water, and a shotgun there. We men will find out who's come and why."

"That's a very good idea," Fidel said.

"Tomorrow I could use some help cleaning up one of those bunkers, then," Rosa said.

"Lili and I will help," Lucinda offered enthusiastically. The pretty almost-sixteen-year-old was so happy to have her future back that she wanted to show her appreciation any way that she could. She looked over at her sister. Eleven-year-old Lili smiled shyly and nodded her head, giving her consent. It was then that Lucinda realized that for the past six weeks, she'd been so wrapped up in her own problems that she hadn't even noticed how with-

The Outcasts

drawn her younger sister had become. Lili had always been the fun one...not quiet and sullen.

"Good," Rosa responded. "Do we have an extra lantern that we can leave there? It's really dark."

"There are more lanterns in the storage building," Antonio informed the group.

Victoria stood up and started collecting the dirty dishes.

"Wait..." Fidel said in a mockingly serious tone. "I forgot something. I just ate the biggest and best-tasting fish I've had since coming here! Who caught that fish?"

Rodrigo sidled closer to the man and looked into his eyes. The boy's head bobbed slightly and his lips tried to form a word...but nothing came out. He lowered his head in frustration, but Fidel pulled his chin up and looked into his eyes again.

"You did good, son. I needed that food and you worked hard to provide it. We need each other. You did good," Fidel praised the boy.

Rodrigo produced a crooked smile...his first real smile since the accident.

Chapter 35

Bright and early the next morning, the camp came to life. New hope had dawned in their hearts, and each person pitched in with renewed strength.

Rosalinda chattered at Alegría as they followed Victoria to the chicken coop to gather the eggs. Victoria smiled, thankful that her little girl had so quickly accepted the orphan from Cerro Alto. She studied the girls. *Alegría appears to be about the same age as Rosalinda, but the similarities stop there.* Victoria grinned. *Alegría's hair is as curly as Rosalinda's is straight. Alegría is sturdily built, but Rosalinda has a slight frame. Alegría is as listless and timid as Rosalinda is animated and confident. But, look what she's been through—losing her parents, and maybe even other brothers and sisters, in that awful mudslide! Maybe this isn't her real personality.* Victoria turned her full attention to the girls and listened in disbelief, realizing that Rosalinda's childish jabbering was in Nala and Spanish! *She's barely begun to learn her own language—yet she's learning a second one as well!*

Armed with a machete, brooms, and a lantern, Rosa led Lucinda and Lili toward the farthest bunker. They lit the lantern and walked down the gradual slope.

"It's made just like the strange houses, but it's under the earth," Lucinda stated in awe. Pointing to two metal fifty-five-gallon drums, the curious young woman asked, "What's in those?"

"The misioneros store gasoline from the 'avión' in those," Rosa explained.

"What's an 'avión'?" Lili spoke up tentatively, for the first time.

"It's a canoe that flies like a bird," Rosa explained with authority.

"Oh," the girls exclaimed in unison, trying hard to imagine such a thing.

"We'll use the empty bunker. Let's go clean that one," Rosa said.

The threesome swept cobwebs from the walls and corners. They inspected every inch of the small room, looking for scorpions, other insects, and snakes. When they began sweeping zealously, years of dirt that had collected on the concrete floor filled the room, causing fits of coughing and sending all three running for breaths of fresh air. After the dust settled, they resumed the task—until they had to rush out again. Rosa sat heavily on the ground, exhausted.

"We'll finish the job," Lucinda offered.

"Okay," Rosa conceded, "I can't move as fast as you two. I'll go help Maamo with the babies. Babies and children seem to multiply around here."

Lucinda smiled at the woman, who tried to sound grouchy, but whose good heart showed through anyway.

Lili giggled. "You should see your faces! I mean, you don't have faces...only eyes!" They all stared at one another and laughed until their sides hurt. As soon as she could, Rosa got up and walked slowly back to the house. *I guess I'll bathe in the river before picking up any babies. Looking like this, I'd scare them to death,* she chuckled. Another coughing fit seized her as her lungs expelled the rest of the offensive dust.

Lucinda sobered. *I never thought I'd laugh again...but there is hope. It's wonderful to see the sparkle back in Lili's eyes, to see her having fun and giggling again.*

Adolfo and his brothers hauled a table and chairs from the storage building into the bunker. "Where do you want these?" Adolfo asked his sisters.

When the girls turned around, the boys burst into laughter. "Your faces are caked in dirt!"

"Just put those over in the corner," Lucinda said with mock indignation.

Adolfo, Daniel, and Rocco set down their loads and then went back to look for more things. Adolfo was amazed by the bed frames and chests of drawers. His mind whirled with ways to make use of the items. Metal was new to him, but the parts and pieces of broken items seemed to have potential, and he relished the idea of constructing things. But for now, they needed to haul all of the stored items to the other bunker so this building could be fixed up, at least temporarily, for their family.

At his house, Chandi was busy with paper and pencil, figuring out the costs for buying extra hammocks and blankets, and the amounts and costs of goods to start their store.

Fidel relaxed in his hammock. The past days had taken their toll, and he didn't have any energy left. In his lap he held Felicidad, who was about two or so. He marveled at the little black girl with her tightly curled hair and huge brown eyes. He spoke to her in Nala, as though she could understand. Soon enough, both she and her sister would, he hoped.

Meanwhile, at Andrés' house, the huge man lounged in his hammock and watched his two new charges. Nacio and Miguel both appeared to be about four years old. They looked like they could have been his sons. Their curly black hair still showed signs of caked mud, and they had sores on their thin bodies from the filth they'd lived in for so many weeks. *I don't know what to do with them. How did I get myself into this?* And then his thoughts turned to Ruby—his daughter—and he resolved to make the boys a part of his life.

"Come on," he said. "We have work to do."

The boys jumped up from the floor and followed him out the door. In the fresh air they seemed to come alive. They ran toward the dogs, smiled, and then patted their backs. All four followed

Andrés to the building next door where Adolfo and his brothers were. Andrés peered up at the makeshift roof they'd put up to protect the items stored in this building, which had also temporarily housed Carlos' family. The tin had been scrounged from the other roofs they'd already replaced. The beams were good, but the rafters were rotten, and Andrés doubted the roof would hold through many more storms. Eventually, this building would be fixed up by the misioneros. But for now, it seemed to be the only available option for Flora and her children.

The little boys quickly tired of standing by Andrés' side while he contemplated the problem.

"Can we go to the river with the others?" Miguel asked.

Knowing that two older boys were guarding the landing, Andrés allowed Nacio and Miguel to join them. Rey and Reina ran happily ahead of the children.

Adolfo had been helping his brothers stack the remaining bedsprings, but he stopped and looked up at the beams that Andrés was staring at. Adolfo had an idea how to fix the roof, but he couldn't speak Spanish. Deep in thought, Adolfo helped Daniel and Rocco take the final load to the storage bunker.

That evening, the group sat around in Fidel's house once more. When they had all finished eating, Andrés brought up the problem about the roof.

The Outcasts

"Rainy season is here, and I don't think that roof is safe enough for Flora's family," Andrés said with concern.

"I promised that house to the misioneros, but I don't know when they'll return," Fidel said. And then in true Nala fashion Fidel recounted for the newcomers the events of the past six months. "The misioneros left Namuro about six months ago. When I returned from taking them downriver, I discovered that Victoria had given birth to twins. So we fled the village and sought refuge at Alberto and Moya's home. But when we arrived, we were told that Alberto had been missing for two weeks. We found him on the other shore, across the Grande. His leg had been badly broken when his canoe capsized. Andrés was caring for him.

"Three weeks later, Dalia, her baby, and Pepe joined us. She had been living at this camp since her canoe overturned while fleeing from Ulgana.

"Diego and Rico discovered us at Alberto's old homestead and tried to kill the twins, but Victoria and Paco fled in different directions with the babies. Antonio, Chandi, and I were returning from this camp when the attack occurred. When Andrés showed up with the dogs to return the canoe, he found the chiefs still looking for the twins. Diego, Rico, and the other men fled. The next day, we moved to this camp.

"The misioneros came with supplies and helped us repair the roof on Alberto's house. After they left, we repaired the roof on this house. Next, Carlos and his family were caught in floodwaters, and their canoe capsized at the same dangerous place where the Namuro River joins the Grande.

"Andrés' place flooded and he's joined our camp. Six weeks later, we found the six children in Cerro Alto, which had been destroyed by a mudslide. And now, Flora, you and your family have joined us.

"So much has happened in such a short amount of time. It feels as though the spirits are angry...and yet we've been protected on every side—not only have we been protected, but we've prospered. The misioneros have shared with us about the Perfect One. Victoria, Maamo, and Dalia have embraced the new trail of the Perfect Son. We want the misioneros to come live with us and teach us the new trail. I, too, believe that the Perfect Son is watching over us. I want to know more about His trail. We don't know when the misioneros will return, but you can use the house that will be theirs until they come back, and then we'll find a permanent dwelling for you. But we have to fix the roof first." Fidel had finished the lengthy chronology.

"I have an idea," Adolfo offered. "Let's go get thatch and poles and repair it with a Nala roof."

"There's no way to tie them into the cement blocks," said Fidel.

"I know," Adolfo countered, "but we could build a frame around the outside of the existing building and roof that frame."

Silence permeated the room as each person envisioned Adolfo's plan.

"That would work," Fidel affirmed. "Good thinking. The only problem is that it will be a lot of work for a temporary solution. The misioneros could come back any day, and I promised them that house."

Again, the group fell into silent contemplation.

Adolfo spoke once more. "We could build a Nala house between Alberto's and this house. It would provide more protection—the three houses would be attached. We'd need poles, bamboo for the two outside walls, and thatch for the roofing."

Flora liked the idea of extra protection.

Antonio spoke up next. "Why don't we go back to our old place and take down the garden house. We can reuse the thatch, bamboo siding, and the poles—all we'd have to gather is vine."

Once again Fidel was impressed. "Great idea," he praised Antonio. "Rocco, Daniel, Adolfo, Antonio, Chandi, Andrés, and I will go early tomorrow. We'll take both canoes. That leaves the women and children with you, Alberto."

Fidel hesitated while he sized up the youngsters; there were five boys who were four to five years old, and Rodrigo, who was eight. Having formulated a plan, he continued, "Rodrigo, you're the oldest. We need you to fish at the river and help watch for anyone who comes. The younger boys will take turns helping you. We have a whistle to blow if anybody comes. That means your father, any other Nala, or any outsider. Do you understand?" Rodrigo nodded his head solemnly.

Rodrigo thought about the shiny whistle on the shiny beaded string that he would be able to wear around his neck. He thought about how important the job would be—he had watched Antonio sitting on the bank with the whistle around his neck. Antonio had explained to him about the danger of any Nala or outsider who might come.

Fidel retrieved the whistle and told Rodrigo he could blow it once now for practice, but that he should never blow it again unless there was danger.

Rodrigo nodded, then blew into the whistle. As the loud, shrill sound permeated the small room, babies cried and little girls covered their ears and sought shelter in loving arms.

The other adults wondered whether Fidel was giving Rodrigo too much responsibility. But as they looked at the five other little boys who were wrestling together on the floor, they realized that their leader had a lot of insight.

Andrés' heart throbbed within his chest. "I have something to say," he blurted out before he could change his mind. "I, too, believe in Jesús. The night that we rescued Rodrigo, I called out to Jesús, the Son of Dios. I realized that I had blamed Dios for the death of my wife and family, but I called out for Him to save Rodrigo, and He did. I don't understand the ways of Dios, but I need Him and I want to know more about Him. I, too, have embraced Jesús and I want to learn more about Him and His ways. I just thought I should make that clear in front of all of you."

The Outcasts

The reflection of the flames from the fire danced happily around the tin roof as Chandi interpreted Andrés' words. All four of the new believers were rejoicing in their hearts, unaware of the great cloud of witnesses who were also rejoicing with them in heaven. The others reflected within themselves. They felt drawn toward this faith—yet pulled by the fear of the unknown, the fear of change, and the fear of losing what little control they had.

Chapter 36

At dawn, the women lit their fires. The men were anxious to get to the canoes and start the trip to Alberto's old homesite to disassemble the garden house for materials. So after quickly downing some cold leftover banana drink, the older boys and men swiftly exited their homes.

All day, Rodrigo remained perched on the bank where he'd been since dawn. He pulled in another fish, pleased that there would be food for the men when they returned. He looked up at the darkening sky which threatened a rainstorm. His eyes darted from the little boys playing farther upstream to the mouth of the river branch, where danger could arrive at any moment. A clash of thunder startled Rodrigo, making him lose the fish that had begun to nibble the crayfish on the hook. Just as he glanced up the river branch again, the first canoe laden with thatch came into his view.

The children scurried out of the stream and ran whooping and hollering toward the houses. But Rodrigo stayed at his post, even as great drops of rain began to pelt him and lightning crackled in the sky.

Fidel disembarked, secured the canoe, and waved for Rodrigo to come. The boy grabbed the vine which tethered his catch and sprinted alongside Fidel toward home.

The second canoe arrived, and Adolfo jumped out and secured it. A flash of lightning and clash of thunder sent him and the others with him running for cover.

That evening sitting around the fire, Fidel gave the account of their trip.

"Nala have been at the old site," Fidel soberly informed them.

"How recently?" Victoria questioned.

"The only footprints we found were inside the garden house... so, sometime before the last rain. The bamboo has grown up quite nicely, but it had been disturbed by whoever came."

Tension filled the room. Victoria trembled; she remembered sweeping the ground inside her house before leaving it. Thunder boomed loudly, adding to the strain that seemed unbearable. Rain pounded relentlessly on the roof as each person processed their own fears of the future.

"Tomorrow, if the weather's clear, we'll start building," Fidel declared. Then he added, "Rodrigo, that fish sure was good. We would have been very hungry tonight without the fish you caught for us."

Rodrigo beamed.

Later that night, Victoria lay still and silent in her hammock. Although exhausted, she couldn't turn her mind away from thoughts of her father. *I can't imagine Dad in Ulgana with* Ramiro! *Ramiro is such a wicked chief. I can't imagine Father no longer being the chief in Luwana! He was a good, strong, and capable man. That is, until he violated Dalia and disgraced himself. That was his ruin. It caused him to send me away—and now he's lost Mother and all the rest of the children! Poor Dad, will he ever be the same man he once was? Is there any hope for him? But...how can I feel sorry for him? He was going to give Lucinda to* Ramiro! Tears slid from her eyes and dropped on Susana's soft black hair as the baby cuddled closely to her mother. *How did my father turn into such a wicked, horrible man? He has beaten Lucinda and Mother, and he tried to hunt down and kill his own grandbabies! I'm afraid. What will he do next? We need help!* Immediately Victoria's mind turned to the Perfect One. *Can You help us? Is there any hope for my father?* Victoria thought about the misioneros, wishing Linda and Roberto would return soon. And in the midst of those thoughts, sleep mercifully claimed her.

Three days later, Flora and her children moved into their new house. Flora was pleased with the large dwelling that was sandwiched between two houses. Gingerly, she swept the dirt floor. She was still very stiff and bruised, and although each movement was painful, it felt good to make this house her own.

Adolfo, Daniel, and Chandi entered the dwelling, each hauling a large cooking log. They placed the logs so their ends met in the middle, where a fire would be built. Rocco arrived with kindling. He dumped it in the corner and then fished into his pocket for the stick matches that had been entrusted to him. With a huge smile, he handed them to his mother and then raced outside to join the other boys, who had already left the house.

Within minutes, the four boys returned, carrying hammocks, dishes, clothes, and other supplies. Flora was overwhelmed! The hammocks looked new, as well as the towels—and a bar of soap! Even though Victoria and Fidel were family, she hadn't expected them to share so freely with her. She tried hard not to think about the years that Maamo had lived destitute—she felt an ache in her heart that she hadn't given her mother-in-law a thought during those years. Tears spilled down her cheeks, her shoulders sagged, and she sighed. *They have accepted us, and have given us their best. They are different, and I want to be like them.*

Andrés carried a wooden table into Flora's hut and set it down in the corner nearest the fire. He wanted to ask where he should put it. He knew the Nala word for "where", but he couldn't force himself to try to say it out loud, so he turned and left. Chairs and benches arrived next, and Flora watched as if in a dream.

The Outcasts

Before her oldest son could leave, she said, "Adolfo, would you hang a hammock for me? I'm very tired."

Her son hurried to string the hammock for his mother. "Do you want me to hang the others now, too?" he asked.

"No, this is fine," Flora said, as she sank gently into the brightly colored, soft folds of woven fabric.

Adolfo watched his mother; he had been very protective of her since his father had beaten her. Although she obviously still hurt, Adolfo saw peacefulness in her eyes—a peacefulness which he hadn't seen for many years. Adolfo smiled and exited the house. If there was any more work to do, Adolfo wanted to help.

Flora lay back in the hammock and looked around her home. Her thoughts turned to Diego and her heart ached. *I don't want to think about him! I hate what he's become! I hate what he did to Dalia and what he became after that! How could he even consider giving Lucinda to Ramiro as a second wife! I did the right thing leaving him there. We had to get away. It was the right thing to do. As mean as he's become, I can't imagine what he'll do if he ever finds us.* A shiver ran down Flora's spine. Then she set her jaw firmly and raised her chin slightly. *Diego has put me through agony since he sent our Victoria away. I refuse to live in fear of that man.*

Chapter 37

Two weeks later, Fidel called a meeting at his house. The delightful aroma of freshly baked yeast rolls wafted into the room as Alberto and his family arrived carrying dozens of hot buns. Alberto tremendously enjoyed supplying his baked goods to the camp. He watched each person savor the bread, and was encouraged by the appreciation that clearly showed on their faces.

The meeting began casually with Maamo's statement, "I think we should name this place."

As usual, Chandi translated the discussion.

"Truly it has become a village for outcasts," Victoria said.

"It's a place of hope," Lucinda added with feeling.

"Yes, it gave me hope...and peace," Dalia said.

"The Spanish word for hope is *Esperanza*," Chandi informed the Nala speakers.

"Esperanza," echoed throughout the room.

"The Spanish word for peace is Paz—we could name it La Paz," Chandi offered as an alternative.

"Ahhh," echoed throughout the group.

"We have a lot of enemies," Andrés voiced. "To me, Esperanza sounds like a weak name for a town."

"What about Fortress of Hope?" Fidel asked.

"Fortaleza de Esperanza," Chandi said in Spanish.

The Nala speakers tried to say it, and laughed at their first efforts. Much to Alberto's surprise, even his wife mouthed the words.

"Let's think about it for a few days and maybe we'll have other ideas, too," Fidel suggested.

"As long as we're talking about names," Rosa interjected, "Dalia, have you named that baby yet? If you keep this up, she'll have teeth and be crawling and we'll still be calling her 'that baby.'"

Dalia blushed, but she had to smile at the laughter from her friends. "I don't know…" she hesitated. "So many names bring back bad memories. I'd like a new name for her—a new name for a new beginning."

Chandi thought, *Hmmm, new beginning. What if we name our village New Beginnings—its name doesn't have to be in Spanish; it could be in Nala. Each one of us has had a new start here.* But he kept the idea to himself.

Andrés sat deep in thought, too. *I wonder… why do the Nala give their children Spanish names? I don't know which names are familiar to Dalia. I'd hate to suggest one that would hurt her in some way.* And then before he could stop himself, he blurted out, "My mother's name is Sofía."

The Outcasts

"Sofía," Dalia whispered. "I've never heard that before. Sofía." She looked down at her precious baby. "She's four months old, but I couldn't bear to name her. I'm afraid for her," the wounded mother confessed.

"We'll do our best to protect her," Fidel offered sympathetically.

"I will name her Sofía," Dalia stated, with a rare smile that softened her features.

For the first time, Maamo realized that the past four months had brought back some youthfulness to Dalia's face and countenance. That hard, older-looking appearance had diminished. Maamo shook her head sadly, thinking, *I should have helped her. I was starving, myself, but if we'd worked together…. I should have helped her.*

In Ulgana, Ramiro was calling a meeting of his own. He blew three short bursts on the conch shell, signaling only the men to meet together in the run-down meetinghouse.

Before Diego could take his seat next to Ramiro, however, he was ordered to sit on the stool in the center!

Diego's jaw dropped. "What is this about?" he questioned gruffly.

"Take your seat," Ramiro boomed.

Stung with humiliation, Diego sat on the small stool.

Ramiro commenced the meeting. "Diego's family has left without permission; he has no control over them. We cannot allow this. Diego has no strength or credibility. He is no longer my co-chief.

"We're going to lose total control. We have to set down harsher rules and regain balance here in Ulgana." Ramiro stopped, pleased with the rapt attention he was getting.

"We know where Diego's family went," Carlos declared. "Let's go and bring them back!"

"From what you've told us," another man retorted, "we can't get back upriver without a motor. How will we get them out of that village of theirs and return here?"

Carlos sat down to think his plan through a little better.

Diego stood up and declared, "This is all Fidel's fault. He's the person we need to get rid of. He *stole* my family away!"

Carlos narrowed his eyes and said, "Lucinda *begged* Fidel to take them away from here. Your own son carried your wife to the canoe. They left you willingly."

Diego sat back down. His pulse raced and his face burned in mortification. But, he was tired of this treatment—he refused to be weak any longer. He bounded to his feet and yelled, "They left because *Ramiro* wanted Lucinda for his second wife!"

Men gasped, and jaws dropped. The room grew deathly quiet as Diego and Ramiro glared viciously at one another.

"You agreed!" Ramiro yelled. "You planned to take a second wife, too. We agreed that Ulgana is dying away. We need more people, more strength, and more power!"

"Stop!" yelled Tomás, one of the younger men. "You two had no right to go behind our backs with your evil plans! Who were you giving to Diego for his wife?" the young man demanded.

Ramiro held his tongue. He had to handle this carefully—to regain control.

"Marta!" Diego blurted out.

"Nooo!" the young man yelled. "Ramiro, how could you? You know that I plan to marry your daughter Marta." Enraged, he lunged at Ramiro, and the room exploded into action.

Older men held back young Tomás.

"Everybody sit down!" Ramiro demanded. "I was going to talk to you today," he lied. "Ulgana is in trouble. We need to build up our village."

Many of the older men began to contemplate the idea of taking younger girls as their second wives.

Tomás was horrified, but silenced himself thinking, *I have to get Marta away from here. I have to rescue her. But what about the other young women—how can I just leave them to this fate?* As the meeting continued, Tomás forced himself to listen, realizing that if he pretended to go along, he might have a better chance to help Marta.

Diego's reprimand had been forgotten, so he sat down on a bench, away from the chief.

Ramiro had gained control and Diego was no longer co-chief, so Ramiro decided to let the man slink away without any punishment.

The darkening sky ended the meeting. Each man had much to think about as he ambled to his own house.

But Tomás, instead of going home, took a detour. He walked toward his family's bathing area. Before he reached the river, however, he sprinted into the jungle foliage toward the chief's family's bathing spot. He hid, hoping to hear Marta's voice at the river. His heart raced, fearing he would get caught and would be accused of spying on the chief's daughters as they bathed. He could hear several people—Marta, her sisters, and the chief's wife. Tomás wasn't sure what to do next. When the women got out of the river and wrapped their skirts around themselves for the walk home, he averted his eyes. When he looked again, Marta was on the path to her house, ready to disappear into the thick stand of trees.

Very softly, Tomás whistled. Marta turned around. He stepped out of his hiding place, and Marta's hand flew to her mouth. Her eyes widened, thinking that Tomás could have been spying on her—that he could have seen her bathing! Her face burned crimson, but before she could scream or run, Tomás spoke quietly. "Wait, Marta—please hear what I have to say."

Something in Tomás' voice stopped Marta. But she backed away from him when he walked toward her.

Tomás stopped and said, "Marta, the men are talking about taking second wives...young women...you're in danger, Marta."

Tears ran down the beautiful young woman's cheeks. Then she said, "Lucinda told me that my father was going to marry her, and that I was to marry Diego. I thought she was trying to cause problems here by saying such awful things. But when she left I wondered whether she had been telling the truth—though I didn't want to believe it! What am I going to do?"

The terror in her eyes was all that Tomás needed to see. "I'll find a way, Marta. I'll take you away from here and we'll be married." Tomás reddened, although in the now-dark sky, Marta couldn't see it. "That is, if you want to marry me. I was afraid that you would marry Raul," Tomás said.

"My father wanted me to marry Raul, but it was you who I wanted to marry," Marta admitted softly. "But how? When? I'm afraid."

"There's some moonlight tonight. Perhaps we can see well enough to get to Luwana. Surely the chief there will put a stop to this," Tomás said.

Suddenly they heard footsteps. "Marta! Where are you?" the girl's mother called from up the trail.

Silently, Tomás slipped back into the dense tangle of trees and vines.

"I'm coming," Marta called out, hoping her mother wouldn't come any closer.

"It's dark out!" the woman reprimanded, as she hurried into the clearing. "Come home now!"

"Yes, mother," Marta said, and walked up the trail, not knowing when or where to meet Tomás.

The young man watched Marta retreat along the trail. He sprinted back to his bathing area and rinsed off in the river. Even though it was too dark to bathe safely, he didn't want to go home without an excuse for the extra time he'd taken.

He walked into his hut and sat down by the fire. His mother handed him a large gourd filled with warm banana drink. He drank it down and then sat staring into the flames, trying to solidify his plans. *It's very dangerous on the trail at night. While we were hunting last week, we saw signs of panthers and of course, snakes. Then, the spirits...* Tomás shuddered involuntarily. He felt like his world had been turned upside down. *What if the chief in Luwana won't help us? We're leaving without permission...what if Luwana has become as evil as this village? I don't know what to do.* And then it occurred to him. *We should try to find Fidel's camp. Carlos said they take in outcasts—that they've all been banished. If we flee from here, we'll be outcasts, too.*

The young man sat in turmoil for many minutes, until his father announced that he was going out for a while. His look told Tomás to stay—and to keep his mouth shut. Tomás knew that he had to move quickly; he felt that Marta and the other young women were in imminent danger. *How many unmarried young women live here?* Tomás wondered, letting his mind take him from one

The Outcasts

hut to the next. Including Marta and his own sister, Amalia, there were five girls of marrying age. *It would be too risky to alert all of them, and we'd never get away without being caught. I should just take Marta and go.* Tomás looked across the fire at Amalia, who sat innocently roasting a plantain in the flames.

He was startled by the male voice calling out, "Tomás!"

"Come in," Tomás responded to his friend, Pedro.

Pedro stood at the doorway and replied, "Let's go find Alec."

Tomás went outside with his friend, but Pedro led him down the path toward the river instead of to Alec's house.

"Tomás, you heard what they said in the meeting. I think the older men, who already have wives, are going to take our young women and leave us with nobody! Besides, I, uh, I've liked Amalia for a long time. I want to marry your sister. I *can't* let this happen!" Pedro's voice was low but emphatic.

"I know. I want to marry Marta. But what about the other young women? You have two sisters who are now marrying age, and Marta has one. Well, at least that's only three households. Maybe we could do it," Tomás said.

"Do you have a plan?"

"We need to take a canoe and find Fidel's village. But I think we have to go tonight. How can we get the word to the girls? The more people we tell, the more likely we are to get caught. And what if they don't want to leave?" Tomás asked, nervously.

Pedro and Tomás sat down on a log near the river. The moonlight sparkled on the rippling water. Tomás' father's large canoe sat enticingly nearby. Wordlessly, they nodded their heads at each other. The unknowns lurked heavily in their minds, but the young men knew they could not live with the repercussions of staying.

"I know!" Tomás said. "Amalia needs some blue thread."

"What difference does that make?" Pedro asked.

"I have a plan—our parents always make us escort our sisters if they go anywhere at night. Go back to your house. We'll come by looking for thread, and you three join us in the search." Tomás stood up and sucked in a deep breath.

Pedro and Tomás hurried back to their homes. The older men were still away. Tomás sat back down near the fire. When his mother went to quiet his baby brother, Tomás got to his feet and ambled over to Amalia.

"Did you say you needed blue thread?" he asked.

Amalia looked blankly at her brother, who was acting very strange. "Yes," she answered.

"I think Marta has some," he informed her.

"No, she doesn't..." Amalia said loudly. But the look on her brother's face stopped her from saying more.

"I'll take you over to see," Tomás offered.

"Okay..." Amalia agreed warily.

"Mother, Amalia needs to borrow some thread, so I'm going with her to find some," Tomás called out, as he prodded his sister toward the door.

Once outside, Amalia said, "What are you doing?"

"Walk," Tomás ordered. "We're going to Marta's for thread."

They called out at Marta's door.

"Come in," Marta's mother offered.

"My sister needs blue thread," Tomás stated. "Do you have any?"

"No, not blue," Marta answered.

"We'll go to Pedro's house, then. Maybe they have some," Tomás stated. "I'm surprised you and your sister aren't asking to go with Amalia; usually you girls love to get out at night, and I'm already stuck escorting." He chuckled.

Marta's mother knew that Tomás liked her daughter. She enjoyed the flirting, and couldn't see any harm in letting her two daughters go look for thread with Tomás and his sister. So the young ladies quickly followed them out of their hut and toward Pedro's house.

The scene was the same at Pedro's, only Tomás said, "Pedro, I'm outnumbered—why don't you come along."

The noisy group walked toward the next hut and asked for blue thread, but when they were turned away empty-handed, Tomás whispered, "Girls, be quiet—really quiet. I want to show you something at the river." He led them back toward the trail behind his house.

When they arrived, he told them to get into the canoe and stay very quiet. The girls all looked skeptically at one another, but Marta had figured it out. She said, "It's okay, get in. We'll explain everything to you." One by one they silently filed into the dugout and sat down. With long poles in hand, Pedro and Tomás pushed them out into the middle of the river and catapulted them swiftly downstream.

"Where are you taking us?" Marta's sister demanded.

"Quiet," Marta admonished. "We're in trouble," she whispered. "Lucinda wasn't lying when she told me that I would have to marry Diego, and that she was going to marry our dad!"

"No!" All the girls in the canoe chorused in hushed tones.

Then Tomás spoke up. "You're all in danger of becoming second wives. We didn't know how else to protect you."

Stunned, they all sat in silence.

"But what about Mother?" Amalia groaned. "Our mothers will be so worried, and I don't want to live somewhere else without my family! Where are you taking us?"

"We're going to find Fidel's village. If any of you decide you want to come back, I'll find a way to get you back here. But maybe our leaving will alert the women to what is being planned, before one or all of you are sacrificed," Tomás told them. "I don't want to take you against your will, though. It isn't too late to turn back now. But all of us have to agree...and I don't think we'll have a second chance."

The young women huddled silently together. They didn't want to leave—but they knew they couldn't stay. In turmoil they watched as the silhouettes of the only homes they'd ever known faded into the dark shadows of night.

Chapter 38

Tomás and Pedro guided the craft to the center channel, allowing the swift current to carry them along. Standing, poles in hand, they watched for rocks in the shallow tributary. Both young men were haunted by the enormity of what they'd just done, yet they could not justify staying.

Time crept by, until finally they neared the mouth of their waterway, which spilled into the Grande River. Tomás and Pedro had traversed these merging currents many times before, but only in daylight; and, they had always gone *up* the Grande River, never down. But the young men had listened raptly to Carlos' tales. With ease, they navigated the canoe into the broad river. They sat down and allowed the swift current to propel them toward their unknown future.

Tomás and Pedro studied the shoreline, watching carefully for the Namuro River. Endlessly, it seemed, trees flashed by, with no sound or sight of the waterway that would signal the closeness of Fidel's village.

The Outcasts

Finally, the five girls began to talk. Gladys said, "Pedro, we didn't bring anything with us. We don't have our hammocks, extra clothes, my chickens! I don't have anything! Are you sure that Fidel will allow us to stay in his village?"

Before Pedro could answer, his sister said, "I don't need blue thread anymore. I don't have my fabric for the new blouse I was sewing."

The girls all giggled—nervous chuckles that somehow released some of the stress.

"Fidel took Lucinda's family back with him, and they didn't take anything with them, either," Pedro said. "Besides, you've heard Carlos' and Edilma's stories—Fidel's group seems to have more things than our villagers have."

"Since when can we believe anything that Carlos and Edilma say?" Marta asked.

Tomás sighed heavily. *I didn't think about* that. His stomach lurched. *We're committed! I need to reassure the others.* "We *had* to leave. If we can't stay there, we'll go to Namuro and get help from Rico, the chief. Ulgana is *not* following the Nala way. Ramiro and Diego *must* be stopped."

"You're right," Marta agreed in her soft, encouraging voice. "It's good that you helped us. We'll all work this out together."

"Shhh," Pedro demanded.

The sound of rushing water greeted their ears. Pedro and Tomás stood and plunged their poles into the dark current. They propelled the canoe toward the shoreline and guided it slowly

The Outcasts

toward the currents of the Namuro River. But the strong Grande wildly swept the craft back again to the middle of the river, away from the Namuro. Tomás and Pedro fought the current, thrusting the boat toward the shoreline again. When they finally stopped the craft, they searched the bank for signs of a village.

But it was very late. No glow from fires lit the sky. No voices or barking dogs could be heard. Only silence.

Chapter 39

At dawn a damp, dense fog enshrouded the camp, entrapping the drifting smoke beneath its thick layer. In each household, crackling flames and the aroma of burning wood enticed the children to bound from their hammocks in eager anticipation of breakfast.

Fidel, however, stayed in his hammock and rocked to and fro. His heart was heavy, weighed down with the enormity of the past months. Slow-paced village life seemed like a dull blur somewhere in his memory. *It all started when I went to Luwana,* Fidel thought. *Is it possible that was only three-and-a-half years ago? Did breaking out of our Nala way bring about all of these disasters? Are the spirits angry? We've been driven out of Namuro, we have enemies on every side, and our twins' lives are still in danger. And Cerro Alto—the whole town was destroyed...everyone except six small children! But, how can I think this way? Many more good things have happened! I have Victoria and our three wonderful daughters. Rosalinda is two-and-a-half years old; she's beautiful, healthy, and happy. Isabel and Susana are nearly six months old—*

chubby and strong, and such joys. I'm so thankful we were able to bring Maamo to live with us. Surely, by now, she would have starved to death in Ulgana if we hadn't rescued her. And the gold that she gave us has saved our lives...she has given so much back to us. Maybe that's what life should be about—passing along good to others.

Why don't I feel at peace inside? Alberto was rescued from his canoe accident, and his family survived because we had to flee Namuro, and we sought refuge with them. It's curious how all of these circumstances have worked together for all of our good. Now we have Andrés, Rodrigo, the six children from Cerro Alto, and of course Dalia, Pepe, and Sofía. Dalia, poor Dalia...it still sickens my heart that two of our chiefs violated that poor girl. And, as if that weren't bad enough, many other men mistreated her regularly after that. I'm so thankful that she has a safe place here with us. Dalia has been different since she declared her belief in the Perfect One. Maamo and Victoria embraced Him, too. I want to know more; I want the misioneros to come live with us and teach us. So much is happening so fast, I feel like things are spinning out of control. I can't do all of this on my own. And I have become a chief. I need help. Perfect One, if You can hear me, I need You.

At mid-morning, the dull hum of an airplane motor caught the attention of the camp. Elated, Fidel realized again how much he wanted to talk to Roberto. He needed the misionero's advice on things, and he also wanted to accept the Perfect Son and learn more about Him. *Surely He is good,* Fidel thought. *Look how quickly He's answered my call for help!*

The red and white plane touched down on the concrete airstrip and slowed to a stop, just past the middle of the long runway. The engine roared as the pilot turned the Cessna around, taxied to a spot near the houses, and turned off the engine. Excitedly, everyone swarmed around the plane, waiting for the misioneros to exit the craft. Victoria hovered near the front of the group, eager to see Linda's new baby.

Bob stepped out first, and reached for his two-month-old daughter. With his free hand he helped his wife from the plane. Kimberly jumped into her mother's waiting arms and then just as quickly wiggled to be let down to the ground. Kimberly smiled broadly and ran to Rosalinda, eager to renew their old friendship. Victoria proudly handed Susana to Linda and reached for the baby in Bob's arms.

"Her name is Lisa," said Linda.

"Lisa." Victoria repeated the name while she carefully looked over the chubby white baby's form. *The poor little thing doesn't have any hair!* Victoria lamented to herself.

"Susana is beautiful!" Linda proclaimed, happy to speak the Nala language again. "Where is her twin sister?"

Rosa stepped forward with Isabel, but the baby howled in dismay at the sight of the white woman. Linda laughed softly and said, "They're identical, and adorable, Victoria!"

"Fidel," Bob said, "what happened to Cerro Alto?"

"A mudslide," Fidel informed him. "When we traveled there to buy supplies, we found only six small children who'd lived through it. We brought them here." Fidel waved his hand toward the retreating group.

The missionary was amazed. "Fidel, we also saw a canoe at the shore halfway between Cerro Alto and this camp. They weren't going anywhere; it didn't look right to us. There were five Nala women and two Nala men. Do you know anything about them?"

"No," Fidel answered. "Nala women don't usually go to town, not five women and two men...unless there's a problem." Deep in thought, Fidel rubbed his forehead. "If they're from Namuro, I can't lead them to our village. But soon enough, I'm sure that everyone will know where we're at, anyway."

Fidel sighed heavily and looked into Bob's eyes. "Roberto," the young man said, "I'm not sure what to do. Our camp is very vulnerable now. I was just calling out to the Perfect One asking for help, hoping you'd come back. And here you are."

Bob's eyes moistened. "I can help you find the Perfect One. He has been waiting for you. And the Perfect Son is the way to the Perfect One. He says, 'I am the way, and the truth, and the life. No man comes to the Perfect Father except through me.'

"All of us have sinned. Do you remember when I talked to you about that?"

"Yes, I know that I've done bad things—I'm a sinner."

"The Perfect One says the penalty for sin is death. But He sent His Perfect Son to die in your place—for your sins. The Perfect

Son died for *you*, Fidel, and He wants you to accept Him and become a child of the Perfect One."

"Will the Perfect Son become my chief? Is that what you mean?"

Bob hesitated for a moment and then said, "In some ways it will be like that, but it's so much more. The Perfect Son is not like any of your chiefs, because He has never sinned.

"He is the way—the trail to the Perfect One. He is the truth— His Book is completely true. He is life—when you trust in Him, you have eternal life.

"I wish I had more Nala words so I could explain it to you more thoroughly. That's why I want to translate the Perfect One's Book into your language, so you can learn all about Him."

"Roberto, I do believe in the Perfect Son—that He died for my sins. I want to walk His trail."

Right there on the airstrip, Fidel nodded his assent and Bob led him in prayer. When they were finished, Bob suggested that they pray again. This time he talked to God about the camp's need for protection and for wisdom about the Nala in the canoe. Fidel was amazed at how easily the misionero talked with the Perfect One, as if He were a friend standing right there beside them.

Fidel remained silent for a few moments. He sighed, then a peaceful smile spread across his face. The *Perfect Son died for me!* Fidel thought, as he began his new life in Christ.

Then Fidel told Bob about Carlos and his family, whose canoe had overturned in the flood waters. And he told him that Victoria's mother and siblings had escaped her father and were living at their camp, too. Bob was amazed, and understood why his friend was overwhelmed. The missionary realized that God was at work among the Nala Nation.

"Well, Fidel," he said, "I think we should go and help the people in the canoe. I believe that the Perfect One wants us to help others, and to rely on Him to help and protect us."

"Okay," Fidel responded, relieved to have his friend's advice.

When they rejoined the group, Fidel addressed them while Chandi translated. "The misioneros saw seven Nala in a canoe downriver from us. They appeared to need help. There are five women and two men, so we don't need to go into the bunker—but be on guard! Andrés, Adolfo, and Chandi—come with Roberto and me."

Victoria had been so caught up with Linda's arrival that she hadn't seen the terror on her mother and sister's faces when the airplane landed and when they glimpsed the white people disembarking from the "canoe" that flies in the air like a bird. Her brothers, too, were awestruck. Two worlds had collided for people whose lives had once been suspended in time by isolation.

Chapter 40

The drone of a boat motor alerted Tomás and Pedro to an oncoming craft. Anxiously, they shielded their eyes against the sun glaring off the rippling, green-blue surface of the water. The girls, still huddled together in the center of the canoe, raised their heads, hopeful to be rescued, yet fearful of the awful noise that they'd only heard about around their fires at night. The group strained their necks, trying to recognize who might be in the speeding vessel.

Moments later, Fidel's canoe pulled alongside the young people. He greeted them and then asked, "What village are you from?"

Tomás said, "We're from Ulgana. We recognize you from your visit to our village—when you took Maamo away."

"Yes," Fidel answered. *I'm sure they do recognize me!* "Why have you traveled so far from home?"

"We need help," Tomás declared. "We heard that you take in people when they're in need. We were hoping to find you. Will you help us?"

Could this be a trap? Fidel wondered. But he looked at the forlorn group. *I wonder if these young women are escaping from Ramiro and Diego's evil plans.*

"Yes, of course we'll try to help you. You can tell us the whole story when we get you back to the camp. Then we'll decide what to do."

Fidel turned his boat around and pulled alongside the other craft. The girls covered their noses to ward off the pungent odor of gasoline. Pedro and Tomás grabbed the coarse wooden side of Fidel's canoe, and the motor revved to life, propelling both of the crafts upriver.

Several hours later, they gathered around the blazing fire in Fidel's house. The peculiar White Ones had been introduced to them as "misioneros," whatever that was supposed to mean. The strange white family was friendly, though, and they spoke their language. The block walls of the house felt cold and confining, but the crackling fire began to have a calming effect on the worn-out group, and the newcomers began to relax.

Tomás knew that it was time to relay the account of their escape. When he began, everyone stared with rapt attention. Lucinda joined the other young women, empathizing with them. Tears streamed down Marta's cheeks as she choked out her apology. "Lucinda, I'm so sorry I didn't believe you when you tried to warn me!"

"I understand," Lucinda responded. "I'm just so thankful that you're safe now."

At those words, however, Fidel's stomach lurched. *Safe, are any of us really safe?* But then he remembered the Perfect One and silently said to Him, *We need you, Perfect One. Please help us. Show us the trail.*

For hours the group talked. Finally the conversation turned to the misioneros. Fidel asked Bob, "Roberto, when are you moving here? Are you ready to fix up your house?" All eyes turned to the white man whose infant was cradled in his left arm.

"I have bad news for you," Bob stated. His eyes moistened involuntarily, and he cleared his throat. "Two of our mission leaders were killed in an accident. Their families returned to the United States. I've been asked to stay in the city and be one of the mission leaders. It..." Bob's voice broke, and he fought to control his emotions. "It isn't what I want, but I believe it's what the Perfect One wants me to do—at least until we get more misioneros who can take the place of our leaders there. But as soon as we can, we'll come here to live and to teach you more about the Perfect One."

Fidel's shoulders sagged. Dalia sank back farther into the dark shadows in the corner where she sat. Tears spilled from her eyes, tears that had threatened their release as more and more people from Ulgana had arrived. In her mind, they threatened to encroach upon the safety and peace of her new life. Discouraged, she contemplated where she could go. She had just begun to feel like a new person with hope for a new beginning, but the old life kept following her around. She looked at the group of young women—

so innocent and hopeful. *They* had been rescued. Dalia sucked in a breath, horrified that for even a moment she could have resented them. *I'm sorry!* Dalia thought. *I'm thankful that they're all safe. I would never want anyone to go through the horrors that I lived through. I'm safe now, too. I like it here—I'm happy. I don't have to live in the past; I am new and I have a new life.*

Bob spoke to the group once more. "I don't know how long it'll be until we can move here, but we'll come for visits as often as we can. I brought a Spanish Bible to give you. It's the Book about the trail of the Perfect One. Chandi, do you know how to read?"

"Yes," Chandi replied. "My father taught Antonio and me to read. We don't have many books, though."

Bob wondered how well Chandi could read. *The Bible isn't an easy book to comprehend, even for an experienced reader,* he thought. *Chandi is obviously very bright, but the truths in God's Word need to be clear to these dear people. And Chandi isn't saved yet. But reading God's Word is the best way for a person to get saved.*

Finally Bob spoke again. "I want to translate the Perfect One's Book into Nala. I had hoped to move here and do that. But the longer I'm away from you, the harder it will be for me to keep the Nala language clear enough in my mind to translate. Would it be possible for Chandi to come out to the city to live with us and help me translate the Perfect One's Book?"

Chandi's eyes widened. He was exhilarated at the mere thought of this new experience. But when he translated the misionero's words, his father's features tensed in dismay. Chandi bit his lip and held his tongue.

Overwhelmed, Fidel addressed the group. "It's very late. We've had a long day, and we have a lot to think about. Tomorrow we'll meet again. We have many decisions to make, but for tonight we need to find space for everyone to sleep."

Rosa rolled her eyes. *Maybe we should stop buying hammocks,* she thought. *Every time we buy more hammocks, we fill them up and then need to buy more again. At least this time they aren't small children. We do have more workers and not just more mouths to feed.*

The following evening, the large group met once again. Fidel began by saying, "First we must decide about Chandi. Should we allow him to go with the misioneros to live?"

Chandi interpreted.

"No!" Alberto demanded.

Chandi lowered his head, and he couldn't meet his father's eyes.

"Chandi," Fidel said, "I agree, we need you here to translate for us. I don't know what we'd do without you. But, we also want to learn more about the Perfect One's trail. Roberto needs help to translate the Book for us, but we need an interpreter here, too."

Discussions erupted around the crowded room.

Antonio spoke up and everyone quieted. "I can speak both Spanish and Nala."

"We need you, too," Fidel said. "You provide the majority of our meat!"

"No," the boy almost stammered. "I mean, I don't want to go with Roberto. I can stay here and interpret like Chandi does."

Chandi breathed a sigh of relief. Thinking that his brother might go instead of him had made his heart skip a beat. He desperately wanted to experience the city, to learn more, *and* to help to translate a book! He felt a small glimmer of hope. But then he looked at his father and saw his narrowed eyes and the stubborn set to his jaw.

Fidel spoke once again. "Whoever is in favor of Chandi going with Roberto, stand."

Once translated, Alberto erupted in anger. "I'm his father and I said *no*! This group *cannot* decide for me what my son should do."

Chandi reluctantly interpreted his father's angry words to the astounded group.

Fidel spoke again. "I'm sorry, Alberto. I forgot that you aren't Nala. This is the Nala way, to decide as a group. I also thought you didn't want Chandi to go because we needed him here as an interpreter. Obviously you have other reasons. Do you want to share those with us?"

Alberto was taken aback by Fidel's compassion. He formulated his thoughts in his head; but, wondering whether he could share his fears so openly, his heart raced. He took in a deep breath and began. "I grew up in an orphanage in the city. It was a horrible place. If Chandi goes and is unhappy, he would have no way to let

The Outcasts

us know, or to get back home when he wants to. The only life he's ever known is here. None of us really know how the misioneros live. The people who ran the orphanage claimed to be religious, too. They were highly respected by many people, but behind closed doors they were monsters."

Moya listened to her oldest son as he translated the account of her husband's past—the past that she had wondered about so often. She knew he had somehow been wounded, but her heart ached at the cruelty he must have endured. Part of her longed to know the whole story, but the other part felt she couldn't bear to know all of the details.

Bob addressed Alberto. "I fully respect how you feel. You're a good father, and you're absolutely right to want to be sure of where you send your son. And you don't really know me. If you would like to come to live with us for a few weeks along with your son, you're welcome to. If you just don't want to let Chandi go, you have every right to say 'no'—you are his father. We'll find another way to translate the Book. Even though Chandi is very gifted with languages, I could translate with a Nala speaker who doesn't know Spanish." The missionary surreptitiously surveyed the group, looking for a possible substitution.

Alberto examined his son's face. *He's such a good boy. He is very talented in languages, and other studies as well. I often wished I could give him a real education, but I don't want him to go to the city. What should I do?* He turned his gaze to his wife and thought, *I wonder how Moya feels about this. I wish I could talk* to her. *How have we lived these years together without communicating?* Out loud he said to Bob, "Are you leaving tomorrow?"

"Yes," the missionary affirmed.

"I need more time to consider this," Alberto stated with finality.

The meeting went on to the issue of Ulgana. After much discussion it was agreed that Tomás, Pedro, and the young women should go to Namuro and tell the chief about Ramiro and Diego's evil plans for their village. The group would pole Alberto's small canoe upriver, and while they were there, they would find out if Fidel would be allowed to come and speak with the village about trading with Namuro, now that Cerro Alto had been destroyed.

Bob had been praying silently through the entire meeting, and he continued his ongoing dialogue with the Lord. *No wonder we've been so burdened for them all these months. Lord, please bless the new believers here, and continue to draw the others to Yourself as they take this huge step. Father, please protect these young people tomorrow, and give them the words to clearly communicate with the village. Lord, please soften the hearts of the people in Namuro. And Lord, I pray for Your protection of everyone here; after tomorrow, they'll be even more vulnerable at this camp.*

Before closing the meeting, Fidel directed his attention to Bob and asked simply, "Would you sell your boat motor to us?"

Bob was caught off guard by the request, but recovered quickly. "You have full use of it—why do you want to buy it?"

"We need a motor to start a trading post here. We'll have to make numerous trips to Avanzada for supplies, and if we trade with

Namuro and sell their crops downriver, we'll possibly have loads of produce to haul. We've only used your motor out of necessity, and we have appreciated that very much. But we need a motor of our own," Fidel explained. "Or, could you buy a new one for us in town and fly it in?"

"It makes more sense for you to buy the one that's already here, especially because we won't need it for a while. Yes, you can buy our motor."

The missionary was pleased that Fidel didn't want to abuse the privilege of using the motor or to take advantage of him. It was a good start for a new believer—a very good start indeed.

Chapter 41

Tomás and Pedro poled the small canoe up the shallow river. As the group rounded the final bend, they heard the laughter of children playing in the first bathing spot of the village. Excitedly, the young ones ran from the river and up the path to alert their families that visitors had arrived.

Rico and three other men appeared at the river's edge to see who the travelers were.

"How did you greet the dawn?" Tomás said.

"Good, and you?" the chief replied.

"Good, too. We're from Ulgana, and we need to speak with you," Tomás informed the men.

"From Ulgana? Nobody has ever arrived here by river from Ulgana," Rico said suspiciously. "And this looks like Alberto's canoe."

"Yes, it is. We'd like to explain everything to you. We need your help," the young man implored, while the five young women cringed as they sat huddled together in the center of the craft.

Rico's eyes narrowed. *They're from Ulgana, and they've asked for our help. We need to at least hear what they have to say. Besides, when they do go, we'll be prepared to follow them. They could lead us right to Fidel.*

"I'll call a village meeting. Come," the chief consented.

Tomás and Pedro ran the canoe up onto the muddy bank, and they all got out. The young men pulled the boat firmly onto the shore and then led the way up a path toward the village that they'd only heard about in stories.

Thud, thud, thud, thud…the rhythmic sound of girls pounding rice met their ears before they arrived at the first hut.

"How did you greet the dawn?" a woman called out from her door, very curious about the travelers.

"Good, and you?" echoed the seven visitors.

"Good, too. Enter," offered the woman. "Sit down. I'll get you some banana drink."

Tomás led the way into the hut and sat on a nearby bench. They answered questions about their family ties. But when barraged by questions about why they had come, and why their families would permit young unmarried people to travel so far alone, they were uncomfortable. Pedro and Tomás exchanged looks and then stood to their feet.

"We'll explain everything at the meeting Rico is calling. We're gone," Tomás said, and led their group out the door.

They greeted people as they headed for the center of the village, where they knew the meetinghouse would be. Tomás'

The Outcasts

group entered the large, thatched-roof structure and sat on benches to wait for people to arrive. Nervously, Pedro scuffed his bare foot back and forth through the dirt, burrowing a hole in the cool, hard earth. Tomás peered through the gaps in the uneven bamboo siding of the structure. Marta ran her fingers along the rough, hand-hewn log that served as the bench that she sat on, while she gazed lovingly at Tomás. Marta's younger sister Erica sat close to Amalia, Gladys and Hilda.

Ooooo, droned the low call of the conch shell, signaling for *everyone* to gather for the meeting. Women hurriedly donned their best blouses and newest wraparound skirts, eager to learn the details about the visitors who'd arrived by river. They took seats in the women's half of the large common building.

Men sauntered in casually and sat in their section. The last person to arrive was Rico.

The chief remained standing and said, "I've called this meeting today because these seven young people have arrived from Ulgana. They have requested our help." He nodded at Tomás, who appeared to him to be their spokesperson.

Tomás stood before the group and introduced himself, explaining who his parents were. He introduced Pedro and his sisters Gladys and Hilda, his own sister Amalia, and then Marta and Erica, the daughters of Ramiro, chief of Ulgana.

Murmurs filled the room.

"They're from Ulgana? Traveling by river?"

"Ulgana allowed unmarried young people to travel alone?"

"The chief's daughters?"

"Why would Ramiro allow his own daughters to travel with this group?"

"We would never allow this in Namuro!"

Tomás waited before he would go on. Eager to learn more, the group quieted.

"Diego was exiled to our village when the people of Luwana discovered that he had violated Dalia. After he arrived, Ramiro made Diego his co-chief." Tomás paused again when another discussion ensued among the listeners.

"Co-chief?"

"The Nala have never had two chiefs at the same time!"

"Who do they think they are?"

But soon the group averted their full attention to Tomás, waiting for his next words.

The young man took a deep breath to calm his nerves. "Ramiro and Diego arranged to take second wives."

"No!"

"It can't be true!"

"Second wives?"

Rico shouted above the din of voices. "Quiet down! Tomás, are you sure about this?"

"Yes. Diego's family fled from the village because his daughter Lucinda was going to be forced to marry Ramiro. Ramiro was furious that she had escaped, so he called a meeting and told Diego that he was no longer his co-chief. Diego was so angry, he

The Outcasts

exposed Ramiro's plan to marry his daughter Lucinda. He then admitted that he himself was going to take Ramiro's daughter Marta as his second wife."

Marta bowed her head in humiliation. Heated discussions broke out all through the assembly.

Rico demanded order and then directed another question to Tomás. "Didn't the other men in the village stop Ramiro?"

"No. Ramiro talked with the men about them also taking second wives. He said that Ulgana was dying away. Later that night, the married men had a secret meeting. Pedro and I escaped in my father's canoe with the five young women who are of marrying age."

Tomás explained about Carlos and Edilma's canoe accident, and how Fidel and his group had rescued them. He told them that when Fidel took Carlos and his family back to Ulgana, Diego's family fled with Fidel to protect Lucinda from marrying Ramiro. Then Tomás filled them in about their own escape and rescue.

"So, you know where Fidel lives?" Rico asked, to get it out in the open.

"Yes," Tomás admitted. "Fidel would like permission to come and speak..." but the crowd's boisterous reaction stopped Tomás from continuing.

After many minutes of heated discussion Tomás declared, "Let me finish!" The harshness startled even him, but it also gave him the courage to stand up for Fidel and to speak his own mind. "Fidel is a good man. Yes, he has veered from some Nala customs—but for good. Ramiro and Diego have veered from other Nala customs—but for evil! We must stop Ulgana, but please consider uniting with Fidel."

"Uniting with Fidel?"

"Who does this young man think he is?"

"He talks like he has authority; this is what comes from a young man breaking away and thinking he knows better than the chiefs and the older men!"

Tomás realized that he had to continue. "Cerro Alto has been destroyed by a mudslide. Now there's nowhere for you to sell your crops or to buy supplies. Fidel wants to help you."

The group fell silent, contemplating Tomás' words.

Rico said, "How can Fidel help us?"

"The spirits have not been angry with Fidel for saving his daughters' lives. In fact, he has prospered. He wants to buy your crops and to sell you supplies, or to trade for goods."

The room exploded at this new information. Optimistically, Luisa searched her mother Ana's eyes. After all, they were related to Rosa and Fidel. Luisa desperately missed her friend Victoria. Hope began to blossom in the young woman's heart.

The meeting continued for hours. The intense afternoon sun parched the bare ground outside and permeated the thatch, producing stifling heat inside. The women sat fanning themselves, with little relief. Luisa fingered the rough, handmade fan which her husband had woven from palm leaves—as it had dried out, the fan had turned from bright green to dull brown.

The Outcasts

She loved Timoteo, but she wished that he were brave enough to stand up with her in behalf of her Aunt Rosa's family. Her heart thudded wildly in her chest as she contemplated pleading on their behalf. She remembered Victoria standing bravely to fight for the misioneros to come live in their village. She looked at the fan again and thought, *If I don't, I'll become as dull and dry as this fan. I must stand up for them!*

Luisa rose to her feet, gaining attention to speak. "We saw for ourselves how wicked Diego is. He came here to avenge his name against his daughter and son-in-law's transgression from the Nala way, and yet he knew he had done worse by defiling Dalia. Now we hear that his wickedness has continued to grow, and he is propagating an evil scheme that will surely be Ulgana's downfall. Or worse, that shamelessness could spread to the rest of our villages!

"Fidel rescued his babies—his flesh and blood. A day doesn't go by that I don't look at my own children and wonder how anyone could have whisked them away and buried them alive. The spirits have not destroyed Fidel, Victoria, or their children. If the spirits were angry about allowing the twins to live, surely they would have destroyed that family. Maybe we were wrong! Namuro is no longer prospering, yet Fidel and his group are. Why?"

Slowly, Luisa looked around the large gathering of men and women—she looked directly into their eyes. "We need them, and they're willing to help us, even after the way we've treated them. It's time to make peace." Luisa sat down. She averted her eyes from her parents and her husband, afraid to see anger toward her, flaming in their eyes. Then the image of Victoria formed in her mind—Victoria standing against the whole village. Luisa lifted her chin in confidence—or at least with determination.

Pedro kept looking through the cracks in the meetinghouse wall. The sun was sinking in the western sky. They needed to leave soon in order to get to the camp before sunset. He didn't want to be on the river again at night and miss the tributary that led to Fidel's landing. But the villagers seemed far from agreeing on the heavy decisions before them. A loud growl from Pedro's stomach reminded him that he'd missed lunch. He longed for a hearty evening meal.

Rico called for order. "We all agree that Ulgana must be brought under control. I'll leave early tomorrow morning to travel to Kala and Luwana. We three chiefs will discuss the bigger issues: whether to dissolve the village of Ulgana altogether, or whether to call a new chief who can run that village with order and respect for our customs. Once decided, we'll go on to Ulgana. Ramiro and Diego will be punished.

"Now, as far as Fidel's group is concerned, it's time to vote. If you vote to trade with them, you will also be voting to make peace with them. However, no matter which way the vote goes, we will not accept them back to live among us. Everybody in favor of peace and trading, stand up...."

Chapter 42

After the vote, Tomás gathered his group quickly, and they headed toward the canoe at the river's edge. They were eager to arrive safely at the camp before nightfall.

Murky water splashed against the sides of the boat as darkness threatened to envelop them. The nightly chorus of insects echoed from the forest beyond the riverbanks.

Finally, the rushing sound of the swift currents of the Grande merging with the Namuro River reached their ears. Pedro and Tomás tensed for the convergence and leaned heavily into their poles. At just the right moment, they released their holds. Swiftly, the canoe sped around the corner, and the men plunged their poles into the muddy bottom of the river, struggling to guide the boat toward the shallower shoreline. They fought to stay near the bank, and then their poles struck rock, just in time to catapult them into the small tributary which led to the camp's landing. As they propelled the vessel safely toward the camp, they breathed a sigh of relief.

Around the warm, inviting fire at Fidel's house, Tomás gave an animated and detailed account of the day's events. Marta listened while her eyes took in the strange shadows of the flames dancing off the peculiar tin ceiling. She ran her fingers along the strange, cold wall; it was smooth with a pattern of rough lines. There weren't any cracks to see through, and she couldn't decide whether it felt strong and protective or unyielding and confining.

Chandi interpreted enthusiastically. Even though he'd been bitterly disappointed when the misioneros flew away without him and he'd barely looked at his father since then, he now realized that, had he gone, he would have missed this event. He had very mixed feelings about the decision that his father would make before the misioneros returned. Suddenly, he appreciated his father and the enormity of the choice before them.

Victoria was so proud of Luisa! She remembered all too well how it felt to stand before the village, sure that she would collapse in fear. Luisa! How she longed to see her dear friend again.

Tomás continued. "Rico said that as far as your group is concerned, they must vote whether to trade with you or not. If they agree to trade with you, they must agree to peace. He said, however, that they will not accept you back to live among them. He told everybody in favor of peace and trading to stand up. After counting the number of adults standing, the chief asked for those who opposed peace and trading to stand. They, too, were counted."

Everyone in the room held their breath—waiting for the verdict.

Tomás continued. "Forty-two people were in favor of making peace, and eighteen were opposed!"

The Outcasts

The room erupted in excitement! Rosa and Victoria hugged each other. Even though they knew that for most the deciding factor must have been the need for supplies, this was a huge victory nonetheless. *My babies are safe*—safe! Victoria's heart rejoiced.

Fidel said, "We didn't do this on our own. I called out to the Perfect One for help, and He heard me. I'd like to talk to the Perfect One."

"That's a wonderful idea," Victoria said."

Although feeling very awkward, Fidel prayed. "Thank You, Perfect One. Please continue to answer when we call out to You. Thank You."

The meeting was over, so each family said goodbye for the night and went to their homes.

Tomás lingered near Marta. As soon as he could, he said, "Can I talk to you outside?"

"Yes," Marta agreed.

The couple went out through the back door. The strong, sweet fragrance of nearby blossoms mingled with the fresh night air. They didn't wander away from the building, so Tomás spoke in hushed tones. "Marta, I want to marry you. Will you marry me now, or do you need to wait until you're reunited with your mother?"

Marta hesitated in order to formulate her thoughts. "I do want to marry you, Tomás." She tilted her head up shyly and gazed into his eyes. "This is so new and strange here at Fidel's camp. Part of me wishes I could go back to what I know—to my mother and the life I've always imagined." She paused and contemplated her next words. "But, part of me thinks that I can never go back. I don't want to see my father—how could I ever trust him again? Tomás, just like Fidel rescued his family, you've rescued me! I'm proud of your courage—I'm so proud of you. It will be very different here—a whole new way of life. But we'll have each other, and we can make the changes together."

Tomás gently encased Marta's small hands in his own. He felt exhilarated touching her so familiarly for the first time. Tomás whispered, "I don't have all the answers, but together we can find our way."

"Yes," Marta agreed.

"Tomorrow, then—I'll ask Fidel if he'll marry us tomorrow."

"Tomorrow," Marta murmured.

One week later, Rico and the chiefs from Kala and Luwana arrived in Ulgana. They were dismayed at the pathetic sight of the run-down village. The huts were in disrepair, and weeds grew everywhere. The stench of rotten banana peels and other refuse stung their nostrils.

Ramiro's chest tightened when he saw them coming, but he put on his mask of composure and invited them into his home. Woodenly, his wife offered the visiting chiefs warm banana drink. Her despondency didn't go unnoticed by the men.

The Outcasts

Immediately Rico took over, calling the village together for a meeting. Once assembled, he surveyed the dismal group. He looked around for Diego, and realized that the pitiful-looking man in the corner was the former chief of Luwana. Rico was shocked. The once-strong and confident chief slouched in the dim shadows. He was filthy, unkempt, and gaunt.

Rico didn't waste any time. He denounced Ramiro and Diego. He announced that Ramiro was no longer chief, and that neither he nor Diego would ever be allowed to become chiefs again. He then gave a detailed account about the seven youths from their village who had escaped and had revealed Ulgana's detestable proposal of taking young women as second wives for their men.

"We have decided to dissolve this village. You will all move to Kala," Rico declared with authority.

Instead of the usual outbursts, silence prevailed.

The women were dumbfounded to learn why their children had disappeared—yet they felt reassured, knowing that the young people were safe. Even though huge changes were about to take place, they felt that anything had to be better than the nightmare of the past week.

The men were chagrined—their clandestine meetings had been exposed! Several had resisted the wicked proposal, but would their wives believe them?

Ramiro was enraged. Diego's stomach lurched. *Kala is where this all began in the first place! How can I face going there?*

Rico addressed the accused. "Ramiro and Diego, you will pay for your evil ways. You will be shunned for two years. Nobody will talk to you or acknowledge your presence. During those two years, you will work Dalia's family's gardens, and you will keep the trails and grounds around the area cleared. A small hut will be built for each of you in the center of the village, where you'll live alone during that time."

Ramiro's jaw tightened and anger flashed in his dark eyes. But Diego's countenance revealed nothing about his thoughts.

The Nala Nation had united to bring Ulgana into subjection—to put a stop to the evil that they felt certain would be the ruin of them all. The chiefs decided that they must become more united as a whole and less independent as separate villages.

The chiefs' eyes had been opened to a multitude of changes which they didn't understand—so they determined to cling even harder to Nala traditions.

But the God of the universe was building His Church among them, beginning at the camp, and one day His Word would spread to the other villages. The Nala Nation would have the opportunity to hear the truth and to know that there is another trail—the trail that leads to eternal life with God in heaven.

Epilogue

SIX MONTHS LATER

Chandi and his father had grown closer through many late-night discussions. Together, they agreed that Chandi should not go and live with the misioneros. Alberto felt liberated from the secrets of his past. He viewed each of his children in a new light, but he was especially proud of Chandi and Antonio. They had carried heavy loads for such young boys—they were well on their way to growing into fine young men.

Everyone at the camp worked hard to open the trading post. After a few residents of Namuro traveled to the camp to buy supplies, the news spread quickly about all the goods which could be purchased. Soon, the village of Namuro brought their crops to sell there, and they became regular customers.

Luisa came with her husband whenever he made the trip, and she relished her time with Victoria, Rosa, and the others. She brought her children with her, and she took home the updates and stories, which she told over and over again at night around their fire.

Adolfo learned to run the motor for the numerous trips to Avanzada. Chandi, Adolfo, and his younger brother Daniel, sold the loads of produce and purchased supplies and goods for the camp and the store.

Tomás and Marta decided to stay at the camp, but the rest of the young people went to Kala to join their families.

When the young people arrived in Kala, Dalia's parents drank in every word about their daughter, grandson Pepe, and granddaughter Sofía. They didn't know how to make amends; their hearts were broken for the daughter they had abandoned in her desperate time of need. But they were so thankful that Dalia was safe now, and they hoped that one day they could see her and ask her to forgive them.

Diego and Ramiro were miserable. They despised the cold stares and obvious disdain. It was demeaning, working like slaves—and for another year-and-a-half! Ramiro loathed his wife and children, who shunned him daily. Diego vacillated between despondency and fury toward the family who'd deserted him. Ramiro had devised a plan: he convinced Diego to help him clear a footpath farther into the jungle each day while they were working in the garden; one day, soon, they would go to the garden and never return.

Andrés' interest in Dalia was increasing, but he was biding his time. He hoped and he prayed that Dalia would fully heal and

The Outcasts

be able to love again. And he hoped that she would be able to love *him*.

Victoria's mother and all of her siblings decided to make the camp their new home.

Maamo was happy and content. Her toothless grin continued to brighten the lives of those around her. Although old and frail, she had a strength that others recognized. Chandi and Antonio spent many evenings by the fire, talking to Maamo. They were curious about the lost village—and the gold that might still be hidden there. They drew a map based on Maamo's stories. Fully aware of how rapidly the jungle reclaimed abandoned village sites, the boys desperately wanted to travel to that area before all remnants of Ulgana disintegrated beyond usable landmarks—but they kept their plans to themselves.

Bob and Linda had made two visits to the camp. They hoped to be free to move there within six more months. On their next trip they would fly in building materials to fix up their house. They were pleased that Chandi was reading from the Spanish Bible and then interpreting the passages into Nala for everyone. Chandi had many questions for the misioneros and desired to know more about the Perfect One. Fidel, Victoria, Dalia, Maamo, and Andrés continued to pray. And they drank in the words from the Book that Chandi read and interpreted for them. They were eager to have the misioneros move in so they could teach them more.

When Isabel and Susana took their first steps, Victoria again thanked the Perfect Son for sparing their lives. Her heart was so full, so thankful at how her life had turned out. She loved Fidel so much—her husband had risked everything for her and for their babies.

Their camp was never really named; it simply became known as "The Trading Post."

Breinigsville, PA USA
01 September 2009
223394BV00001B/2/P